Kyoto Stories

Kyoto Stories

Steve Alpert

Stone Bridge Press • *Berkeley, California*

Published by
Stone Bridge Press
P. O. Box 8208, Berkeley, CA 94707
TEL 510-524-8732 • sbp@stonebridge.com • www.stonebridge.com

This is a work of fiction. The names, characters, businesses, places, events, and incidents in this book are either the product of the author's imagination or are used in a fictitious manner.

Cover design, book design, and map by Peter Goodman. Cover art: "Rock Garden of the Ryoanji" by Kamei Tobei; obtained via PICRYL and cited as a work in the public domain. Map background from Shutterstock.

Printed in the United States of America.

First edition 2022.

p-ISBN 978-1-61172-074-7
e-ISBN 978-1-61172-955-9

Contents

KYOTO
MT.
Shu
Daitoku-ji
KAMOGAWA
Kinkaku-ji
Ryoanj-ji
Komyo-ji
Imperial
Palace
Ginkaku-
Kyoto
University
Tetsugaku
no Michi
Myoshin-ji
ARASHIYAMA
Sento
Gosho
Shogo-in
Marutamachi
KAMOGAWA
Heian Jingu
Nijo
Castle
Nanzen-ji
OMIYA
SHIJO
TERAMACHI
GION
Kawaramachi
Gojo-dori
Kiyomizu-dera
HI NO OK
Higashi
Hongan-ji
HIGASHIYAMA
Shichijo-dori
Kyoto Tower
Katsura
YAM
Kyoto
Station
UJI

The Ice Box

IN 1975 I LIVED IN a big one-hundred-and-fifty-year-old Japanese house in Kyoto. I shared it with my American girlfriend and one of her American friends from her Japanese tea ceremony school. The rambling old house had once been the centerpiece in a traditional family compound just behind the Shogo-in temple near the Kyoto University Hospital. The compound's owners had done the modern thing. Moved out to a fancier part of town, subdivided the old house, and rented out the pieces separately.

One day my girlfriend Pattie let me know that she had invited a guy named Ed from her Zen meditation sessions at Daitoku-ji to live with us. A month later I was asked to move out and I no longer had a girlfriend.

I admit I took it badly. For the first few weeks I was unable to function normally. I had been teaching English to a housewife in Yamashina, Mrs. Shimokawa. I did it for very little money as a favor to a friend. Mrs. Shimokawa took pity on me and let me stay in her house until I could find someplace to live. She seemed to think I would be a good role model for her nephew, Yuichi, who lived with them. Yuichi was twenty-five and worked in the Shimokawa family construction business.

Yuichi was hopelessly in love with a bar hostess. I was doing my best to get over being hopelessly in love with Pattie Wilson, the all-American blond girl of my dreams. Pattie, a psychology major from the University of Washington, had moved to Kyoto after graduation from college to study Zen Buddhism and tea ceremony. She and I had lived together in Kyoto for about a year.

Yuichi was perfectly happy with his situation and didn't particularly want or need a role model. He was good-looking, and he was fit from working at his job outdoors. The Shimokawa construction company specialized in building drainage systems for public swimming pools, ice skating rinks, and nuclear power plants. Yuichi spent all of his monthly salary visiting the bar where the girl of his dreams worked. Their relationship, which existed only at the bar as long as Yuichi paid for the girl's time, was harder on Yuichi's family than it was on him. His family wanted Yuichi to start thinking about finding a real girl to marry and begin a family of his own. An arranged marriage with the right girl would have made the family very happy.

Yuichi, a straightforward guy who always said what he was thinking, understood that his obsession with a bar hostess was probably not a good thing. But it was his obsession and his money, and he was resolved to see the girl as often as he had the money to do it. It was supposed to be my role to talk him out of it. Instead I talked to him endlessly about Pattie, which probably made him decide he was better off seeing a bar hostess.

The Shimokawas ran a free-range household. The house had been Mrs. Shimokawa's parents' home, a traditional Japanese house to which her husband had appended a very new, three-story building that they called the Annex. The Annex was connected to the main house by a covered passageway. The ground floor of the Annex contained a small but spectacular family bath and the office of Mr. Shimokawa's construction business. The second floor was being used for storage and had empty space in it that was earmarked for future bedrooms. Yuichi occupied the third floor by himself until I showed up. He seemed not to care about having a roommate. He was neither happy nor unhappy about it.

Mr. Shimokawa was a burly, earthy, good-natured man. He

and his wife had three kids. They all lived in the older, traditional main house. Mrs. Shimokawa's mother had lived with them. Mr. Shimokawa took out a loan to build the Annex to avoid the Japanese inheritance tax, as people in Japan with property do. But the mother-in-law died just as the building was being finished, and the Shimokawas never moved into the new building. Everyone seemed comfortable in the main house. So they invited Yuichi to live in the Annex.

The family ate dinner together in the largest Japanese room in the main house. After dinner, everyone sprawled on the tatami floor watching TV and playing card games. The adults drank beer or sake. Yuichi left to visit his bar hostess if he still had money left over from his monthly paycheck. While I lived there I was free to join the family for dinner, but most days I rarely even bothered to get out of bed. In this way I lost all my part-time jobs teaching English.

The Shimokawas' bedroom in the main house was separated from the big room where everyone ate by sliding *shoji* screens. The children, two girls seven and nine, and a boy five, shared one room at the back of the house. But no one in the family ever seemed to sleep in their own room. On those rare days when I joined the family for dinner, I played cards with the children afterward and then fell asleep on the floor watching late-night TV. As the children fell asleep in the main room, Mrs. Shimokawa simply covered them with blankets and they slept the night where they lay. I would wake up at three or four in the morning and find myself covered with a blanket and surrounded by small sleeping bodies.

Most of the time I slept upstairs in the Annex. If I was awake when Yuichi came home from visiting his hostess, we talked.

"Have you ever had sex with your bar hostess?" I asked Yuichi.

"No. She let me kiss her a few times. Once when we had too much to drink she let me feel her breasts."

"In front of other people?"

"No. In the back stairway of the building where the bar is."

"Do you ask her to have sex with you?"

"Of course. But she always either changes the subject or just says no."

"If she said yes, where would you go? A love hotel?"

"No. We would go to an *onsen* somewhere."

"Have you ever tried other bars?"

"Before Yoriko, sure. Not since I met Yoriko."

"That's her name? Yoriko?"

"Yes."

"Is that her real name?"

"I don't know. What difference would it make?"

"Do you know her surname?"

"No. Why would I?"

When Yuichi asked about Pattie, I explained how she had taken all my money, found another boyfriend, invited the new boyfriend to move in, and then kicked me out of my own house.

"But you still want to see her again, right?" Yuichi asked. "If she wanted you back you would go, right?"

"I do want to see her again. But I know I shouldn't. What I really want is to be over her. I think if I see her I'll have a hard time doing that. So I'll have to make sure not to see her."

"You think that's what I should do about Yoriko?"

"I guess so. Everyone assumes she's playing games with you. I mean, it's a business and that's what bar hostesses do. But what about you? Suppose Yoriko agreed to sleep with you. Then what? Are you planning a relationship with her outside of the bar? Do you see her as a girlfriend or lover or future wife? How do you even know what she's really like if you only see her in a bar over drinks?"

"I never think about it."

"Suppose you did think about it?"

"Well, maybe I'll never sleep with her. Maybe she'll find a customer who's richer and who she likes better. Then Yoriko might stop seeing me and I'll have to find another bar and someone else. I won't end up like you, with no place to live and no money and sleeping all day."

When I realized that Yuichi was more worried about me than he was about himself, I knew it was time to snap out of it and move on. Yuichi brought me the English-language version of the *Yomiuri Shimbun* every day. He thought that reading the newspaper would give me an excuse to get out of bed. Or connect me back up to the real world.

SADAHARU OH WAS STILL PADDING his home run record and the Yomiuri Giants in Tokyo, perpetually in first place and passionately hated in Kansai, were on their inevitable march toward another Central League pennant and Japan Series trophy. In the world of sumo, the college-educated duo of Yokozuna Wajima and Ozeki Takanohana were doing their best to keep down the newly promoted bad boy Yokozuna Kitanoumi who had never made it past the eighth grade. It was graceful style and classical technique vs. sheer bulk and meanness. Bulk and meanness was winning.

I knew the only way I could reliably expect to earn money was by teaching English. In the help-wanted section of the *Yomiuri Shimbun* newspaper I came across an ad for a live-in teacher at an English-language school. The position seemed to answer all my problems at once. The school, the Oxford Academy of English, was in downtown Kyoto near the train station. When I showed the ad to Mrs. Shimokawa, she looked at the address and made a face.

"What?" I asked.

"Nothing," Mrs. Shimokawa said.

"So why the face?"

"Well . . . the neighborhood. . . . It's not a good neighborhood."

"Really? It's downtown near the train station. Convenient to public transportation. It's on the sixth floor, so it must be in a newer building. What could be wrong with the neighborhood?"

"It's . . . not good."

"Not good why?"

"Just . . . not good."

I could see that Mrs. Shimokawa wasn't going to tell me what made the school's location a bad part of town. I thought about the area, which I passed through now and then. There was virtually no street crime in Kyoto, so that wouldn't be it. There was nothing about the area that struck me as any different from other parts of Kyoto. It couldn't be a secret red-light district because it bordered a major avenue and was too visible to passing traffic. The old red-light district near there was farther north along the little Takasegawa river. At most, the area where the school was located was old and a bit run-down, but not unusual for Kyoto. To get a better answer I asked Yuichi.

"*Eta*," Yuichi said.

"*Eta*?"

"*Eta*. It's not exactly a polite word, so don't go trying to use it. You'll get yourself into trouble. *Burakumin*. Do you know that word?"

"*Burakumin*? Village people? It's an area where peasants live? Country bumpkins?"

"Not peasants. Undesirables. Unclean people. Lepers."

"People with Leprosy? Actual lepers?"

"No. In the old days when everyone was Buddhist, certain people did the unclean jobs."

"This is the twentieth century."

"Maybe. But not here. If you're a *burakumin* you can't marry a regular Japanese person."

"Seriously?"

"Yes."

"Do they look different? How would you know?"

"They live in certain areas. They work in certain professions. Slaughtering animals, making leather, shoe repair. That kind of thing."

"But that's centuries ago. They don't still do the same jobs anymore do they?"

"Yes. Even if the family used to do it, but the children don't anymore, they're still considered *eta*. It's always been the same families that have always done that work. That part of Kyoto is one of the places where they live."

"The same families who used to do 'unclean' tasks still live in the same part of Kyoto?"

"Yes. It's near the railroad tracks. When railroads get built in places where people already live, whose land do you think they take first? Who lives near the railroad tracks?"

"And the very same people, they still continue to live in that area? For generations?"

"They do. Sometimes they change their names, but it's the same people."

"So if I saw *burakumin* walking around on the street, would I recognize them?"

"No."

"But you would?"

"Just by looking? No."

"So how . . . ?"

"There are ways of finding out."

"How?"

"Sooner or later you do. You just do. If your son or daughter is marrying into a family you don't know, you hire a detective. It's not unusual."

I decided to answer the ad. The man who took my call sounded normal and reasonably well educated. I arranged to go for an interview.

—

THE OXFORD ACADEMY OF ENGLISH was housed in a newish, narrow, six-story building in a neighborhood of older, run-down buildings. Most of the neighborhood consisted of grimy one- or two-story prewar buildings. They housed businesses that had gone or were about to go defunct. The ground floor of the newer, taller building that the school was in housed a real estate office and an elevator. A sign next to the elevator listed the other companies in the building. The English-language school occupied the building's top floor. The other companies in the building seemed to be the kind of businesses that last for a few months and then disappear, their staff unpaid and the owner in jail or fled to another part of Japan with a new name.

I got into the tiny elevator. It was barely big enough for two people. I pushed the button for 6. When I got to the top I saw that half the floor was the apartment of the school's proprietor, and the other half was the school. I tried the door to the school and found it unlocked. I peeked inside. The room was empty. I went across the hall and knocked on the proprietor's apartment door.

The man who answered, Ohno-san, the head of the Oxford Academy, was a thin, bespectacled man. He seemed genial and easygoing. He led me back across the hall and into the school. The classroom had a comfortable sofa in it and we sat.

Ohno-san asked me only a few basic questions, all of which could have been answered by simply handing him my passport. Name, Don Ascher. Age, 26. Citizenship, the United States of America. Satisfied, he then offered me the job. Apparently the only real requirements for the job were that the teacher be an actual *gaijin* and be willing to live at the school, and work for the proposed salary. Previous teaching experience was not required, but that wasn't unusual for English-conversation classes in Kyoto.

I didn't ask about the school or its students. I needed the job and a place to live. Ohno-san assured me I would have enough time off between classes to study Japanese and pursue other interests. I accepted the job and got a tour of the premises.

The classroom consisted of a large room set up as a living room. Part of it had a sofa and some comfortable armchairs in it, ideal for smaller groups. There were about a dozen metal folding chairs scattered about the room for additional seating. More of the metal folding chairs were stored leaning against one of the room's walls. At the back of the room was a closed-off six-mat tatami room. Sliding *fusuma* closed the room off for privacy and for sleeping. The back part of the tatami room had a sliding glass door that led to a narrow balcony.

The balcony overlooked Shichijo-dori and faced north and east. It was at the top of the tallest building in the neighborhood and had a commanding view of the grime-covered tile roofs that made up most of this part of Kyoto. I could see out as far as Higashiyama. The view from the other side of the building in Ohno-san's apartment would have been Higashi Hongan-ji, Kyoto Tower, and the western mountains near Arashiyama.

There was a separate bathroom out across the classroom. It had a nice, large Japanese-style bath in it. It was extremely clean and modern compared to the hundred-year-old Japanese house I had been living in with my now ex-girlfriend Pattie. There was even hot water that you didn't have to light a wood-burning fire to summon up.

There was no kitchen in the apartment. Only a counter set against one wall of the classroom containing a hot plate and a toaster. Ohno-san explained that the live-in teacher would take his dinners with his family in the apartment next door. Ohno-san lived with his wife and two small children. I would be on my own for breakfast and lunch, but dinners were included as part of the teacher's pay. Ohno-san promised to buy a small refrigerator for the eating area, and he assured me it would be in place by the time I moved in and reported for work.

I returned to the Shimokawas' to tell them I had found a job and would be moving out. They seemed happy for me now that I was beginning to get myself together and move on. There was a farewell dinner for me with an enormous platter of take-out sushi and plenty of beer and sake. I told Yuichi I would be back to go drinking with him once I got settled in my new job and residence. Mrs. Shimokawa thanked me again for being a positive influence on Yuichi. She was sure Yuichi would soon stop wasting his money on a bar hostess and find himself a real girlfriend.

I had few possessions, so moving out of Yamashina was simple enough. Once I'd settled into the Oxford Academy of English, I discovered that Ohno-san and I together were the entire school. I had incorrectly assumed that there would be other teachers. There were none.

Ohno-san taught small classes in the living room in the apartment on his side of the building. I taught larger classes in the living room/classroom on my side of the building. I had never heard Ohno-san speak English. I had a hard time imagining that Ohno-san could speak it well enough to teach it to others. But I was prepared to give him the benefit of the doubt.

Dinner in Ohno-san's apartment was a purely functional and mirthless affair. Ohno-san was rarely present. Mrs. Ohno didn't seem to like me much. I knocked on the door, entered the apartment, and was seated at the table in the kitchen. I never got past the kitchen to see what other rooms there were in the apartment. Plates of food were set out on the table. I sat alone eating on my side of the table while three sets of eyes watched me eat.

Ohno-san's daughter was about eight years old and very shy. She helped her mother prepare the meal and then bring in the food and clear the plates afterward. She never ate until I was finished and sat quietly in her place staring at me. Mrs. Ohno would install her infant son in his highchair and start spooning food into the baby's mouth. She never ate until I was finished eating and the baby was finished eating.

At the table, Mrs. Ohno was taciturn and mostly mute. She was a round woman of medium height. Between delivering spoonfuls of boiled carrot mash to the infant, she eyed me suspiciously as I ate. If I asked where Mr. Ohno was, the most I could get out of the wife was that her husband was out on business. The meals were ordinary home-cooked Japanese food. The kind you might get in a college cafeteria. I tended to finish them quickly without the distraction of conversation.

Eventually Mrs. Ohno got used to me and began to talk. This proved to be less pleasant than when she was silent. What she had to say at the dinner table I mostly found disturbing and mildly depressing.

Mrs. Ohno had grown up in a poor family in rural Kyushu. As a young woman she had been naïve and inexperienced when it came to men. Her first experience with sex got her pregnant. The man refused to marry her because he was already married. She refused to have an abortion and her parents kicked her out of the house. She decided to end her life by jumping off a cliff. She chose a well-known suicide spot in a forest near Mt. Fuji. She said she had always wanted to see Mt. Fuji before she died.

Ohno-san had been a friend of the man who got Mrs. Ohno pregnant. He convinced her not to kill herself. He said they were both young and had their whole lives ahead of them. They could run away to Osaka together and make enough money to see Mt. Fuji and all of the rest of Japan. Ohno-san didn't mind bringing up another man's child.

Life was hard in Osaka and the romance faded. Living conditions were difficult. Osaka was filthy compared to rural Kyushu and the Ohnos rarely had enough to eat. Ohno-san had a job as a door-to-door English-language encyclopedia salesman. He was on the road most of the time. Mrs. Ohno stayed at home and raised the baby. She also worked from home doing piecework for a clothing factory.

Selling encyclopedias turned out to be a rough business. Ohno-san would offer Volume 1 of the encyclopedia to a customer for free if the customer purchased Volume 2. He said that there was no obligation to buy further volumes, and any purchased volumes could be returned for a full refund at any time. Customers could keep Volume 1 even if they returned the others. But in reality, if customers stopped buying further volumes, or tried to return any of the volumes, they would receive a visit from a muscular, tattooed collection agent. Customers who were visited by collection agents almost always continued to purchase the complete set of encyclopedias.

The encyclopedia sales business continued to go well until the company that published the encyclopedias discovered how they were being sold in Osaka. Ohno-san and his family then had to move to Kyoto. The family wasn't named Ohno when they lived in Osaka.

Over dinner every night as Mrs. Ohno fed her infant son, I heard more stories about the schemes Ohno-san had carried out or planned to carry out in order to cheat people out of their savings. I worried about what I had gotten myself into and wondered if I should already be trying to get myself out of it. These were people who viewed life from a different perspective than I was used to. From the way Mrs. Ohno related her stories, it was clear she had no idea that she and her husband were doing anything wrong. She looked out for her own family and other people ought to do the same.

While Mrs. Ohno was becoming comfortable enough with me to tell me about herself, she also pumped me for information about myself. She was especially interested in hearing about my family and where they lived. Once when she had me describe my parents' house in detail, I had mentioned that they had a cherry tree in the yard. That was the only thing I ever said about myself or my parents that seemed to strike her as interesting.

My parents had selected a house in semi-rural Connecticut that was under construction in a small tract of new homes. They had a free hand in selecting the plants and trees to go with it as part of the construction. They were city people and knew nothing about vegetation. They didn't know that the soil that was used to fill in the swamp on which their house sat was particularly unsuited to fruiting trees, or that the shady spot they chose for the mature cherry tree they planted was precisely the wrong spot for it. Even so, in its first year the tree produced an avalanche of bright red fruit. In its second year the tree produced only a few sad dark cherries. In its third year the tree died.

But for Mrs. Ohno, that cherry tree that I had only casually mentioned became something of a symbol. It was a detail she fastened on and often mentioned. The tree in her mind was not the sad tree that lived for three seasons, began to rot, and then expired. It was a shining image of an unobtainable and nearly unimaginably perfect life.

I hadn't expected my life as a live-in teacher to be pleasant. I needed the money and a place to live. I knew I wasn't qualified to be a teacher of anything, but I expected to do my amateur best. If the students weren't satisfied, they were free to find a better school. There were a lot of places like this in Kyoto. I wasn't comfortable with the idea that I might be helping someone to cheat them. But I had also never asked Ohno-san how the school functioned or what had been presented to the students or what claims he had made about the classes. Even if this part of Ohno-san's scheming wasn't entirely above board and honorable, I was pretty sure nothing about it was illegal.

Most of the school's evening students were ordinary working people with low-paying jobs. The day students were mostly housewives. The school's main selling points were its convenient proximity to Kyoto Station and that it offered a very flexible plan for classroom attendance. The students were told that they could come to class whenever they wanted between the hours of eleven a.m. and nine p.m. They paid a small monthly fee and were allowed to show up and be taught English any time during the school's operating hours. They were told that whenever they showed up, a class would be in progress that they could join, and that almost all the classes would be taught by a qualified native speaker. Since I was the only native speaker at the school, I wondered how this was going to work in practice. I wasn't planning to be available to teach continually from eleven a.m. to nine p.m.

The students of the Oxford Academy of English displayed a surprisingly high tolerance for being lied to. They seemed unsurprised when the operation of the school differed from the way it had been advertised. Had the school operated as advertised, it would not have been a good way to learn a foreign language. There was no class continuity, no program, no texts, and no guarantee that the students in a class would all be at the same or even comparable levels of ability. Advanced students sat idle while the beginners in the class struggled to form basic sentences. Less advanced students couldn't understand any of the conversations between the teacher and the more advanced students. Students simply showed up and did their best to talk to the *gaijin*.

After the first two weeks of trying to manage the chaos of teaching students at different levels of ability in a single class, I decided to change the system without consulting Ohno-san. I got a rough feel for who tended to show up and when, and I posted specific class times for each level on the bulletin board in the classroom. Not a single student of the Oxford Academy of English ever complained that it was not the program they had signed up for.

Since no one complained, I began telling students which classes they could attend and which ones they couldn't. What evolved was a private class in the late morning or early afternoon for a group of housewives, two big evening classes, and an occasional second class in the afternoon. As long as no one was complaining, Ohno-san didn't seem to mind the changes.

The evening classes were the biggest, and started at about six and lasted until eight, or nine if I was feeling generous and still in the mood to teach. Some students were teenagers who had lived for a while in the US and wanted to keep up their language skills. Some were college or high school graduates who wanted to use English at work or to get a better job. Some were older people who viewed the classes as a kind of club. Most of them had day jobs.

None of the students expected me to do any actual teaching. All I had to do was talk or let other people talk. Whenever I attempted to do any teaching, they seemed to regard it as a kind of bonus. I tried assigning homework, but none of the students ever did it.

The classes were so large that it was impossible to eliminate all the differences in ability levels altogether. Advanced students sat quietly and patiently while the less fluent struggled with sentences like "Yes I would like some coffee please. Thank you very much." Sometimes when a slower student labored to get out the words of a sentence in English, I would doze off while standing at the head of the class. I was astonished to discover that it was possible to fall asleep while standing up in front of people.

There were five women who came regularly to the day class, at least two or three times a week, and formed the core of the class. I enjoyed my conversations with these five women. When I realized that I could do whatever I wanted about reorganizing the classes, I stopped allowing anyone other than the five women to attend the day class, telling the others to come only in the evening. Again, no one ever complained.

The class with the five women was small enough that we could sit on the sofa and the easy chairs and just chat. Most of the conversations were in English, but some were in Japanese. If someone had something they really wanted to say and decided it was easier to say it in Japanese, they just said it in Japanese. The classes even began to feel like friends getting together for an informal discussion group. Often I talked so little I was no more than just an observer.

The women weren't actually all housewives. Two of the women were unmarried. Mrs. Tanaka was a barber. She and her husband, also a barber, had a barber shop up on Gojo-dori near the Keihan train station. Mrs. Watanabe lived in one of the "bed towns" between Kyoto and Osaka. Her husband was an executive in a large manufacturing company. Mrs. Ogawa's husband ran a family business in textiles that had been passed down for generations. Miss Itoh worked for the phone company. She was a telephone operator on the night shift. Miss Katoh lived with her parents in Himeji but kept a small apartment in Kyoto, where she performed as a soloist and first cellist with the Kyoto Municipal Symphony Orchestra.

The women could all more or less speak English. Mrs. Tanaka, the barber, and Miss Itoh, the telephone operator, were the least fluent. They quickly switched to Japanese when they couldn't find the words in English. The conversations got personal very quickly, and all the women encouraged each other to talk. Secrets were confessed. Intimate details flowed freely. The English language had become a kind of prophylactic, insulating the speaker from embarrassment and from caution. I was sometimes amazed at the kinds of things the women would confess to me and to each other when speaking English.

Mrs. Ogawa suspected her husband of seeing another woman. Mrs. Watanabe's husband's company paid for him to take private English lessons. He was sleeping with his young, blond American English teacher. Miss Katoh the cellist spent most of her time practicing. She complained that she hadn't had sex in almost a year. The last time had been with the orchestra's guest conductor, a foreigner and a married man. Her parents had arranged *omiai* for her several times. The potential husbands she met in this way had expected her to give up her career as a musician. She was hoping for a man who would just show up at night for the sex and not interfere with her practice and concert schedule.

Miss Itoh said that working the night shift made it hard for her to meet people. It also made it very hard for her parents to arrange *omiai*. At twenty-five, she was the youngest in the class. She was slim and fit, and one of the very few females I'd seen in Japan wearing jeans. She liked disco dancing. Her job at the phone company had put an end to that and to dating. She thought she might be falling in love with another woman, a co-worker on the night shift.

Mrs. Tanaka, the barber, said little during these conversations, though she always seemed interested in what the others were saying. I assumed it was because she had trouble expressing herself in English.

The evening classes were much harder to get through. I felt sympathy for many of the evening-class students and often wanted to help them. But teaching them English the way the classes were set up was an unrewarding, miserable slog. Not good for the teacher. Not good for the students. The teacher who was being paid for it seemed to mind it more than the students who were paying.

For the most part the evening classes were an endless series of repetitions of basic English spoken in slow motion. When no one who could actually speak showed up to break the monotony, I sometimes asked the students questions that amused only myself. Was Nietzsche right when he said, "To live is to suffer, to survive is to find some meaning in the suffering"? Is the meaning of the universe really forty-nine? Who in the class can tell me why death exists? Do frogs dream? If cows had wings would there still be ice cream?

Sometimes I would discover something about the lives of the people who sat in front of me, eagerly waiting for me to somehow magically enable them to speak English, and I would recover my sense of humility. The burly guy in the front row worked long hours as a butcher's apprentice and was hoping to have his own butcher shop someday. The heavily made-up girl at the end of the second row was a hair stylist who didn't make enough money to live on her own and was saving up to earn a degree in cosmetology. The soft-spoken guy in the third row was an apprentice kimono dyer. The woman with short hair next to him was an assistant tea roaster. The skinny guy at the back of the room was a junior tax accountant. They all dreamed of doing something different in their lives, and weirdly, learning English somehow played a part in their imagined futures.

I finally began to accept the possibility that no one really expected me to actually be able to teach them English. All that was really expected of me was that I be there at the front of the classroom, that I continue to be a *gaijin*, and that every once in a while I say something in my native language. It was part of the students' magical sense of what learning English meant to them. This realization made me feel less bad about my part in the school's taking their money. When I discovered students who seemed like they might actually be able to learn the language, and who might actually want to try, I took them aside after class and advised them to find a better school.

At night, alone in my futon bed, I thought about Pattie. We still lived in the same city. She had said when we parted that we were still friends and that I should come and see her. Thinking about her made me not want to go out and see other people. Not going out and seeing other people made it hard to get over her. Being a teacher didn't count as seeing people.

When I did go out, I did so only at times when I knew I wouldn't see anyone. I went on solitary walks in Kyoto in the early mornings or late at night. I enjoyed the anonymity of the large crowds on Shijo-dori or Kawaramachi. Sometimes I stopped and talked to the homeless men who lived under the bridges along the Kamogawa river. They often had campfires going and liked to chat.

Sometimes I would sit on the concrete banks of the river just watching the reflections of the passing Keihan Railway trains in the swiftly flowing water. From the bridge at Sanjo in the early morning I could see the shoulders of Mt. Hiei looming in the distance. Even though Kyoto was far inland, swarms of gray-and-white seagulls frolicked along the river rummaging through the bits of garbage that people had left behind.

I supposed I could go back to New York and start graduate school. There were worse fates.

—

ONE DAY AS THE WOMEN of the afternoon class were heading for the door, Mrs. Tanaka, the barber, lingered. When the others had left she asked if she could stay and speak to me privately. She seemed nervous, slightly embarrassed, and shy about making the request. She had asked in English, so it took her some time to get the words out.

She sat on the sofa. I sat in one of the easy chairs facing her. She spoke softly and hesitantly, and I had to lean forward to catch her words.

Mrs. Tanaka did not look like a barber. She also did not look like a housewife. Her age was somewhere between thirty and forty. She was not plain but she was not beautiful. She was not thin nor fat nor tall nor short. She wore slim-fitting slacks and plain blouses to class. Her hair was thick and wavy and cut fairly short. It was not a particularly stylish cut. She had on enough makeup that you could tell she was wearing makeup, but it was minimal. There was a cross on a thin gold chain around her neck, a very small gold watch on her left wrist, and a modest diamond engagement ring and a matching gold wedding band on her thin artistic fingers. Many Japanese women wore crosses. Usually it had nothing to do with Christianity.

Mrs. Tanaka was normally very direct when she spoke. I was never sure if it was because that's how she was, or if it was because her English wasn't very good. In class Mrs. Tanaka had mentioned that she hated being a wife in a traditional trade in a neighborhood where everyone knew everyone else's business. But she seemed to be a happy, normal, well-adjusted, and extremely upbeat middle-class woman. When the personal revelations began to flow in class, Mrs. Tanaka rarely joined in.

"Asha-*sensei*, may I ask you a question?" Mrs. Tanaka began.

"Yes Mrs. Tanaka, of course."

"It is rather . . . a personal question. I hope you don't mind it."

"All right, why don't you ask, and we'll see if I do mind it."

She blushed and seemed reluctant to go on.

"It's fine," I said. "Please ask what you like, Mrs. Tanaka. I'm sure I won't mind."

"All right then. Thank you Asha-*sensei*. You see, what I wanted to ask is . . . that is . . . my husband and I, we . . . we . . . well, we belong to a group. Our group meets every week. Usually on Sunday. Uh, maybe group is not the right word. I'm sorry my English is very poor. It's a group, or . . . what do you call it? . . . ah . . . a club. Yes, I think you call it a club. Maybe club is the correct word."

"I see. And what sort of club is this?"

"Well, yes, ah . . . well, we have talked about this, my husband and I, we discussed it and we would both very much like for you to join our club. To be members with us."

"I see. That's very nice of you. But what sort of club exactly is this?"

"Oh, well I understand you have these clubs in America too. . . ."

"Yes, we have many clubs in America. We have book clubs. We have sports clubs. We have bird-watching clubs. What type of club is yours, exactly?"

"Oh, well I think they call it a . . . uh . . . a . . . uh, a swappers club."

"A swappers club?"

"Yes, a swappers club. Do you know?"

"No, not really. Do you mean a kind of club where you bring certain things that you have that you don't want or don't need anymore, and then you trade them to other people in your club for things that you do want? Is that it?"

"Uh, no . . . not exactly that. You don't have that word in English? Swappers?"

"Well I think I get the meaning of the word, but I'm not quite sure what it is, exactly, that you mean by it."

"Would you mind if I say this in Japanese please?"

"Sure, please go ahead and say it in Japanese. Maybe that would be best."

Mrs. Tanaka looked extremely relieved. She relaxed and began to speak more comfortably and with less hesitation.

"I thought swappers was an English word. I was sure it came from America. It seems like it would be an American word."

"Yes."

"You see, a swappers club is a club for married people. Well, most of the people are married. And you go to the swappers club with your husband or wife, and then you swap them for another partner, with someone else in the club, and you have sex with the other partner, the one that's not your husband or wife. You see?"

"Ah. Um . . . yes. I *have* heard of that. I didn't realize that's what you meant, but I do think I've heard of . . . swapping."

"So would you like to join? My husband and I would really like you to join us."

"Um, well, would it be all right if I asked a few questions about the club?"

"Oh yes, please."

"Well, where does this club meet?"

"Oh, well, one of our members is very rich. He has a very big house in Arashiyama. They have lots of space and several unused bedrooms. We usually meet there. Some of the other members have big places and we meet there sometimes too."

"So you just pair off right there? With the other people's husbands and wives?"

"Yes we do. Or sometimes we plan to meet somewhere outside later on. When the club meets, we have drinks first. We all sit around and talk. Then we find partners and get together."

"I see. You and your husband? You both go?"

"Oh yes. He very much welcomes you to join."

"You know I'm not married? I don't actually have a spouse to swap with anyone."

"You could join with your girlfriend. You talked about your girlfriend in class. My husband agreed that it would be fine if you joined with your girlfriend."

"Ah, I see. Well . . . my girlfriend and I are not exactly together now. But even if we were together, I'm very certain she would not want to join. At least, I think she would not want to join."

"Well that would be too bad, but my husband and I talked about that too."

"You and your husband discussed this?"

"Yes. And he said it would be fine if you wanted to join alone. Just you."

"I see. You already discussed it and he's fine with it if I join without my girlfriend?"

"Yes."

"And are there other foreigners in your group? Would I be the only one?"

"Yes. You would be the first one! So would you like to join our club?"

"Well, I . . . I would like to, but . . . I . . . I really don't think I can. I just don't think I can."

Mrs. Tanaka sighed and sagged slightly on the sofa.

"Oh, I see," she said with obvious disappointment.

"I mean . . . please understand this Mrs. Tanaka. It's very important. This has nothing at all to do with you. It's not that I . . . that is, that . . . that I don't find you . . . or uh . . . the idea of your club . . . I mean . . . well, this is a very bad time in my life, and . . ."

Mrs. Tanaka began to perk up again. She leaned forward in her chair and reached for one of my hands with both of hers. She had very nice, soft hands.

"You don't have to answer now. Please think about it," Mrs. Tanaka said. "Think about it some more. It would be really nice if you joined. It would make me very happy. And I think it would make you happy too."

"Well I . . . you know, Mrs. Tanaka, I really, really appreciate your offer. I really do."

She squeezed my hand a little.

"And it's a very, very appealing offer. But I think probably, in the end, I won't be able to accept it. I want to, but I can't."

Mrs. Tanaka released my hand.

"You can't join? But why can't you?"

"I can't join a spouse swapping club because . . . because . . . because it's against my religion. I'm sorry, but I should have mentioned that from the beginning. It's against my religion."

"It's against your religion?"

"You see, I'm a Catholic. Catholics are absolutely prohibited from joining spouse swapping clubs, and . . ."

"But I thought you told the class that you were Jewish?"

"Jewish? Uh, yes. Jewish. I'm both Jewish and Catholic. I'm Jewish but I'm also Catholic. Many Americans are Jewish and Catholic."

Mrs. Tanaka looked sadly at me. I looked sadly at her. I noticed how her small but firm breasts rose and fell beneath the thin blouse she had on. I noticed the shape of the no-nonsense bra she wore that was clearly visible beneath the blouse. I noticed the full curve of her hips, the appealing plumpness of her thighs and the attractive shape of her legs. She had a smooth round face with full, moist, kissable lips. It was only really just beginning to dawn on me that this fine-looking woman was offering to have sex with me. My first instinct had been to say no.

"Asha-*sensei*," Mrs. Tanaka said, "may I tell you something? May I tell you a secret that I have never told anyone? That I never even told my husband."

I nodded.

"There was a German man. He lived in Tokyo and used to come to Osaka sometimes on business. He would come to Kyoto and we would arrange to meet. I first met him at an *onsen* in Izu. I was there with some of my girlfriends. We were on a little vacation for women only. After the German man and I got to know each other, he would let me know when he was coming to Kyoto and we would spend the afternoon together in a hotel room near Kyoto Station. It was very, very nice to be with him. Very special. He didn't speak much Japanese. I don't speak German. We both speak a little English. When he went back to Germany I was sad that I couldn't see him anymore. It was sad not to have our meetings to look forward to. I never told my husband. It was different from what we do at our club. But better in many ways."

Mrs. Tanaka looked hopefully at me.

"Please join the club," she said. "Please join. But don't answer now. Please think about it. Don't say anything now. Think about it and tell me later when you decide."

I said I would.

Mrs. Tanaka stood up to go.

I stood up and walked her to the door.

She said she would see me in class. I said I would see her in class.

She got into the elevator and she was gone.

That night in bed I thought about her offer. I was dreaming about what it might be like to have sex with Mrs. Tanaka. It was a pleasant dream. Exciting new possibilities. An adventure. Learning about new things and new people. Then Pattie entered the dream and Mrs. Tanaka was no longer in it. It was no longer a pleasant dream.

Mrs. Tanaka continued to come to class as usual after that. She gave no indication that we had sat together holding hands and had a conversation about wife swapping. Now and then I caught Mrs. Tanaka looking at me with a question in her eyes. I wondered if there was still an opening in her club for a brand-new member. There were so many reasons to have said yes. But I said no. I was too young to understand that a random sexual encounter might have the power to change or alter the course of a life, for better or for worse. So it wasn't that that was holding me back. I had no idea what was.

—

EVENTUALLY OHNO-SAN BEGAN TO EXPRESS dissatisfaction with the class schedule. He felt the school could accommodate more students and he wanted to increase my course load. But by now I realized that

I could simply refuse. Once, a young man showed up at the afternoon class with the women. He said he had been told by Ohno-san that he could join. I ushered him out into the hall and told him to come back for the evening class. Ohno-san stormed in to protest, and he and I went back out into the hall to discuss it.

"Ohno-san," I said in my best tough-guy Japanese, "this class is full. If you want more students at this time of day, you can teach them yourself. Do you understand? If you don't, we could go back inside and have this conversation, in English, in front of the students. Shall we?"

Ohno-san's English wasn't good enough to understand one tenth of what I said to him in English. I assumed that if he had to carry on an actual conversation with me in English in front of the students they would immediately realize what a fraud he was. I didn't understand that Ohno-san was someone probably used to other people being mad at him, and to verbal abuse. He wasn't bothered in the least by my anger. The students would probably not have cared that he didn't speak English well enough to teach. Ohno-san simply made a calculation. Push the *gaijin* past his limit and try to find a *gaijin* to replace him or concede defeat.

This time he was willing to allow me to win. If new students could only attend the day class, he taught them himself. Otherwise, new students came to the evening classes only. With only one exception.

On a particularly fine Thursday morning, I was sitting in my room having my usual breakfast of two fat slices of the white bread known as *shokupan*, toasted and plain, washed down by a mug of instant coffee with Creap, the Japanese powdered substitute for real milk. I had the *Mainichi Shimbun* from the day before spread out before me and was circling ads for small refrigerators in the "for sale" columns.

The sad state of my morning meal was due to the fact that Ohno-san had never provided the small refrigerator that he had promised to buy for me when I took the job. There was no place nearby to buy food. There wasn't even a coffee shop in the neighborhood. If I wanted anything perishable to eat for or with breakfast, like cheese, yogurt, butter, or milk, I had to have a refrigerator.

I was tired of drinking my instant coffee with powdered artificial milk and of not having anything to go with my toast. I decided I had no choice but to just go ahead and buy a small used refrigerator with my own money, of which I had very little. I would worry later about how to get Ohno-san to pay for it.

As much as I disliked Ohno-san and his way of earning his living, I was also beginning to feel a little sorry for him. Once, at dinner when his wife had told me another one of the sad stories of her life with her husband, I suddenly found it too much to take. Normally I just sat passively, chewed on a tough piece of *tonkatsu* or day-old *kaki-furai* and listened. But this time I suddenly objected.

"I can't believe that there aren't ways of making your way in the world without hurting other people. There are honest ways to earn a living you know."

Mrs. Ohno looked up at me sadly and seemed to be thinking about it.

"It's not always possible to choose the world you live in," Mrs. Ohno said.

"Everyone has choices," I said.

Mrs. Ohno fixed me with a weary look that seemed to question if I could really be that naïve.

"Yes," Mrs. Ohno said. "How nice it must be to be an American. How nice it must be to have choices. How nice it must be to always have a beautiful house with a cherry tree to go back to."

I had to admit, I really was nothing but a tourist in her world. I was thinking about this as I drank my instant coffee with Creap and circled ads for secondhand refrigerators. Just then Ohno-san came into my room without knocking. I hated that Ohno-san never knocked before entering. The door had a lock, and I kicked myself for again forgetting to lock it.

"Good morning Mr. Ascher," Ohno-san said.

"Ohno-san, do you see what I'm doing here? I'm looking at ads for small refrigerators. Do you remember that you promised me you would buy a refrigerator for the room? Can I expect you to honor your promise?"

"Yes, of course. I'm very sorry, but I will take care of this very soon. Soon. Very soon. Please be patient, Ascher-san. I haven't forgotten."

"Then you *will* get me a small refrigerator?"

"Yes."

"Soon?"

"Yes, very soon. But listen, Ascher-san, I just came to tell you that we have some new students coming over today. Two young men, and they are going to be in a class by themselves. Just the two of them, separate from the school's normal program. They're going to have their own schedule. Two-hour classes. Daytime only. You can work out the exact times with them."

"I see. Who are they?"

"They're two young men who want to learn English. Please just teach them well."

"What if other students come when they're here? Don't we promise the other students they can join any class that's in session when they come?"

"This is a private class. If anyone else comes, I will teach them."

"Great. When do we start?"

"They'll be here in ten minutes."

"Ten minutes? You're kidding? I haven't even finished eating breakfast."

Ohno-san got up and left. I went into the bathroom and filled my one-cup kettle from the sink and then brought it back and set it on the hotplate. When it boiled, I made myself another cup of Nescafé, added some white powdered Creap from a jar, and spooned in some sugar to kill the taste of the artificial milk substitute. Then I went back to scanning the ads. The instant coffee tasted very bad. It was a leap of the imagination to think of it as coffee at all.

There was a knock at the door. I got up to open it and found myself face-to-face with two unusually well-dressed young men in their early twenties. They bowed very correctly and addressed me politely in Japanese.

"Good morning. Are you Asha-*sensei*?"

"Yes."

"We have come to learn English. May we come in?"

I looked them over and then nodded them into the room. The pair bowed themselves in and took seats on the sofa. I put away the newspaper and sat down in one of the big chairs opposite them.

We sat in silence for a few minutes. I continued to look them over. They sat patiently and looked back at me.

One of them was thin and tall and had his hair carefully greased and combed back. He had long arms and very large hands. The other was round and stout and had hair cropped close to the scalp. The thin one wore a shiny dark blue suit of an artificial material, a navy shirt, also of artificial material, and a narrow white tie. The stout one seemed to be made entirely of solid muscle. He wore a light brown polyester suit, a white shirt with a wide collar open at the neck, and no tie. Instead of a tie he had a heavy gold chain. They both wore stylish, narrow leather shoes, very highly polished.

The two young men seated opposite me bowed deeply. The thin one did all the talking.

"*Sensei*, please teach us English."

More bowing.

"I am Aizawa and this is Ihara. We are here to master English. Please teach us."

"I see. So, how much English do you know already?"

I asked this in English and got back blank looks in return. I switched to Japanese and asked again.

"We are starting from zero."

"From zero?"

"Yes, we never studied any English before."

"None?"

"No."

"Not even in kindergarten or elementary school? I thought everyone had to study some English?"

"*Sensei*, school has always been a weak point for Ihara and myself."

"You know the alphabet? ABC? Can you read a little?"

"No."

"I see. So, could I ask you why you want to learn English? Is it related to your work or is it just a kind of a private hobby?"

"I think both and neither."

"I see. Then could I ask you what it is you do for a living? Your work? What your jobs are?"

Aizawa leaned forward.

"*Sensei*, do you know what a numbers game is? Like the national lottery, only not run by the government. A kind of private lottery."

"Uh-huh, yes, I think I have heard of that."

"Well, our work is connected with that. Our job is to collect the cash."

"That sounds like a very interesting job."

"Interesting? No, to be honest, not really interesting. We work at night. We go to the same places every night. We see the same people. We hang around. We wait. There's not much conversation. We pick up the earnings. We count the cash. We issue private receipts. Then we drop the funds off at headquarters. It's a lot of waiting around. Very dull."

"I see. But it can't be that simple. You're being modest. For example, what happens if someone doesn't hand over the money? What do you do then?"

"*Sensei*, you've been watching too many movies. Everybody pays."

"Everybody?"

"Of course?"

"No danger at all?"

"None."

"OK, so what do you want to learn English for?"

"*Sensei*, Ihara and I have a dream. We want to move to Hawaii and open a restaurant. A *tonkatsu* restaurant. Do you know *tonkatsu*?"

"*Tonkatsu*, yes. Deep-fried pork cutlets. Very tasty. But why Hawaii?"

"Too many *tonkatsu* restaurants in Japan already. Very hard to start one up here. Very expensive. Rent expensive. Equipment expensive. Pork expensive. You have to pay off the building inspectors, the health inspectors. Get licenses. Pay protection money. Very expensive. My uncle lives in Hawaii. Things are still very open there. Lots of Japanese in Hawaii. America is still cheap. Hawaii is very beautiful. I hear Hawaii is beautiful. Is it?"

"Yes, I suppose so, but can you just pick up and move to Hawaii and start a restaurant?"

"Yes, my uncle will help arrange everything. Ihara and I are still young. We can do it."

"OK. So you need to learn English to live in Hawaii and run a restaurant. That's a very good reason to learn. So how long are you prepared to spend to learn English?"

"Our plan is to master English in exactly two months."

"Two months? Are you joking? You can't master English in two months. Look, it's just not realistic. If you guys are going to spend your hard-earned money to do this, I want you to understand clearly from the start, you cannot possibly learn English in two months. Not from zero. I'm sorry, but I want to be fair to you. Nobody could do it."

"*Sensei*, we are prepared to give our utmost effort. We will study hard and we have a good teacher. If we, and you, *sensei*, all give our utmost effort, we will master English in two months. We have complete confidence in you."

Visions of an early death ran through my brain. All that I really knew about these kinds of guys, about *yakuza*, came from TV and the movies. That and from some anecdotes I had heard from a Princeton professor, a documentary filmmaker, who had had to work with *yakuza* to make a film about nightlife in Tokyo. I had heard that *yakuza* were the most traditionally minded of all Japanese. They maintained a clear and definite social hierarchy and had an iron-clad code of behavior. They lived and died by their code. They were calling me *sensei*. I assumed that meant I had been fixed in their hierarchy and placed in a position high enough for me to talk to them any way that I pleased. In theory, I should be able to say whatever I wanted to them, however I wanted to say it. I hoped very much that I was right about that.

"Idiots!" I said with conviction. "No one can master English in two months."

"Please *sensei*. We are prepared to give our utmost effort."

"Look, you're starting from ABC. Even if you could already talk just a little, which you can't, you can't get anywhere in just two months. If you're serious about this, and you really want to learn enough to get by in Hawaii, then expect to spend at least a year. A year of hard work. Absolute minimum. Do you understand that?"

Aizawa leaned forward again. His voice was just a little bit harder than before, and his body language just a bit more taut.

"*Sensei*, we have two months. We are prepared to work very hard. You will teach us what we need to know in two months."

"Listen to me. I'm not negotiating with you or trying to bargain with you. I am telling you as a professional, as a professional teacher of English, that you cannot learn the language, or even a little piece of it, in two months starting from zero. I am telling you, as a person who knows, that it cannot be done. Simple fact. Not possible. Do you understand me?"

Aizawa looked up at me.

"Thank you, *sensei*. We appreciate your concern for us. We have two months. We will work very hard. You will teach us."

"You'll be wasting your money."

"It's our money."

"Then why not do it right? Don't expect to do it in two months. Do it right and let it take as long as it takes. What's magic about two months?"

Aizawa looked at me very hard and moved just a little closer to the edge of the sofa. His voice was very low and firm.

"*Sensei*, we have two months to master English. Just two months. We have complete confidence in you. We place ourselves in your hands."

The two of them bowed deeply again.

I didn't like it. Clearly there was nothing I could do about it.

"All right gentlemen. Then let us begin."

"Thank you, *sensei*. We will not let you down."

Them letting *me* down was not at all what I was worried about. I arranged for them to come in for lessons four times a week for three hours at a time from ten in the morning, the earliest they said they could make it. I had them down for Mondays, Wednesdays, Thursdays, and Saturdays.

"*Sensei*, we can come every day."

"No, I'm giving you homework. If you're going to get anything out of coming to class, you have to learn to do your homework and do it on your own. You have to practice before you come here so you don't waste your time or mine. You promised to work hard, now let's see if you can do it."

"*Sensei*, we promise to do our best."

I began with the basics. By the end of the first lesson we had almost mastered the alphabet. I was glad to discover that hours of watching *Sesame Street* with my baby sister had not gone completely to waste. I wanted to ask, if they should fail to learn any English at all in two months, would they be expected to cut off any fingers or would I? I decided not to ask. I wanted to get to know them better before discovering if *yakuza* had a sense of humor about these things.

Aizawa and Ihara were true to their words about their motivation. Their drive to actually learn English surpassed anything I had seen in any of my other students. If learning were just a matter of motivation alone, they were bound to succeed.

"*Sensei*," Aizawa said to me after their first class, "we have a car. We have a car and free time during the day. If you ever need us to drive you anywhere, it would be our pleasure to do so. Please ask for our help whenever you need us."

"OK," I said. "Let's go up to Maruzen on Kawaramachi and get you some English study tapes to listen to. The tapes are your homework. Maybe we can find you a good beginning textbook there too."

"Thank you, *sensei*. We are in your debt."

AIZAWA AND IHARA ALWAYS ARRIVED precisely on time for their lessons. And they always dressed exactly the same, or more or less the same, as when I had first met them. Either they didn't own a lot of clothing, or they saw their clothing as a kind of uniform. I tried to picture them dressed in their Japanese *yakuza* clothes in Hawaii.

Aizawa and Ihara were extremely good-natured about everything and always very polite. I had a hard time imagining them working their regular job, collecting bags of money, providing friendly warnings to slow or late payers, or dealing with the non-payers. I assumed that at their day job, which took place at night, they were models of professionalism and efficiency. As students of English they were completely hopeless. Hopeless, but cheerful.

Ohno-san had never made good on his promise to provide me with a refrigerator. I finally found an ad for one in the newspaper "for sale" columns that I could afford. When I called the number in the ad, an oily-voiced middle-aged man confirmed that the price was ¥5,000, as advertised, and that the machine worked perfectly, as advertised, and that if I wanted it, I would have to come and get it. He couldn't guarantee how long it might be before someone else came in and wanted it, and he wouldn't hold it for anyone. Not for a day. Not for an hour. The location of the appliance seller was all the way on the other side of town. The cost of having it delivered, or even a taxi ride to and from, would push the price well beyond my ability to afford it.

There was something about the man's voice that made me want to just forget the whole thing. But I was very tired of living without in-house refrigeration and the price was right. How to go there and get the thing? All the way to Kitaoji to the north and west of Kyoto. And then I remembered that Aizawa and Ihara had a car and had offered to drive me anywhere, any time.

"Guys," I said when the pair arrived for class, "do you remember telling me you would be happy to drive me anywhere in your car?"

They brightened perceptibly. Either they really liked driving around Kyoto in their car or they were just sick of basic pronunciation drills and would have done anything for a break from them.

"Yes, *sensei*. Would you like us to take you somewhere?" Aizawa said.

"Well, as a matter of fact I have to go over to a place all the way out on Kitaoji to pick up this refrigerator I want to buy it for the room here, and . . ."

"Of course, *sensei*. It's no problem at all. We have a car and we are at your complete disposal. When would you like to go?"

"Well, the guy said that if I didn't come to get it soon he couldn't guarantee that it would still be there, so . . ."

"Fine, then why don't we go right now?"

"Right now? You don't mind?"

"Of course not. Shall we?"

"OK. Maybe we can do some grammar drills in the car."

I was supposed to be on call for other lessons after my class with Aizawa and Ihara. But I guessed that Ohno-san was not likely to object to my leaving in the company of two of the school's most prized students. Taking his approval for granted, I left without telling him.

Aizawa, Ihara, and I got into the building's tiny elevator and went downstairs. Out on the street it was sunny and pleasant. People were out and about and doing this and that. I wasn't used to the brightness of the outside. Everything seemed a little strange to me.

Their car was parked illegally on a side street. It was a nondescript black Toyota sedan. An older model, but very clean and apparently in good shape despite its age. We got in.

I sat stretched out in the comfort of the back seat. Ihara drove and Aizawa rode shotgun. Their arms hung out the open windows. Cigarettes dangled from their lips. They were the kings of all they surveyed and happy to be on the move. I hadn't often been in a private car in Japan, and it felt a little strange. Riding in a private car in Kyoto somehow gave me a different perspective on the city.

Riding on public transportation in Japan makes you feel a part of the general population. One of the people. Part of the normal tapestry of regular life in your city. Riding in a private car lets you feel that there's an entire other world out there. A world that's not open to just anyone. You feel just a little bit like Alice on her way down the rabbit hole. Unexpected things can happen.

As the car made its way through Kyoto's heavy downtown traffic and into the north part of the city, the wider roads became narrower roads and the general atmosphere became less commercial and more residential. We entered an area where there were lots of small mom-and-pop shops crammed together. Narrow alleyways ran through the neighborhoods and drying laundry hung from the back and side windows of most of the buildings. There was not much here to indicate that this was a part of the ancient city of Kyoto. It felt like just some ordinary part of anywhere Japan. There were no temples, no shrines, no castles, and no historical houses. For Kyoto this was unusual.

The car pulled into a local shopping street. Most of the buildings were shops below and residences above. The surrounding area behind the shopping street was densely packed with small private homes. Just beyond the houses was an area of small farmers' fields that seemed completely out of place within the city limits of one of Japan's largest cities.

Ihara parked the car.

"*Sensei*, shall we come in with you."

"No, please just wait in the car. This should take just a minute or two. I'll come and get you if I need help lifting the refrigerator."

I got out of the car, found the address the man on the phone had given me, and went in. The place was a kind of junk shop. A shop selling worn and half-broken electric appliances, dusty curios and antiques, and miscellaneous bits of domestic housewares. It was as if someone had decided to start up one kind of business, then changed his mind midway, and then changed again. At the back of the shop sat a fat man in a sleeveless undershirt and baggy tan slacks. He was fanning himself slowly with a cheap paper fan. It was hot in the store.

"Hello," I said. "I called earlier about the small refrigerator."

The man looked me over slowly, continuing to fan himself. He had a sour expression on his face. He pointed to his left with the fan.

"There."

I stepped over and looked at the refrigerator. I opened the door. It was clean inside. It seemed OK as far as I could tell.

"Does it work?"

"Works fine."

"OK, then, I guess I'll take it."

The man eyed me with apparent disgust. I was unsure if the man disliked me in particular, humanity in general, or just anyone who happened to come into his store. I reached into my pocket and took out the ¥5,000 that was most of the money I owned in the world. When I moved to hand it to the man, he looked at it and shook his head.

"The price is ¥10,000," the man said.

"No, I think there must be some mistake. On the phone you said ¥5,000. The ad in the paper said ¥5,000. I made sure of that before I came all the way over here."

"It's ¥10,000."

"Is this the refrigerator we talked about on the phone?"

"Yes, it is."

"Then we agreed on ¥5,000. You told me ¥5,000. I came all the way across town, all the way here because you said the price was ¥5,000."

"It's ¥10,000."

"Listen, I haven't even got ¥10,000 and I really need this refrigerator."

"Not my problem. ¥10,000."

I began to get angry. The man seemed to be amused by my anger. He sat in his chair slowly fanning himself and chuckling.

"¥10,000. Take it or leave it."

"Look, we agreed on ¥5,000. You said ¥5,000. ¥5,000 is all I'm going to pay you. ¥5,000 is what you agreed to on the phone. You agreed to it and that's what it is."

The man fanned himself and smiled.

"That was then. This is now," he said. "You want the refrigerator? It's ¥10,000. Up to you. I don't care either way."

"Listen you . . . you . . . you . . . you shit-eating fuckwad."

I had to switch to English for the last part. I regretted that there was no equivalent in Japanese, or at least I didn't know one. I did my best to sound threatening, but it wasn't working very well, and it wasn't getting me any closer to owning the refrigerator.

"Look, come on," I said, trying to switch tactics. "I'm a guest in your country. I'm here working hard to learn your language. Don't you think you could cut me a break and sell me the refrigerator for ¥5,000?"

"As I already said, the price is ¥10,000. Take it . . . or leave it."

I got mad all over again and started screaming at the man in English.

"Goddamnit! You agreed! You goddamned fuckhead! You agreed to it! I'm buying this fucking refrigerator for ¥5,000! You agreed! You agreed and you are going to do what you fucking agreed to! Here! Here's the money! Take it! Take it you . . . you . . . you . . . fuckwad!"

I held out five ¥1,000 notes in front of the fat man's face, my hand trembling with rage. The fat man was sitting in his chair, calmly fanning himself and smiling pleasantly. But suddenly a look of surprise came over the fat man's face. He wasn't looking at me anymore. He was looking just behind me, and his smile had vanished.

A voice reached me from behind. It was Aizawa.

"*Sensei*, is there a problem here?"

I turned to look at him. Aizawa and Ihara had followed me into the shop. The fat man was looking up at them. He looked puzzled and he looked worried. His mouth was opening and closing like a fish gasping for air. Words wanted to form but wouldn't.

Before I could say anything, the fat man was out of his chair, up on his feet, bowing and trying very hard to get a smile to form on his greasy face. His lips twitched with the effort.

"I . . . I . . . I . . . No. No, no. No problem at all. No problem. We . . . we were just concluding . . . uh . . . concluding the sale of this . . . this refrigerator. Five . . . five thousand yen I . . . I believe the price was. Five thousand yen, yes. Yes."

I was already so used to Aizawa and Ihara that I had forgotten the effect they might have on a stranger. Was it really that simple? You only had to look the part? Or being the genuine article, did you project it? Whatever it was, it was working.

"No," I said, "I believe you told me the price was ¥2,500."

I put three of the ¥1,000 notes back into my pocket, replaced them with a ¥500 note and handed the money over to the fat man. The man looked as if he were about to complain, but then he thought better of it. The smile was trying to come back on.

"Uh . . . uh . . . why, yes, yes. ¥2,500. Yes."

"We have a car outside," I said. "Please carry it out to the car for us."

The man seemed to be looking for something, a hand cart possibly, but with three pairs of eyes staring down hard at him he grew flustered and gave up. He heaved a great sigh, leaned down, and picked up the refrigerator and then hauled it outside. If the fat man was angry, he had decided to save it for after his customers had left.

Ihara showed him the car and popped the trunk for him. The fat man hoisted the refrigerator above the trunk, gingerly placing it inside. When it was in, he stood to the side with his head slightly bowed as Ihara took his time checking to make sure there was no damage to the appliance or to the inside of the trunk. Satisfied, Ihara shut the trunk again and then held the door for me as I got into the back seat. No one smiled. Aizawa and Ihara got into the front seat and the man said nothing, still keeping his eyes to the pavement. He was sweating profusely.

Ihara took his time finding the key and starting up the engine. He was in no hurry. When the car finally pulled away from the curb, I turned back to look at the fat man who continued bowing until the car was out of sight. I wondered, was the man overreacting? What exactly could my two affable, good-natured students have actually done to the man? Was it really so important to keep completely off of the *yakuza*'s radar?

Though I was happy to finally have a refrigerator for cold drinks, yogurt, butter for my toast, and real milk for my instant coffee, I began to feel a little guilty. Surely a person with a home to go back to, one with a cherry tree in the yard, could have afforded to be more generous and paid the full ¥5,000. Surely I could have.

A few months later I got a postcard from Aizawa and Ihara in Hawaii. A month after that there was a short letter and a snapshot of them in front of their own *tonkatsu* restaurant.

By that time I was well on my way to being completely over Pattie. I had already arranged to spend a few months in Tokyo before starting graduate school in New York.

Wendy

I STUDIED THE JAPANESE LANGUAGE at the Kyoto Japanese Language School. It was an odd little place that in the past had trained some of the world's best-known students of Japanese art and literature. There were more prestigious programs in Tokyo run by well-known universities. But for those seriously studying Japanese in Kyoto, this was the place to be.

The school was off an alley just across from the Old Kyoto Imperial Palace, a giant park that surrounded two walled-in imperial palace compounds. The school was in what had become an upscale residential neighborhood. It was one of the few areas in Kyoto where property owners had not hesitated to update the buildings that sat on their property. The Kyoto Japanese Language School was the only building anywhere nearby that wasn't someone's house.

The school building was a hundred-plus-year-old wreck of a place. If it had ever been a private residence, nothing to indicate its original purpose remained. It retained the aura of a bygone era. You half expected it to still be Meiji Japan inside. The floorboards moaned when you walked on them. A nearly vertical narrow flight of wooden stairs led up to a second floor. Even the school's bathroom was old-style. To reach the single-sex stalls that held old-fashioned squat toilets, male and female students had to pass the tile wall with a metal trough at its base that served as a urinal.

You took off your shoes at the *genkan* and stored them in a shoe cabinet with many shelves. The shelves had once had little wooden doors, probably with wooden keys, but these were long gone. Directly across from the entrance was a bulletin board with information about class assignments, homework assignments, grades, rooms to let, roommates sought, English-conversation teaching jobs, kerosene heaters for sale, motorbikes for sale, used books for sale, and the location of good cheap local restaurants.

I had Japanese class for three hours a day, three days a week. The classes were small. You usually knew everything there was to know about your classmates. In Japanese-conversation class, what was there really to talk about for hours at a time except ourselves? We always tried to find out as much as we could about the teachers, but they were better than the students at keeping their personal lives to themselves.

Kyoto was the kind of place where new people were always arriving and people you had just gotten to know were leaving. One of my first classmates was from Ireland. Her name was Saoirse, which she pronounced "*sir*-sha like inertia." Her Irish accent made her Japanese almost completely unintelligible to me, but the teachers seemed to understand it. Saoirse had a part-time job at a restaurant up in the hills behind Kiyomizu-dera.

Sam Orbach from New Jersey came from some place called Matawan that was near the Jersey Shore. He had graduated from Princeton and was now a graduate student at Columbia University studying Chinese and Japanese literature. He wanted to be a translator like his two idols, Donald Keene and Burton Watson. Donald Keene had told him to forget about translation because it was insufficiently academic. Burton Watson had dropped out of academics and was driving a taxi in either New York or Tokyo depending on which rumor you believed. Keene told Sam if he wanted to really learn about Japanese literature he had to spend time in Kyoto as Keene himself had done. And here he was.

Sam had scholarship money from Columbia and didn't need to do part-time jobs. He spent nearly all of his time studying. Wherever he went he carried around with him a stack of cards containing the ten new *kanji* characters he was making himself learn each day, plus twenty or thirty of the ones he had learned over the past two weeks. He was the kind of person who could read a dictionary for pleasure. I was in awe of his discipline and his ability to speak, read, and write Japanese. His presence was a source of shame for me. A reminder of how I should be using my time in Kyoto but wasn't.

We had a different teacher for each class. All the teachers in the school were women. Hirata-*sensei* taught reading and writing. She was a compact, pretty woman in her early twenties, just out of teachers' college. All we were able to get out of her was that she was originally from up north somewhere, Tohoku or Hokkaido, that she lived in a rented room all the way up in Otsu, and that she didn't have a boyfriend.

Nishimura-*sensei* taught grammar. She might have been alive during Japan's Meiji period, or at least she retained the social norms and manner of speaking from that era. She was an excellent teacher.

Watanabe-*sensei* taught Japanese conversation. She was about thirty years old and very beautiful. She had the face of a Pre-Raphaelite beauty that might have been painted by Dante Gabriel Rossetti had he ever wanted to put an Asian female into one of his lush landscapes. Watanabe-*sensei* never joked around in class or even smiled. She was all business.

Her beauty and the fact that Watanabe-*sensei* seemed to be trying to hide it was a topic of conversation after school. She dressed herself in shapeless ankle-length woolen skirts and oversized sweaters. She parted her dense, lustrous black hair in the middle so it fell in thick unruly clouds to her shoulders. She wore large round glasses with black plastic rims. And she wore a large silver cross around her neck, the kind that that signified an actual connection to Christianity and not just a casual bit of ornamentation. There was a rumor going around the school that Watanabe-*sensei* had once been a Catholic nun and had lived in a nunnery.

Springtime in Japan brought both cherry blossoms and a new

semester at the Kyoto Japanese Language School. Saoirse had gone back to Dublin and Sam Orbach was back in New York. I arrived at school and headed to the bulletin board to check out my new class assignments. I ascended the creaking flight of wooden stairs to the second floor for my first class, intermediate Japanese conversation with Watanabe-*sensei*. There would only be two students in the class, myself and a new student named Wendy Anderson.

The economics of the Kyoto Japanese Language School were a mystery to me. The student body was small. The tuition for a semester of classes was reasonable enough that you could afford it doing a few part-time jobs teaching English. How they were able to stay in business and pay the teachers and the upkeep on the building from the money they charged for tuition seemed like some kind of minor miracle.

When I reached the small upstairs classroom my new classmate was already there. She was seated at one of the too-small desks. She was pale, trim, and she had an unkempt mop of long, naturally bright orange hair. Her hair was such a brilliant shade of orange I was momentarily stunned when I entered the shabby classroom.

I took a seat next to the pale female and she extended a hand for me to shake. The hand was very white and the grip was very firm.

"Wendy Anderson from the University of Wisconsin."

"Don Ascher, Cornell University, most recently anyway."

"Is Don short for Donald?"

"No. It's actually short for Sheldon. A name I truly despise. I don't usually confess that to someone I've just met. Don or Donnie if you don't mind."

"Oh."

"So, is Wisconsin also where you're from?"

"Green Lake Wisconsin. It's in the Upper Peninsula. We moved to Lodi when I was in high school. Do you know where that is?"

"Near Ann Arbor?"

"No. That's in Michigan. I'm in Chinese History. You?"

"Undetermined. *Chinese* history you said? You do realize this is Japan we're in now?"

"Yes. My graduate program requires two languages. I've pretty much done my Chinese requirement. Japanese will be my second language."

"Are you Scandinavian or Irish?"

"Have you ever been to Wisconsin?"

"One night in Spring Green on my way to San Francisco. To see the famous Frank Lloyd Wright house there."

"Did you see it?"

"No. It was dark and I had just driven there with a friend from Cleveland. A friend of another friend had a job at the famous house as a caretaker on the property. We had to leave early in the morning. We spent the night in a converted barn on the property. The caretaker's residence. It was a really terrific barn."

Wendy had a habit of chewing on loose strands her red hair when she was uncomfortable. I hoped it was about learning Japanese and not about me.

"How long have you been here?" Wendy asked.

"About nine months," I said.

"Nine months! Gosh, I just got here last week."

"Yeah? Where do you live? Did you find someplace nearby?"

"Well, the school helped me find an apartment. I guess I got here kind of late to really find anything good, or close to the school. My stipend doesn't provide too much for housing. I'm kind of out of the main part of town. Kind of west I guess, and maybe north. Could be south. I'm not really good with maps. There's a great big temple nearby. Myoshin-ji, I think. I guess it must be. That's the name of my stop. The train stop. I think it might be a Zen temple. I'm not sure."

"Yeah, that's a pretty big Zen temple."

"Is it? Oh. Well I haven't seen it yet. It's on my list of things to do. I take a bus to Omiya and then that cute little train that goes all the way to Arashiyama. I get off at Myoshin-ji. The train stop, I mean. Not the temple. I have my map. I can show you."

"No, I know where it is. It's kind of a landmark. So then you're living in a traditional working-class part of town, right?"

"Is it? I guess so. It seems kind of run-down. Where do you live?"

"Hi no Oka."

"Hi no Oka? Where's that?"

"East. Almost to Yamashina."

"Oh. Where is Yamashina? Gosh, I really have no idea where anything is. This place is a whole lot bigger than I thought it would be. Is Hi no Oka a nice place to live? I haven't been anywhere yet. I've never heard of any of these places. I should really take some time and study my map, I guess."

"Hi no Oka? Yeah, it's all right. Well, there aren't any thousand-year-old Zen temple complexes clogging up the neighborhood. It's more residential. *New* residential. Maybe traditional is a better way to get to know Kyoto. You might be onto something."

Just then Watanabe-*sensei* came in. She plunged right into the lesson without any welcome chit-chat. In conversation class Watanabe-*sensei* couldn't be baited, provoked, or embarrassed, though it was fun to try. It was extremely hard to get her to smile, but worth it when she did. She had a dry sense of humor and was skeptical of every assertion her students made. She had a way of making you talk and teaching you things as she did.

Watanabe-*sensei* and Wendy did not seem to get on well from the beginning. Whatever Wendy's other talents were, she was not good at speaking Japanese. Armed with a dictionary, stubborn patience, and some time, Wendy could work her way through almost any written text. But hearing and speaking the language were real problems for her.

Other teachers were gentle with students who seemed insecure and tentative in class. Watanabe-*sensei* was not. Wendy seemed to resent being treated roughly when she couldn't master a sentence pattern or a verb tense. As a result, Wendy often clammed up in class and had to be forced to speak. I had a part-time job in a Japanese restaurant and interacted in Japanese with Japanese people almost every day. Wendy spent most of her time outside of class studying her texts. As the weeks passed she began to fall behind.

One day Watanabe-*sensei* asked me to stay after class for a few minutes. After Wendy left, Watanabe-*sensei* asked me if I had noticed that Wendy was falling behind.

I said yes.

Watanabe-*sensei* said she was worried about Wendy. It surprised me very much to learn that Wendy and Watanabe-*sensei* had begun meeting in the afternoon for tea. I had the impression that they disliked each other. Now I supposed I'd been wrong about that.

Watanabe-*sensei* had begun giving Wendy free private lessons. She said Wendy was working too hard but just not getting it. Wendy needed extra tutoring but she couldn't afford it. She was too proud to ask for help. She spent too much time alone in her room with her textbooks. Watanabe-*sensei* wanted me to help her. Would I be willing to spend time with her and show her better ways to study? Would I introduce her to Japanese people she could practice with?

I said I would. I liked Wendy very much. But Watanabe-*sensei* . . . I probably would have jumped off the roof of the school building if Watanabe-*sensei* had asked me to do it. But all Watanabe-*sensei* wanted was for me to help Wendy. I said I would try and separate Wendy from her books. I said I would encourage her to get out and experience more of Kyoto. I had already invited Wendy to join me for dinner, or lunch, or to go out and visit one of the big famous temples in the city, but she had always refused, saying she would love to but that she had to go home and study. I said I would ask Wendy again and not take no for an answer.

A few days later I asked Wendy to go with me and have a look at Myoshin-ji, the major Zen temple right in her neighborhood. Wendy, to my surprise, said yes. I supposed that she had had the same talk from Watanabe-*sensei* about getting out more.

We settled on a day when neither of us had class. After a few months of living in Kyoto, Wendy had still never walked down to look at the world-famous major Zen temple a few streets over from where she lived.

THE *TSUYU*, JAPAN'S RAINY SEASON, had begun. The balmy days of May had not led to summer heat. Instead, June brought chilly weather, cloudy skies, and the kind of rain that never reaches the level of honest downpour. It went on for weeks, casting a damp pall over everything. It felt like a kind of regression in the steady forward march of the seasons. A kind of disappointment after the cherry blossoms in April and the flowers in May.

Early one chilly, overcast morning, I set off on my yellow Honda motorcycle to meet Wendy. Wendy had drawn me a map to her rooming house. In Japan, no invitation to someone's house was a real invitation unless it was accompanied by a map of how to get there. Even in the relatively well-ordered city of Kyoto, where the street addresses even gave some clue to a building's location, without a map it wouldn't have been possible to find an address for a first-time visit.

It was only eight-thirty in the morning when I arrived at the X on the map that Wendy had given me. I had passed very near the impressive gates and crumbling walls of the Myoshin-ji complex of Zen temples. Nearer to the temple's front side, where the main gate was, the houses were mostly traditional and imposing. But toward the rear of the complex, the neighborhood became a jumble of small houses, a mixture of old and new. There were even tiny farmers' fields, clearly distinguishable from just ordinary people's communal gardens by the relentless fastidiousness of the way the professional farmers arranged and cared for their plots.

Wendy's building was old in the sense that it was built using traditional methods, and it was beat up, ramshackle, and run-down. It was new in the sense that it was a kind of rooming house, which in

Japan, especially in Kyoto, was not really a traditional building. This one was two stories tall and held about a dozen individual one-room apartments. The entrance to each of the one-room apartments was on the outside of the building. A wooden stairway led to the second story. A second-story wooden walkway, not wide enough to be a porch or a terrace, went around the outside of the building.

The walls of the building were made in the traditional Japanese way, with mud and straw and a kind of plaster pressed into a wooden frame. The dried mixture had now aged to a cracked and faded yellowish brown. The walls groaned and sagged under a roof of heavy, slate-gray ceramic tiles. The endcaps bore the floral design of some family's crest, a sure sign that they had been recycled from something older.

There was a muddy dirt parking area in front of the building. It was strewn with beat-up secondhand bicycles and motorbikes, some standing and others fallen over. One side of the building was bordered by a small but thick grove of tall bamboo trees. On the other side was an outhouse that announced its presence by its unmistakable odor.

I parked my motorcycle, climbed the stairs, and knocked on the door of unit number 202. It opened, and there was Wendy, dressed in sweatpants and a sweatshirt holding a mug of tea.

"Hi. Come on in. You found the place OK?"

"Sure. You drew a good map."

"It's the only way anyone could ever find this place. I don't understand why they don't get a better system here. Why can't they just number the houses in order?"

"Because it's Japan."

Wendy held the door for me and I stepped inside her room. There was a very small square of cement floor at the entrance, about six inches lower than the rest of the room, that served as the *genkan*, or at least, as the place you took off your shoes and left them. Wendy had been standing in this *genkan* in a pair of rubber sandals. She stepped back out of them and up onto the tatami to make room for me. The room was a standard six-mat tatami room. As I removed my shoes Wendy had to lean back across me, barely keeping her balance, in order to stretch over and close the door. I did my best to keep out of her way, but couldn't in the tiny space.

"I could have closed it for you," I said.

"It's OK. Come on in."

I stood on Wendy's rubber sandals and placed my hiking boots next to hers in the *genkan*. I stepped out of the rubber sandals and up onto the tatami.

At the back of Wendy's room was a bed that consisted of a thin mattress laid over a sheet of plywood supported by yellow plastic crates. The crates had "Kirin Beer" printed on them in large red letters. At the right side of the room was a small sink with a single faucet and knob for cold water only. Next to it was a linoleum-topped counter. On the counter sat a single-burner hot plate, an open box of tea bags, and some other boxes containing sugar cubes, Ritz crackers, Saltine crackers, and Pop Tarts.

Under the counter was a small refrigerator that had seen better days. A makeshift bookcase full of textbooks took up the opposite wall of the room. In the center of the room was a low *kotatsu* table. The bed was blocking a traditional Japanese futon closet, though it looked like you could still get at the contents of the closet from the bed. There wasn't much space in the room to move around. Water was boiling in a kettle on the hot plate.

"You want some tea?" Wendy asked. "I just made myself a cup."

"Looks like you're already boiling the water."

"Oh. Oh no, that's not for tea. That's for the cockroaches."

"For the cockroaches?"

"Yeah. That's how I kill them. Let me show you."

I walked over to the sink with Wendy. There was a pot sitting in the sink, and in the pot were five plastic boxes that were divided into internal sections. In each of the sections there were bunches of cockroaches of different sizes. Some were alarmingly large.

"I put out traps for the cockroaches every night. Then in the morning I collect them, and they're always all full. Full! The traps fill up with cockroaches and then I don't know what to do with them. I catch them in the traps, and then what? I can't just throw out the traps because I need them to catch more cockroaches. So I decided this is the best way to kill them."

"You boil them to death?"

"Yes. Well it seemed like the cleanest way to do it. I don't know how else to kill them. And if they're boiled I don't mind so much having to handle the traps again afterwards."

"So . . . you get about five traps worth every single night?"

"Oh no. No, there are about thirty traps. Here, I was just collecting them when you knocked."

Wendy went over to the bed, reached underneath and pulled out another trap. It was full of big black cockroaches moving around, antennae wiggling anxiously, trying to find a way out of their prison.

"What do you do with them after they're boiled?"

"Dump them onto old newspapers, wrap them up and throw them out. It's part of my morning routine. I hate cockroaches."

"You seem to have quite a lot of them."

"I suppose so. So, would you like some tea?"

"Uh, no thanks. I'm good."

"OK, well let me finish mine and we can get going."

Wendy sat down next to the *kotatsu* and I sat on her bed.

"So, today we're going to look at Myoshin-ji. Is that okay?" I said.

"Yeah. That's what you said. Zen temple. Honestly, if it were up to me to think of things to do, I probably would never leave my room. I don't feel comfortable exploring on my own. I know it's bad, but I feel guilty doing anything but studying."

"I think if you start doing things you'll feel more comfortable doing things on your own."

"Maybe."

"So, no bath here? No bathroom?"

"No. That's kind of a pain. There's nothing so bad as having to go downstairs to that outhouse, you know, to use the toilet in the middle of the night. I really hate it."

"I guess so. The bath?"

"There's a *sento* down the street. I really love the public bath. Really. It's great. I get to practice my Japanese, but it's also so relaxing to get completely clean and soak in a hot bath. And I always meet the same old ladies there. Mostly old ladies. The first day I went, an old lady came over and started washing my back. I was so freaked out! She just came over and started doing it. And I just let her do it. I didn't know what else to do. She even seemed surprised that I was freaked out. And then I noticed that they do that for each other in the public bath. Sometimes. Women wash each other's backs. Normally I would find that kind of creepy. But here it seemed OK. I think I actually like it. Do men do that too?"

"So far as I've discovered, they don't. I used a public bath for a while when I lived in Tokyo. You sometimes get *yakuza* with incredible tattoos. Nobody tried to rub my back. I think I would have been freaked out by that too. I wasn't sure that it was safe to just stare at the *yakuza*, and those tattoos. But I think they like to have them admired. Anyway, a *gaijin* can get away with it. Women in the baths don't have tattoos, right?"

"I never saw any. Maybe you need to be in a different part of Kyoto."

"So who else lives here? Who are the other people who live in the building?"

"All students. The ones I've met go to Kyodai and Doshisha. I'm the only girl."

"So you've made friends in the building? The only girl, you must be very popular."

"At first I guess they were curious. One of the Doshisha guys asked me out to a local bar with him. But my Japanese isn't good enough to really talk and his English wasn't very good, so it was hard. Otherwise I know everyone by sight. And their girlfriends. You sort of get a feeling of community from seeing them on the stairs on the way to the bathroom in the middle of the night, if you know what I mean."

"I suppose."

"Anyway, it's cheap and it's quiet and I get my work done."

"Yeah, but . . ."

"But what?"

"Nothing. You know, maybe if you're done with your tea we should get going."

"All right. All right, but listen, I'm going to change now and you have to look the other way and promise not to look at me."

"OK, I understand. Turn around and don't look at you."

"I mean it. You have to promise. Promise you won't look at me."

"I promise I won't look at you."

"Really. If you look at me while I'm changing I'm going to kill you. You understand? I'll kill you."

"I understand. I see how you boiled the cockroaches and I know you mean business. If I look at you, you'll kill me. Understood."

"All right. Now turn around and don't look until I say you can."

"I could wait outside."

"Please just shut up and turn around."

I turned and faced the door. I noticed that under the sink, and under the bookcase, and here and there under things in the room, there were more of the plastic cockroach traps. Behind me I could hear the futon closet open and shut and then the rustling of clothes.

"Don't look. I'm watching you."

"OK, I get it. I'm not looking. I'm counting the cockroach traps."

I thought Wendy was getting carried away. Maybe she had some kind of birth defect that she didn't want anyone to see. It was hard to believe that anyone who used a common outhouse and went to a public bath would be that worried about being seen in a state of partial undress.

As I was thinking this there was a loud knock on the door and Wendy let out a brief, high-pitched yelp.

"Why do people only show up when I'm getting dressed? Who could that be?"

"I don't know. Do you want me to go and see?"

"OK. OK, I almost have my jeans on. OK. OK, there. Yes, go see. Go see who it is. Just open the door a little. And don't look at me. I'm not dressed yet."

I went to the door and opened it a crack. A postal worker in a blue postal worker uniform and white helmet hat was standing there with a small package.

"Mailman," I reported back to Wendy. "Looks like a package. You want me to get it?"

"Yes, OK."

I opened the door a little more and greeted the mailman.

"Are you Wendy Anderson?" he asked.

"Yes," I told him. "What have you got for me?"

The postman looked up at me skeptically and then shrugged and handed me the small package. Then he thrust a thin white slip of paper at me.

"Sign."

I signed the paper "Wendy Anderson" and handed it back to him. He tipped his helmet cap and hurried off down the stairs to his waiting red post office motorbike. He had left the engine running. They always did. I couldn't understand how it was that no teenage juvenile delinquent ever hopped on one of them and took off on it for a joy ride.

Wendy came over and tapped me on the shoulder and I turned to face her. She was dressed, and she held out a hand for the package.

"You forgot to tell me it's OK to look."

She didn't say anything and I gave her the package. Her carrot-colored hair was neatly brushed and held in place at the front by a pale blue plastic clip in the shape of an upside-down U. She was wearing a rust-colored sweater and her eyes looked very green. She now seemed crisp and refreshed, although all she had done was change out of her sweatshirt and sweatpants and into regular clothes. She took the package, looked at the sender's address, and then tore it open.

"It's a tape from Judy. My best friend in the world. Do you mind if I play a little bit of it before we go? I haven't heard from her in ages."

"Sure."

We sat down again, Wendy by the *kotatsu* and me on the bed. Wendy went to the bookshelves and brought back a portable tape player. She popped the cassette into the player and turned up the sound.

> *Hi Wendy! It's me. Wendy . . . Wendy you'll never guess what happened. You know this guy Ron that I've been going out with? The one who's studying to get his CPA? Well we're really starting to get serious and guess what! We had this big fight and decided to break up. But then we had make-up sex, and it was GREAT! I had an ORGASM! Yes, I really had . . .*

Wendy let out a one-syllable, staccato shriek at the word "orgasm" and stabbed at the off button on the tape machine. Her face turned an amazing shade of crimson. She was so upset her hands and neck and every visible part of her had turned red. Tears filled her eyes. She looked as if she had peeled and eaten a dozen raw onions.

"Wendy, don't tell me you're embarrassed by the word . . ."

"Don't you say it. Don't you dare say it."

"But . . ."

"Don't."

"OK."

We sat for a few minutes in silence. Wendy's face began to resume its normal color, a very pale white. The tears subsided.

"That's not the kind of thing she usually puts in her tapes."

"OK. Why don't we go? You can listen to the rest of it later."

"All right."

Wendy and I moved to the *genkan* and took turns putting on our shoes. I finished lacing my boots outside Wendy's door. Wendy came out and closed the door behind her.

"Aren't you going to lock it?"

"I don't think it does have a lock."

"I see."

It was a very gray morning. Chilly and gray. Just as we stepped off the bottom stair a very light drizzle began to fall. It was really no more than a fine mist. Tiny particles of moisture swirling in the air.

"I know we said we'd walk around here, but now I'm thinking we might go over to Ryoan-ji instead. It's a weekday morning and the weather isn't good and it's in between Japanese tourist seasons. It's probably about the best chance you'll ever get to see Ryoan-ji without a crowd of people ruining the atmosphere of it."

"What's Ryoan-ji?"

"You don't know? Even better. Come on, were going by bike."

"On your motorcycle?"

"Sure. See, I carry an extra helmet. Put this on."

We put on our helmets and I got on the bike and put down the passenger footrests behind me. Then I kick-started the engine. Wendy looked doubtful, but she got on behind me.

"Where do I hold on?"

"You put your arms around me."

"Isn't there someplace else I can hold on to?"

"No, there isn't. If you don't want to fall off, you put your arms around me and hold on like you mean it. Look, think of it like the *sento*, like the old lady scrubbing your back. It's just how it's done. It's the custom. This is how you ride as a passenger on someone's motorcycle."

Wendy put her arms around me, clasped her hands tight at my

waist and leaned her body against mine. Then she rested her chin on my shoulder. I put the bike in gear and accelerated, probably a little faster than I needed to. We were off.

RYOAN-JI WAS EVEN LESS CROWDED than I had thought it would be. From Wendy's place it had taken less than twenty minutes to get there. The big parking lots were so far almost empty and there were no tour busses at all. Just a few private cars.

Wendy and I got off the bike and walked into the temple grounds. There was a large pond and a scattering of walled temple compounds with signs saying they were off limits to the public. Other signs pointed to the steep path that led up to the famous Zen garden. The garden was part of a small sub-temple at the top of the hillside complex. The path to it was narrow and made of smooth flat stones pounded into the dirt. No concrete. The path was bordered on both sides by fences made of woven bamboo.

At the intersection of several pathways, a more formal stone stairway led steeply up through a large wooden gate to the garden's entrance. Through the gate and at the top of the stairway was a ticket booth where I paid for two tickets. Then Wendy and I took off our shoes, exchanged them for slippers from a large cardboard box full of slippers, and went up the three steps into the temple reception area. Ignoring the rooms of the building that were on open display and the art on the walls, and the small area where souvenir items were for sale, we padded out onto the wooden veranda in our slippers toward the famous garden. Four other couples were sitting there on *zabuton* cushions and silently watching a narrow enclosed garden of nothing but rocks and stones, some covered with various kinds of moss.

Wendy and I each took a *zabuton* cushion from a stack of them. Some unwritten code in Japan requires each group of people sitting in a public place, a park, a river's edge, or a temple's veranda to space themselves precisely equidistant from each neighboring group. I was never able to work out quite how they managed this. Instinct I supposed, since I had never seen anyone actually measure. As *gaijin*, Wendy and I proved somehow incapable of following the pattern. We sat as far away as possible from the others, in a corner at the end of the veranda.

The light drizzle had turned steady and the morning was chilly. Our corner was only just protected from the rain by the temple's roof.

"What do we do?" Wendy asked.

"Just look."

We sat for a while, just looking at the rocks. The rectangular garden was enclosed by a very old and picturesquely crumbling earthen wall. The wall was topped with weathered gray ceramic roof tiles of the same sort used on temple roofs. The garden consisted of a few very large stones and rocks, maybe a dozen or more, and here and there were patches of dense moss at the bases of the largest stones. The rocks were surrounded by an ocean of carefully raked light-colored pebbles. The marks of the rake were left intentionally prominent and formed roughly concentric circular patterns that seemed to suggest either rows of waves lapping against islands in a sea, or the pathways of unseen karma guiding all living beings, or the powerful but invisible forces alive in the universe that shape human destiny, or possibly just nice-looking rock patterns with no particular meaning. That part was up to you. It was Zen.

As we sat looking, a metallic tape-recorded voice of a young woman came crackling over a very out-of-date, very poor-quality loudspeaker system:

> *Welcome to the Ryoan-ji Temple. This Zen garden, a type of Zen garden called a dry garden, is a designated Very Important National Cultural Treasure of Japan. It was designed by the famous Zen landscape architect Soami in the late fifteenth century. The garden is designed for*

> *meditation. Please sit quietly and enjoy the garden in silence. To appreciate the garden's true purpose, allow your mind to settle upon its features. Let it wander freely over the garden's patterns of stone and gravel. Relax your mind. Think of nothing. The fifteen large rocks of the garden may seem to you like mountains in the sea. Or like tiny grains of sand. Please meditate on their true meaning in silence. Thank you. Please enjoy the garden.*

Wendy burst out laughing, and then tried to suppress it.

"I might be able to enjoy the garden if that recorded lady would shut up," she said.

"It's a loop. They do it alternately in Japanese and English every few minutes. After a few times you just get used to it and you can ignore it."

"Doesn't it spoil the effect?"

"Not once you get used to it."

"If you say so. Seems to defeat the purpose."

"Try ignoring it."

"How?"

"Don't pay attention to the words. Think of it as ambient sound."

Wendy looked skeptical. Then she slumped a little and relaxed. I turned and arranged my legs under me to be more comfortable sitting on the *zabuton*. Wendy and I sat and watched the garden.

In the intervals between the repetitions of the recorded message, there was only the sound of gently falling water on stone. The sudden absence of the tinny recorded voice made the quiet in the garden more distinct. It was comfortable and dry under the shelter of the eaves, and that made a contrast with the damp and chilly space beyond. The wooden floor on which the *zabuton* rested had been polished by the slippered feet of millions of visitors shuffling over its planks, by the people who had come to have a look at this inordinately famous rock garden. The veranda was smooth where people had walked, but the edges of the veranda, off limits to visitors, exposed to the weather and roughed up by the sun and rain, looked to be made of a completely different material. The sheltered and polished wood seemed an entirely different thing from the same wood exposed to nature.

I looked out at the garden. I looked over at Wendy trying to concentrate on trying to watch the garden. I looked back at the garden. The mist had become a very light rain. The sound of the rain was becoming more distinct. After a little while I forgot about the people sitting quietly at the other end of the veranda. After a while I forgot about Wendy sitting next to me. I watched the garden. I listened to the rain.

The sound of individual droplets striking the little white bits of stone came to seem like a muted sizzle. The sizzle grew louder and began to resemble the churning and heaving of tiny ocean waves. The little stones that made up the carefully raked rows of white gravel formed unbroken lines around the big rocks. Each stone seemed to have its own rock-like identity. They were not all white after all. Some were greenish, or pinkish, or almost translucent when wetted by the rain. These millions of tiny individual stones, sizzling and grinding against each other when struck by tiny droplets of water, were producing an almost familiar sound. Between the sound and their barely perceptible movement the little stones seemed to come alive.

The sound coming from the stones grew louder. Their movement began to form into waves. The waves grew taller as they surged toward the large rocks in the garden. The moss at the base of the large rocks had appeared to be a soft but solid mass of green. Now I could see that there were at least a dozen different kinds of moss. There was dense underbrush-like deep-green moss. There was a reedy grass-like moss. There was stouter tree-like moss. The tree-like moss stood taller than the other moss. Its leafy moss crowns took on the shape of ancient pine trees defiantly leaning into onshore winds.

Behind the tree moss the weathered slabs of bare rock were like steep cliffs facing the sea, sheer walls of steely gray reaching for the heavens. Each of the big rocks was a windswept, rain-swept, wave-beaten island sitting in the middle of an ocean, far from any other land, big slabs of the earth's crust thrust up out of a primeval sea. Riding on the backs of these island boulders was a teeming host of living matter, sucking in air and drinking in life. All of it still seeming fresh and new from the dawn of creation and a million years from the world of man.

The sea began to calm itself. The illusion of islands in a primeval sea was suddenly and startlingly complete. As it became so, the whole scene seemed to recede and then shrink so that it could all be taken in at once. Waves pounded in at the shores, but now with less urgency and force than before. The winds died down. The rain stopped. Flocks of shrieking seagulls wheeled overhead riding on breezy currents. Schools of fish roiled the water. The air smelled of salt and brine. Sweet, basic, and pure.

And then almost as quickly as it had risen out of the sea, the illusion of the islands passed. Just passed and became a pile of wet rocks and moss in a light spring mist, surrounded by row upon row of neatly raked pebbles. The rain was no longer falling. The air was damp and cool. I was aware of my legs folded underneath me. My left foot had fallen asleep. A tinny mechanical female voice in the background was offering advice on how to appreciate the garden. A few people were sitting nearby on cushions looking at the rocks. The wet air felt fresh and sweet.

I looked up at Wendy and she looked dreamily back at me, her eyes half closed. I wasn't sure exactly how much time had passed.

"Great, huh?" I said.

"Yeah."

"Impossible to see it this way once the tour busses get here and the place fills up with tourists."

We sat there for almost another hour until the place did fill up with tourists. Then we left and found a local *kissaten* and had some reasonably good coffee and *omuraisu*, a rubbery omelet stuffed with rice and covered with ketchup. We sat and talked until the rain, which had begun again, let up enough to ride back to Wendy's place. I left Wendy to her studying and drove back to the eastern part of town to earn my ¥600 an hour as a waiter in an upscale *shabu-shabu* restaurant. You had to be lucky to catch Ryoan-ji nearly empty, and to see it the way it was meant to be seen. You just never knew when it would happen.

—

IN SEPTEMBER, MY CLASS WITH Wendy became a class of three. Kyle Johnson from Duluth, Minnesota, joined us mid-term. He was a graduate student in Chinese history at Washington University in St. Louis. He had lived in Japan for a few years as a kid and he could speak Japanese fairly well. It seemed to come naturally to him. His father had been a Christian missionary. When the family joined the mission in Japan, the children attended ordinary Japanese public school.

Kyle, like Wendy, was Midwestern and socially conservative. He never swore and never drank alcohol. He was all business in class and had no discernible sense of humor. He had a solid, no-nonsense body. Erect posture. Dressed formally. No jeans, ever. He wore his reddish-brown hair short and sported a moustache that never really grew in all the way. He was arrogant and had an abundance of self-confidence. I pretty much hated him from the first time I saw him.

For reasons which I could not understand, Wendy and Kyle seemed to hit it off right from the beginning. Watanabe-*sensei* seemed to like Kyle too. Kyle was good at Japanese; he worked hard and never joked around in class. In the three-person class, now with Kyle in the mix, Watanabe-*sensei* was less patient with my fooling around and much less patient with Wendy when she failed to get something right after only one or two tries.

Wendy and Kyle often ate lunch together, bringing in lunches they had made themselves from dinner leftovers. I usually preferred to eat lunch at one of the nearby Doshisha University student cafeterias where I could flirt with the female students. Sometimes when the weather was exceptionally fine, I bought something to eat and took it out to the park surrounding the Kyoto Imperial Palace, stretching out to read or have a nap afterward in one of the fenced-off grassy areas in front of a sign that read: "Entrance into the Grassy Area Is Forbidden."

Kyle, like Wendy when she first arrived, had little interest in and no time for visiting Kyoto's famous temples and gardens. He made it clear that he thought that the Chinese originals would be worth seeing, but the Japanese versions were merely inferior copies. But Wendy had changed his mind and wanted *me* to take the three of us to someplace interesting.

The obvious choice was one of the imperial properties right across the street. There was the Old Kyoto Imperial Palace and there was the Sento Gosho Detached Imperial Place. The official policy of the Kunai-cho, the government agency that managed the emperor and his imperial properties, was that to visit these properties you had to submit your request in writing and they would inform you when you would be allowed to visit. The waiting list for foreigners was about three months. The waiting list for Japanese nationals was two years. The Kunai-cho managed four properties in Kyoto: the Old Kyoto Imperial Palace, the Sento Gosho, the Katsura Rikyu Detached Imperial Palace, and the Shugaku-in Detached Imperial Palace.

The Imperial Household Agency had an office in a small building discreetly secluded at the back of the northwest corner of the big park that contained the Old Imperial Palace. I had discovered, by simply strolling into the office, that any *gaijin* could just show up there and make a same-day reservation to tour any of the four imperial properties. You just had to show up in person and prove you were a *gaijin*. The tours were conducted twice a day at 11:30 and 1:30. The tour guides were Kunai-cho new hires, usually men in their mid-twenties with graduate degrees in Japanese history from Tokyo University or Kyoto University.

On a clear, chilly November morning, Wendy, Kyle, and I strolled across the street and up to the Imperial Household Agency office, passports in hand, and made reservations for the 11:30 tour of the Sento Gosho. Then we headed through the big park to join our tour.

We passed through the huge front gate of the palace, one of the few massive gates serving as the entrance to a temple or a castle in Japan that was still connected to its imposing walls. The gate still served its original purpose of sealing the place off completely while providing an impressive entrance to something you couldn't see into but could only imagine. The stony-faced guards nodded as we displayed our document with the official Kunai-cho seal that granted us entry.

On the other side of the wall we were directed to a ramshackle wooden building where the people taking the 11:30 tour waited for the tour to begin. There were old-fashioned wooden lockers where you could leave anything you didn't want to carry with you as you strolled the grounds. Gorgeous picture books of the Sento Gosho and other imperial properties were for sale, along with souvenir picture postcards and official guidebooks. Spectacular trees that had been groomed and shaped for maybe hundreds of years blocked the view into the spectacular garden beyond.

The twenty or so people who had been signed up for the tour assembled, and the tour began at 11:30, exactly on time, as things do in Japan. The beauty of seeing a property like this was that you were seeing something special and important and the twenty people in your group were the only other people present. Unlike every other important cultural property in Kyoto, it wasn't swarming with tourists whose primary interest in the place was having their pictures taken next to something famous. The Japanese people in our group had waited two years to be here.

Wendy, Kyle, and I were the only *gaijin*. A young man in a dark suit came out to lead the tour. The explanations, and the questions and answers, were all in Japanese and there was no translation. But an abbreviated guidebook had been handed out with descriptions of the Sento Gosho in Japanese and English. For other foreign languages you had to buy the official guidebook.

The guide began by explaining that the Sento Imperial Palace was completed in 1630 for Emperor Go-Mizunoo's retirement, along with the Omiya Palace for the Empress Dowager Nyoin. Both palaces had been destroyed by fire. The Omiya Palace had been reconstructed at the beginning of the Meiji period. It was where the current emperor stayed when he visited Kyoto. Queen Elizabeth had stayed there on her most recent visit to Kyoto. Because it was still in use, the Omiya Palace and its pond and grounds were off limits for the tour.

Our tour began at the entrance to a large pond. I had taken the tour twice before. But now it was November, the time of year when Japan's spectacular display of autumn foliage was at its height. The area bordering the Sento Gosho pond and its carefully choreographed meandering pathways had been planted with trees selected for the range of autumn colors they would produce. The effect of seeing them at their full peak was simply breathtaking. Even the tour guide, who must have done this tour dozens of times, seemed awed into silence.

At first the tour guide gave us a quick history of the garden and a detailed explanation of the nearest of the two remaining original structures on the property, a rustic teahouse called the Seika-tei. Then he released us into the garden to ogle the autumn leaves on our own, and for those of us who brought cameras, to take photographs. The guide had let us know that the gardens had been designed in 1630 by the landscape artist Kobori Enshu. The Seika-tei was a spare little structure with clean modern lines that might have been someone's small house. The roof had a ridge of ceramic tiles and was covered with thin handmade tiles of cedar bark that would cost a small fortune to maintain and a larger fortune to replace.

The group began its meander around the pond following the clearly marked and approved route. Everyone was visibly awed by the display of autumn colors planned by someone three hundred years earlier. The tour guide brought up the rear to pick up stragglers. The pond had little islands in it connected by paths and stone bridges that were off limits to the visiting public. The ancient Japanese maples beamed their reds and yellows at us. Gnarly cherry trees broadcast burnished orange. Massive ginkgo trees sizzled yellow against an achingly blue sky. In several places there were artificial hills designed for providing views of the pond. Most of the trees closest to the pond were pines and willows that had been trained and groomed to form pleasing shapes and were among the oldest trees in the garden. There was a small shrine on one of the islands and a variety of stone lanterns along the way.

The garden was a masterpiece of crafted natural beauty, and for the most part there wasn't much for the guide to say. At this time of year there was nothing he could say. The trees and the landscape were doing all the talking for him. He simply allowed his charges to wander along the roped-off route admiring the scenery and taking photos. We came to a large and intricately constructed stone bridge covered in an impressive wisteria trellis. This was the only bridge in the garden we were allowed onto. As we lingered and enjoyed the view, most of us with cameras out, the guide explained that it had been built in 1895. The famous wisteria had shed its purple flowers months before.

A section of the pond's edges had been designed to evoke an ocean shore. It was an expanse of smooth, flat stones. The guide explained that as far back as the Heian period certain landowners were allowed to pay their taxes in special stones like these to be used as ornaments in the imperial gardens. The stones were "farmed" in local rivers and transported by the taxpayers to the imperial capital.

At the other end of the pond we encountered the second teahouse, the Yushin-tei. The Yushin-tei resembled a small rustic farmhouse walled off by a simple bamboo fence. It had a massive country-style thatched roof and seemed to have been implanted in the garden perfectly intact from somewhere in rural northern Japan. The side facing the pond had a large round window that a country farmhouse or actual rustic hut would not have had.

The paths in the garden had been designed to afford perfect views of the garden's special features. One part of the pond seemed to have been arranged to form the Japanese character *kokoro*, the heart, but it was hard to tell. It was a common conceit in Japanese pond design to add a little esoteric flavor to the design. Every little hill, every island, every tree, and every stone or rock in the garden would have been perfectly placed. Then successive generations of gardeners and caretakers would have had to deal with two or three hundred years of nature's resistance to the human plan.

"I think the garden is supposed to represent some kind of Buddhist Paradise," Kyle said. "Something about Chinese immortals riding on a turtle's back."

"It's so beautiful here," Wendy said.

"How old did you say it was?" Kyle asked the guide.

"1630," the guide said.

"So during the Edo period. Isn't that when they had an empress and not an emperor? Empress Meisho, right?"

The guide looked uncomfortable.

"So where did Empress Meisho live? In the Kyoto Gosho just north of this place?"

"Yes," the guide said. "The Kyoto Gosho was the site of the Imperial Palace until it was moved to Tokyo in the Meiji period."

"But Empress Meisho would have been what, five or six years old then? And I thought this whole area belonged to some loyal Tokugawa *daimyo* during Edo."

"Perhaps you know a little too much about Japanese history," the guide said to Kyle in a low voice. "I don't think this is the place for those kinds of questions."

So saying, the guide walked off toward the building where we had left our things in lockers. Most of the people followed him.

"Gosh," Wendy said to Kyle, "you know a lot about Japanese history."

"These Kunai-cho guys always give you the official version of Japanese history. Their version of it," Kyle said. "I don't understand why they don't just admit that the Tokugawa made the emperors irrelevant and made them live in poverty outside the city."

"Yes," I said, "and while they're at it, they should also admit that the entire Japanese imperial family came from Korea."

"What do you mean 'their version of it'?" Wendy asked.

"The old Japanese temples and the Imperial Household Agency always seem to have versions of their own history that don't quite match what academically trained historians have to say."

"Such as what?" Wendy said.

"Well, a good example is Anraku-ji. Watanabe-*sensei* showed me a brochure from that temple that says that the temple's founder, Anraku, was executed by the emperor because he, Anraku, insisted on adhering to his true religious beliefs even if it meant death."

"Watanabe-*sensei* did?" Wendy asked.

"We were talking about religion in Japan. She thought it would interest me."

"In class? I don't remember that coming up."

"Anyway, the emperor at the time happened to be a supporter of a rival Buddhist sect. The imperial records say that Anraku was a dangerous religious subversive and sought to undermine the government. Academic historians on the other hand say that Anraku was a charismatic public speaker drawing large crowds to his lectures and sermons. He was especially popular with women, and with women in the imperial court in particular. He gave these women special, individual audiences. Anraku apparently had certain relations with one of the emperor's favorite concubines. The emperor found out about it, and he had him executed. Everyone agrees that Anraku was a great public speaker and that he was beheaded in public by imperial order down on the banks of the Kamogawa, where they usually executed people."

"So," I said, "in other words he was either killed for preaching a version of Buddhism different from the official imperial version, or he was killed because he was caught having sex with the emperor's favorite concubine, depending on whose version you believe?"

"Exactly," Kyle said. "A story like that could be ambiguous. Either side could be the truth. But it just bothers me that the Kunaicho guys refuse to acknowledge the possibility."

"Well, Wendy said, "it's a very beautiful garden, and I think we're lucky to have seen it like this. With just a few other people. I might buy one of the official guidebooks with all the pictures in it. I bet it's gorgeous here in the spring when the cherry blossoms are out."

"You can," Kyle said. "Just don't be fooled by the historical nonsense they put in it. In their version of history the Japanese emperor, not the Tokugawa shogunate, was the real power in Japan during Edo. How ridiculous is that?"

We made our way back to the little shack near the entrance gate and collected our things from the lockers. I suggested we adjourn to a *kissaten* for coffee or down to the Sokoya, a *gaijin* hangout bar, for a beer, but Kyle and Wendy said they were sorry but they had other plans. As I watched them head up to Imadegawa to catch a streetcar, I could tell from their body language that they were more than just friends or classmates. They weren't holding hands or anything like that. But it was clear enough.

IT WAS A LITTLE MORE than a month after the trip to the Sento Gosho. Wendy seemed to be having a very, very bad day. Kyle was absent, and it was just me and Wendy again in Watanabe-*sensei*'s class. Watanabe-*sensei* was usually tough on Wendy when she got something wrong or didn't seem to be picking up a new lesson quickly enough. Wendy usually soldiered through the tough love. But today Watanabe-*sensei* seemed to have her claws out, and Wendy seemed angry about the rough treatment.

Wendy was struggling with the nearly impossible double-indirect-passive-honorific-pluperfect-female version of the verb "to be" when Watanabe-*sensei* let her have it.

"I see, so now Anderson-san no longer wishes to speak like a woman. You've given up on trying to behave like a woman and you've decided you might as well just speak like a man. Haven't I told you many, many times that a woman, a woman who wants to sound like a woman, should . . ."

"You know what?" Wendy said in English, interrupting the teacher, "I don't care what a woman is supposed to say in this situation. I don't care what a woman is supposed to *say* or *do* in this fucking country! I . . . don't . . . give . . . a . . . FUCK! I don't! I just don't anymore!"

As she said the word "fuck," Wendy's face turned a bright shade of red that you don't normally see on a human being. Swearing was not something Wendy ever did. Words having to do with sex embarrassed her. The words "fuck" or "orgasm" or "penis" rendered her speechless. I suppose even the word "dick" was out of bounds, unless it was being used as a man's name. Now she was simultaneously so angry and so embarrassed that she was shaking.

Watanabe-*sensei* looked over at me as if Wendy's meltdown were *my* fault.

An uncomfortable silence filled the room. Wendy snapped her textbook shut, got up, and left the classroom. Watanabe-*sensei* looked accusingly at me again. I looked back at her, silently professing my innocence.

"Ascher-san, are you sure you didn't say anything to upset her?"

"Me? No. Absolutely not. Not me."

Watanabe-*sensei* looked at me skeptically.

"Not me. Really. I don't know, but maybe sometimes you can be a little hard on her and . . ."

"Me? As a professional teacher I think I understand what to say to help my students learn Japanese properly. But if you think you know better . . ."

"No, that's not what I meant at all. I . . ."

"Shall we go on with the lesson, then, you and I? Or would you like to curse at me too in a voice loud enough for everyone in the school to hear?"

"No. Sorry. Please continue."

We went back to the lesson and somehow managed to continue more or less normally up to the end of the period. Watanabe-*sensei* looked angry, but she did her job with perfection, as usual. I was unhappy to be blamed for Wendy's outburst. But I was unable to hold that against Watanabe-*sensei*. Great beauty can be, and is usually, forgiven for everything.

WENDY EVENTUALLY TOLD ME WHAT happened to her after her outburst in class, though she never admitted to what caused it. She couldn't believe she had told Watanabe-*sensei*, in class and out loud, to go and fuck herself. She said she was sure she'd never used the word fuck before. She said she had no memory of picking up her books and leaving the classroom. The next thing she knew she was just outside and on her way home.

At home Wendy took off her shoes and then threw herself down on her bed and cried. When she got up again it was early evening. She put up some water for tea and began absently going through her afternoon routine of collecting cockroach traps. She had just lifted one of the traps into the sink when it broke open and the cockroaches inside spilled out onto her and began racing frantically all around her body. Wendy swatted at them and beat at her clothes to get them out, and they probably were out. But she couldn't shake the feeling that they were still crawling around inside her clothing. She needed a bath. She was running behind schedule.

Wendy gathered up her bath things and walked down the road to the public bath. In the changing room she took off each item of her clothing carefully and examined it to make sure it was cockroach-free. When she got everything off and had checked it thoroughly, she rechecked everything again and then folded it all up and put it into one of the changing-room baskets for street clothes. Then she took the blue plastic pail with her soap and shampoo, and her little towel that covered almost nothing, and walked naked into the ladies side of the bath.

The bath was more crowded than usual. She was there later than her usual bath time. Wendy had been going to the public bath for a while now and she was completely comfortable with its familiar rituals. She went over to the row of faucets to begin washing. But as she entered, the lively chatter that echoed off the high ceiling and ceramic-tiled walls abruptly came to a halt. The ladies in the bath stared at Wendy, an unfamiliar alien, a pale-white presence. The old ladies who usually came over and washed her back and chatted to her were not there.

When the conversation in the bath began again in whispered asides, the word *gaijin* was about the only word Wendy could clearly make out.

Wendy went through the familiar Japanese bathhouse rituals less mechanically and less automatically than she usually did. In a room full of strangers watching her every move, today especially, she didn't need their whispered disapproval for being a stupid, ignorant *gaijin*, unable to manage the proper Japanese way of doing things.

As Wendy approached the large, steaming hot soaking bath, the conversation in the room again stopped. Wendy looked up and saw that every woman in the room was staring at her.

"They probably expect me to dump bubble bath into the pool," she thought.

Wendy eased herself into the bath. It was very, very hot. Much hotter than usual. Her legs and feet were screaming pain. All eyes were on her. No one spoke. No one moved. Wendy looked back at the women in the bath staring at her. When she moved, the hot water felt like shards of broken glass tearing at her legs. And then . . . she just snapped.

Wendy sloshed back to the edge of the bath. She got out of the bath, snatched up her bucket and little towel, and faced the women staring at her. Then she started screaming at them in Japanese.

"What is the *matter* with you people?!! Why are you staring at me?!! *Minasama, nani wo miteimasuka? Watakushi wa ninjin desu. Minasama to onaji. Ninjin desu!* What are you *looking* at!?! I am a human being!! I am just like you!! I am a human being! A HUMAN BEING! I am a HUMAN BEING!!!"

As she said this the women stared at her in amazement. Wendy stomped naked, dripping wet and still furious, out of the big public bath and into the changing room. The women continued to stare at her.

Wendy realized later that she had made a mistake. The Japanese word for "human being" is *ningen*. *Nin* means "person." But another word for "person" is *jin*. Many beginning students of Japanese put the two together as *nin* - person, and *jin* - person, and get *ninjin*, which means "carrot." Wendy had been screaming at the women in the bath "I am a carrot! I am a carrot!"

The story of the naked white lady with bright red hair who claimed she was a carrot and ran screaming from the bath passed into local legend in the Hanazono district of Kita-ku in Kyoto. It was over a week before Wendy could summon up the courage to go back.

FOR THE LAST FEW CLASSES before the New Year's break we were down to two again. Wendy and me. And we had a new teacher. The petite and upbeat Hirata-*sensei.* When I first heard the rumors that Watanabe-*sensei* had eloped with Kyle and left with him for St. Louis, I thought it was too crazy to be true. Then the rumors started to acquire the status of news, having been filled out with factual, verifiable content. Watanabe-*sensei* and Kyle were married.

No one at school had the slightest idea that the two of them had been seeing each other. They had married over a weekend in a private church ceremony in front of Watanabe-*sensei*'s relatives and a few old friends of hers from her school days. None of the teachers at our school had been invited. Nor any of the students.

I was sitting in the deserted classroom, about ten or fifteen minutes early, looking over the day's lesson. It was a gloomy, chilly, gray morning. Hirata-*sensei* always arrived on the dot of nine a.m. Rarely earlier. Never later.

Wendy came in and sat down. She dumped her book bag and plopped heavily down in her seat. I didn't look up, pretending to be concentrating on the textbook. We didn't speak. Wendy sighed heavily.

"All right," Wendy said. "Go ahead and say it. Let's get it over with."

"I never liked him."

"I suppose everyone thinks I'm shattered."

"No, no one thinks that."

"Oh come on."

"OK, they all think you're a wreck. Completely ruined. Broken hearted. Crushed. Possibly suicidal."

"Suicidal?"

"I made that up. Look, everyone thinks . . . they think you've suffered a . . . um . . . a . . . disappointment."

Wendy sighed.

"All right," she said. "I did like him. I had no idea he was seeing anyone else. Certainly not our teacher. I suppose I could tell there was something not right the last few weeks. Still . . . oh fuck."

"That's the spirit. Oh fuck is exactly it."

Wendy sighed again. And she looked, only for the very briefest second, as if she might cry.

"It wouldn't be so bad if everyone weren't watching me all the time. I think they're waiting for me to snap or something."

"I don't think so. People really like you. They just want you to be OK. They mean well. And they don't know what to do. You know, they want to help if they can, but they want to give you your space. And besides, everyone has heard the story about the bathhouse, so they know you've already snapped once and probably got it out of your system."

"That's not funny."

"It is actually, but I appreciate that you might be sensitive about it. So, how about the traditional remedies?"

"Which are?"

"Heavy drinking or large quantities of junk food."

"I can't afford junk food. Or drinking."

"Sex with a stranger."

"You're not a stranger, if that's what you're thinking."

"Well I don't like seeing you unhappy."

"Thanks, but I don't think so. Anyway, wouldn't it cause problems for you with the tea ceremony bitch?"

"The tea ceremony bitch? Whoa! First it's 'oh fuck' and now 'the tea ceremony bitch'? Next you'll be talking about your . . ."

"Don't you dare say it. Don't you *dare* say that word!"

"All right. Relax. I won't say it. But I like it when you talk dirty. And anyway, to tell you the truth, things are not so smooth now between me and the tea ceremony bitch."

"Oh? Are you suffering a disappointment too?"

"I feel one coming."

"Feel one coming? Like what?"

"Well, she's been making, or hinting at . . . I don't know."

Wendy smothered a laugh. I hadn't seen her smile in a while, so I hesitated before warning her about laughing at my misfortune.

"I've never met your girlfriend, but from everything you've ever told me about her, she sounds like a money-obsessed phony. You'll have to forgive me for telling you you'd be much better off with someone else. So what kind of weird things is she hinting at?"

"I think she wants me to have sex with Hirata-*sensei.*"

"Hirata-*sensei*? Our Hirata-*sensei*?"

Wendy smothered another laugh.

"What's funny about that? She's a very attractive young woman."

"What do you mean she wants you to have sex with Hirata-*sensei*? How do you hint about something like that?"

"She said I should ask her to give me private lessons. But I think that's what she means."

"You mean, she might feel better about breaking up with you if she thought you were . . . involved . . . with someone else?"

"Yeah. I guess that's the idea."

"But why Hirata-*sensei*? Have you ever mentioned that kind of interest in Hirata-*sensei*? I don't get the connection. Your girlfriend doesn't study Japanese. Not for real, anyway. How does she even know Hirata-*sensei*?"

"Well this guy that moved into our house a few weeks ago, a guy studying Zen in Pattie's meditation class, he takes private lessons from Hirata-*sensei*. She comes to the house now a couple times a week. Pattie thinks Hirata-*sensei* has a crush on him."

"So she wants *you* to get together with her? He moved into your house? Your girlfriend thinks Hirata-*sensei* has a crush on him, so she wants *you* to start going out with her? That's bad. Bad for me too. Now everyone will be looking at *both* of us."

"You think so?"

Suddenly Wendy leaned over and hugged me. I was too surprised to even hug her back. I don't think I had ever touched Wendy before, except once when she rode on the back of my yellow Honda motorcycle.

"Does this mean we're going to have casual sex to forget our troubles?"

"No, it does not. Tell me about this guy."

"Well, he's a bit older. From an old wealthy family in the south. Alabama or Georgia maybe. Graduated from Princeton. Engineering degree from MIT. Worked for NASA designing rockets. Then joined a big famous consulting firm for a huge salary and they sent him here to do projects all over Asia. He had some kind of a nervous breakdown and decided he wanted to spend the rest of his life seeking the 'truth.' He quit his job. Entered a Zen temple. Now all he does is meditate and study Zen. And take Japanese lessons."

"And he's rich?"

"Well, he doesn't seem to worry about money, though that could be part of the Zen thing."

"He's rich. You need to dump her. Or be prepared for her to dump you. You're screwed. I hope you realize that."

"Maybe."

"Are you going to have sex with Hirata-*sensei*?"

"I don't think so."

"Too bad. If you did, then you could get married and take her back to Connecticut with you. That would be just perfect."

"Too bad there are no male teachers in this school."

Wendy looked at me hard and for a few long beats. Then she hugged me again.

Hirata-*sensei* came in while we were still hugging. When we both looked up at her we started laughing.

Hirata-*sensei* had no idea what we were laughing about.

The Extra

I WAS SLEEPING IN MY room at the International Students Residence when Hashimoto-san, the dorm's RA, came knocking on my door to say that the front office had received an emergency call. It was just before six a.m. The Toei Studio west of Nishi-Oji needed a *gaijin* extra for one of their B movies and they needed him ASAP. They had already dispatched a car to fetch me and I had about half an hour to shower and dress.

Being an extra in a Japanese B movie was great work if you could get it. It was one of the things my Australian friend Peter Franks handed off to me when he began to prepare for his return to his homeland. During his time as a student at Kyoto University, Peter had an enviable career as an extra in Japanese B movies. He had even appeared in a joint Japanese/Hollywood movie called *The Yakuza*, featuring Robert Mitchum, a genuine American movie star in the twilight of his career, and the perennial Japanese film icon Takakura Ken.

Together with Peter, I had tortured Japanese prisoners of war and run a few of them over in a truck. On my own I had been an American mobster at a Japanese banquet who nearly got into a fight with a *yakuza* boss. I had played a foreign engineer at a Japanese electronics plant. I stood in a commuter train that was attacked and then eaten by Gamera, a relative of Godzilla.

The pay for a day's work in the movies was ¥20,000. That was what they paid you whether you worked for an hour or all day. In those days it was a lot of money. It was more than I could make in two months teaching English or working at the *shabu-shabu* restaurant where I had a part-time job.

My first job acting as an American GI with Peter had taken the whole day. Peter and I had reported to Toei and were immediately sent to wardrobe. We were outfitted as WWII American soldiers. The filming took place in an unpopulated mountain area outside of Kyoto. Peter and I spent most of our time in our uniforms waiting for our scenes to be shot. We practiced running over and killing rubber stunt dummies in an actual US army truck from the 1940s. Peter had refused to shave his handlebar moustache, so the director made him ride shotgun where his face would be mostly in shadow. I knew how to operate a stick shift, so I got to drive. I had to drive the car while keeping my full face visible in the driver's side window so the film-going audience could see that the truck was operated by a genuine American *gaijin*. Other than that, acting was entirely optional.

The job as a mobster at a *yakuza* banquet consisted of only one scene that had taken the better part of an afternoon to film. After an hour of make-up and wardrobe, my fellow American Mafiosi and I were led onto the set. The gray hair and paste-on moustache I was given seemed comically fake, but I was assured it would look just fine on film.

All the food and drink at the banquet table was real. During multiple rehearsals, a bevy of gorgeous Japanese actresses, dressed either in kimono or ball gowns, served the foreign guests and their *yakuza* hosts with real food and real champagne. It was the kind of food that, as a student in Japan, I would never have been able to afford. The assistant directors encouraged us to eat and drink, and we all did.

The main figure in the scene, a *yakuza* crime boss, was played by a very famous Japanese actor. He was so famous that even I would have recognized the man on sight if I had seen him. During rehearsals, his part was played by a stand-in.

The scene was rehearsed about five or six times and then practice-filmed twice. The dinner party continued between takes.

We extras and minor part actors consumed a dozen bottles of chilled French champagne, three-quarters of a sliced roast beef, several platters of fried shrimp, most of a platter of smoked salmon garnished with capers and chopped onions, half of a large Camembert cheese, numerous slices of Swiss cheese, Italian salami, bunches of red and white grapes, sliced and peeled apples, and three bowls of mixed nuts.

The female extras were directed to flirt with the banquet guests. They sat on laps, poured drinks, and stayed in character between takes. By the time the star of the film came out for his single five-minute take, the supporting cast was very drunk and stuffed to the gills. The scene required me to stand up, argue with the *yakuza* boss, try to throw a punch at him, and end up being restrained by some of the *yakuza* in the room. Face to face with the star, who I certainly did recognize, I was awed by his presence. My punch started out as an attempt to shake the famous man's hand until I managed to remember what my character was supposed to do in the scene. I made a half-assed attempt to hit the famous actor in the face and was roughly seized by two genuine *yakuza* who were playing *yakuza* as extras. Then I was slammed, for real, back into my seat at the banquet table.

The director yelled, "*Katto!*" and, to my surprise, he declared himself satisfied after only one *honban* take. The cast was dismissed.

I watched sadly as the food on the table was whisked away and the lovely women in gowns and kimono stopped behaving amorously. We extras returned to wardrobe to give back our costumes, peel off fake moustaches, remove hairpieces, wash off makeup, and get back into our street clothes. Then we all walked over to the accounting department to collect our pay envelopes. Inside mine was a payroll slip that showed the gross amount of my pay and the after-tax net amount that exactly equaled the two crisp ¥10,000 notes nestling pleasantly inside the envelope. All salaries in those days were paid in cash.

On the day of my early morning emergency call, the studio car got me to the main lot a little before 7:30 a.m. I told the guard at the gate that I was on call for a shoot. The guard found my name on a list attached to a clipboard, and I was told to report to the commissary. The assistant casting director who would be my handler for the day would come and get me.

The commissary itself was like a scene from a movie. Bulky tattooed *yakuza* and Edo-period villagers in rags were sitting at communal tables having breakfast with green space aliens and women in skimpy superhero costumes. Silvery metallic robots struggled to eat hardboiled eggs and fat slabs of white toast in their unforgiving costumes. Women in kimono with elaborate hairdos were eating scrambled eggs with bacon. Samurai warriors drank coffee from mugs with the studio's logo printed on them. I helped myself to coffee from a big urn and some toast and a few hardboiled eggs from a steam tray. Then I sat at a table to eat and wait for my handler.

As I sat and ate and took in the room, I noticed that there were a number of very attractive women in diaphanous, semi-see-through negligees sitting together in small groups. Perhaps a soft-core porn movie was being shot somewhere on the lot. I wondered if it might be possible to sneak onto the set.

The man who eventually came to get me was named Yamamoto. Yamamoto-san was in his mid-thirties. He was medium height and good-looking. He struck me as the kind of person who was in training to be a film or TV star or a game-show host. He was a fast talker who avoided answering questions. He said he was the assistant casting director on the film. When I asked what kind of movie I was going to be in, or how long the shoot would take, Yamamoto-san was vague. Either he didn't know or didn't want to tell me. He said only that I would be playing an American.

I was handed off to wardrobe where I spent over an hour being dressed in a WWII American soldier's uniform. I had done this before, but this time an actual tailor came in to make sure the uniform's fit was both perfect and period-correct. In my previous role as a GI, I had been issued an ill-fitting uniform off the rack in the wardrobe closet. This time the uniform they gave me looked broken in, authentic, and fit me perfectly. The jacket and the shirt had military insignias sewn on and pins and colorful bars affixed to the jacket's lapels and pocket flaps. I was no expert in WWII insignias, but the only thing that I thought might be off was that I seemed to have been made a corporal in the Shinto Shrine squad.

At the end of the fitting I was issued a handsome pair of black army boots and a jaunty cap, both of which also fit perfectly. I had to be shown how to tie the necktie that went with the uniform. Finally I was handed an open pack of chewing gum, an open pack of Lucky Strike cigarettes, and a small handful of 1940s Japanese coins. I was told to put these into uniform jacket pockets. I put my own clothes and other possessions into a locker in the wardrobe section's changing room. There were no locks or keys for any of the lockers. Most of the people using the men's locker room that day were *yakuza* who were either extras or just hanging out for the day, showing off their tattoos and muscles. *Yakuza* were known to be reliably honest. No one was concerned about theft when they were around.

I was now entirely period-correct and set to perform my role in the film. When I looked in the mirror I was awed to discover that I now had that jaunty young American soldier just-returned-from-the-Big-War appeal that I had often seen in black-and-white newsreel films. The kind of appeal that allowed you to grab random young women off the street and sweep them into a kiss and suffer no objections. Yamamoto-san came back to collect me. He drove me to the far end of the main lot in a golf cart where I got my first look at the set.

The set was an elaborately constructed section of what appeared to be a market street that might have existed in prewar Japan. Most of the shops and buildings were facades only, but one of the larger buildings in the middle of the street, a Japanese *ryokan*, had actual interiors. It was an exact replica of a prewar inn except for one detail. Only the front part of the building had a roof. Where the roof would have been, there was an elaborate metal framework holding cables and wires and lights and microphones. The overhead grid also supported a small-scale railroad that ran on tracks and allowed a large-format movie camera, along with a cameraman, the director, and two assistants, to glide above the rooms in the building and film whatever was happening in them.

"So what kind of film is this?" I asked again.

"It's a period piece," Yamamoto-san replied. "Postwar Japan. Kobe. You're a soldier in the American Occupation. You're in this part of town for some R&R."

"R&R? Like what?"

"Why don't I explain that later. For now let's get you into the set."

We abandoned the golf cart alongside another dozen or so identical golf carts and walked down the commercial street of small shops and businesses and came to the front of the inn. From the outside, the inn looked like a cheaper, seedier version of a traditional Japanese *ryokan.*

"Okay," Yamamoto-san said. "Let's go in."

We entered the inn. The *genkan* was full of beat-up men's shoes. Men's shoes only.

"Take off your boots and leave them here please," Yamamoto-san said.

I removed my genuine, handsome, black WWII US army boots and left them in the *genkan* with the other more ordinary shoes. I took a step up into a pair of beat-up leather slippers marked with the name of an inn. Yamamoto-san moved to the far edge of the *genkan* to remove his shoes. He slipped them into a cabinet so they would be out of sight. He came up from the *genkan* without taking a pair of slippers and led me down a narrow hallway. I looked up through the open top of the building at the tangle of wires, cables, klieg lights, and microphones. The tracks for the movie camera formed a semicircle that ran through it all. Technicians were climbing all over the overhead structure, making adjustments and using hand-held meters to take light and sound readings.

Yamamoto made a right turn into another corridor and slid open the third door he came to. He entered and I followed him in, abandoning my slippers just outside the room. The room was Japanese style, with worn, shabby tatami mats on the floor. It had a very genuine old-fashioned feel to it. It might have been constructed piecemeal out of actual antique parts. The only furniture in the room was a small writing desk with a wooden chair. There was also a double set of futon laid out on the tatami floor. The futon looked as if it had seen better days.

"So it's a brothel?" I asked.

"Well . . . yes," Yamamoto-san reluctantly agreed. "This is actually a mock-up of one of Kobe's 1940s red-light districts. They were illegal of course. But then, as now, they did exist."

"And what will I be doing here?" I asked.

Yamamoto paused, apparently wondering how to begin answering the question.

"I'll be explaining your role in the film in detail later on," Yamamoto said. "But for now, please take the things out of your pocket and lay them on the table. Then take off your jacket and hang it on the back of the chair."

A lot of trouble had been taken to fit me into that jacket. I was surprised by the request. I hesitated, but I did as I was instructed.

"Can I chew the gum or smoke the cigarettes?" I asked.

"I wouldn't," Yamamoto said. "I think they're really from the period. Not just fake props. The cigarettes are probably stale. And the gum . . . "

"Can I at least get a little more information about what exactly is going to happen here?"

"Please be patient and wait. I have to leave now, but I'll be back soon."

I waited. I watched the crews overhead at work. I examined the prewar money. I sat at the desk. I paced around the room. A wristwatch was the one period item I had not been provided with. It seemed that a lot of time had passed.

Above, in the space where the building's roof and ceiling should have been, the lighting and sound technicians were scurrying around in the scaffolding making adjustments. The director and the camera operator sat in chairs that were attached to the camera, poring over a script. Outside in the corridor I could hear other actors being placed in other rooms in the brothel.

When Yamamoto came back into the room there was an attractive young woman with him. She was wrapped in a terrycloth bathrobe about two sizes too big for her. The robe lacked a sash to keep it from opening at the front. Where it fell open I could see that under the robe the woman wore a shortish, semi-transparent negligee like the ones I'd seen earlier in the commissary. My heart began to beat a little faster.

The woman looked to be in her early or mid-twenties. About my age. Maybe a few years older. She seemed to be unhappy about something. Her displeasure was directed in equal parts at Yamamoto, at the room, and at me.

Yamamoto left the young woman in the far corner of the room and told her, and then me, to be patient and wait for further instructions. Then he went out, shutting the door to the room behind him. My new roommate eyed me with a mixture of suspicion and displeasure.

I studied the female across the room from me. It seemed natural to try and speak with her, so I moved closer to do so. She clutched her robe to her and looked alarmed.

"Are you cold?" I asked. "There's a jacket over on the chair you could use. I don't think they'd mind until they start filming."

There was no reaction. Just wary eyes looking back at me with suspicion and even mild contempt.

The activity above was increasing and intensifying. The walls of the fake brothel were very thin, and I could now hear flirtatious conversations between men and women in the other rooms. I looked again at the young woman in the corner.

"Are you a student?" I asked. "College student like me? Just doing an *arubaito* to make some extra money?"

This got a laugh. More of a snort really. And a look that said, "What kind of idiot are you?" But no answer.

Yamamoto came back into the room.

"All right," he said. "Here's what you'll be doing."

The young woman and I moved in to listen to him.

"It's just after the end of the War. The American soldier is in Kobe during the American Occupation. This is a brothel. A very low-class brothel. The soldier is on leave and a customer. The woman is a prostitute servicing a client. As you see, the cameras are overhead and filming everything from above. The main action will be taking place outside, in the corridor there. Both of you please come over here and have a look."

The woman and I joined Yamamoto next to the door to the room. Yamamoto slid the door open.

"Two *yakuza* are having a fight to the death. In one long cut they will start their fight way back there at the end of that corridor. The two of you are lying on the futon on the floor when you . . . "

"Just a minute," the woman interrupted.

This was the first time I had heard her speak. It was a voice you could not possibly mistake. Harsh. Angry. Crude. Stereotypically, a shop girl from a lower class neighborhood.

"Am I . . . ?" the young woman continued.

"Please do not interrupt," Yamamoto said sternly to her. "I'll get to that part later. For now just listen to what I have to say. You can ask questions later."

"Yes, but . . . " the woman tried again.

"*Listen* to me!" Yamamoto barked. "If you are going to keep interrupting me I can find another female to do this and you can leave. If you want to stay, you will *listen* to your instructions and do as you are told."

The woman looked sullen, but she didn't say anything else. Yamamoto slid the door closed again.

"Now . . . the two of you are in bed together over there. The

American soldier hears a commotion outside. He gets up to investigate. The woman follows. He slides open the door just a crack to see what's going on. She sees that it's a fight between two *yakuza*. She immediately slides the door closed and drags the soldier away from the door and back to bed. He resists, but she's able to get him to come back to bed with her. Now I would like you to please try it. For now, just the part next to the door here."

I had more or less stopped listening at the words "the two of you are in bed together." So I was tentative when we first practiced cracking open the door and seeing a fight. By the third try we had it down. The woman practiced forcing the door closed and pulling me back. She seemed less than eager to practice the part that involved getting me back into bed with her.

Yamamoto delivered his critique of our performance.

"I'd like the American soldier to react a little more strongly to what he sees outside. Two men are fighting *to the death*, okay? His reaction needs to be *bigger*. The cameras are above and they have to see his reaction. So please do it bigger. The prostitute needs to make more effort to get her customer back into bed. She's afraid of the *yakuza* and she doesn't want any trouble. He's an American soldier. He might do something rash. She *needs* him back in bed. Got it? Now try it again."

I practiced sliding open the door and reacting more extravagantly to the imaginary fight outside. The woman made more of an effort to get me back to her bed. In doing this her robe came open, giving me a good look at her body. She had to struggle to keep the robe closed as she practiced the scene. She wasn't wearing much underneath the robe.

Yamamoto looked up at one of the director's assistants who was watching us from above. The man joined the tips of his fingers in front of his face, making an O with his arms. The Japanese sign for OK. Yamamoto looked back at me.

"Very good," Yamamoto said. "Now remember, we'll run through this a few times and it's a long scene. The camera will be capturing what's happening in all of the rooms here from above. During the run-throughs, there will be no actual fight of course. Two of the director's assistants will move through the corridors where the fight would be taking place. In the *honban*, when they shoot the scene for real, the real actors will be having a real fight. Okay? Got it?"

I nodded and the young woman nodded.

"Good. We'll run through the rest of your part now."

Yamamoto directed me and the woman to move back toward the futon on the floor. He told the woman to take off her robe. She seemed about to object, but Yamamoto gave her the hard "I can get someone else" look and she removed the robe and handed it to him. She was wearing a kind of short, mostly transparent negligee. You could see her bra and bikini underpants through the gauzy material of the outer garment. She had the kind of body that I had only known from magazines with centerfolds.

I was instructed to take off my shirt and tie and drape them over the jacket on the back of the desk chair. I hesitated. I should have expected it, but I didn't. Now Yamamoto was giving *me* the "I can get someone else" look, but with less conviction. I had been fitted by an actual tailor for my uniform and they had taken pains to have it look correct. Why would they do this if I was just going to take most of it off? It bothered me, but I glanced over at my lovely partner in the upcoming brothel scene and did as I was told.

"All right," Yamamoto-san said, "the American soldier lies down on top of the futon on his back."

I did as instructed.

"Now the woman lies down on top of him."

The woman hesitated, but then did as she was told.

An attractive female who was good-looking enough to be a centerfold, and ostensibly of legal age, now draped her minimally clothed self on top of me. The synthetic material of the negligee, which had looked fetching enough, felt stiff, scratchy, and unpleasant to the touch. The female body on top of me was cold, stiff, and very heavy. Her perfume was like a combination of Mr. Clean and powdered sugar. The chemical hairspray that held her hair in place made it brittle. The woman's face, now hovering just inches from my own, had on it an expression that made it seem she had just been asked to lie down on top of a bed of freshly eviscerated squid or mackerel. Not exactly how I had imagined it.

The woman on top of me ceased moving altogether and assumed the aspect of a cadaver, hard, cold, and clammy. In the fantasies of the uninitiated, all brothels are safe, clean, high-class, and the female employees are happy in their work and go about it with cheerful enthusiasm. This was the vision I was trying to keep in my head for my role in the film.

"Okay," Yamamoto-san said, "this isn't complicated. He's male, she's female. He's paid for this. He's chosen her. She has a customer she needs to please. There are other women in the brothel. She wants to keep this customer. Please proceed. With feeling. So the camera can see it."

I put my arms around the clammy female lying on top of me and hugged her to me. The woman continued playing dead and allowed me to explore her body as I pleased. For the most part she didn't react to anything I did, only squirming a little when one of my hands got into someplace normally out-of-bounds between couples who had only known each other for five or ten minutes.

I looked up into the maze of lights and wires above. I could see the assistant director looking unhappy.

Yamamoto looked up and saw him as well.

"Please," Yamamoto said, "show a little more passion, you two. We want the camera to see a man and a woman vigorously engaged in sexual foreplay. It's a very brief scene and we really need to be able to see it. It has to register clearly in just the few seconds it takes for the camera to pass over. Once more please."

I took further liberties with the ice-maiden's womanly parts and fondled them with some enthusiasm. My partner squirmed a bit in response, but the feeling I got back was more of controlled malice than erotic joy.

Yamamoto looked up at the director's assistant. He was also feeling no joy and summoned Yamamoto with a gesture.

"We'll try this again later," Yamamoto said. "Both of you please wait here. I'll be back."

Yamamoto left, taking the young woman's robe with him. She retreated back to her corner.

Time passed. I studied the woman in the see-through negligee and abbreviated underwear. She kept me at a distance with the look in her eyes. I decided to try again for a friendly conversation. I approached. She shielded her body with her arms and looked skeptical.

"So, have you done this before?" I asked.

The skeptical look became a flash of anger.

"Sorry. I didn't mean . . . What I meant to ask is, have you worked as an extra in the movies before? Are you a professional actress, or . . . ?"

The woman relaxed a little and sighed. Hopeless, her face seemed to say.

At first I had thought that she was about my age. Now up close I could see that she was older than I had originally thought.

Yamamoto came back into the room and took me aside. He walked me back toward the desk.

"The director thinks the scene would look more natural if you took off the undershirt."

I hesitated. I looked over at the woman, who was watching us intently. I reluctantly removed my undershirt. Yamamoto took it, placed it on the chair, and fiddled with it to get the placement right. Then he went over to the woman.

"The director wants the negligee off. He wants more of you

showing. He wants you looking like a prostitute, not a horny housewife."

"Why?" she said in the rough voice that didn't match the rest of her. "I already took off the robe. It's cold in here. I want to keep it on."

"And do you also want to get paid for today?"

"I'll take it off when they're ready to shoot."

"You will take it off now. I'm not going to ask you again."

The woman glared at Yamamoto. Then she removed the negligee and handed it to him. Her body was now covered only by a plain white bra and little white bikini underpants. Her skin was toothpaste-commercial white. Probably she didn't get outdoors much.

Yamamoto tossed the negligee on the floor and looked up at the director's assistant for confirmation. Then he left the room again. The woman retreated to her corner of the room looking angry. I went back and stood next to the desk and tried not to be just staring at the female in her underwear across the room. I watched the technical crew above busily doing their work. From time to time I noticed some of them pausing to stare down into one of the other rooms in the sprawling set.

Yamamoto returned and came over to me.

"Listen, I'm sorry to ask this, but we're going to need the pants off."

"My pants?"

"Yes."

"But the tailor went to a lot of trouble to fit me into these pants. And I'm wearing 1974 underpants. Fruit of the Loom cotton briefs. I don't think . . ."

"It's fine."

"But they spent so much getting the uniform right. Why . . ."

"Look, it's how the director thinks you should look in the scene."

"But . . ."

"We really need to get going. May I please have the pants?"

It wasn't exactly that I was unhappy about appearing as an extra in a movie clad only in my underpants. I didn't like the feeling that they were trying to put something over on me. Had they intentionally not told me in advance that this would be how it would go, or was it something they were improvising, working it out as they went? If they had told me this was what I would be doing from the beginning, would I have agreed to do it? Yes, I realized. For ¥20,000 I probably would have. But I wasn't happy about it.

Yamamoto held out a hand for the pants. I took them off. He arranged them on the floor near the desk.

"Okay," Yamamoto said. "Now we're going to do a practice take. The soldier and the woman are in bed when the camera passes slowly overhead. The woman is on top. As soon as they hear the sounds of the fight in the hallway, the American soldier rolls the woman off of him and heads to the door to see what the commotion is. The woman slides the door shut and drags the American away from the door and back toward the bed. By that time the camera will have already passed and your part will be over. Any questions? No? Okay, let's go over to the futon and take our positions there."

Yamamoto, the woman, and I moved to the bedding on the floor. The woman and I got down onto the futon again.

Dressed only in underpants and socks, I lay on top of the futon looking up at the tangle of wires and scaffolding and camera and lighting equipment. I again had a mostly naked woman on top of me. Her body felt cold and heavy as before. I was nearly overwhelmed by the cloud of cheap perfume and chemical hairspray that came with her. She lay stiffly on top of me and didn't move. Apparently she was playing her role in the film as a large dead fish. So far.

Yamamoto looked up at the assistant director who was watching us from above.

"Okay," Yamamoto said, "you'll hear the director's assistant shout 'action.' When you hear that, the soldier and the prostitute will begin engaging in sexual activity. When you hear the commotion in the hall, the soldier and the prostitute will get up and then proceed as we rehearsed. Please wait here in position until you hear the call for action. And please remember, you're having sex and we really need to see it."

Yamamoto left the room. The woman lay stiff and motionless on top of me. The time passed very slowly. The woman and I lay there silent and feeling each other breathe, in and out. Once the camera started rolling forward, we were going to pretend to be having sex. The elements of that rare and special thing that I thought of as sex were in place. In spite of everything, the body resting on top of me registered as delectable and female. There were acres of smooth, pale, womanly flesh at my fingertips. I was being asked to do what I had probably fantasized doing more often than I would care to admit. And yet, something was missing. Somehow, the element of joy was missing.

The set grew quiet. There was giggling coming from one of the other brothel rooms but someone shushed it with a harsh whisper, and a few minutes later the director's assistant yelled, "*Renshu ban* take one! Action!"

I looked up and could see the large movie camera with its three-man team of camera operator, director, and director's assistant slowly rolling forward on its track above the set. I allowed my hands to explore the woman's body. She squirmed only minimally in reaction to my touch. Her stiff bra dug into my chest. Her brittle hair had the smell and feel of cotton candy and irritated my face when she moved. I soldiered on and did my professional best to grope the woman thoroughly and with enthusiasm.

The sounds of a commotion came from down the hall. I rolled the woman off me and rushed to the door of the room. I slid it open a crack and saw Yamamoto and one of the director's assistants stomping along in the hallway shouting and making fighting noises. The woman slipped in beside me, forcefully slid the door shut, and placed one hand on my shoulder and one on my arm. She tugged at me and pulled me back toward the bed. I ad-libbed a few lines in a loud voice in English saying, "Wha . . . what in the dag nab . . . why the heck . . ." The woman surprised me by ad-libbing her own lines in broken English, saying, "Bahddo . . . beri, bahddo . . . America *heitai* no look . . . beri beri bahddo . . ." Perhaps she *was* an actress after all.

When the camera stopped moving, the woman released me and retreated back to her corner. From the other rooms I could hear laughter and bursts of nervous conversation. A woman was telling someone to keep his hands to himself. Another was telling someone not to touch her *there*. There was even some heavy breathing as if one or two of the couples had warmed to their roles and were staying in character between takes.

Yamamoto came back into the room and gave us his critique of our performance.

"Look," he said. "You've both had sex before, correct? Could you both please, *please*, put a little more feeling into it? Move a little more and use your hands and arms more. Don't be shy. It has to be bigger. The camera needs to see that, that the American soldier is really having sex with this woman. Can you do that?"

"Yes," I said. "Sorry, I guess I can."

The woman nodded sullenly.

"Okay, the next pass is going to be the *honban*, the real take. So please, put some more energy into it. It's sex. Try to enjoy it. We need to see it."

The woman and I got back down on the futon. Yamamoto paused and looked down at the woman and me again in position laying on the futon. Then he looked up at the director's assistant in the scaffolding above. The assistant was making a gesture that I couldn't quite see.

Yamamoto leaned down and began unhooking the woman's bra. She squirmed on top of me and tried to stop him. Yamamoto gave her a stern look and she stopped squirming.

"The director wants this off. He thinks it will make your American lover a little more passionate."

The woman slumped on top of me. Yamamoto unhooked and

removed her bra and tossed it on the floor. Her naked breasts spilled out onto my chest. They were medium-sized, neon white, and bouncy. The nipples were purple and rock hard. Her breasts were the only warm, soft parts of the woman's body that I had encountered so far. No makeup. No powder. Just fine, smooth female flesh.

"Now *please* show me how you'll do it this time around," Yamamoto said. "The camera needs to see it. The next take is the *honban*."

I gave it my best shot, placing a hand on the back of the woman's head and pressing her face to mine. We fake kissed passionately with our mouths closed. My hands took their liberties and for once my partner reacted. To an outside viewer it might have seemed like passion. But what I could clearly feel was anger. Yamamoto was satisfied.

That's more like it!" Yamamoto-san said. "Okay. You can relax now and save it for the *honban*."

Yamamoto left and the woman resumed pretending to be a corpse on top of me. We held our positions. We waited. I felt the rise and fall of a naked chest and hard nipples as the woman breathed in and out. I closed my eyes. Sounds of giggling and whispered conversation drifted in from the other rooms. An excited woman's voice again said, "Take your hands *out* of there!" There was laughter from the nearby rooms. Then it was quiet.

The director's assistant called out, "*Honban* take one! Action!" The camera began to move slowly forward.

The woman on top of me began to writhe. She had suddenly come to life and was behaving as a living person. Her movements were exaggerated. Sometimes she was an amateur belly dancer. Sometimes she was having a mild epileptic seizure. We kissed passionately with our mouths closed. Maybe it was the naked bosoms, but the body on top of me was beginning to feel much more compellingly female.

The camera crawled slowly forward. I looked up. And then, all of a sudden, the entire universe and time itself began to slow down, almost to a complete stop. I could hear the sounds of people having simulated sex in the neighboring rooms. The mostly naked female on top of me was writhing in slow motion. My brain seemed to begin seeing things with great clarity. I was on my back on a *futon* in my Fruit of the Loom underpants looking up. It was almost like I was out of my body watching the scene unfold.

I began to imagine what the camera was seeing as it rolled toward me. I thought I could see how I must have looked to the camera. I was in a soft-core porn movie. Other couples in the other rooms were laying down a visual montage of sex in a brothel with a Japanese sex-video soundtrack. There was female squealing and male grunting. There was moaning, sighing, and heavy breathing. I realized that I had been so focused on the mostly naked female in the room that I had lost track of everything else.

My sex partner began to up her game. She added high pitched girlish moans and squeals. The grinding of her hips became more purposeful. My hands rampaged through the acres of exposed alabaster white, smooth, womanly flesh. In a burst of spontaneous actorly inspiration, I yanked down the woman's white bikini underpants so that her naked bottom was exposed to the approaching camera. A frisson of alarm coursed through her still squirming and grinding body. She tried to squirm the underpants back up without using her hands. But it wasn't working. She growled and gyrated forcefully. She slammed her hips against me. She fake-kissed me so hard that her lips almost parted.

The two of us had finally hit our actorly stride. The director could not but be pleased. However . . . at this point none of what we were doing was being filmed. The camera above in its relentless slow crawl forward had not yet reached our room.

The woman and I were just about to come into frame. Time slowed nearly to a stop. My newly awakened brain began to broadcast warnings. Did I not realize that I was about to be immortalized forever on film in my Fruit of the Loom underwear in a brothel having sex with a prostitute? Was this really a good idea? Who might someday see this movie? Friends? Relatives? My teachers at school? My unborn children? I didn't exactly have a starring role in the production. But a permanent record on film was being made. Did I really want that to happen? Had I even agreed to this? Hadn't I just been maneuvered into it step-by-step without realizing exactly was going on? Hadn't I allowed myself to be trapped by a ridiculous adolescent fantasy? Was this really worth ¥20,000? What the hell was I doing?

The camera inched forward on its gigantic dolly. I could see the director and the cameraman peering down at the rooms that were in frame as the camera moved. The director's assistant was scanning the rooms just ahead that were about to come into frame. The camera couldn't quite see me yet.

I removed my hands from the writhing woman's undulating naked buttocks and placed them in her hair. I pressed her face to mine. We fake-kissed passionately. And just as the camera approached, I seized handfuls of the woman's brittle, cotton candy hair and completely covered my face with it. Through the veil of the woman's rust-colored hair I could see the assistant director pointing down at me with a look of panic on his face. His look of betrayal was even comic. As the camera passed over, the director's face registered mild surprise. The camera could not possibly see my face through the woman's hair.

The sounds of tumbling and crashing bodies came from the corridor outside. I pushed the woman's body off of me and rolled her to the side of the futon. I did that possibly a bit more enthusiastically than how we'd done it in practice. The few seconds it took for the woman to try to get her underpants back up made her slower to get over to the door than when we had rehearsed it. I raced to the door with my head down and my shoulders forward so the camera couldn't see my face from its angle above. I slid the door open a crack and the woman, still struggling to pull up her underpants, rushed over to join me and missed getting the timing of closing the door right.

I had a moment of unscripted time to watch two massive *yakuza* outside the door wrestling and beating the crap out of each other while executing impressive martial arts moves in the narrow space of the hallway. One of them held a short sword and their fight revolved around trying to get control of the blade or trying to keep from being slashed by it. I was fascinated by how skillful the men were. When the woman finally moved to slide the door shut, I resisted her for real.

"Baddo . . . beri . . . ah . . . baddo . . . no! . . . no . . . America *heitai* no! . . . you no . . . uh . . . *miru na! Bakayaro!*" the young woman screamed at me with real feeling as she struggled to shut the door.

We never made it back to the futon.

The noise of the fight moved on toward the brothel's *genkan*. After some more loud crashing and the sound of the battle continuing, someone from above finally yelled, "*Katto*!"

The woman retreated rapidly to the futon and got under the covers. Up in the scaffolding I could see the director's assistant having an animated discussion with the director while pointing a finger angrily down at me.

Ten minutes later Yamamoto came into the room accompanied by a female assistant. The female assistant picked up the bra and negligee from the floor and handed them, along with the terrycloth robe, to the woman. The woman got out of bed, retreated to her corner, turned her back on the room, and got dressed. I got permission from Yamamoto to gather my clothes from the back of the chair and get dressed again in my army uniform.

"It seems there was a minor problem with the take," Yamamoto said dryly. "Apparently," he said looking at me, "your head was covered by the woman's hair and the camera couldn't quite see your face. They discussed shooting the scene over again but decided against it."

Yamamoto held me with his eyes for a moment and then turned to look at the woman.

"So," he said to both me and the woman, "you are now finished for the day. We have to ask you to wait until they finish the next scene and then you can go up to wardrobe and return your costumes. Then you may proceed to accounting to collect your pay envelopes. You can wait in here, or you can go outside and watch them complete the fight scene, as long as you don't get in their way."

The woman immediately grabbed Yamamoto and started complaining.

"I want to be paid more because I was naked," she said. "You said I wouldn't have to be naked. If you're naked you have to be paid more. That's the rule! You said I wouldn't be naked. I want to be paid more."

Yamamoto tried to escape the woman but she wouldn't let go of him. I decided to leave them to their discussion and go outside and watch the conclusion of the fight scene being filmed.

The two *yakuza* who had been fighting were sitting comfortably on the edge of the brothel's *genkan*. A movie camera and lights had been set up facing the *genkan* and microphones hung from wires just outside of the camera's range. Many of the extras who had been in the brothel formed a semicircle on either side of the camera to watch the scene being shot. I found myself standing next to one of the script girls, who seemed more than happy to explain to me everything that was going on in hushed stage whispers.

"These are rival *yakuza* in love with the same woman," the script girl said. "Now they are going to have a fight to the death. These fight scenes are really tricky. They're carefully choreographed but the men really have to do all the fighting moves. With a set like this, everything has to be shot in as few takes as possible. At the end of the fight, the guy in the plaid jacket is going to stab the guy in the green jacket in the chest and the blood from his heart is going to explode into the sky like a bright red geyser or a fountain of blood. See the girl over there next to the director? She's in charge of the exploding blood sacs they wear under their clothes to make the effect. It's going to be terrific. You'll see."

The *yakuza* got up and resumed their positions inside the brothel. The director's assistant yelled "*Honban!*" and "Action!" and the fight resumed. The battle was exciting and skillfully executed. The combatants battled rolling on the ground and leaping in the air. At the last minute, the *yakuza* in the plaid jacket got the better of his green-jacket rival, flipped him onto his back, and plunged his sword into the man's chest. The green-jacket *yakuza* looked grief-stricken and surprised, but he was resigned to his fate. His body relaxed and he expired manfully. The plaid-jacket *yakuza* looked vaguely melancholy and also surprised. His body relaxed and he removed his sword from the other man's chest. A stream of crimson blood gurgled down the green-jacket *yakuza*'s pants leg.

"*Katto! Katto!*" the director's assistant screamed.

All eyes turned to the girl standing next to the director. Her head hung low and she began to weep. The weeping became wailing. One of the other script girls took her to the side and began massaging her back and trying to comfort her. A small discussion circle formed around the director.

"The blood sac didn't explode properly," the script girl next to me whispered. "Now they have to decide what to do. I saw this happen before. The director will want to reshoot the scene, but they'll have to go all the way back to the beginning of the fight. The producers won't let him do it."

"Why can't they just redo this scene. The final one here in front of the brothel?"

"Because when they fought out here on the ground they completely destroyed the clothes they were wearing. They can't start the scene with their clothes already dirty and ripped. They'll have to change clothes and start all over again."

"Don't they have back-up pairs of the same clothes in case something happens? Can't they just wash them?"

"No. It's a low-budget production. Getting the clothes cleaned properly and trying to match them will take time, and unfortunately in this business time is also money. They'll either have to try to have the clothes cleaned quickly and repaired and then redo the scene or redo the scene here with different clothes and hope the audience won't notice or won't care. Or they'll have to just give up on the exploding spray of blood."

In the end, they gave up on redoing the scene and called it a wrap for the day. I walked back to locker room and changed into my own clothes. Then I went back to wardrobe and returned the army uniform. By the time I got to the accounting office to pick up my pay envelope, all the women in see-through negligees had already left the premises.

Sado: The Way of Tea

I FELL IN LOVE WITH Kyoto the very first time I saw it and decided to stay. I was living in Tokyo and had a part-time job with an advertising agency translating ad copy for Canon cameras. On my first visit to Kyoto, in the space of a single day, and with an incredible amount of luck, I enrolled in a school where I could study Japanese and I found a place to live.

The school was the Kyoto Japanese Language School, which I heard had trained some of the world's best-known students of Japanese art and literature and was the place to be for those seriously studying Japanese in Kyoto. I'd just dropped in on a whim and asked if I could sign up for classes. The head of the school said yes, and that by the way, she happened to know about an international students' dormitory where I might get a room. She wrote me a letter of recommendation and called to say I was coming. She said if I hoped to get a room there, I had better get over there ASAP, because when there were openings, they were snapped up immediately.

The International Students Residence was the only three-story building in a neighborhood of upper-middle-class single-family homes on the eastern outskirts of Kyoto near the town of Yamashina. The nearest tram stop was Hi no Oka on the Keihan Line. The International Students Residence was a large, rectangular building made mostly out of concrete. It had all the charm of a Stalin-era building in Soviet Russia.

I found the administration office for the dorm just to the right as

I entered the building. It was a big room full of metal desks and office equipment. Almost the entire wall of the room facing the entrance was glass, so you could see into it and the people inside could see whoever was entering the building. Next to the entrance was a sliding-glass window and a counter for depositing mail or packages. A woman sitting at one of the desks looked up as I entered.

The sliding-glass window was open, and I leaned in to address the woman in my finest formal Japanese.

"My name is Don Ascher," I said. "Someone at the Kyoto Japanese Language School called to say I would be coming to see about a vacancy here."

The woman got up, came over to the glass window and looked me over head to toe. Her assessment of me was decidedly negative.

After a pause she said in English, "Come around the corner. The entrance to the office is over there."

I did as I was told.

"Sit," the woman said, indicating a chair in front of her desk.

I sat. She sat and then studied me for a bit longer.

"Kobayashi," the woman said, not bowing or extending a hand to shake. "I'm in charge of this dormitory."

Miss or Mrs. Kobayashi was about five feet two inches tall and wiry. She was eerily pale and dressed entirely in black. She might have been in her mid-forties, though she could have been ten years younger or ten years older. She had a raspy Marlon-Brando-in-The-Godfather voice. Her black hair was flecked with gray and pulled back into a tight ponytail. She looked more like a member of an all-female motorcycle gang than an administrator of a dormitory operated by the Japanese government.

As Kobayashi-san regarded me with a look of extreme skepticism, she took out a little black cigarillo from a package on her desk and lit it with a wooden match from an old-fashioned matchbox. Her ashtray was full of the butts of cigarillos. For a few minutes

Kobayashi-san just studied me, blew smoke in my face, and flicked ash into the ashtray.

"So, Donald Ascher," she said, "what is it you've come to Kyoto to study?"

"Ah . . . actually the full name . . . the one on the passport . . . it's Sheldon, not Donald. Don is short for . . . "

"And . . . ? Studying what?"

"Japanese," I said. "I'm here to study Japanese."

"And what else?"

"Uh . . . just Japanese."

"You're what? American is it? You're enrolled at some American university?"

"Columbia in New York . . . that is . . . when I get back from Japan."

"Studying what?"

"Japanese literature."

"Why?"

"I love Japanese and Chinese poetry. I'd like to maybe someday translate Japanese poetry into English."

"So you're taking advanced Japanese lessons?"

"More intermediate I would say."

Kobayashi-san sighed. She flicked more ash from the cigarillo into the ashtray.

"You have a student visa?"

"Yes."

"Show me."

I took out my passport and handed it to her. She studied it and handed it back to me.

"And you planned to live here in Kyoto for a year or two is it?"

"Yes."

"And you came here with no place to live? You didn't think to correspond with the school here before you got here and have someone there help you find a place?"

"Well actually, I've been living in Tokyo for about a month. I was planning to go to school at a university there, but . . . but visiting Kyoto . . . I don't know, I just . . . spontaneously I guess . . . just decided that if I'm going to spend two years in Japan studying Japanese, I would rather be here in Kyoto doing it."

"So you dislike Tokyo?"

"No, but . . . if I have only two years I'd rather spend them here."

"I see."

There was a long pause. Kobayashi-san sighed again.

"The rent for a room here is ¥3,000 a month," she said.

"That seems very reasonable."

Kobayashi-san laughed. It was more of a cackle actually.

"We bill you every month on the first of the month," she said. "If you don't pay on time, you're out. No excuses. We have strict rules here. Hashimoto-san is the head RA of the dormitory. He will explain the rules to you. All of our residents are students. Many from third-world countries. Japan is expensive. Some of them find it necessary to take temporary part-time jobs to make ends meet. Student visas allow that to some extent. It's a privilege. So don't abuse it. The teaching of English conversation here is a big business. We discourage our residents from doing it. A class or two from time to time we accept. But if we find you're doing more teaching English than studying Japanese, you're out. If you break any of our rules, you're out. Is that understood?"

I said that it was.

"Fine. I'll have Hashimoto-san show you your room. We'll do the paperwork when you move in. I should tell you that we're not particularly fond of Americans here. Don't make me regret letting you live here."

I said that I would try not to.

Hashimoto-san was a graduate student in American Literature at Kyoto University. Oddly, he seemed to share Kobayashi-san's dislike of Americans. He was tall for a Japanese. Thin but clearly not athletic.

He struck me as more of a bureaucrat than an academic. In showing me around my future home, he was an odd combination of business-like, friendly, and standoffish.

Hashimoto-san explained that the International Students Residence was a great place to live in Kyoto if you were a student and didn't have money. The rent was cheap and the facilities were good. You had your own room, access to hot water showers, and a very large, fully equipped kitchen. You had a phone number where you could be reached and someone would take messages for you. The world's international student population was well represented. The dorm's policy was to allow no more than two students from any country to be in residence at the same time. This was a boon for students from the less well-off nations for whom Japan was an impossibly expensive place to live.

Hashimoto-san provided me with a five-page list of the dorm's rules. He made sure I understood that if I broke any of the rules I would be kicked out. He said that Kobayashi-san ruled the dorm with an iron fist. She didn't approve of her residents doing part-time jobs. Residents were supposed to be in Kyoto to study. Having a part-time job, other than something nominal or that could also be considered a mutual exchange of cultural ideas and understanding, was against the rules of the dorm. Having someone of the opposite sex sleep over in your room was against the rules. Sexual intimacy between the residents of the dormitory was forbidden. Did I understand that?

I thanked Kobayashi-san and said that I did.

Besides the administration offices, the first floor held a kitchen and a large dining room. A part of the dining room at the back had sofas and easy chairs and could be partitioned off to use as a kind of common room for activities other than eating. There was a wing off of the first floor in the back for female residents. The second and third floors were where the male residents lived. Everyone had their own room. Mine was on the third floor.

My room was already vacant when Hashimoto-san showed it to

me. It was a Spartan, monk-like cell. There was a narrow single bed in it, a small wooden desk, a bookshelf, and a small closet. Its one window was open. With the door to the room open, a breeze cooled the room. I walked over to the window and looked out. The dorm was up on a hill so it had a good view. A sea of single-family homes stretched to the horizon. The pine-covered green slopes of Higashiyama anchored one side of the view. Just behind it, unseen from this vantage point, would be Kyoto proper. To the east were the commercial buildings of the town of Yamashina. At the edge of the horizon a silvery white *shinkansen* Bullet Train was just slithering into the tunnel that led to Kyoto Station.

It was a fine view. I supposed it would be spectacular at night as the sun was setting and the lights in all the houses were coming on. It was south-facing so there would be sunrises and sunsets.

Hashimoto-san walked me out of the dorm, and as I left, I waved at Kobayashi-san in her office puffing away on a cigarillo. She ignored me.

I went back to Tokyo, tendered my resignation at my part-time job, explained to the university that had sponsored my student visa why I would not after all be enrolling in the fall, packed my few belongings, and moved to Kyoto.

I was one of only two people in the dormitory not attending an actual Japanese university in Kyoto. Most were students at either Kyoto University or Doshisha University. The two Sri Lankans in the dorm attended a science and technology university in Osaka. The only other American in the dorm, Pattie Wilson, was studying the Japanese tea ceremony at a tea ceremony school called Honsenke. I thought it was odd that there was a university of tea.

I saw Pattie Wilson around the dorm sometimes, but I never went over to talk to her. She was a perky blond and seemed to me like a typical college sorority girl. She looked like someone who might be more comfortable waving pom-poms and leading cheers at a football game than studying how to make Japanese tea. She was trim and athletic-looking. Very polite. Smiled all the time. And she was very pretty. She also seemed to be very busy, and whenever I saw her she was in motion, on her way to or from somewhere.

When I first moved in, Kobayashi-san, the tough, cigar-smoking woman who ran the dorm, reminded me that she would be keeping an eye on me. But after my first week she ignored me. She seemed to have forgotten who I was.

The first friends I made at the International Students Residence were two Australians, Peter Franks and Judy Martin. Peter Franks had been in Kyoto for nearly two years studying fermentation methods at Kyoto University's agricultural science department. Peter was tall and thin and had longish hair and a moustache. He had the quick sense of humor people expect from Australians. He was from Sydney and was getting ready to go back there to finish a graduate program in food science.

Judy Martin was from Queensland, the least populated part of northeastern Australia. She grew up on a large farm which she referred to as a ranch. She was studying English literature at Kyoto University. I found it difficult to understand why anyone would come to Japan to study English literature. Judy's Japanese was truly terrible. Besides her impenetrable Australian accent, she seemed to have little grasp of the basic rules of Japanese grammar. She made spoken Japanese sound like a bad computer translation of Australian English. But she did know a lot about English literature, and for some reason poisonous snakes. She could talk about poisonous snakes and the myriad varieties of kangaroos in Australia for hours if you let her. I supposed that if you lived in the remote Australian outback, having a good supply of reading material would be important. The snakes I never understood. The kangaroos I did.

Judy was easygoing and relentlessly calm. All of her clothes seemed to have been designed by Peter Max: colorful, free-flowing, and New Age appropriate. Her chestnut-colored hair fell to her shoulders in a cascade of unrestrained curls. Her brown eyes were warm and welcoming. She loved Japan and was curious about everything having to do with it. But she made it clear that that there was no place she would rather live, or would ever live, besides her ranch on the far northeast coast of Australia.

Peter and Judy and I had dinner together in the dorm's dining room two or three times a week. Sometimes we were joined by the two Germans in the dorm, Wolfe and Gunter. Wolfe was tall, blond, handsome, and very fit. He was studying law at Kyoto University. Gunter was small, bearded, and very precise about everything he did. Both spoke English perfectly. Pattie Wilson seemed to take all her meals out and was never present at dinnertime.

Peter had a mostly live-in girlfriend named Satoko. This was against the dorm's rules. Peter's room on the second floor was identical to my room on the third floor. It was very small and contained only a narrow single bed and a desk and dresser. It was hard for me to imagine how Satoko managed to live in the dorm. The big bathroom and showers on the second and third floors were male-only. The women's bathroom was downstairs in the much smaller women's wing on the first floor. Besides Pattie Wilson and Judy Martin, there were only four other women in residence.

Peter's girlfriend Satoko was stunningly beautiful. She was so beautiful that people in the dorm wondered out loud what she could possibly see in Peter. She had been a stewardess for Japan Airlines International at a time when beauty and poise were the main hiring criteria for the job. Japan's national airline regarded its stewardesses as ambassadors of Japanese culture. Satoko had retired early from JAL and was currently working for the JTB, the Japan Tourism Bureau, as a uniformed hostess and tour guide. She was so beautiful you sometimes had to remind yourself to stop gaping and speak when she spoke to you.

As a professional, Satoko was probably used to male attention and knew how to deal with it. She was genuinely modest, sweet, considerate, and very intelligent. She clearly cared for Peter. She appreciated his sense of humor. She appreciated his straightforward frankness. Satoko was also straightforward and frank. She said exactly what she thought and didn't water it down or soften it. If she had an opinion on something, she told you what it was. That was very unusual for a Japanese female.

My friendship with Peter changed my life in two important ways. Peter for some reason owned two small motorcycles. Since he only needed one of them, he sold the other one to me. It was a very old Honda. Because it had been repaired so often, and so many of its parts had been replaced, the exact age of the motorbike was undeterminable. Peter only charged me ¥1,000 for the bike. At some point the motorcycle had been painted a bright yellow. Though old, the bike was a totally reliable form of transportation, at least when it wasn't raining too hard or snowing. It could defeat any traffic jam the city could put up. Nothing got you where you were going quicker. Pleasanter depended on the weather.

Peter also made me his designated successor to the part-time jobs he worked to support his studies in Kyoto. Peter knew the Japanese agent who hired extras for the movies. He had appeared as an American bad guy in a score of B-grade Japanese films. I found it funny that the Japanese considered him a quintessential American despite his thick Australian accent. Peter also held the world's best-ever English teaching job in Osaka. I inherited that from him too.

There was a weekly poker game that began at around ten p.m. and lasted all night. The stakes, and the chips used for betting, were featherweight one-yen coins. Peter invited me to join, and I became a regular player. One night I won ¥1,432, which was the dorm record that stood for as long as I lived in Kyoto. I have to admit that it was more a matter of luck than skill, since most nights I usually lost.

The real point of the game was the drinking and the conversations that accompanied it. Gunter, one of the two Germans in the dorm, was from a small village near the city of Gütersloh in the north of Germany near the border with Holland. He complained constantly that the Japanese failed to do things properly. His poker playing was unfailingly conservative, and he rarely lost much or won much. The other German in the dorm, the blond, athletic, handsome, and affable Wolfe, was a very bad poker player and always lost quickly and left the game early.

The usual winners in the game were Markar from Sri Lanka and Rudy from the Philippines. Rudy's field of study was nuclear engineering and Markar's was business administration. Markar was seeing Angelica, one of the women who lived in the dorm, a violation of the dorm's rules that all the residents knew about but the administration seemed not to. She was a very enthusiastic and very voluptuous Japanese-Brazilian. She sometimes sat in on the game, the only female, and when she decided it was time to leave, Markar left with her, unless he was losing.

Ali and Mohammed, the two Iranians in the dorm, were studying engineering at Kyoto University. They complained bitterly about the Shah and his friendship with Israel. They were both in the army and in Japan on Iranian Army money. Ali was from a wealthy family. Mohammed was working class.

"I don't understand why we are killing Iraqis when we should be killing Jews," Ali would say with real feeling.

Then Mohammed, the less volatile of the two, would apologize to Peter, who was Jewish, and calmly explain that Ali only meant the Zionists and had nothing personal against individual Jews. Both Ali and Mohammed were terrible poker players. They got drunk after one or two beers and always left the game by midnight. Peter and I both took a special pleasure in winning money from them, though we tried not to show it.

MY FIRST FEW TRIPS TO my Japanese-language school were by tram and streetcar. It took forever to go back and forth that way, and the charm of riding the picturesque, aging green-and-tan streetcars left over from another era was beginning to wear off. That problem was solved as soon as I started riding the yellow Honda. The trip on the motorcycle was a joy, even in the rain. The one-way trip took less than half an hour. Although it was illegal, motorcycles skirted traffic jams by sneaking along the left edge of the road, creating a de facto motorcycle lane that moved when the rest of the traffic did not. The rule of law in Japan seemed to be that if everybody did it, the police wouldn't stop you.

My first classmates at my Japanese language school were Saoirse Ryan and Victor Reitman. Saoirse like inertia was Irish from Ireland. Victor was from New York City, born and bred. He was a graduate student at Harvard studying Chinese and Japanese politics. He said he had chosen Harvard because he wanted to work for the State Department. He said Harvard connections got you into the Foreign Service, Yale connections got you into the CIA, and Princeton got you a job in academics. Given his field, he should have been in Tokyo. But since everyone else was there, he preferred to be in Kyoto.

Victor had generous scholarship money from Harvard and didn't need to do part-time jobs. He spent most of his time studying and was vague about what he did the rest of the time. He lived in a farmhouse in the north of Kyoto with his girlfriend who was in Kyoto studying Zen Buddhism and martial arts. She was blond and beautiful and could do forty push-ups the hard way, on her fists. She could do it without breaking a sweat or breathing hard. It was something she liked to demonstrate.

Once over dinner and sake at Victor's farmhouse, Victor warned me about the half-dozen Americans in Kyoto who he said worked for the CIA. He said they were there keeping tabs on Red Army members and student activists. One of them was a surfer from California who ran an organic bakery and coffee shop near Arashiyama, someone whom I had met a few times. The bread and the pastries were really good, but sadly, the store was too far away to visit on a regular basis.

Even on my motorcycle. Another was a guy named Lee who ran a bar in downtown Kyoto that was a hangout for *gaijin* and Japanese motorcycle gangs.

Saoirse had a part-time job at a Japanese restaurant way up on Higashiyama. Her husband Sean, who spoke very little Japanese, worked nearly full-time teaching English to support them in Kyoto. Sean had a car and drove Saoirse up to and back from her five-days-a-week restaurant job.

—

LIVING IN KYOTO I WANTED to visit all of its famous temples and shrines. It was said that if you just visited the most famous ones, two or three a week, it would take you more than twenty years to see them all. Victor lent me his favorite book on Kyoto, titled *Kyoto: A Contemplative Guide* and written in the 1950s by a Princeton graduate named Gouverneur Mosher. I started with that. In it, Mosher identified some of the best examples of temples and other cultural relics that had managed to survive each of the broad eras that made up Kyoto's history. The book provided a brief history of each temple and its period, a map by which to explore it, and a summary of its outstanding qualities.

Most of the important temples, and the most interesting ones, were tucked away in the mountains or foothills surrounding Kyoto and took some getting to. If you lived in Kyoto you could pick the exact season and time of day that allowed each of these places to show off what it was that made them famous. You could bask in the atmosphere of the art and culture that existed when the temples were built, and marvel at the civilizations that made them. Or you could just sit and marvel at the nature that still surrounded them and with which they were designed to be at one.

I also found places near the dorm in Hi no Oka where I could hike in the woods for hours without seeing a person or a building. It surprised me that, in a city as old and as densely populated as Kyoto, there were still wild places in the hills where no one lived or even visited.

One beautiful Sunday morning I had just headed out of the dorm for an early morning hike in the woods when I bumped into Pattie Wilson, also headed out for a morning walk. I had been up all night playing poker and had won about ¥30.

Pattie was a natural strawberry blond. She had piercing blue eyes and a disarming smile. Her skin had a healthy, golden glow, like someone who spent time outside but not enough to get really dark or sunburned. Pattie seemed fit without being overly athletic. There was a tennis court behind the dorm, and I'd seen Pattie play. She was good. She didn't overpower her male opponents. She outsmarted them and outlasted them.

On this particular Sunday, Pattie was dressed in tan khaki slacks, a plain cotton blouse, a cotton cardigan sweater, and white tennis shoes. She was the kind of person who seemed to think wearing blue jeans was un-feminine and wrong unless you worked on a farm or did manual labor.

"Where are you headed?" Pattie asked.

I had certainly seen Pattie around the dorm, but I'd never spoken to her. She was attractive. She spoke English. She was the only other American in the dorm. But I'd always had the feeling we were living in different worlds with no possibility of overlap. She was in Japan studying the Japanese tea ceremony, which I had to admit I found utterly ridiculous.

"Where are you headed?" Pattie asked again.

"I . . . um . . . just out toward the woods at the top of the hill over there. No particular destination in mind."

"What's up there?" Pattie asked. "Is there anything worth looking at? An old temple or something?"

"No. Not really. Just woods. Trees. The trails up there go on forever. You could go through the woods all the way to Nanzen-ji in one direction and over the big mountains all the way to Otsu in Shiga

Prefecture the other way. And . . . oh yeah . . . there's a canal up there that goes all the way from Lake Biwa to Nanzen-ji and then becomes part of the Tetsugaku no Michi."

"A canal? What do you mean a canal? Like the kind boats go on?"

"More of an aqueduct. It's made out of brick in the places it isn't buried in the ground. It looks like some of it was built in Meiji, or maybe just improved then. It's supposed to have existed in one form or other all the way back to Heian times. It's how they got water from Lake Biwa to the Imperial Palace in Kyoto. Or so they claim when you take the official tour."

"And you can follow it all the way to Nanzen-ji?"

"Yeah. It's a pretty long walk from up there."

"And in the other direction you can walk along it all the way to Lake Biwa?"

"Uh . . . no. In that direction it goes as far as Yamashina and then into a tunnel. There's a few of those traditional flat-bottomed canal boats, *takase bune*, tied up by the mouth of the tunnel. I guess you could steal one and make your way underground through the tunnel to the lake."

"Steal a boat?"

"Borrow."

"Did you ever go all the way to Nanzen-ji?"

"Once. But not along the canal. Through the woods. It took about three hours. There are a lot of interesting old buildings behind the main temple complex at Nanzen-ji. You're not really allowed back there, so if you come in through the main entrance you wouldn't be able to see them. But you can if you come in through the woods."

"How did you know about this?"

"I didn't. When I walk in the woods up there I try to see where the trails go. There seem to be a lot of them, actually. A few of them are well-worn, but I've never seen anyone else there. As far as I can tell, there's nothing up there but woods."

"No buildings or anything?"

"Nope. Apparently in this part of Kyoto, a city that has been continuously occupied for about the last 2,000 years, no one has ever built anything. I read somewhere that maybe 1,200 years ago religious hermits lived in all the mountain areas leading up to Mt. Hiei. And bandits. That would include this area, though we're pretty far from Mt. Hiei. If you go off-trail sometimes you can find the remains of old houses. Small huts. The stone foundations they were built on are still there."

"Why would you go off-trail?"

"Just curious."

"So that's where you're going now? Up there into the woods to hike?"

"Uh huh."

"Can I come with you?"

"Uh . . ."

"Are tennis shoes OK, or do you need good hiking boots like yours?"

"For the canal, the tennis shoes would be OK. You would have to climb a fence to get up there."

"Fine, let's go."

I hesitated. My plan for the day was to smoke half of a Thai Buddha stick and then do some hiking. My classmate Victor knew a guy who sometimes showed up at the monthly Toji flea market and sold marijuana or hashish to people he trusted. He only dealt in very small quantities. If I was going to be accompanied by Miss All-American Cheerleader, I supposed I would have to give up on the idea of smoking the joint. There didn't seem to be an easy way to revoke an invitation that I hadn't made.

I said okay, and Pattie and I walked up together past the few houses at the top of the hill that bordered the woods just above the dorm building. Kyoto's municipal water department managed the aqueduct. There was a sturdy five-foot-tall chain-link fence we had to climb over. The canal wasn't visible until a good ways past the fence.

Once we cleared the houses and the water department property, there was a nice view of Hi no Oka and the hills on either side of the tram line. We paused to take it in and then went on until we reached the woods. After a hundred yards of bushwhacking we came out into an open area and then reached the aqueduct. This part of the aqueduct was dug into the ground, the way it is along the Tetsugaku no Michi, the famous walking path that runs between the temples Nanzen-ji and Ginkaku-ji. On either side of it there was a well-worn trail.

Pattie and I paused to look at the water as it flowed steadily past. It was crystal clear and provided a perfect view of the bottom and sides of the canal. Clumps of bright green moss stuck to the faded red bricks in places. The canal itself was maybe five feet across. It was almost narrow enough to jump over, but not quite. An athlete could probably do it.

"What is it you do up here besides walk?" Pattie wanted to know.

"How do you mean?"

"I had the feeling you didn't want me come with you. I'm not used to rejection."

"No, I mean . . . "

"Is it my imagination," Pattie said, "or do you come up here to get high?"

"Now why would you think that?" I asked.

"Do you?"

"I . . . "

"Because if you do, I would really want to join you. It's been a long time, and I miss it."

"Well . . . I . . ."

"Look, I understand," she said. "I know no one thinks I'm the type to smoke pot. But I am, okay? Whatever people think of me is probably wrong. I can be as naughty as anyone else."

"Uh huh."

"Look, I don't want you to get the wrong idea. I like to smoke and drink just as much as anyone. Maybe I'm old-fashioned. Maybe it's how I was brought up. I just don't think a girl should be seen doing it. That's all. What you do in private is your own business. If there's something you only do in private, I don't see the point of advertising it."

"Right. So what else do you do in private that you don't want people to see you doing?"

"Not anything you're going to find out about just because we shared a joint out here in the woods."

"I see."

"I hope so."

I hesitated, but then I brought out the joint I had planned to smoke from the pocket of my shirt along with a box of wooden matches.

"Hold on," Pattie said. "Right here? You're just going to do it right here where anyone passing by could see us?"

"I think I mentioned that I've never seen another person in all the times I've been up here. There isn't even any way to get here without climbing a fence. Not at least until almost to Yamashina."

"But this path looks well worn. Like it's used."

"Well, it's hundreds of years old. I suppose the water company guys do inspections."

"It just feels too . . . out in the open."

"OK, if you'd rather do this somewhere more secluded, there's a clearing in the trees over there. You can't be seen once you're in it. It's a good place to rest and just appreciate the woods. The view from there is kind of pleasant."

We walked over to the clearing, found some big rocks to sit on and I lit the joint. Then we passed it back and forth. When it was down to a tiny nub, I snuffed it out, wrapped it in tin foil and put it back in my pocket.

We were quiet for a while, just listening to the rustling of leaves and watching the clouds float by in the sky above.

"It's so quiet up here," Pattie said. "You really never appreciate how not quiet it is everywhere else until you bump into someplace quiet like this. Is that why you come up here?"

"Not really. I just like to walk."

We sat for a while, not talking.

"When I first came up here I just followed the aqueduct," I said. "Walking back toward Yamashina I noticed this stone fence. Every time I passed it I wondered why there would be a stone fence like that up here. It looked old. It was made out of individual pieces of stone. Hard, like granite. Kind of like what you see in Japanese cemeteries sometimes. I mean, there's nothing up here besides the canal and these woods. So why put up a stone fence?"

"What kind of fence? You mean like a wall?"

"No, more of a fence. It's about chest high. With a little effort, anyone could just climb over it. So it's not providing security or anything. And there's nothing on the other side of it but trees, so it's not obviously signifying or demarcating anything."

"So you climbed over it?"

"I did."

"And what did you find?"

"At first nothing. It was just woods and scrub brush. But as I got farther from the fence I could see it had once been part of something. A formal garden. The remains of a pond. Mucky and overgrown, but you could see it had once been a kind of ornamental pond. I poked around more, and the farther I got from the fence, the more I could tell that the place had once been something."

"Like what?"

"Yeah, that's what I wondered. So I kept wandering. After a while I got to another stone fence. More of a wall. And it was more modern. And on the other side of it there was a little hut. Like a guardhouse. So I crept up on it, and sure enough, it was a guardhouse. There was a guard in uniform in it asleep."

"What kind of uniform?"

"A police uniform. Yeah. So then I was a little worried about maybe trespassing on something, so I crept back through the woods back to the stone fence and climbed back over. When I got back to the dorm I had a look at my map of Kyoto. It's a Japanese map, and pretty detailed, and there, right where I was walking around, it's marked as the tomb of Emperor Tenji. A Japanese emperor from the seventh century."

"You were trespassing on an imperial tomb?"

"Can you believe it? I mean, if you really thought about it, the nearest tram stop, the one after Hi no Oka, is Misasagi. You never really pay much attention to these funny old names, and Misasagi . . . you could try for a million years and never figure out that Misasagi is the way to read the *kanji* for the tram stop if they didn't also have it in *romaji*. But however you pronounce it, the meaning of the *kanji* is clear enough. Imperial tomb is what the name means."

"Yes, if you know how to read Japanese characters."

"Right. But the thing is, how weird is it that at the front of the tomb, at the entrance, they have a guard, and probably a real fence? But at the back of the tomb, anyone can just hop over an old stone fence and tromp all over Emperor Tenji's tomb. I just love that about this country. All they have to do is put up a token fence and everyone stays out. No worries. It's protected. There's a fence."

"It didn't seem to keep *you* out."

"Yeah. They didn't plan for *gaijin*. That's why they don't like us. We don't follow the rules. Assuming we even know what they are."

"*Some* of us don't follow the rules."

"Point taken."

We were quiet again for a while. After that I don't remember exactly what else we talked about. I believe I summed up my entire life for Pattie. That took maybe five minutes. Then Pattie told me something about hers.

Patricia Wilson was from Seattle. She was Trisha or Trish to her sorority sisters in college and to her cheerleading squad teammates, but Pattie to her oldest friends and now to people she knew in Kyoto. Her parents always called her Patricia.

Pattie was living in Japan as a full-time student of the Japanese tea ceremony, variously referred to by its practitioners as *sado* or *cha no yu*, the Way of Tea. In order to practice the art of tea, Pattie had a cultural visa, not a student visa. Every weekday Pattie attended classes in tea ceremony at Honsenke. Honsenke was a large traditional, commercial, and, as Pattie maintained, spiritual purveyor of Japanese culture based in Kyoto. It was the biggest school of tea in Japan. Founded by the historical figure Sen no Rikyu, Honsenke had been in operation for about four hundred years. In its modern version it licensed tea ceremony teachers and practitioners all over Japan. It also ran a tea ceremony school in Kyoto.

With an eye toward becoming an international institution, Honsenke began looking to license practitioners of the art of the tea ceremony outside Japan. An international branch of the Kyoto school was opened to teach the tea ceremony to foreigners who would then be licensed to teach it to others in their home countries. It was called the Murasaki no Kai. Pattie was one of its first students.

The Japanese tea ceremony was theoretically one of the essential pillars of Japanese culture, along with the arts of ikebana and kimono. If a Japanese woman truly wanted to be a Japanese woman, she needed to be familiar with, or even master, these three true and essential Japanese arts. There were levels of mastery of the tea ceremony, each evidenced by a formal license issued by Honsenke. The system of levels and formal certificates was like the ranking system in judo or karate or sumo. Licensing the practitioners and the teachers of *cha no yu* was a very, very big business. Along with selling the things that were needed to properly perform a tea ceremony.

Pattie's tea ceremony classes also included ikebana, calligraphy, and the correct way to wear a kimono. She learned how to prepare the basic *kaiseki* meals that were sometimes served with a tea ceremony. There were courses in understanding and appreciating how the tea was grown, dried, and prepared for drinking. There were courses in understanding and appreciating the pottery that was used in the tea ceremony, and the bamboo that was used for making the utensils and implements used to prepare and serve the tea. There were music appreciation courses for the *koto*, the *ichigen koto*, and other traditional Japanese musical instruments. And there was training in the complex etiquette of the tatami room. Though Pattie couldn't speak much Japanese, and didn't know much about Japanese history, she was becoming the quintessential traditional Japanese woman.

Honsenke's instructors were grand masters of tea. They were elegant and refined and came from the oldest and wealthiest traditional business families in Kyoto. The head of Honsenke, called the Oiemoto, was Sen Sosuke, a direct descendant of Sen no Rikyu, the man who established, or created, the tea ceremony in the late 1500s. As part of her program, Pattie attended lectures on Zen Buddhism and weekly meditation sessions at the large and famous Daitoku-ji temple.

"Honsenke pays me a living stipend," Pattie said, "but it's not really enough to live on. If I ever lost my place in the dorm I'd be in trouble. I couldn't afford to live anywhere else. I teach English to make ends meet, and I have a few ideas for a business that might make some money."

"A business?"

"Do you know anything about *washi*? Japanese handmade paper?"

"No."

"It's so beautiful. They make such beautiful things out of it. And no one in America has ever heard of it. I sent some to friends in Seattle and they loved it. You can't even buy it in America. It's very strong and durable stuff, even though it's paper. You can make really nice things out of it."

"How do you find time for all this? You're also taking Japanese lessons, right?"

"No, not really. I have one hour of Japanese-language class a week. If I tried to learn Japanese, it would take me forever. I pick up what I need to know from the other classes and from being with Japanese people."

"You're studying the Japanese tea ceremony and you don't have to learn Japanese?"

"It would take too long, and I don't have that much time."

"Yeah, it does take time."

"I admire people who are learning it. Like you are. I wish I could."

"But you do wear kimono and everything when you're doing the tea ceremony?"

"Not at first. Not until you've learned to wear it properly. But then of course you have to. The etiquette of a tatami room is really based on wearing a kimono. The exact way to sit. The way to go from one position to another. The way you have to elegantly move the sleeves of the kimono that are always getting in the way. There are rules. There are so many rules. And you wouldn't believe what everything costs! If I had to buy any of the things I use every day . . . I don't think I'll ever have that much money in my whole life. I've used tea ceremony bowls that cost more than $100,000. One of the kimonos they gave me to wear cost more than most cars."

"I thought the idea of the tea ceremony was to keep everything simple and basic."

Pattie fixed me with her smile.

"Sometimes that's the most difficult thing to do," Pattie said. "Pure and simple. Just the essentials."

"It sounds like a strange world to be a part of for a *gaijin*. The traditional Japanese part of it I mean."

"I'm not so sure it's all that different from anywhere else. How the very rich behave," she said. "They live in a world apart. They live by a different set of rules. The only way to learn the rules is to be a part of it."

"Unless you were born into it."

"Yes, unless you were born into it."

After that, Pattie and I sat there for a while just watching Sunday morning become Sunday afternoon. Then, feeling the need for something physical to do, we got up and walked into the woods. The woods were full of old trails to explore. I had been up there enough times that I felt comfortable letting one take me wherever it wanted to go. But Pattie had an afternoon lecture to go to at Daitoku-ji and after that an English conversation class to teach, so we cut the walk short and headed back to the dorm.

We parted ways as soon as we got back. Pattie said we should do this again. I said we should.

The next time we saw each other it was like the Sunday in the woods had never happened. We said hi to each other when our paths crossed. That was it. But we were no longer complete strangers either.

I WAS OFTEN OFFERED JOBS teaching English conversation, but I had so far managed to resist accepting any. I didn't have too many expenses. I had a part-time job working at a *shabu-shabu* restaurant up on Higashiyama. All the Americans I knew living in Kyoto supported themselves at least in part by teaching English. If I could do it, I wanted to accept only the kind of part-time work that allowed me to practice and improve my Japanese.

One early autumn afternoon, I was returning home from a day of Japanese classes when Kobayashi-san, the woman who managed the International Students Residence, saw me on my way in and rapped on the window of her office to get my attention.

"Ascher-san," Kobayashi said, sliding open the reception window to the office, "a word."

The residents of the dorm were all afraid of Kobayashi-san. So was I. She was a hard woman who spoke Japanese like a *yakuza* and regarded the people who lived in the dorm with the kind of skepticism employed by homicide detectives interviewing murder suspects.

If Kobayashi-san called you into her office it was never about anything pleasant. If you were a student and didn't have much money, the International Students Residence in Kyoto was a great place to live. The rent was laughably low and the facilities were very good. Even "rich" Americans like myself feared losing a valuable place in the dorm. If you were called in to see Kobayashi-san, there was a good chance the discussion would be about your being kicked out for some reason.

Kobayashi-san didn't approve of her residents doing part-time jobs. We were supposed to be in Kyoto to study and not to work. Having a real part-time job was grounds for being kicked out. I always thought I could make a good case for my job at the *shabu-shabu* restaurant since it involved speaking Japanese and learning about certain important aspects of Japanese life, but I hoped I wouldn't have to.

I entered the office and Kobayashi-san motioned for me to sit in the chair facing her desk. Her wire-rimmed glasses with thick lenses made her eyes look much larger than they were. I sat and Kobayashi-san spent a few silent minutes just looking me over with her plus-sized eyes. I waited and she puffed away on one of her little cigars. With her hair pulled back tight against her scalp into a single salt-and-pepper ponytail and dressed all in black, she was one seriously tough, seriously intimidating woman.

Kobayashi-san tapped cigarillo ash into a big ashtray on her desk.

"What have you been up to lately, Ascher-san?" she asked.

"Me? Nothing in particular," I said. "You know, studying Japanese mostly."

"Remind me again, what is it you're studying at your university? Cornell isn't it?"

I had to pause, because I couldn't remember what I had said I was studying when I had applied to live in the dorm. I also wasn't actually affiliated with Cornell anymore.

"Well you know," I said, "I'm really concentrating on learning Japanese right now."

"Art history, wasn't it? Have you been out looking at art?"

"I do try to get out and see as much art as I can. And as many of Kyoto's famous temples and gardens. But today it was class. Japanese-language class. But yes, there's so much to see here in Kyoto you know. It's like a full-time job, trying to see all the famous places here."

"Yes," she said, blowing smoke from the cigar in my direction. "And money? Are you all right with money?"

"Oh, the rent. Um, that's not a problem. Sorry it's a little late this month. I just haven't got around to . . ."

"Someone from the neighborhood asked me if one of our residents would be interested in teaching an English class. Two evenings a week. You could teach it here. By eight p.m. no one uses the dining room. It's five students. All women. Two teachers at the local elementary school. The other three teach at the junior high school. The one organizing the class is a Miss Yamada. Here's her number. Please give her a call."

Besides me there were three native English speakers living at the International Students Residence: the other American, Pattie Wilson, and the two Australians, Judy Martin and Peter Franks. The residential area around the dorm was full of people who wanted to study English. They were aware of the stream of foreigners going up and down the hill to and from the Hi no Oka tram stop. Kobayashi-san probably got a dozen or more requests in a month for English teachers or private tutors, all of which she immediately turned down. It was unusual for her to say yes to one.

Because the students were women, it seemed even more unusual for Kobayashi-san to trust *me* to teach them. The most natural choice would have been Pattie Wilson. Kobayashi-san made no secret of the fact that she disliked Pattie, who had somehow managed to be admitted to the dorm after Kobayashi-san had initially rejected her application. Judy Martin had an Australian accent so thick that most Japanese people would be hard-pressed to recognize her speech as English, although that didn't stop her from having jobs teaching English. Kobayashi-san liked Peter Franks and he would probably have been her first choice, but she knew he was already fully booked teaching private classes in Osaka and would be leaving Japan soon.

"I don't know," I said. "I'm not much good at teaching English. I'm not sure it would be fair. . . . "

"You have Miss Yamada's number. Call her."

"I . . . all right. And thank you. I guess I could use the money. I'll do my best. Just out of curiosity, the three junior high teachers, do you know what subject they teach?"

"English."

Kobayashi-san took a drag on her cigarillo and dismissed me with a look and a puff of smoke. I thanked her again and got up to leave. She watched me leave while tapping ash from her cigar into the ashtray. She watched me all the way out of her office.

After dinner I gave Yamada-san a call. She sounded pleasant on the phone. She asked if she could come over to talk about the class. I said sure, and she came over the next night.

Keiko Yamada was one of the elementary school teachers. She was about twenty-seven or twenty-eight years old. Most people would probably consider her pretty. She seemed like a very serious person. She had a round face and a way of tilting her head to the side and looking up at you that gave her an air of perpetual concern. Her head seemed just a touch too large for her body. Otherwise, she was average height and medium build. If you saw her on the street and had to guess her profession you would probably guess nurse. She had the look of someone who was concerned for the welfare of others.

I never really saw Keiko Yamada smile. Smiling would have undermined the level of passion she brought to whatever it was that she was doing. I imagined her joining picket lines and peaceful protests in her spare time. She wore blue jeans to our first meeting, and usually to the classes that followed. Women in jeans were rare in Japan. Kyoto women generally favored drab practical clothing and seemed to be immune to fashion trends like the Country Ma'am craze I'd seen when I first arrived in Tokyo.

Along with the jeans, Keiko Yamada wore a loose-fitting peasant blouse and clean white tennis shoes. Her medium-short black hair came down in bangs and mostly covered her left eye when she tilted her head inquisitively. Her face had a healthy glow without any hint of makeup, or at least not any that I could detect. She spoke clearly and distinctly in both Japanese and English, which I supposed served her well in her job as an elementary school teacher. She taught second grade.

Keiko Yamada and I agreed that the classes would be on Tuesdays and Thursdays at eight, and that they would last for an hour and a half each time. To begin with, we would do simple conversation. Later we might decide to use some kind of text, or possibly read a book and talk about it in class. I tried to think of things the women might like and could easily read in English like Steinbeck's *Of Mice and Men* or *The Pearl*. I assumed the other women in the class would be more or less like Keiko Yamada.

My pay for teaching the class was ¥10,000 per week. That was good money for teaching English, especially since I didn't have to go anywhere to do it. Keiko Yamada would collect the money from the other women and pay me after the Thursday class. I walked her out the front door of the Residence and told her I was looking forward to the classes. We shook hands.

On my way back inside I encountered Pattie Wilson heading for the common kitchen and dining area. She was carrying a paper bag and a tin of tea.

"Hey," Pattie said, "who was that cute Japanese girl I just saw you with? New girlfriend?"

"A student. I'm teaching English now."

"I thought you said teaching English was beneath you."

"I don't know that I put it exactly like that, but . . . anyway, now I have a few students."

"How sad. You've sunk to the bottom with the rest of us. Well, good luck with it. It's not as easy as you probably think it is, but if all your students look like her, you might actually enjoy teaching."

—

I DISCOVERED I DID NOT enjoy teaching. The first class was easy. Each of the women introduced herself and then I did. For a while I had fun extracting personal information from them. But once we settled into conversation, the differences in the skill levels of the women began to emerge. The books and short stories I assigned for reading were no problem for the younger teachers. But they were for the older ones.

The three junior high English teachers were ten or more years older than Keiko Yamada. All five of the women were unmarried. Etsuko Saito was about the same age as Keiko Yamada and taught kindergarten. Etsuko was energetic, outgoing, and flirty. She was the elementary school teacher in your school who lasted a year or two before being snagged by a successful suitor and carried off to become a suburban housewife. Or maybe she was the art teacher who got into trouble for having an affair with the married math teacher.

Etsuko had shoulder-length hair with faint reddish highlights, the stray ends of which always seemed to need pushing away from her face. She had the body of an athlete or a dancer. She was the unpaid assistant coach of the girls' junior high basketball team. She played the *shamisen* and enjoyed *rakugo* and Kabuki. She refused to say whether or not she had a boyfriend. Keiko Yamada, who answered any question you put to her directly and with complete sincerity, said she did not have a boyfriend.

Both Etsuko and Keiko were pretty much fluent in English. Etsuko spoke well enough that anyone would assume she had lived abroad, though she had not. Keiko spoke well enough to express anything she wanted to, though her English had a distinctly Japanese flavor. I knew I was supposed to give everyone in the class equal time to speak, but the older teachers made that difficult. They had trouble getting even a basic sentence out. And they were very, very slow. It was much easier and much more enjoyable to talk to the two younger women who could actually speak. I had to keep reminding myself that I was being paid and therefore had an obligation to all five women in the class.

By the sixth week of classes the older women stopped showing up. Keiko Yamada stayed after class to tell me that it was now just her and Etsuko and that she couldn't continue paying me what she had promised. She said she very much enjoyed the classes and hoped I would still be willing to continue for a lower fee. I said I enjoyed teaching her and Etsuko and told her to reduce the fee to whatever she could comfortably afford to pay.

Two classes later, Etsuko Saito, the other elementary school teacher, dropped out. She had a boyfriend after all. One who objected to the extra time she was spending on English lessons. From then on it was just me and Keiko Yamada.

I suggested that we just forget about the class altogether, but Keiko insisted she wanted to continue. I insisted that she cut the fee in half, but she refused. She said she thought she knew other teachers who might be interested, and that we should just continue for a while and see what happened. Others might join in later.

Meeting twice a week, one-on-one, I began to feel like Keiko and I were becoming friends. She told me a lot about her personal life. I told her about some of my old girlfriends. Keiko was only a few years older than me. Unlike me, Keiko said she was worried about what the rest of her life was going to be. She loved children and loved teaching them. She wanted to find the right partner and marry and someday have a family of her own.

Keiko had come from a small town in neighboring Shiga Prefecture and had gone to college in Osaka. Her college boyfriend had gotten a job with a big electronics company after graduation and was immediately transferred to their Tokyo office. He proposed. Keiko was sure she didn't want to live in Tokyo. She also didn't want to be the wife of a Japanese salaryman who did whatever his company told him to do and would go wherever his company asked him to go. The boyfriend still wrote to her but she didn't answer his letters. She lived alone in a small apartment near the train station in Yamashina.

Keiko was very fond of the poems of Robert Frost and wanted me to tell her what it was like to live in New England. I told her that the way I lived was probably different from how Robert Frost lived, but Keiko was happy to hear what the trees were like in autumn and how it was in winter when the snow covered the ground and the lakes and ponds froze over. She wanted to know if people really rode in one-horse open sleighs in the winter.

Oddly, I had done that once.

My high school girlfriend's ninety-year-old grandfather had some land, kept horses, had a sleigh, and maintained a trail for it that he'd long ago blazed through his Connecticut farm. A sleigh ride through the snow with her grandfather was a Christmas tradition for my girlfriend, along with the heavily brandied eggnog that followed it. Boyfriends were allowed to join, as long as they got along with the dogs and helped wiping down the horse and putting away the vintage harnesses and other gear that went with the sleigh.

I told Keiko it was not a common experience anymore.

"Is spring in New England yellow? In 'The Road Not Taken' it is."

"Well," I explained, "yellow in New England is usually the color of early autumn. The line in your favorite poem 'leaves no step had trodden black' suggests falling leaves in autumn."

"But," Keiko asked, "isn't a choice of paths something a young person makes earlier in life? Shouldn't the poem be set in spring?"

"Maybe the season doesn't matter," I said. "I guess roads not taken are happening all the time in our lives."

"But the poem says the road less traveled by has made all the difference. Doesn't that mean that the choice happened early and the results came much later?"

"I guess it could mean that. I don't know if Frost meant that or if he meant that people have the one big choice that determines everything that follows. I think in the course of a life we have more than just one big choice that we have to make. We have lots and lots of choices and we're making them all the time."

"Oh," Keiko said. "I don't think that's true in Japan. I suppose we Japanese have fewer choices."

"Maybe," I said. "Small country, big population, not very many places where the leaves are not already trodden black."

"Yes, in the big cities. But in rural areas, like where Frost lived, maybe there are more," Keiko offered.

"No," I said. "In rural areas in Japan I think it's all quiet ponds and startled frogs."

"I'm sorry Don-san, I don't understand. What do frogs have to do with it?"

"Sorry. I was just making a bad joke. You're in love with the poems of Robert Frost. I'm in love with haiku by Matsuo Basho. Anyway, I think Frost is urging people to not just do the thing you're expected to do, or that everyone else does. I think Frost's parents wanted him to be a lawyer."

"My parents want me to be married."

"And you don't?"

"Yes, I do, Don-san."

"They liked the college boyfriend?"

"Yes."

"They thought you should have married him and moved to Tokyo?"

"Yes."

"So, why didn't you?"

Keiko blushed a charming shade of pink. Probably it was a question I wasn't entitled to ask.

"It wasn't the life I wanted for myself," she finally said. "I don't believe you have to give up everything for money to be happy. I think you have to be willing to take a little risk sometimes or end up regretting that you never even tried to have the life you wanted."

"And you don't regret letting the company man get away?"

Keiko hesitated.

"No," she finally said. "And maybe yes. We can't help making the choices we do, but sometimes we don't realize that until we've made the choice. We're forced to choose and then we know right away if we've done the right thing. Frost says he will be telling about this 'ages and ages hence.' But he's already telling it and it's not ages and ages hence. He already knows he chose the right path."

"Four Pulitzer Prizes for poetry."

"The prizes don't mean anything if you haven't made the choice to do what you know you want to do. The real prize is having made the right decision. Whatever comes of it."

"I'm sure you did the right thing. I think whoever gets you will be getting a real prize. I hope whoever it is realizes it."

Keiko blushed a deeper shade of pink and looked away. I hadn't meant to embarrass her. After a short silence, she said she didn't want to discuss poetry anymore.

I was beginning to find that I enjoyed talking to Keiko. I enjoyed it so much that I felt bad that she was paying me. I tried again to get her to forget about the money, but she refused to consider it. She said if she didn't pay me she wouldn't feel comfortable taking up my time. I argued, but in the end I had to let her have it her way. I didn't want to miss out on having her come over to see me twice a week.

ON AN EVENING THAT WAS unusually hot and sultry for October, Keiko arrived as usual for her lesson. It was the kind of day that in Connecticut we would call Indian Summer, when the cool of autumn suddenly reverts to August's heat for a few days. In Kyoto, the summers can be very, very hot. The International Students Residence was not air-conditioned. All the sliding doors that led from the dining area to an outside patio were open and two very strong portable fans were laboring mightily to at least circulate the warm, humid air. The breeze they generated didn't begin to approach cooling.

Markar, the chemical engineering student from Sri Lanka, was hosting some kind of a party in the dining area. The place where Keiko and I usually found a quiet corner to sit and talk was now occupied by a large group of lively and energetic Indian subcontinent exchange students drinking beer and eating hot-sauce-drenched raw onions with their fingers.

I told Keiko that the only quiet place I knew of in the dorm where we could go and have our conversation lesson was up in my room on the third floor. Keiko thought that was a good idea and up we went. The hallways in the residential part of the dorm had rooms along one side and glass windows all along the other. When we got to my room, I switched on the room's overhead light and took out one of my huge Japanese *kanji* dictionaries to prop open the door to the hall. All of the hall windows that could open were already open. I opened the window in my room as wide as it would go. The faintest hint of an evening breeze filtered in.

Keiko walked over to the open window and looked out at the view. The rooms in the dorm all faced south. There was a sweeping view across Yamashina and out to the border with Kyoto at the base of Higashiyama. At the western edge of the sky, the last fading ribbons of rose-colored light from the setting sun edged the horizon. Commuter trains sped back and forth across the landscape in the distance. The *shinkansen* made a quick appearance as a stream of white on its final glide into the tunnel that led to Kyoto Station. Stars were beginning to appear in the hazy lavender sky. The lights in people's houses came on slowly and added a cozy, restful element to the scene. It was a warm night and everything outside was quiet and completely at peace.

"Oh!" Keiko said. "What a lovely view you have from up here. You can see all of Yamashina and even a bit of Kyoto. Is that the *shinkansen* over there? You're so lucky. Don-san, why don't you turn off the light. Turn off the light and then come back over and look."

I did as requested.

"Yes," I said, "we have a very nice view from here. Sometimes I just sit up here and look out at it."

We knelt on the floor and leaned against the window frame and watched the outside in silence. From time to time a brightly lit train would slither across the landscape in the middle distance. You could just make out the people in the lighted interiors. We watched a train as it emerged from a tunnel in the hills and then plunged back into another tunnel to disappear from sight. I had grown accustomed to this night view and taken it for granted. But Keiko staring out and appreciating it made me see it fresh again. Keiko pointed out places that she knew; small temples, her school, and a park where she sometimes took the children to play. For a long while we just looked out the window without talking.

"So many little lights out there," Keiko finally said. "And each one a house with a family in it. You can't help wondering about the people on the trains. Where they're going, and why. I can't see anything like this from where I live. Such a nice view. It's very pretty tonight, don't you think?"

I said I thought so too. I remembered that I was being paid for my time and I asked Keiko to take a seat on the bed. There were two places to sit in the room; the bed and the wooden chair at my desk. I thought the bed would be the more comfortable choice for a guest. Keiko sat, and when I went to turn the room light back on, she stopped me.

"It's cooler with the light off," she said. "We can see each other all right with the light from the hall coming in. We don't need the light to just talk. I like your room the way it is now."

"Yes," I said. "This way you can't see that I never clean it."

I pulled the desk chair over to the bed to get closer to Keiko. Keiko sat on the edge of the bed leaning forward.

"I think we're very lucky to be living in a place like Kyoto," Keiko said.

I had to agree.

"So much important history has taken place here," Keiko said. "And somehow little bits of it, temples and gardens and things, have survived here for hundreds of years. Japan's traditional arts are still alive here as well. There's almost no place in the city where you can't see mountains. There are so many places to visit. Arashiyama is a part of the city but so different from the rest of it. Little mountain villages like Ohara. Or Kurama. Do you know Kurama?"

I said I'd heard the name but had never been.

"Kyoto is very hot in the summer," Keiko said. "But if you can always see mountains it makes you feel cooler even if you don't actually go there. In November, the *momiji* leaves in Kurama are at their peak and beautiful. You can have lunch there. Some of the restaurants have wooden platforms that overlook a clear little stream that tumbles down through the town from the mountains. The restaurants are famous for their *soba*. I think they have the very best *soba* in Japan. You can sit there eating *soba* right next to the river. It's so nice. I love the sound of rushing water in early November. Maple leaves fall into the stream and float by. Bright orange, bright red, and bright yellow. So beautiful. So very beautiful."

I looked at Keiko sitting on my bed imagining the autumn leaves at Kurama. Sitting in the dimly lit room, she seemed somehow transformed. Keiko placed the palms of both hands on the bed and eased herself back so that she was leaning against the wall. It was hot and sultry in the room. Quiet. The air in the room was very still.

Usually Keiko wore blue jeans and a white peasant blouse to our class. I sometimes tried to imagine her dressed more formally for her teaching job, but never could. On this night Keiko was not wearing her usual jeans. She had on a short denim skirt, a loose-fitting sleeveless blouse, and beat-up rubber sandals on her bare feet. As she continued to tell me about Kurama, Keiko sat relaxed on my bed with her back to the wall, letting her legs drift slightly apart and allowing her feet to dangle over the edge of the bed.

As Keiko spoke of the beauty of Kurama, my eyes drifted down to take in the beauty of this lovely young woman draped casually over my bed. I don't think I'd ever noticed how lush and moist and ethereally white her skin was. Or the shape of her lovely long neck, naked shoulders, and the roundish swell of her breasts peeking out over the edge of her loose-fitting blouse. Her smooth, plump thighs were now exposed most of the way up. A sandal dangled precariously from one naked foot at the edge of the bed.

Keiko was murmuring something about the cool mountains around Kurama. She looked over at me with dreamy eyes. She sat languidly on my bed, leaning against the wall looking up at me. She was waiting for an answer to a question that I had not heard. I slowly got up to join her on the bed. Keiko followed me with her eyes but didn't move or change her position.

When I sat down on the bed next to her, Keiko turned to look at me. We sat quietly looking at each other for a few seconds. Then I leaned very slowly toward her. The dreamy eyes followed me as I moved closer. Keiko leaned toward me. Her lips parted ever so slightly. I placed a hand on one of her bare legs and one on her bare shoulder. Our eyes met. We moved closer together. Keiko closed her eyes. And then, just as our lips were about to touch, a sudden gust of warm night air rushed in through the open window, fluttered the papers on my desk, and slammed the door to my room shut with a ferocious bang.

Keiko jerked back in surprise. Her eyes snapped open. They'd lost their dreamy glaze. I froze where I was. I looked at Keiko and smiled. Keiko smiled back at me. It might have been the first time I had ever really seen her smile. I hesitated and then leaned toward Keiko to kiss her, but she put out her hands to stop me.

"No, Don-san. We shouldn't."

"Yes, Keiko, I think we should. I really think we should."

"No," she said, "We shouldn't. We mustn't. Please. I'm sorry. I think I had better go."

"No, Keiko, please, you don't have to go. I didn't mean to . . . well, I *did* mean to . . . that is . . . it just happened. It just happened, but . . ."

Keiko was looking at me with her head tilted to the side. She was giving me her look of perpetual concern. It had been a while since I had seen it.

"Look," I said, "why don't we forget what just almost happened and continue talking? I'll go back to my chair and we'll go back to talking. I won't apologize for wanting to kiss you, because I really did want to do that, and I thought you wanted me to."

"It's all right, Don-san," she said. "There's nothing to apologize for. But I should go."

"But was I wrong? Did you not want me to kiss you?"

"I'm sorry, Don-san. I have to go now."

"Please don't go."

"Yes, Don-san, I have to go."

Whatever had almost happened between us had passed. Keiko stood up, put her foot back into her loose sandal, and smoothed her skirt.

"You don't have to go," I said. "We could just sit here and talk."

"No, Don-san. But thank you for saying it."

I wanted her to stay, but Keiko was going. I said I would walk her to the tram station. She said no. It was a firm, uncontestable no. Keiko turned to leave. I held the door for her. I watched her walk down the hall and then disappear down the stairs.

I closed the door to my room. I sat down on my bed. I didn't believe in divine intervention, but I couldn't help wondering about that sudden gust of wind. Even now when I think back on it I wonder, but for that gust of warm wind would my life have changed somehow and been different in some important way? Or not?

I had a candle in the room and some incense. I had bought a small hand-forged iron candle stand at the big *mingei* Japanese crafts shop in town, and also a ceramic incense burner. At one of the famous Zen temples I had visited I had bought a fat devotional candle and some incense sticks. I had bought all these things because I thought that creating the proper mood in my room would help me understand Zen Buddhism. The religion that had caused most of the famous temples I had been visiting to be built. The sudden change in the room caused by Keiko's departure had left me feeling the need for something, if not completely spiritual, at least soothing. A candle and some incense seemed like they might do the trick. Perhaps it was a good time to sit quietly and contemplate the mysteries of the universe.

I got up and placed the candle on its stand and the incense stick in its holder. I lit the candle with a wooden match from a little matchbox from the restaurant where I worked. I lit the incense stick. Then I sat back down at my desk to look out the window and contemplate the universe. After a while of contemplating the universe, I moved over to my bed to continue contemplating the universe while horizontal. The universe seemed unwilling to give up any of its secrets.

I WASN'T SURE HOW MUCH time had passed when there was a knock at my door. My first impulse was to ignore it. Then I thought it might be Keiko. I thought, maybe she'd changed her mind and had come back. The knock came again. A bit more insistently. I got up and went to the door and opened it. Pattie Wilson was standing there looking unhappy.

"Is this a bad time?" she said. "Can I come in for a minute? I know it's late. I'm sorry. But I'm glad you're still awake. Something happened and I . . . I just need to talk to someone."

I stepped aside and Pattie came into the room. She looked at me and then she looked at the door. I closed it.

"Why is it dark in here?" she asked.

"I was just contemplating the universe. At least, the part of it you can see out this window. Shall I turn on the light?"

"No, this is fine. It never really gets completely dark in a city, does it? I like this. You have that candle going. And incense. It's kind of nice."

Pattie went and sat on my bed and I sat back down in the desk chair.

"Has something bad happened?" I asked.

"I'm really sorry to bother you with this. It was nothing really. Nothing important. But somehow it just really got to me. I don't know why I let it. I just have to talk to someone."

"Sure. So . . . ?"

"Just one of my English classes. I've been teaching this English conversation class for three months now. Downtown at the big English-language school. Do you know it?"

"Yeah. A lot of *gaijin* in town teach there."

"The students are a mix of businessmen, housewives, and high school students. Tonight was the last class. I really like the class and most of the people in it."

"Even the businessmen?"

"Yes. They're all very nice. Very sweet people."

"Okay."

"Since it was our last class, they wanted to take me out to dinner. We went to one of those beer hall places near Sanjo. One of the nicer ones by the river. It wasn't bad. It was a nice place for a class dinner. Everyone came over and took turns sitting next to me to chat. It was nice."

"Sounds nice."

"At the very end of the dinner, most of the people in the class had already said good-bye to me and had left. The very last to leave was one of the high school students. A sweet boy and my favorite student in the class. He waited for everyone else to leave and then he came over to me. He's very shy. 'Miss Wilson,' he says. 'There is something I . . . ' He was too shy to get out what he wanted to say. I said 'Come on Seiji-san. What have I taught you? If you have something you need to say, just go ahead and say it. What kind of a teacher does that make me if you're not confident enough to use what I've taught you?' So he takes a deep breath, gathers up his courage, and then he reaches out, just like *this*, and grabs my breasts. Very hard."

Pattie reached out and twisted her hands in the air, one clockwise and one counterclockwise, to demonstrate how she had been assaulted.

"He grabbed me hard enough that it hurt. But more than that, I was stunned. Before I could say anything or react at all, he ran out of the room. I thought what he was going to say was what a great teacher I was and what a privilege it had been to have me as his teacher. I thought he was going to say that he appreciated having me as his teacher and that he had learned a lot and that he had been encouraged to continue trying to improve his English. That's what I expected. It just made me so . . . "

"Angry?"

"No. Not angry. Sad. Very sad."

"So, basically this kid had been staring at your chest in class for three months and wondering what it would feel like to touch your breasts. This was his last big chance to do it, and he couldn't let it go by without giving it a shot. And because he doesn't have much experience handling female breasts, it came across as mauling instead of caressing. Is that it?"

"I guess."

"Adolescence. It's a tough time to get through."

"You wrack your brains and give your students everything you've got to try and teach them English and it just doesn't seem to matter whether you teach them anything or not. It makes me wonder, why? Why am I doing this? Why am I spending my time trying, giving it my best effort, to teach these people English? Why am I even here? Japanese tea ceremony? What is that? Who's going to care about a ceremony for Japanese tea in America? Why am I doing any of this? Why am I? Why?"

I didn't know what to say to her. I wasn't prepared for a second existential crisis in one night. I didn't know anything about tea ceremony but it sounded stupid to me. I didn't think I should say that.

"Do *you* ever feel that way?" Pattie wanted to know.

"No," I said.

"No? You don't wonder if what you're doing with your life is the right thing?"

"No."

"Never?"

"No."

"Could you come over here and sit on the bed with me?"

Pattie patted the bed next to her.

"I really need a hug," she said.

I hesitated. I looked at Pattie watching me and the flickering light of the candle reflecting off her face. I wasn't used to hugging as a thing. I grew up in New England, and New England people don't really hug. But I stood up and went over and sat on the bed next to Pattie. She put her arms around me and rested her head on my shoulder. Then she hugged me.

The hug was not sexual, but it was very close to the border between sexual and friendly. Not knowing exactly how to hug properly or what to do with my hands, I made a weak attempt to massage Pattie's shoulders and back. Pattie placed her hands behind my head and drew me to her.

We sat on my bed hugging. The candle on its hand-wrought iron stand glowed warmly atop my bookcase. The delicate fragrance of temple incense wafted through the air. Wrapped together in a hug we slowly tilted over to one side. The hug became horizontal. We had to intertwine our legs to keep from falling off the narrow bed. Somehow this was still a non-sexual hug. We might have kissed, but I'm not sure. After a while we just fell asleep like that on my bed.

By the time Pattie got up to go back to her own room, the sun was just beginning to rise. We hadn't really done anything sexual that night. That came later.

I ENDED UP SPENDING A lot of time in Pattie's room. Her room was cleaner and nicer to be in than mine. And because it was on the ground floor it was easier for me to slip into without being noticed than it would have been for her to stay over with me on the third floor. Pattie and I did our best to maintain the fiction that we weren't seeing each other. Sex between the residents was a violation of the dorm's rules. We knew we were in danger of losing our places in the dorm if we were found out.

In my experience, women in a relationship may or may not accept you for who you are, but they always feel they can improve you. They appreciate the raw material they've been presented with and want to help you become the person they think you should be. Did I dress badly? Did I not pay proper attention to grooming? Was I not living up to my economic potential? Was I insufficiently ambitious? Yes. But Pattie realized she could help me fix all that once we'd started sleeping together.

Pattie spent most of her waking hours practicing or thinking about tea ceremony and Zen Buddhism. They were ways to live in the world unconcerned with material things. They preached indifference to wealth. You had money or you didn't have it. It didn't matter. What mattered was how you lived your life.

But Pattie's relationship to money was complicated. She didn't come from it. She liked being around it. She kept it at arm's length. On the wall just above her desk, Pattie had taped a handwritten note. The note said, "Do Not Envy the Rich." I thought, if you need a note that you see every day taped to your wall to remind you of something, that something, or the opposite of that something, must be a problem for you.

Zen Buddhism defies understanding, possibly because not understanding it is part of its doctrine and perhaps one facet of its mystique. Most of the Americans and Europeans I knew in Kyoto had at least tried it out. Some of my friends were devoted to it. But tea ceremony? What really was tea ceremony to Pattie? Was Pattie just taking advantage of a rare opportunity to be funded while doing something interesting? Did she believe that her meditation at Daitoku-ji and her mastery of the tea ceremony would lead her to a state of enlightenment? I didn't know.

But I did know that she was less interested in studying the culture that gave birth to these things and whose language she couldn't speak and whose history she knew next to nothing about. Was it just foreign and exotic to her and to the people in the world across the ocean that she came from? Could she be creating a kind of shell that protected her from something? Was she fleeing something back home? That was the kind of suspicion people sometimes faced who had decided to abandon the country of their birth. Or had Pattie just happened to find something in a foreign culture that appealed to her for reasons obscure and unidentifiable? I just didn't know.

It was however clear, at least to me, that Honsenke, the home of Pattie's university of tea, was a commercial enterprise and on a very large scale. Most of the Japanese people I knew considered the tea ceremony to be a kind of Ponzi scheme that took advantage of ordinary Japanese women. Like Zen Buddhism, foreigners seemed to respect or even revere it, but to most Japanese people it was a joke. Ordinary Japanese people came into contact with Zen priests or Zen monks when someone died or when some ritual relating to a dead relative needed to be performed. Then they witnessed first-hand the difference between Zen practice and Zen theory.

The head of the sub-temple of the famous Daitoku-ji in northern Kyoto where Pattie went to practice Zen meditation was a very famous and charismatic Zen priest who gave public lectures and appeared on TV. He was sometimes featured in the Japanese press.

His outsized public persona seemed to contradict his claim to be no more than a simple monk. He was a powerful and influential head of a major Zen temple.

Pattie was one of a handful of practitioners at her sub-temple who were chosen to be instructed personally by the *shike-sama*, the famous priest, himself. Once, when Pattie reported to the *shike-sama* in a one-on-one meeting to discuss her assigned *koan*—an esoteric question to meditate on—the famous Zen priest had tried to have sex with her. Pattie was not surprised or offended. She knew how to take care of herself in situations like this and found the famous priest much easier to fend off than other men she had known back home in America. Despite the inappropriate behavior, Pattie's respect for the priest and his Zen teachings was undiminished. She wrote off his unwanted advances as the Japanese male's inability to resist the overwhelming temptation of the blond female *gaijin*. He had tried. She said no. And that was that.

Though Pattie and I thought we were successfully hiding our relationship from the people in the dorm, the other women in the dorm at least, had quickly realized that Pattie and I were a couple. I made every effort not to be seen going into or leaving Pattie's room. I didn't think that I had been. But women just have a way of sensing romance. Soon everyone in the dorm knew about us. Pattie and I continued to keep up our pretense that we were not seeing each other. The other dorm residents were considerate enough to play along with the pretense. Nothing could have been more Japanese. You know something exists, but as long as no one speaks of it out loud, or admits to it publicly, it doesn't exist.

Pattie's room was identical to my own, only much cleaner, and more artfully arranged. The room at night was bathed in a gentle amber light that came from an asymmetrical floor lamp made of Japanese handmade *washi* paper. Pattie rarely spent money on things, but she had a special weakness for *washi* and anything that was made from it. She also liked objects that had been made by someone famous. The lamp was made by a Japanese designated Living National Treasure.

The bed in Pattie's room was always made and the sheet and light blanket covering it were taut and perfectly tucked in. The blanket was something she had picked up in a *mingei* shop in downtown Kyoto and was made out of a blue-and-white antique cloth from Kyushu called *kasuri*. Her small desk was uncluttered and also very neatly arranged. Next to the desk was a small but handsome bookcase. It was not one of the standard-issue bookcases that came with each room. She had it mostly filled with art books, books on Zen Buddhism, and books on tea. Some of the books were attractive and in Japanese, so, books Pattie could not read.

On top of Pattie's bookcase was a handsome burnished-wood tray. On it sat an expensive-looking teapot, two teacups, and a rough earthenware vase containing a single flower. On the wall above the desk was a Japanese calendar with a picture of a woman performing the tea ceremony in a simple rust-colored kimono. On the wall above the bed was a handsomely framed Japanese ink painting of a crude circle that seemed to have been swiftly executed in a single fluid brushstroke. There was a woven bamboo mat on the floor next to the bed.

Although I was skeptical, I thought I needed to try and understand what Pattie saw in the Japanese tea ceremony and Zen Buddhism. Pattie had a scholarship from the Monbusho, Japan's Ministry of Education, for the study of the tea ceremony. She believed that Zen Buddhism was essential for a true understanding of the practice of *sado*—the way of tea. I cared for Pattie very much and I thought it was important to make an effort to appreciate the things that she cared most about.

Japanese bookstores allow customers to stand in the aisles, or even sit, freely reading the books and magazines for sale there for hours. I made use of this practice to learn about the tea ceremony without buying the books.

The tea ceremony was said to have been created in the sixteenth century by the tea master Sen no Rikyu. Pattie's tea ceremony school, Honsenke, was founded by and still run by a descendant of Sen no Rikyu. Sen no Rikyu conducted tea ceremonies for Oda Nobunaga and Hideyoshi, the two historically important shoguns who are credited with unifying Japan into a single nation. Rikyu was from a merchant family and had received training as a Buddhist monk at the Daitoku-ji Zen temple.

Shoguns and samurai warriors lived in an era of nearly constant warfare and valued the discipline of Zen Buddhism. Nobunaga, whose control of the newly unified country was less certain, respected the orderly restraint and self-control of the tearoom, and the quiet and the clarity that came with it. Hideyoshi, whose military power was more secure, appreciated the entertainment value of the tea ceremony. The tea ceremony under Hideyoshi became more lavish. Rikyu, Hideyoshi's tea master, counseled *wabi* and *sabi*, the Japanese aesthetic concepts of understated simplicity, the dark patina of age, and muted melancholy. Hideyoshi planned tea ceremonies for five hundred guests and had his tea ceremony utensils plated in gold. Rikyu was not happy.

Hideyoshi had his gardeners obtain rare plants from abroad so that he could display them at his tea ceremonies. He once acquired iris bulbs and had them planted in a special garden. He wanted to be informed as soon as the famous flowers came into bloom so that he could be the first to see them. When the day arrived, Rikyu got there first and destroyed all the flowers but one. Hideyoshi learned of this and was not happy. He paid a visit to his tea master. He found Rikyu sitting in his teahouse serenely contemplating a single, perfect iris, perfectly presented in a two-hundred-year-old Korean earthenware vase in the tearoom's *tokonoma* alcove. Hideyoshi contemplated the flower in the vase. Rikyu sat next to him smiling benevolently.

Hideyoshi understood and possibly even appreciated the lesson that Rikyu had prepared for him. Still, he didn't like people fucking with him. He let Rikyu choose between committing public *seppuku*, ritual suicide, under a blossoming cherry tree while composing a poem, or watching his entire family being tortured to death, having his estate burned to the ground, and being boiled alive in a large cauldron of hot oil.

Rikyu chose ritual suicide. His grateful family went on for generations propagating the tea ceremony and the legend of Sen no Rikyu. At some point there was a rift in the house of Sen. The family divided into three rival schools of tea, Honsenke, Urasenke, and Omotesenke. All three became vast commercial empires in the modern world. As a kind of counterpoint to the Meiji and Taisho and early Showa periods' emphasis on Western ways and Western values, more conservative and nationalistic Japanese insisted that the practice of tea ceremony, along with kimono and ikebana, were essential to becoming a true Japanese woman. *Cha no yu*, the way of tea, was also embraced by certain practitioners of Zen Buddhism.

The tea ceremony school that Pattie attended was run by Honsenke. Honsenke made its money through tea ceremony classes conducted by certified Honsenke tea ceremony teachers. Each teacher paid to be certified. Each student paid a fee to Honsenke for a certificate of completion for Honsenke-approved courses. There were levels of accomplishment just like in karate or judo. If a student completed a certain number of courses, the student could become a certified teacher. Only certified Honsenke teachers could teach Honsenke courses.

Honsenke also certified and sold the implements and vessels needed to perform a tea ceremony. The highest levels of instruction took place at the Honsenke University of Tea. Its special students were usually the children of Kyoto's wealthiest traditional business families. This was one of the places where the scions of these families made connections and honed their skills in the traditional Japanese arts while being groomed to take over the family business. Pattie's group, the Murasaki no Kai, was the first step in Honsenke's plan to expand into foreign markets. Pattie Wilson was one of the Murasaki no Kai's very first students.

After all of my extensive reading on the subject, I was very eager to experience an actual tea ceremony. Pattie had assured me that once I had seen a complete tea ceremony properly done, I would appreciate its unique value in preserving an important part of living Japanese culture. Although Pattie had performed parts of the tea ceremony for me in her dorm room, she said this was only a hint of what a real tea ceremony properly performed in a real tea ceremony room would be.

It was true that watching Pattie kneeling on the floor of her room, her strawberry-blond hair tied up at the back of her head, dressed in the oversized Pink Lady T-shirt I had given her as a present, I had begun to feel that I was becoming a fan of the tea ceremony. There she sat, her lovely arms and delicate fingers managing the sleeves of an imaginary kimono as she pretended to scoop out imaginary powdered green tea from the expensive, Honsenke-approved cherry-bark tea caddy she kept in her room. She skillfully and gracefully handled the age-burnished bamboo tea scoop, and the bamboo tea whisk, and the ¥100,000 tea bowl she had on loan from Honsenke, her face a mask of concentration and oneness with her task.

And then the day for me to experience a true tea ceremony finally arrived. The Murasaki no Kai was hosting a formal tea ceremony in a three-hundred-year-old teahouse in the nearby town of Uji. Each of the foreign students in Pattie's class was allowed to bring a relative or friend. Sen no Rikyu himself had once used this perfectly preserved teahouse, and it was designated an Important Cultural Treasure by the Japanese government.

Early one Sunday morning, Pattie and I left the International Students Residence and strolled down the hill to Hi no Oka to catch the tram to Sanjo Keihan Station. Trains from Kyoto to the sleepy town of Uji on the Keihan Line ran sporadically on most days. On Sundays there were even fewer trains. It was a lazy, sun-drenched morning. There were only a handful of other people on the train to Uji when we got on.

Free of the pretense we had to keep up in the dorm, Pattie and I held hands and watched Kyoto go slowly by through the train windows. The Uji line used older trains that had been retired from the main Kyoto–Osaka line. The floors were made of solid wood and the heavy window frames, also made of wood, opened to let in the morning air. Kyoto early in the morning didn't resemble the tourist magnet it would become by ten in the morning. Once the train veered off the main line toward Uji, things became even more peaceful and charming.

The Uji train station seemed to belong in some remote part of rural Japan and not the greater Kyoto area. That impression ended once we left the station and began to stroll toward the town center. Every ten yards or so we encountered another of the wooden plaques that memorialized some historic event or personage. We crossed the Uji River on the bridge that had once been the site of a famous battle between the Genji/Fujiwara clan and the Heike/Minamoto clan. It was an event that every Japanese schoolboy or schoolgirl knew of.

As we stopped to look out over the Uji River, I wondered how such an important battle could have taken place in such a confined space. At least three other famous historical battles had taken place here. The river was not broad and shallow the way most Japanese rivers are. There wasn't a lot of room for swinging Japanese swords. The current bridge was steel and concrete, but it was doing its best, by design and coloring, to evoke the one that had been there when the famous battle took place in the year 1180.

Near the center of town, the information plaques took on a more commercial tone. Modern Uji was mostly known for producing the best tea in Japan. Uji was where the *matcha*, the powdered green tea in Japan's tea ceremonies, came from.

The designated meeting place was a famous tea shop in the center of Uji. Since it was Sunday and still early, most of the other stores and shops in town were still closed. A woman from the tea shop wearing an expensive kimono welcomed us and showed us into a private room in the back of the shop. Pattie and I were the first to arrive. The kimono woman offered us tea. It was a special kind of morning tea brewed from leaves grown only a few hundred yards from where we sat.

Out the back window of the shop I could see the edge of what was probably a very beautiful and very large Japanese garden. As with so many things in Kyoto, a casual passerby would have had no idea that something so spectacular sat behind the row of shops that lined the quiet street. I stood up and went over to look at it. The garden had a little pond. A path led to a rustic teahouse on one side of the pond. The trees and plants in the garden seemed to have been trained and nurtured for decades, or even longer, to create the effect of a perfectly natural garden.

I returned to my seat in the shop. Pattie and I sipped the tea, which was very good. We were soon joined by an affable man in his mid-forties. He was dressed casually and comfortably, perhaps for a round of golf. He introduced himself and explained that he was the tenth-generation owner of the tea shop. He said his family had been tea growers and tea merchants in Uji for many, many years.

"It must be a heavy responsibility to carry on that kind of tradition," I said. "Uji's tea is Japan's very best, and I was told that this shop is where Uji's best tea is sold. I guess you have to work very hard to maintain the standards and keep up the quality."

"Yes," the man said, "I suppose you could say that. As you probably know, we tend to do things exactly as they've been done for centuries. It's not something that requires a good deal of innovation. Someone figured out the best way to grow and prepare tea a few centuries ago. Now the challenge is to keep doing it that way. To do exactly what they did."

"So, it's not challenging then?"

"Oh no. Doing things exactly as they were done hundreds of years ago isn't so easy these days. Our basic business and our basic process may not have changed and may not need to change. But other things have changed. People have changed. Not many people are still willing to do the kind of work it takes to do things the traditional way."

"You mean you can't use modern labor-saving methods to grow and process the tea?"

"Exactly. Green tea from other parts of Japan can be produced more cheaply, but it lacks that certain something that you get by doing it the old-fashioned, labor-intensive way. We're the Rolls-Royce of the tea industry. If we did things any other way we wouldn't be Rolls-Royce anymore."

"So your problem is to find people willing to work and do things in the old way?"

"There's that. But the real problem is real estate values. The price of land has shot up so much that the sons and daughters of the farmers whose land is used to grow the tea don't want to grow tea when they can sell off bits of their fields for enormous sums of money. As Uji's landowners age and die off, the number of acres used to produce Uji tea declines. This is the real problem. The younger generation prefers to live simply by selling off land, not by growing tea. Sadly, they've developed a taste for expensive foreign cars, Italian clothing, and Swiss watches. What was once prime tea-producing farmland is becoming residential subdivisions for people working in Osaka. If we don't do something to stop it, Uji tea won't be coming from Uji anymore. It will be coming from someplace in Asia. China even. Who knows?"

"What can you do about it?"

"Well, Honsenke is helping us. Both of you are from Honsenke, isn't that right?"

"Yes," I said.

Pattie looked uncomfortable. Her Japanese wasn't good enough to follow most of the conversation.

"Honsenke bought some of the properties that came onto the market when the prices were still somewhat reasonable. Now they're using their political connections to get the Japanese Diet to designate Uji's tea-growing areas as Important National Resources. Then the only thing you can do with that land is to grow tea. Your *iemoto*, Sen no Sosuke, has been very helpful in promoting the legislation."

"So Honsenke has enough political clout to get that done?" I asked.

"Certainly. Honsenke is a huge business. Politics is all about money isn't it?"

The welcome woman in the expensive kimono came in to announce that the other guests had begun to arrive. The man stood up and said he had to leave. He shook hands with me, and with a nod to Pattie he left.

Pattie's other classmates from the Murasaki no Kai were all women. Elizabeth Parsons from Cleveland, Ohio, was deciding what to do with her life after graduating from Smith College. Karen Hall from Chevy Chase, Maryland, was taking her junior year abroad from Vassar. Dorothy Yamamoto was from Honolulu and wanting to get in touch with her Japanese heritage. Jeri-Ann Morasky, the fifth member of the small class, had a previous engagement and had asked to be excused from the weekend event.

Elizabeth Parsons brought her parents, who were visiting from Cleveland. Karen came with her boyfriend Ron from Dartmouth, who had taken a semester off to be with Karen in Japan. Dorothy had her parents from Honolulu. The Parsons and the Yamamotos were staying at the Miyako Hotel, Kyoto's finest and most expensive Western-style hotel. Mr. Parsons had arranged with the Miyako Hotel to have a van bring everyone to Uji. Elizabeth Parsons had offered to have the van come and pick up Pattie and me at the dorm, but Pattie said she preferred to take the train.

George Parsons was an expansive, over-large man in his late fifties. His wife Beverly, also on the large side, seemed perpetually embarrassed on his behalf. Henry Yamamoto and his wife Malia were laid-back Hawaiians. Karen's boyfriend Ron found everything in Japan fascinating and bewildering. He was a psychology major.

"Hello, hello, hello! George Parsons from Shaker Heights, Ohio," George Parsons said. "This beautiful young woman must be Pattie Wilson who my daughter Lizzy has been telling us about. And you are?"

"Don Ascher," I said introducing myself.

"Are you here visiting too?"

"No, I live here."

"Live here? My Lord! Don't know how you kids do it. Haven't had anything decent to eat since we got here. Had some of that Kobe Beef last night. It wasn't half bad, but what it cost! Good God! No wonder everybody here eats fish. Imagine how much it would cost if they actually cooked the fish!"

"George!" Mrs. Parsons said.

"Daddy!" Elizabeth said. "Please. Do you have to behave like a textbook ugly American *everywhere* you go? The food here is wonderful. And it's really good for you too. Can you *please* stop embarrassing me in public."

"Well that's fine for you, Lizzy, and for you other girls as well. But a man needs to eat meat. Isn't that right, Don?"

George Parsons winked at me.

"Absolutely," I said. "I wouldn't eat anything other than red meat if I could afford it. The tofu and little bits of tree roots and seaweed that people here eat, you can hardly even call it food."

Pattie shot me a dirty look.

"You see what I'm saying!" George said. "This man *lives* here and he knows what he's talking about. That meal you dragged us to the other night, what was it?"

"*Yudofu*," Elizabeth said. "Okutan is one of the finest restaurants in Kyoto."

"Well it was darned expensive. Boiled cubes of that *toe-foo* stuff, and you had to cook it yourself! And you would think that for that kind of money you wouldn't have to sit on the floor."

"The garden was very lovely," Mrs. Parsons said.

"Yes, the *scenery* was fine," George Parsons continued. "But the *food* was terrible. And there was hardly much of it. I had to have something at the hotel afterwards."

"Daddy!"

"What? It's true. Am I supposed to pretend that it isn't? We're among friends here. We should be able to say what we think."

I nodded in agreement, and all the women and even Ron the boyfriend gave me dirty looks.

The lady in the kimono was back to explain that since we were a large group, there would be two separate tea ceremonies. Pattie and I along with the Parsons were assigned to the first group. Karen and her boyfriend and the Yamamotos would be in the second group. Group one was instructed to follow the lady in the kimono into the garden.

A door at the rear of the reception room led to the garden. Each visitor was instructed to remove his or her shoes and socks and put on a pair of outdoor wooden *geta*. The open-toed wooden platform sandals were laid out in neat rows just outside the door. The kimono woman gracefully stepped out of her lacquered indoor sandals and slid effortlessly into a pair of the wooden *geta*. The foreigners took off their own footwear and did likewise, but not gracefully.

The garden was small but spectacular. There were dwarf trees that could have been a hundred years old or more. The smooth stones that paved the pathways had probably been harvested from the Uji River and were formed into interesting irregular patterns. Large lichen-covered rocks sat in the shade of the carefully pruned and sculpted trees. Colorful *koi* casually swam across the pond, breaking the surface of the water with their mouths wide open and hoping to be fed, as they did whenever they sensed a human presence. The five visitors and their guide strolled slowly down the moss-lined path. The guide in her kimono with mincing graceful steps. The foreigners on their wooden *geta* doing their best not to topple over.

The garden path led to a rustic bamboo gate that screened the entrance to the teahouse from view. From the outside, the teahouse resembled an idealized vision of a peasant's hut. It had a large, flattened conical roof of exquisitely thatched cedar bark. The structure was supported by age-polished posts of cedar and had walls of compressed clay and mud.

The kimono lady paused to offer a brief commentary on the garden's features. Since I was the only one in the group who seemed to understand it, I translated for the others.

"She says all the land in Uji belonged to the Fujiwara clan dating back to the 900s. The pond in this garden may have been part of their original Heian-period estate. The teahouse in the garden dates from the mid-1500s and is a designated Japanese Important Cultural Treasure. Sen no Rikyu himself once performed tea ceremonies here. Because the teahouse is so old and so fragile, and because of its historical and artistic importance, it can only be used for tea ceremonies no more than four or five times each year. Tea ceremonies have often been performed here for members of the imperial family and their guests."

Passing through the gate, we came to a very large, flat stone that sat just below the entrance to the teahouse. The entrance was about one-third the size of a normal door. The kimono woman slipped out of her *geta*, again very gracefully, and placed them neatly facing outward on the flat stone. She bowed low and demonstrated the proper way to enter the teahouse. Pattie followed her and entered the teahouse with grace and agility. Once inside she turned to me.

"Bend from the waist as you enter. You need to be aware of everything around you as you come in. See those little flowers planted just to the side of the entrance? Notice the fragrance. The purpose of the small door is to make you express humility and allow for the heightening of the senses."

I did my best to execute a less feminine version of what Pattie had done, while being aware of my surroundings.

"I can see how it would have been difficult to get in here with a sword," I said.

"You're supposed to concentrate on appreciating the special beauty of the teahouse," Pattie said. "Entering the door of the teahouse represents a break from the normal everyday world."

Inside the teahouse I found myself in a narrow corridor. The floor of the interior was all tatami mats. The tatami inside the teahouse were new. You could tell by the grassy fragrance they gave off. But the tatami had apparently been woven from a special dark strain of bamboo grass, so that even though they were new, they looked old.

There was only room enough in the corridor for one person to pass through it at a time. The wooden beams in the frame of the teahouse glowed with the patina of age. An open wooden lattice-framed window looked out onto the pond and was the only source of light for the teahouse. It also framed a picture-perfect view of the garden.

The guide passed through a low narrow door. Pattie followed her and I followed Pattie. I could hear George Parsons struggling in the narrow space behind me and complaining about the smallness of the entrance and the run-down state of the teahouse. His wife and daughter were trying to shush him.

The tearoom was cozy and compact. Some of the light that came through the window in the corridor reflected off the pond and gave the space a shimmery feel. In one corner of the room, an elegant woman in a gorgeous but tastefully restrained kimono sat tending glowing coals in a small fire pit that had been cut out of the tatami floor. A handsome hand-forged artisanal iron pot sat on an attractive hand-forged artisanal iron tripod above the coals. To the side were several ceramic tea bowls, each costing more than an Italian sports car. Other museum-quality implements and utensils sat neatly arranged on the tatami floor.

Pattie and I were instructed to seat ourselves near the back wall of the room, opposite the woman tending the coals. Pattie immediately merged gracefully with the tatami and took up the formal *seiza* position, sitting upright on her knees with her legs tucked economically underneath her. Pattie had shown me how to sit like this in her room at the dorm, and I knew I wouldn't be able to do it right and that it was going to be painful. I hoped that doing it in a real tea ceremony room would be easier. It wasn't.

"Don't embarrass me," Pattie whispered.

I looked over at George Parsons now doing his best to settle onto the tatami. Compared to the embarrassment that George was about to inflict on his daughter, whatever rules I violated would seem like nothing. Focusing on George's extreme discomfort took away some of the pain in my legs. The Parsons were instructed to sit next to Pattie and me, forming a neat row facing the tea ceremony lady. The guide in the kimono sat opposite the guests and next to the woman making the tea. They formed a perfect photo-ready picture of Japanese feminine grace and elegance. Sadly, Pattie had forbidden me to bring my camera.

Getting George and Beverly Parsons into the *seiza* position proved impossible and they were given permission to sit as they pleased. I looked hopefully at Pattie. Her stern glance said nothing doing. *You* are going to do this correctly.

George leaned with his back against the wall of the room with his legs sprawled out before him. The kimono lady guide shuddered involuntarily when George's large body touched the centuries old wall of the teahouse. Little bits of three-hundred-year-old mud and clay trickled gently onto the tatami.

In a series of graceful motions, the gorgeous kimono lady began to arrange her implements and to make tea. She ladled water out of the iron pot and then poured it into one of the tea bowls. Having warmed the tea bowl, she transferred the water into a larger ceramic bowl. The tea ceremony, like Japanese cuisine, required the use of quite a lot of exquisitely beautiful earthenware pottery.

The gorgeous kimono woman scooped some powdered green tea out of a little tea caddy and into the warmed tea bowl with an age-burnished bamboo scoop. She added boiling water from the iron pot. Then she began vigorously mixing the tea and water with a bamboo whisk. When she finished, she set the bowl of tea down on the tatami and turned it so that the front faced Pattie. And finally, in one smooth movement of balletic grace, the gorgeous kimono woman bent from the waist, and without releasing her body from its formal seated position, slid the tea bowl across the tatami floor delivering it precisely in front of Pattie at the correct distance for Pattie to just be able to reach it. All of this was doubly impressive because the woman had to do it all while managing the inconveniently long sleeves of her kimono.

The kimono woman, her face expressionless, bowed. Pattie bowed. The kimono woman resumed her original position. Pattie leaned forward without leaving the *seiza* position and drew in the tea bowl so it sat on the tatami in front of her. She then turned the tea bowl so that the front of it faced away from her. Then she bowed to the tea bowl and took it up in two hands. Without looking at me she whispered instructions.

"Watch what I do, and you do exactly the same when it's your turn."

Pattie brought the tea bowl to her lips and sipped the tea with a very loud slurping sound. George Parsons guffawed. His women shushed him. Pattie noisily sipped again, and George Parsons issued a muffled guffaw. Pattie slurped at the tea a third time, the exaggerated noise of it making clear that she had finished all the tea in the tea bowl. She placed the tea bowl back on the tatami in front of her.

"*Kono mono wo haiken itashimasu,*" Pattie said loudly, formally announcing her intention to examine the tea bowl.

Pattie picked up the tea bowl, an insanely expensive piece of antique ceramic art, and raised it above her head so she could study the bottom of it. Having turned the bowl in her hands and thoroughly admired it, she put it back down on the tatami and turned it so that the front was facing the gorgeous kimono lady. Pattie then slid the bowl across the tatami, returning the tea bowl to the kimono woman and herself to the *seiza* position with a look of satisfied serenity.

The gorgeous kimono woman repeated the complete ritual for each of the rest of us in line after Pattie.

When it was my turn, the handsome tea bowl I got was rough and very irregular. It was easy to spot as a product of the ancient pottery village of Shigaraki. Its unglazed orangish-brownish surface was flecked with little bits of white impurities. The bowl bore the marks of fire from the kiln and streaks and drips of green where melted ash from the high-temperature wood firing had dripped down onto the bowl. It was a complex, nuanced, and infinitely interesting piece of ceramic art. Venerable and ageless. But I couldn't tell exactly what part of it was the front, and I wasn't sure if I could keep track of that part of the bowl to return it properly.

"Exactly three sips," Pattie whispered, "and you have to drink *all* the tea."

My legs ached from sitting in *seiza*. Japanese legs were made for sitting in *seiza*. American legs were not. Despite the stiffness and pain, I managed to get the tea bowl up and take the first sip. I made the loud slurping sound. The tea tasted bitter, but I liked it. It was denser and more concentrated than regular Japanese green tea. It had a nutlike pleasantness to it. The texture and mouth-feel of it seemed to go perfectly with the bowl it was in. But I was so focused on getting the procedural part of the ceremony right that paying attention to the taste of the tea seemed like an unnecessary extravagance.

After my second sip I realized that I had underestimated the amount of tea in the bowl. Sip number three was going to be more of a big gulp. With effort, I managed to get it all down and issue the proper slurping sound at the end. I put the bowl back down on the tatami.

"*Kono mono wo haiken itashimasu*," I announced.

Then I picked up the tea bowl again and studied it. The tea bowl was a seriously impressive object, simultaneously crude and complex. It had a weighty feel. The apparent casual randomness of the bowl's design was intentional. Its features were purposely made to look accidental. You didn't have to see it to appreciate it. You could feel its specialness just by touching it. It was not a thing of the modern world. Important people long dead would have once used it. I would really have liked to spend more time just handling and appreciating this object, but I was worried about remembering all the remaining ceremonial steps I still had to perform.

I hoisted the bowl above my head as Pattie had done and immediately understood the importance of drinking *all* the tea. I turned the tea bowl over and examined its foot. The fingerprint of the craftsman who had created it in what had once been wet clay was still visible. The kimono lady had chosen a more masculine bowl for me than she had given to Pattie.

I returned the tea bowl to the tatami and turned it, hoping that I had remembered which side was the front. Then I leaned forward to slide it across the tatami. When I did that, I nearly toppled over. I hadn't noticed that the pain in my legs had disappeared. That was because my legs had completely gone to sleep and I could no longer feel them.

I looked at Pattie. She still looked mildly serene, so I figured I was OK.

None of the rest of us were able to perform as gracefully as Pattie had. Elizabeth did fairly well, though she failed to slurp up all of the tea, and when she held up the tea bowl to examine it, some of the green tea dripped down onto her silk blouse.

George made no attempt to execute the ritual moves and when he tasted the tea, he gagged.

"Oh My God! This is terrible," George bellowed. "I'm sorry, but I'm going to need milk and sugar to get this down. Would somebody please ask her."

"Oh, Daddy, PLEASE! Please stop it. It's a tea ceremony."

"I don't care what it is. This stuff is terrible."

George looked around the room for sympathy and found none.

"I'm sorry, I don't mean to offend anyone, but to be honest it tastes terrible. I really don't know how the rest of you can drink it. Maybe you have to get used to it. I don't know. But we came here to drink tea didn't we? It's a simple request. It's just tea. I need milk and sugar or I can't drink it. I just can't. And I'm not apologizing for asking."

The two women in kimono sat impassive and continued to look serene. George returned the tea bowl without drinking any more of his tea. The gorgeous kimono lady accepted it graciously.

Beverly Parsons skipped most of the steps in the ritual. She nearly gagged when she took the first sip of tea but she soldiered on and finished it all, though she had to use more than the mandatory three sips and didn't make the required slurping noise. She returned her bowl unexamined to the kimono lady who, ever serene, accepted it as if the ritual had been accomplished perfectly.

The elegant kimono lady bowed to the group, holding the deep bow for a very long time. Then she got up and left the room. The guide kimono lady then informed us that it was time to leave.

When I tried to get up to follow Pattie out of the tea ceremony room, my legs objected. They began to wake up and were radiating a tingling, high-voltage electric pain. Walking normally was difficult. I managed to get up and wobble over to the low narrow door that led to the narrow hallway. My feet and legs were transmitting no information about the floor. I just had to assume that except for the pain, they were functioning normally.

George Parsons was rumbling along just behind me. He seemed very uncomfortable in the confined space of the teahouse and eager to get out. He grunted, and I looked back to see that when he'd reached the narrow doorway, he'd failed to turn sideways, which he needed to do in order to get his considerable bulk through it.

"What is it with this country?" George bellowed. Can't they even make doorways big enough for a normal person to fit through?"

"Daddy!"

"George!"

George Parsons lowered his shoulders, and still obstinately front-facing, surged forward through the narrow doorway. The doorway briefly resisted. Then he popped out the other side. When he did, his momentum carried him right into me. I felt his large body hit me from behind like a massive ocean wave. I lost my balance and went crashing into the six-hundred-year-old wooden lattice window frame just in front of me.

The world began to move in slow motion. The wooden frame of the window made a brief and unpleasant tearing sound and came loose from the wall. It was ejected like a cork out of a champagne bottle toward the pond. The lower part of the wall stopped me from following it out. I was left hanging half-way in and half-way out of the newly gouged hole in the Japanese-government-designated Important Cultural Property where Sen no Rikyu had once performed the tea ceremony. I studied the arc of the wooden frame as it sailed through the air and slammed into the pond and then sank. If the *koi* in the pond had detected a human presence and ventured to the surface hoping to be fed, some of them may have been dispatched to the great pond in the sky by the flying window frame.

The second round of tea ceremony guests were just making their way along the path toward the teahouse. As I extricated myself from the hole in the wall, I saw looks of horror and astonishment on their faces. I turned and saw unhappiness deeply etched into Pattie's lovely face. Everyone in the group was looking at me with reproach and accusation in their eyes.

"No," I said. "Not me. It was George. George pushed me."

Several gardeners came rushing over from the back of the garden. The elegant lady in the gorgeous kimono stood on the garden path looking at the teahouse. For once she seemed unable to look serene.

"Why is everything in this country so flimsy?" George was saying as his wife and daughter led him away. "I am not apologizing. It absolutely was *not* my fault."

On the way out I noticed packages of Uji green tea wrapped up specially as gifts for the visitors from Honsenke. I was very sad that Pattie and I would not to be able to claim ours as we left the tea shop ahead of schedule for the train back to Kyoto.

On the train back to Kyoto Pattie held my hand. We didn't speak. She seemed sad about the way the morning had unfolded. But later on she said that at least I'd gotten to see how a real tea ceremony was performed. She didn't seem to blame me at all for my role in the destruction of Sen no Rikyu's teahouse. For that, I felt a very deep gratitude and appreciation for the teachings and tenets of Zen Buddhism. The philosophy that made it possible to not attach too much importance to the transient events of everyday life.

The Whirlpool

MY CLASSMATE AT THE KYOTO Japanese Language School, Saoirse Ryan, had a job as a waitress at a Japanese restaurant. When she was getting ready to go back to Ireland she asked me if I would take over the job when she left.

"I don't think I'll look as good as you do in a kimono," I said. "Won't they be looking to replace you with a female *gaijin*?"

"They are. But they'll never find one. The restaurant is difficult to get to. There's no busses that go anywhere near the place. My husband Sean has to drive me all the way up there and then he has to come back and get me after work. You've got your own motorbike. They'll settle for a male *gaijin*. It's worth a look. It's a proper restaurant. Very expensive. They don't pay much to work there, not nearly as much as teaching English. But you'd be practicing your Japanese. And that's why you're living here in Kyoto, isn't that right?"

"True. Okay, where is it?"

"It's just up Higashiyama. A bit above Kiyomizu-dera."

"*Above* Kiyomizu-dera? There's nothing but trees above Kiyomizu-dera."

"Exactly. There's the trees. And there's this restaurant."

"What does it pay?"

"¥650 an hour. It's three times or more what they'd pay a Japanese person to do it. And you'd be learning things about Japan and Japanese food. The people are nice. I learned the proper way to manage a real kimono. But of course you wouldn't be doing that."

"What kind of restaurant is it?"

"*Shabu-shabu*."

"*Shabu-shabu*? That's putting thin slices of Kobe Beef and some raw vegetables into boiling water. What can you learn about Japanese food from that?"

"Ah, you'd be surprised. I'll give the owner your name and you can go up and have a look. Take my word for it. You'll be thanking me for this."

I was skeptical but I told Saoirse I would go and see.

A few days later I rode my old yellow Honda motorcycle up to the *shabu-shabu* restaurant. It was called Higashiyama Sanso. Just as Saoirse had said, the restaurant was up on Mount Higashiyama above one of the most iconic Kyoto Buddhist temples, Kiyomizu-dera, and right in the middle of a national forest.

There were only two ways to get to the restaurant. The most direct way from downtown Kyoto was to follow Gojo-dori as far east as it went, merge onto the Yamashina highway connector, and take the first exit onto the old Yamashina road. The trouble with that was, between the connector and the old Yamashina road, you had to get onto a brand-new toll road that went far up into the Higashiyama forest. The toll was a hefty ¥600, and for that you'd be on the toll road for less than the sixty seconds it took to reach the first exit. Customers of the restaurant could afford the taxi to and from, and the ¥600 toll both ways. Restaurant workers could not.

You could also reach the restaurant from the other side of the mountain. From the center of Kyoto it was a more roundabout way. The other end of the old Yamashina road connected to a little-used lane that ran behind the Miyako Hotel and was very near to the International Students Residence where I lived. This end of the old Yamashina road wound its way up the mountain and passed in front of the restaurant before it reached the toll road. It was inconvenient if you were coming from Kyoto proper, but for me coming from Hi no Oka, it was shorter, and it was free.

The old Yamashina road climbed Higashiyama in a series of lazy, wide switchbacks. The big trees along the way, unlike most of the lower mountains and foothills in Kyoto, were wild and not planted with row upon row of cypress trees. There were no houses or farms along the road. No shrines or temples. Just big beautiful trees, rugged valleys, and steep slopes. There was the afterglow of sunset in the late afternoon. Brilliant twinkling stars at night. And sometimes a fine view of the moon, fat and round and just emerged from a veil of wispy clouds over the tops of giant pine trees.

On my first visit I was amazed to find a restaurant tucked away all on its own in the middle of a national forest. Its presence was announced by a small, tasteful sign. A gravel road led into a compound arranged around an attractive pond. The small parking lot was screened off by trees and shrubs so as not to distract from views of the pond.

At the back of the pond there was a building that was a modern replica of Kinkaku-ji, the Temple of the Golden Pavilion, but minus the gold. You didn't realize until you got much closer that the Kinkaku-ji replica was only half of the building. The part hidden by the tasteful placement of shrubbery was a modern Japanese residence. From the parking lot or from the restaurant you only saw the Kinkaku-ji part, its reflection mirrored appealingly in the still water of the pond.

To the right of the pond was a formal stone walkway that led to an older, very traditional wooden Japanese building that might also have been someone's house. Beyond that, a path led on to another much-older-looking traditional Japanese building that was almost completely hidden by trees and tall bushes.

I entered the restaurant. No one was around. I called out "*Gomen kudasai*" in the loudest and most manly voice I could muster. An attractive young woman in a simple country kimono came out. She was in her mid-twenties. Her face was unusually expressive. She could probably have carried on an entire conversation without speaking. The face was asking me, "Yes, and what can I do for you?"

I said I was Saoirse Ryan's classmate. I got back an indulgently patient and inquisitive look.

"RAI-ahn-noo-san," I said.

Still nothing.

"Sasha. Sasha-san," I said. Saoirse like "inertia" became "Sasha" in Japanese.

The lights in the pretty face came on.

"Ahh," the young woman in the kimono said. "*Sasha-san no tomodachi desu ne.*"

A barrage of questions followed in rapid-fire Kansai-accented Japanese. The young woman asked one question and then launched the next question without waiting for an answer to the first. I didn't catch most of it, except that her name was Mieko.

"You're Sasha-san's friend," Mieko said. "Why didn't you say so? Don't just stand there. Come in. I'll go and get Emi-san. She's the owner. You sit over there and wait."

Mieko took off about as fast as you can go wearing a kimono. I took a seat at one of the guest tables and studied the restaurant while I waited.

The restaurant was divided into three separate areas. There was an area with three private tatami rooms that were closed off by some very fancy hand-painted, possibly antique sliding *fusuma* panels. There was an area in a separate room that had a small bar. And there was an area with chairs and tables that seemed to be a Western-style dining room.

The bar had chairs around a raised *irori*, a kind of fire pit in a rural Japanese farmhouse that would be the center of everyday life there, where the cooking was done and the eating, and where the heat in winter would come from. A large antique hook on a decorative wooden arm hung over the *irori*. In the farmhouse it would have been for hanging cooking pots over the heat.

The small dining room had six solid wooden tables in it, each with four chairs. Every table had a gap in the center where the cast-iron *nabe* would be placed over a gas burner to cook the *shabu-shabu.* The interior of that part of the restaurant was mostly done up in a kind of *mingei*, Japanese folk art, style. It was all thick, age-burnished beams and pillars with traditional mud-stucco walls. The idea was to create the feel of an old and traditional Japanese farmhouse but updated with electricity and other modern conveniences.

There was art on the walls. Colorful modern woodblock prints. Most of them by the artist Clifton Karhu, whose work was easily recognized. Tucked into purpose-built niches and alcoves, there was *mingei*-style pottery by Kawai Kanjiro, a Kyoto native, or Hamada Shoji, both *mingei* movement craftsmen whose works, if you could find them, would cost about the same as a small house on Lake Biwa. Things you would mostly expect to find in high-priced antique shops.

After a ten-minute wait, a woman in her mid-forties wearing gray wool slacks and a black cashmere sweater came in and sat down next to me at the table. She said her name was Emi, which she pronounced Amy in clear and unaccented American English. She owned the restaurant. She had lived in California and she spoke English fluently.

I introduced myself. Amy asked, in Japanese, if I could speak Japanese. I said I was learning. She asked if I had ever tended bar. I said I had taken a famous bartending course at Columbia University but only actually tended bar once at a private alumni function. Amy asked if I had a car. I told her I had a motorbike. I was hired on the spot.

"I have to go now," Amy said, "but if you have any questions you can ask Miyata-san, the head of the waitstaff, or Mieko who you already met. I'll send Miyata-san out to speak with you. I think it's a good idea for you to work when Sasha-san is here. She can show you how things work."

Miyata-san was tall and lean and wore thick, black-rimmed glasses. I liked him immediately. He worked at the restaurant part-time to help pay tuition. He was an English Literature grad student at a local university. Miyata-san spoke in a measured voice and could not be hurried or his train of thought interrupted or derailed. He had a very dry, deadpan sense of humor. He also seemed to possess an encyclopedic knowledge of a wide range of subjects. As I later learned, when you worked long hours in a restaurant that had few customers, you had a lot of time to talk.

In the time I worked at the restaurant I heard Miyata-san talk about Kierkegaard and the Leap of Faith. He explained the historical significance of Sakamoto Ryoma and the *shishi* who helped engineer the Meiji Restoration that ended the Tokugawa Shogunate. He knew how long it took Herman Melville to write *Moby Dick*. He told me how much Charles Dickens got paid to write *Bleak House*. He showed me the exact and precisely correct way to enter a tatami room and place a *nabe* over a gas fire and fill it in front of paying customers. He taught me the correct way to wash and stack the Mashiko-*yaki* bowls used for the *shabu-shabu* dipping sauce. He was a patient teacher, and he would eventually leave the *mizu shobai* (restaurant) business and become a college professor.

Miyata-san explained how much, how, and how often I would be paid. It was less than even the lowest-paying English-teaching job, but more than what Saoirse was being paid and also more than what the other waiters in the restaurant were paid. Miyata-san explained matter-of-factly that men in Japan were paid more. Unlike America, he said, gender equality was not a Japanese concept. Japanese-speaking *gaijin* were rare, and therefore got paid more. When I added up the hours I would be working, I figured I would be earning about half of what I could earn teaching English and spending many more hours doing it. But I would be using my Japanese and learning a lot. That was the theory.

The restaurant was only open for dinner. An exception was made when a private party booked the restaurant for lunch or for a late afternoon. The restaurant closed when the last guest left. If a party of guests decided to remain until two a.m., the restaurant would stay open until two a.m. If the last guest left the restaurant at eight p.m.

and there were no reservations, the restaurant would close at eight p.m. None of the staff left the restaurant until everyone left. That was the Japanese way.

There were only three things on the restaurant's menu. There was *shabu-shabu* with Kobe Beef. There was *kani mizutaki shabu--* with Hokkaido King Crab legs. And there was *tori mizutaki shabu-shabu* with chicken instead of beef. Each choice came with a bamboo basket of raw, thinly sliced beef, crab parts, or chicken chunks, and a bamboo basket of vegetables, rice noodles, and blocks of tofu. The serving size depended on how many guests there were, but the minimum order was for two. If one half of a couple dining at the restaurant wanted crab and the other beef, they were out of luck unless they ordered portions for four and did the cooking in two separate *nabe*. The menu had prices for the basic course and then for additional plates of beef, crab, or chicken and baskets of vegetables.

That was the menu. The prices of everything on the menu were high. *Shabu-shabu* was usually expensive. The main ingredients were expensive. Kobe Beef and Hokkaido King Crab legs were very expensive. But the prices at Higashiyama Sanso were expensive even for *shabu-shabu*. This was a seriously high-class restaurant.

On my first night at work I was shown around the restaurant. I was issued a blue *happi* coat with the restaurant's name and logo on it in white. I wore my only pair of pants that weren't jeans. I traded my hiking boots for a pair of the restaurant's slip-on sandals. Gradually I got used to the restaurant's routines and began to look forward to going there.

The restaurant opened at six but there were rarely any customers until eight. When I arrived, Mieko and Saoirse would be upstairs somewhere putting Saoirse into her kimono. The entire upstairs was off-limits to men. Putting on a real kimono for anyone without extensive experience was a two-person job. Mieko seemed to live in her kimono and it was hard to imagine her dressed any other way. Like most *gaijin*, Saoirse never looked exactly right in hers.

The kimonos Mieko and Saoirse wore in the restaurant were the kind of plain, everyday kimonos women in Japan used to wear back in the days when it was actually what most women wore. The restaurant's kimonos were working-women's kimonos not housewives' kimonos. Country kimonos in rough but folk-craftsy fabrics and patterns.

Miyata-san showed me the bar. Dessert was included with the meal and customers had their dessert in the bar. There was one choice. Fresh strawberries dipped in chocolate melted in a small iron pot over the coals in the *irori*.

If anyone ordered a mixed drink it would be my job to make it. I expressed my concern. This was an expensive restaurant. I had no real experience making mixed drinks. I didn't like mixed drinks, and the only time I had ever had one was at the bartending course I once took. Miyata-san told me to relax.

"Ninety-nine percent of the customers order something straight up," he said. "Brandy or whiskey or wine. If your mixed drink is off, Japanese customers won't know the difference. If there is something not right about the drink and a *gaijin* had made it, they will assume the problem is with them, not the drink."

Next was the kitchen. I had worked in kitchens in America in high school and in college. They were chaotic and filthy, and the chefs or the line cooks were extroverted, sadistic bullies. There was a hierarchy and I was always at the bottom of it. The kitchen at Higashiyama Sanso was all cleanliness and serenity. It was more spic-and-span than a TV chef's on-air kitchen. Everything was neat and organized. It was brightly lit. And there were only two classes of people in the kitchen. The restaurant's chef and everyone else. Omote-san, Amy's sister, was the restaurant's chef.

The kitchen was very large and well equipped. Much too large and well equipped for a kitchen that only turned out sliced meat and sliced vegetables and occasionally a new batch of *gomatare*, the sesame-based *shabu-shabu* dipping sauce. A broad counter served as the kitchen's main workspace and divided the kitchen in two. There was Omote-san's domain at the back and there was the section at the front where the waiters placed orders or retrieved baskets of ingredients that were ready to go out.

Opposite Omote-san's counter was another counter where the waiters washed and dried the dishes and put them away in cupboards. Waiters washed and dried the dishes by hand and put everything away before the restaurant closed up each night. No one left until everyone left. The restaurant had to be clean and ready to go for the next day before everyone could call it a day.

Along a narrow corridor and behind the kitchen was the staff room. It had lockers where the staff exchanged their clothes for the restaurant's *happi* coats and sandals. There was a table where the staff had dinner. Dinner before work was an added perk. Omote-san cooked it for us. The food was much like what college students ate at their university cafeterias. Curry rice. Yakisoba. Kaki fry. We never tasted the *shabu-shabu*. Not even once. If there were uneaten or even uncooked leftovers, they were thrown away. Sometimes seeing perfectly good Kobe Beef thrown out reduced me to tears.

Omote-san lived above the restaurant with her husband who was a real estate agent and the only male allowed up on the second floor. He must have been a traveling real estate agent because he was almost never there. Saoirse once told me that there were nicely appointed guest rooms upstairs. The restaurant had originally been built as an upscale inn just before the Tokyo Olympics in 1964. The idea had been Amy's. The property the restaurant was built on belonged to Amy's husband. Amy was the businessperson in the family.

Amy's husband's father had been a long-time employee of the Imperial Household Agency. He had been Emperor Hirohito's butler. When he retired, he was granted a small piece of an imperial property in the middle of a national forest with two little houses on it and a pond. When Amy married her husband after returning to Japan from California, her husband was living in the smaller Japanese house near the pond. Amy introduced the concept of taking out a mortgage and building a modern house at the back of the pond. Then she started thinking about what kind of businesses they could operate to pay off the loan.

Amy thought that well-to-do foreign visitors to the Olympics would not want to leave Japan without seeing Kyoto. She took out another loan to build the inn. The inn would be an upscale establishment where foreigners would feel comfortable. It would be Japanese but not uncomfortably Japanese. It would have Western-style rooms with Japanese taste and sensibility. Olympic visitors to the inn would spread the word and the inn's reputation would grow. But the inn business never really took off. The restaurant was all that was left of it.

Omote-san was a woman of few words. When an order came in she cut up the vegetables, went into the giant walk-in refrigerator, and brought out a slab of Kobe Beef and ran it through the slicer. She went back in and got the rice noodles and a huge block of tofu, cut that up, made everything pretty, and sent it out with one of the waiters. Then she filled an antique ceramic sake bottle with the special *shabu-shabu* broth that the meat would be cooked in at the table. She kept the broth in a large urn behind her. The recipe for the broth was a highly guarded secret, as was the recipe for the special *gomatare*, the dipping sauce for the cooked slices of *shabu-shabu* beef.

Once a month Omote-san made the *gomatare* from scratch. The other choice for dipping the cooked beef was called *ponzu*, a blend of soy sauce and vinegar. That came in a bottle. The restaurant bought it from a wholesale supplier. Except for making meals for the staff, making the *gomatare* was pretty much all the cooking Omote-san did. After a month on the job I learned that the special *shabu-shabu* cooking broth consisted only of water and *kombu*, a kind of seaweed. Only.

Ninety-five percent of the restaurant's business occurred in the three tatami rooms. Even *gaijin* waiters were expected to know exactly how to behave as a server in a tatami room. Even though many of the customers themselves did not know, to do my job properly, I had to know.

The tatami rooms were one step higher than the floor of the main dining room. You slid open the *fusuma* door and stepped up into the tatami room while gracefully losing your slippers. You pivoted, knelt, and slid the *fusuma* door closed. Then you bowed, stood up and went wherever you were going. It was improper to bend over from a standing position in a tatami room to do anything. You picked the spot where the doing would occur, you knelt there, and then you did whatever it was you had to do.

In the middle of the room was a long, low table made of handsome aged wood. There were three cutouts in the middle of the table outfitted with gas burners where the cast-iron *nabe*, the cauldrons that held the *shabu-shabu*, were placed. One waiter brought in the *nabe*, the number of *nabe* depending on the number of guests, and set them down on the burners. It was the only task in the room you didn't have to kneel for. Another waiter came in with the earthenware jar of the special broth and filled the *nabe*. The first waiter came back with a box of the restaurant's wooden matches and lit the gas under the *nabe*. The waiters were mute by design but could respond minimally when questioned.

Next, one of the women in kimono, Mieko, or Sasha-san, came into the room, introduced herself, and explained how the meat and vegetables would be cooked and consumed. The guests could do the cooking themselves or the kimono women could do it for them. For the most part this was a fake option. The kimono women were quick to do everything for the guests, placing cooked beef or vegetables from the *nabe* into whichever diner's bowl was the least full before the diner realized it was being done. In this way, anyone who was a slow or a light eater, or was shy about being seen to eat too much, or who resisted taking the last cooked slice of Kobe Beef from the *nabe*, was encouraged to eat more and to eat faster.

A mute waiter was stationed in the room to execute drink orders or to provide other assistance if needed. The kimono girls and the mute waiters also patrolled the table to make sure that everyone's drinks glasses were always filled.

When I finally got to watch Mieko at work I was enthralled. She was casually graceful in her kimono and moved as if the kimono was part of her. She converted the dinner service into a kind of graceful food ballet. She did it despite the inconvenience of being wrapped in exactly the kind of garment that you would not want to be wearing while serving a meal of any kind, let alone hovering over a pot of boiling water and dishing out slices of extravagantly priced beef. Her management of the long, bulky, baggy sleeves of her kimono while serving seemed effortless.

Mieko made navigating the complex rules of the tatami room seem a thing of grace and beauty. When she stepped into the tatami room she seemed to transform herself. She was witty. She was graceful. She kept up a constant banter to amuse her guests while moving the meal along and making sure everyone ate and drank more than they wanted to and were happy to do it. She was the perfect hostess. Outside the tatami room Mieko was sometimes bad-tempered, sometimes coarse, always everyday practical, and often funny.

Saoirse also handled herself admirably in the tatami room. A *gaijin* wearing a kimono always looks somehow wrong in it. But once she started to move, Sasha-san got you past that. She wasn't as natural as Mieko was, but she was very good at it. For the conversation part, Sasha had an advantage that Mieko didn't. Sasha-san didn't have to keep up a running monologue. Most Japanese people didn't get to meet *gaijin* who spoke Japanese, so they asked a lot of questions. Sasha-san didn't quite give the impression of being in charge the way Mieko did. But she was a talking *gaijin* in a kimono, so the customers were always satisfied.

Sometimes the guests in the room were all Japanese men. When they had had too much to drink, which they always did, they would invariably ask Sasha-san if her pubic hair was the same rust-orange color as the hair on her head. Then the silent waiter in the room would know it was time to escort Sasha-san out of the room and bring Mieko back in. Mieko was also a genius at handling drunks.

On my first night at the restaurant, once the guests started arriving, Miyata-san got busy and I was delivered into the hands of Yoshida-san, one of the other waiters, for my basic instruction. After Miyata-san, the next most senior waiter was Nakagawa-san. Normally Nakagawa-san would have been the one to teach me, but he disliked *gaijin* and resented the fact that *gaijin* were paid more money to do the same job as the Japanese waiters. He had refused to instruct me.

Nakagawa-san was very handsome, fit, and trim. He was originally from Osaka, but he had graduated from a reasonably good college in Tokyo. Now he was back in Kansai studying to become a tax accountant. He had played rugby and captained the rowing team in college. He belonged to a karate club where he held a first-degree black belt. He was proud of the fact that he spoke no English, and he made it known that he thought that Japanese people were altogether too fond of foreigners and foreign things.

Yoshida-san was relatively tall and also very good-looking, but he took himself far less seriously than Nakagawa-san. Yoshida had a habit of saying out loud whatever it was that he was thinking, which in some cases could be uncomfortable. But if you wanted to know something about someone that should not be said aloud, all you had to do was ask Yoshida-san. Yoshida had warned me that Nakagawa and Mieko were an item and that I should be careful not to get too friendly with Mieko. Once when I was talking to Mieko about something, I got the same message from Nakagawa, only non-verbally. "Hands off my woman," his eyes were saying to me.

When nothing in particular was going on in the restaurant, Miyata and Nakagawa stood stoically silent. Yoshida liked to fill the void with conversation, or with his own observations. One night during a lull, Yoshida asked me if I had ever worn women's pantyhose.

I said no.

"You know," he said, "people would think I'm a faggot or something if they found out I wear women's pantyhose under my pants.

But in the winter, when it's really cold in here, pantyhose keep you warm like nothing else. The dining rooms are heated in the winter, but not the back part of the restaurant. Omote-san has a little space heater, but the rest of us are freezing our asses off. I don't like to be cold. Pantyhose just work for me and I don't care what people think about it. Why should I care what people think, right?"

"But . . . when you have to take a leak say . . . isn't it a little . . . inconvenient?"

"Yeah, okay. It is, a little. But how often do you have to pee when you're here? Not that often. I don't anyway. I'd rather be warm."

Once Yoshida-san asked me if I knew what *shabu-shabu* meant in Japanese.

"I don't think it means anything. It's just a sound, right? Isn't it supposed to be the sound the meat makes when you swish it back and forth in the boiling water to cook it?"

"That's right. But it has another meaning in Japanese."

"Okay . . . what's the other meaning?"

"It means to fuck. It's the sound your dick makes when it's poking around inside a woman's pussy."

Yoshida-san then re-explained in detail, with accompanying hand gestures, how the *shabu-shabu* sound was the sound a penis makes when inserted into a female vagina and is vigorously engaged. I verified this with Miyata-san who assured me completely deadpan that Yoshida-san was correct. *Shabu-shabu* in Japanese slang means to fuck, he said. It occurred to me that I had never been aware of any sound like that when having sex, and I began to wonder if I might be doing it wrong somehow.

"So," I asked, "how does someone know when you say *shabu-shabu* that you mean the food and not fucking? I mean, let's say you've picked up a girl for a date and you ask the girl, what should we do tonight? Shall we go for *shabu-shabu*? Couldn't you accidentally get yourself in trouble by being too . . . ah . . . direct?"

Miyata and Yoshida considered this carefully.

"I think when you mean it to say fucking," Yoshida said, "you say it twice. *Shabu-shabu, shabu-shabu.* Then it means fucking."

"Yes," Miyata said. "I believe that is generally correct."

I worked at the *shabu-shabu* restaurant three or sometimes four days a week. Most of the time I was there, there were very few customers and I wondered how the restaurant was able to stay in business. But when there were guests, they were always the kind of guests who ordered big, ordered more, and drank a lot. Also, the guests were usually very interesting. The woodblock print artist Clifton Karhu was a friend of Amy's, and he sometimes ate at the restaurant. His framed prints decorated the walls of the restaurant and were for sale in the restaurant's antiques store at the side of the pond. Karhu, originally from Minnesota, had lived in Kyoto for decades. He lived in a very old Japanese-style house and famously only wore kimono. When he had visitors from Tokyo or the US or entertained Kyoto friends, he came to Higashiyama Sanso.

Amy collected Imari porcelain and used it in the restaurant. She also sold it in her antiques shop. One Saturday when I arrived for work, Amy took me over to the antiques shop and showed me some of the things she had. There was a lot of antique pottery and some handsome wooden *tansu* chests. From time to time we had wealthy foreign visitors in the restaurant. At the end of the meal Amy would bring them over to look at the antiques. Amy said that sometimes she might not be there to show foreign guests around and she wanted me to understand the things she had in the shop so I could explain them to potential customers and make the sales. I learned to recognize Imari, Nabeshima, Arita, and Kutani porcelain at a glance, and how to tell real antiques from modern imitations.

Sometimes we had guests who were famous Japanese politicians or the head abbots of the major temples in Kyoto. Buddhists were not supposed to eat meat, and the secluded Higashiyama Sanso was the ideal place for them to not be seen doing it. When important guests were in the restaurant Amy always took care of them herself with only Mieko and Miyata-san to assist her. *Gaijin* could not be trusted with the seriously famous clientele, probably because we could not be relied on for absolute discretion. Private restaurants in Japan were where deals and meetings that could not face public scrutiny were carried out. Some of them happened in our restaurant.

Mieko always went out of her way to teach me about things in the restaurant. I was aware that she was flirting with me. I thought it was more for Nakagawa's benefit than anything to do with me. But I enjoyed it. Her charm, when she felt like using it, was irresistible. I had seen that side of her in front of guests in the tatami rooms. I continued to be amazed at how she would enter the tatami room and the charm would snap on as if someone had thrown a switch. And then as soon as she slipped out of the tatami room her face relaxed and the charm vanished.

It was rare for Mieko to turn on the charm outside the tatami room or when there were no guests. But she sometimes did it for me. She could also do something with a kimono that I had thought impossible. She could make it seem sexy.

WHEN I WAS WORKING AT the restaurant I was living in the International Students Residence in Hi no Oka. My girlfriend, Pattie, also lived in the dorm. I sometimes spent the night in her room in violation of the dorm's rules.

My friend Peter Franks had moved back to Australia with his girlfriend, now wife, Satoko. Satoko didn't know about me and Pattie and encouraged her younger sister, Mariko, to spend time with me. I reluctantly accepted an invitation to have dinner with Mariko, and her mother, at their home in the south part of Kyoto. I got the date wrong.

I was in Pattie's room when Mariko, furious at being stood up, delivered the meal her mother had prepared for me to the dorm. I was paged multiple times on the dorm's PA system. I couldn't come out because I would be seen leaving Pattie's room. The paging went on for about twenty minutes. Then Hashimoto-san, the dorm's RA, knocked on the door to Pattie's room and delivered the meal to me along with a message from Mariko ostensibly expressing concern for my health but which in reality meant "fuck you, asshole."

The next day Kobayashi-san, the woman who ran the dorm, called me into her office and told me that Pattie and I were kicked out. We had until the end of the month to leave. I accepted it as inevitable. There were advantages to living in a well-managed dormitory. But you were sheltered from the slings and arrows of real Japanese life, and you ended up using your English way too much.

Pattie said she would have someone from her tea ceremony university call the dorm to change their minds. It didn't work. Kobayashi-san disliked Americans in general and Pattie in particular. The call from Honsenke made Kobayashi-san sure the decision to kick us out was the right one. We had broken the dorm's rules. We were out.

I checked the bulletin board at the Japanese-language school where I was learning Japanese. There was nothing. Kyoto was a tough place to find somewhere to live on a budget. You had to get really far out of town and accept something very run-down to get a place.

I reported for work at the restaurant and found Amy, the restaurant's owner, in the kitchen talking to her sister, Omote-san, the restaurant's cook. Amy asked how I was and I told her I was losing my room at the International Students Residence at the end of the month. Amy asked me why and I told her. She said that that was too bad, but that she might have a solution for my problem if my girlfriend and I didn't mind living in a very old Japanese-style house. I said we would love to live in a Japanese house. Amy said she would make a phone call and get back to me.

I changed into my *happi* and reported to the kitchen where Omote-san had me spend half an hour grinding sesame seeds for her special *gomatare* sauce. That task completed, I then joined Miyata-san, whom I found standing at the waiters' station. He was watching Nakagawa-san and Mieko at the far end of the dining room. They seemed to be having an argument. Nakagawa-san was trying to pull Mieko into the bar. Mieko was resisting.

I asked Miyata-san what was going on.

"Nakagawa's been telling everyone that he and Mieko are engaged to be married," Miyata-san said. "He did it without asking her first. It seems that she doesn't agree that they are engaged to be married or that they ever will be engaged to be married. Now they are discussing it."

"Should we do anything?"

"No. I think Mieko can handle the situation."

I stood next to Miyata-san and watched Mieko and Nakagawa arguing.

"I just spent a half hour grinding sesame seeds for Omote-san," I said. "She's making a fresh batch of *gomatare*."

"Omote-san doesn't usually allow anyone in the kitchen when she makes the *gomatare*. Grinding the sesame seeds is hard work. She dislikes physical labor. But she doesn't want anyone to know how she makes the *gomatare*. She must have thought a *gaijin* would have no idea what she was putting in it."

"She was right," I said.

Nakagawa came storming past us and into the kitchen without even looking at me or Miyata-san. We could hear Omote-san yelling at him as he passed through the kitchen and into the back room. Mieko came over and stood next to us. Her face was flushed and she looked angry.

After a few minutes, Nakagawa came out from the kitchen dressed in his normal street clothes. Without a word or a glance behind him, he walked straight out of the restaurant. When he was gone, Mieko and Miyata-san looked at each other. Miyata-san was studying Mieko's face. I couldn't even begin to guess what he was seeing there, but after a few moments they both turned and went into the kitchen. Omote-san yelled at them as they passed through on their way to the staff break room.

Amy came back into the restaurant.

"Was that Nakagawa-san leaving already?" she wanted to know.

"I think so," I said.

"Where are Mieko and Miyata-san?"

"I think they're in the back."

"One of them should be out here. We have guests arriving at eight."

"I'll go and get them."

"Before you do, I came back to tell you I have good news. The friend I mentioned would like to rent her house out. She prefers renting to foreigners. You probably don't know how real estate laws work in Japan, but when you have Japanese tenants and you need them to leave, it's almost impossible to get them out if they don't want to go."

"Ah."

"This is a traditional Japanese house near Kyoto University. It's been in my friend's family for a long time. They moved out four or five years ago and divided up the property so they could rent it out. Part of it is rented now, but my friend is saving the main house for her son. Her son is in medical school in Boston. When he finishes his residency in the US, she wants him to move back into the family house. She won't rent it to Japanese, but as long as you understand you have to move out once the son is ready to come back, she's willing to rent it to you."

"That sounds great. When do you think the son might come back?"

"Please don't ever tell my friend this, but someone who has lived in America will never want to live in an old traditional Japanese house like that. But I'm sure you will enjoy it. My friend can show it to you tomorrow."

"Thank you. I really appreciate it. Tell me where and when and I'll be there."

—

PATTIE AND I WENT TO look at the house the next day. Amy's friend, Ohta-san, met us at the house.

The house was a faded beauty. Like a concubine living out her old age in some long-forgotten temple in a remote mountain village. Obscure now. Would have been something grand once.

The house was located just north of Marutamachi, off Higashi-Oji and across from the Kyodai Byoin, the Kyoto University Hospital. It had once been part of a family compound. The compound was now carved into individual units to be rented out, but the main house stood intact, its wood heavily darkened with age under a proud mantle of steel-gray ceramic roof tiles.

The neighborhood around the house had an unpretentious residential feel. It was full of older houses that had probably been converted to rentals for Kyodai medical students or nurses at the nearby hospital. This had once been a neighborhood of well-off people. But those who still had money had moved to leafier, less congested parts of the city. The streets here were narrow and there were many poorly maintained buildings not handsome enough or functional enough to have survived in other parts of the city. The neighborhood was hemmed in by big shrines and temples. The high back wall of the Heian Jingu ended it to the south. The Komyo-ji temple compound ended it to the east. And to the north there remained parts of the now vanished Shogo-in that gave the area its name.

There were no shopping areas or stores nearby. The closest place to buy groceries was all the way down to the Nishiki market at Shijo Teramachi, a brisk thirty-minute walk or more. Either the area had been too classy to allow ordinary commerce within it or the expansion of Kyoto University had eaten up its market streets. A small enclosed room jutted out from a crumbling old house at the edge of the alley that led to Ohta-san's house. An ancient man sat on a raised platform of tatami mats in the room. From here he sold cigarettes, candy, and lottery tickets. Sometimes his wife was there doing the selling. That was the only commercial enterprise in the entire neighborhood.

The one-room shop had a pay phone in its window through which all purchases were made. Anyone in the neighborhood who didn't have their own phone used the pay phone at the little shop. Almost no one in the neighborhood had their own phone.

The alley that led to Ohta-san's house dead-ended there. The compound that contained the house had a wall around it. Its formal gate was long gone. Pattie and I stood looking at the house. Ohta-san's black Mercedes was parked next to it. In its prime, a novel by Tanizaki Junichiro might have taken place there. The house had belonged to Ohta-san's husband's family for generations. Considered a new property by Kyoto standards, the house had been rebuilt and "modernized" sometime during the last hundred years.

Pattie and I introduced ourselves to Ohta-san. She gave a nod that was not quite a bow and quickly moved to unlock and slide open the front door to the house. I wondered if locking a door this insubstantial was a waste of energy. Even a mildly determined intruder would have no trouble breaking in. What kept a house like this secure was the presence of people inside, not locks.

The stately old house had a large *genkan*. Ten people could easily rest their shoes there before donning slippers to go up into the house. All of the rooms in the house were tatami rooms. There was a ten-mat tatami room just off the *genkan*, and just off that room, a kitchen. The kitchen had a big sink, a counter for food preparation, and three gas burners for cooking. At the back of the kitchen was a small room with a dirt floor that you stepped down into. This had probably been the house's original kitchen. Now it had a small Japanese washing machine in it.

On the other side of the first tatami room, a set of very steep wooden stairs led to the second floor of the building.

"This would have been the family dining room," Ohta-san

explained. "My mother- and father-in-law lived in this house. They died about three years ago. It's never been rented out before. My son used it for a while. I suppose the house had memories for him from his childhood. What do you think so far?"

"It's really a great house," I said.

Pattie looked skeptical.

"The tatami are a little old," Pattie said. "They're not that bad, but . . ."

"If we were renting to Japanese people, of course we would have to change all the tatami in the whole house. The rent we're proposing takes into account the fact that we won't be doing that."

"How much would the rent be?" Pattie asked.

"¥24,000 per month," Mrs. Ohta said.

Pattie and I were each paying ¥3,000 a month for our rooms at the International Students Residence. We both knew that was impossible to duplicate elsewhere.

"For such a big house, that seems fair," I said.

Ohta-san laughed.

"I see you haven't tried to rent a house in Kyoto yet," Ohta-san said. "You wouldn't find anything close to that even in the worst neighborhoods, let alone in a central part of Kyoto. Shall we look at the rest of the house?"

We spent the next half hour immersed in a tour of a faded remnant of Meiji Japan. Electric lighting seemed to be the house's only concession to the twentieth century.

The house was designed so that any of the rooms in it could be closed off completely by sliding *fusuma* screen panels. In this way, two or more of the rooms could be made into a larger room. In winter, the smaller spaces would be easier to heat, and in summer, the larger rooms could be opened to the outside of the house.

The rooms at the outer edge of the house were bordered by a narrow hallway. Its floor was made of finely joined slats of a burnished hardwood. The outside walls of the hallway were sliding wooden doors with glass panes. On the other side of the glass panes was a small garden. When we walked through the hallway, the wooden slats beneath our feet moaned and squeaked.

"This is the traditional *roka*," Ota-san said. "The large room at the end here would have been the main bedroom. The noise the wooden floor makes when someone walks on it is called the 'nightingale voice.' It has a poetic name, but its purpose is to prevent the sleeping master of the house from being surprised by assassins or thieves."

"Or possibly a poetic excuse not to fix or replace the floorboards," I said.

"Yes," Mrs. Ohta said, "that is also a possibility. Ascher-san I understand you know something about Japanese literature. Perhaps you've read how Japanese poets would sit on the edge of the *roka* in the morning looking into their gardens, sipping tea and writing poetry?"

I went over and looked down into the garden. There was a long wooden plank that served as a step leading down into the garden. A worn pair of wooden *geta* and a pair of rubber sandals sat in the garden waiting to be used. Part of the garden was tiled and part was just dirt. A high mud-and-lattice wall topped with ceramic roof tiles kept the garden invisible from the street. A few large earthenware pots were scattered around at the base of the wall. The pots had dirt in them but no plants. A few scraggly bushes clung desperately to life on the south and west sides of the wall.

"As you see, we haven't really kept the garden up. It could be a nice project for someone who enjoys gardening."

Mrs. Ohta looked at Pattie. Pattie smiled back at her.

The wooden *roka* made a right turn around the side of the master bedroom and then a left into a narrow hallway. There it dead-ended into a wall that did not seem to be an original part of the house. One side of the hallway had sliding wooden doors with glass panes that looked out into the garden. The other side had solid wooden sliding doors. Ohta-san slid back one of the wooden doors to reveal a very lovely blue-and-white-ceramic antique Japanese toilet. I had one of these in my Tokyo apartment when I first arrived in Japan. This one was much larger, much finer, and much older. There was a large white ceramic tank bolted to the wall near the ceiling. A chain for flushing the toilet hung down from it. At the end of the chain was a very handsome blue-and-white-ceramic chain pull.

I looked at Pattie and expected to see revulsion on her face. Instead there was a smile.

"We have these at Honsenke," she said. "I even know how to use one wearing a kimono."

"Pattie studies tea ceremony at Honsenke," I said.

"Yes, I'd heard that from Emiko-san. A house like this must be perfect for you then," Ohta-san said, looking at Pattie.

Pattie smiled back at Ohta-san.

"Shall we go and see the upstairs?" Ohta-san said.

We went back toward the entrance and climbed the steep set of wooden stairs at the front of the house. Each step was a beautifully burnished slab of dark wood, polished over the years by the passage of slippered and stockinged feet. The room at the top was very large and very bright. Two sides of the room had the same wooden *roka* corridor as below. Instead of the sliding *fusuma* to close off the room, there were sliding wooden doors with glass panes on both sides of the *roka*.

When I went over to look outside, I was amazed. There were very few buildings in the immediate area that were two stories tall. From this room there was a view out over the entire neighborhood. It was like being in a low-flying spaceship looking down over an alien culture.

For the most part the view was of Kyoto's distinctive gray ceramic-tiled rooftops. They spread out in every direction like melancholy waves on a rainy sea. Wedged into the neat but densely packed warren of alleys and houses were tiny little gardens and oddly cantilevered, jerry-built wooden decks. None of these would have been visible from the street. The gardens were stuffed with bundled-up objects for which there was no storage space inside the houses. Their value as gardens and morning inspiration to tea-sipping poets seemed to have been lost.

Seen from the back, Kyoto houses gave a true picture of the life going on inside them. It was a partly sunny day, and nearly every house I could now see had people's laundry hanging out to dry. Even the small temple two streets over had laundry hanging out in its walled-in garden. From this vantage point, I could see that if I lived in this house and spent time in this room, I would soon know everything about what kind of clothing my neighbors preferred, including their underwear.

The other surprise was that nearly every house that I could see had large collections of *bonsai* plants. They were not so much in the gardens, but on the cantilevered roof decks and on planks attached to the windows of the buildings. Everywhere I looked, there were forests of miniature trees in pots. Some of the pots the little trees were in were themselves miniature works of art.

"It's a very nice view, isn't it?" Mrs. Ohta said. "My father-in-law used this room as his study. He was a banker, but he wrote poetry after he retired and he liked the way the light reflected on the roofs in the evening."

"It's a nice view," I said. "Uniquely Kyoto."

"So the house doesn't have a bath?" Pattie said.

"Oh yes," Mrs. Ohta said. "I almost forgot. Let's go back downstairs."

We followed Mrs. Ohta back to the family dining room. In the corner of the room there was a *fusuma* door that I had taken to be a closet. It opened into a small room. The floor of the room was tiled, and embedded in the floor was a large iron pot of the type cannibals use to boil jungle explorers in cartoons. A single faucet with a single knob extended out from the wall and could be swiveled into position to fill the iron pot. Built into one wall at about waist height was a wooden shelf with a mirror above it. Just below the shelf was a little wooden stool and a little wooden bucket.

"Is that a hot water tap?" Pattie asked.

"No," Mrs. Ohta said. "There's a gas heater that makes hot water for the sink in the kitchen. But only enough to use in the sink. You can't make hot water with that to heat the bath. Let me show you how we heat the bath."

We followed Mrs. Ohta back to the *roka* and out into the garden. Mrs. Ohta slipped into the rubber sandals and I put on the wooden *geta*. Pattie sat on the step and watched us.

Once I was down in the garden I could see that under the corner of the house where the *roka* began were three separate wood piles. I could also see the bottom of the iron bath cauldron. One stack of wood was made up of very neatly cut up and nearly uniform-sized wedge-shaped logs. Another pile was of smaller thick pieces of wood. The last pile was of slender wooden shards. There was a metal platform under the cauldron and resting on top of it a large rusted metal oven.

"You bring out some newspaper with you when you do this," Mrs. Ohta advised. "Then you stack up the wood in the metal box with the smaller pieces on the bottom and the bigger ones on top and the newspaper underneath. You light the newspaper and you shouldn't have any trouble getting a fire going."

"I was a Boy Scout," I said. "I know how to make a fire."

"Then you should be fine. It takes about a half hour to heat up the bath. Depending on the weather and how many people are bathing. You might sometimes have to come out and add more wood. We have a man who comes every few days and replenishes the wood supply. He's very reliable and he also takes care of odd jobs here and any repairs to the house and to the other houses in the compound."

"So your husband's family owns the whole compound?"

"His parents did. This was all once one big family compound. But my husband had to divide it up and rent or sell off parts of it. Do you know about the inheritance tax in Japan?"

"I'm sorry, I don't."

"Let's just say it's a big problem when you own property."

"Who lives in the other parts of the compound?"

"There are three other units. A single man lives in the one next to you. He's very quiet and he travels quite a bit for business, so he's really not there much. Across the courtyard where my car is parked is a smaller unit. A young married couple with a baby live there. The one on the corner is rented to two women. I think they belong to a Buddhist temple. Nuns in training or something like that. As you can see, it's a very quiet neighborhood. So tell me, what do you think? Do you like the house?"

"I like it very much."

I looked over at Pattie who was watching us and smiling.

"Pattie and I will talk it over and we'll let you know tomorrow. But I think we'd love to live here."

—

PATTIE WAS A LITTLE LESS positive about the house than I was. Where I saw sunsets over a sea of gray-tiled roofs she saw a collection of ramshackle rooms that needed dusting, cleaning, and hours of maintenance, no more hot showers, and no access to a fully-equipped modern kitchen.

"¥24,000 a month is a lot of money," Pattie said. "I don't think you and I could afford that. Why wouldn't you let me try to bargain the price down a little? If she's not willing to rent to Japanese tenants, who else can she find to rent the place?"

"Bargaining down the price would be bad faith and bad manners. We were offered this because of my connection with the restaurant. She already gave us a spectacularly low price."

"If you say so. Doesn't your school have connections for places to live?"

"Yes, but you might not want to live in the kind of place we could find through the school. It's mostly single rooms. They're in odd locations and some of them are kind of primitive."

Pattie seemed unconvinced.

"You can't be so passive about it," she said. "You have to try harder. You don't get what you want by not giving it everything you have. Let me talk to people at Honsenke."

Pattie consulted her classmates and her teachers at Honsenke. That finally convinced her that if nothing else, Ohta-san's house was an incredibly good deal.

"How would you feel about sharing the house?" Pattie asked. "The two of us and one more roommate?"

"It's a pretty big house. Sure. That could work . . . with the right person. Do you have someone in mind?"

"One of my classmates at Honsenke. Jeri-Ann Morasky. She's a bit older than we are. She's nice. I think you'll like her. If we split the rent three ways, I think we can manage."

"Where does Jeri-Ann live now?"

"She has a small room somewhere. She doesn't speak Japanese. She doesn't do much besides study tea. I think she's lonely. I think she needs a little more human contact."

"Sure. The three of us then."

I called Ohta-san. I thanked her for her kind offer to rent her house. And I asked her when we could move in.

As a bonus, Mrs. Ohta said if we didn't mind used things, she would let us have some of the old futon sets, *kotatsu*, pots and pans, and kitchen things she had from the house that were in storage and that no one was using. I gratefully accepted the offer.

LIVING IN A LARGE OLD Japanese house was a big change from living in an international student dormitory. As one of a few dozen residents of a dormitory I had settled into a comfortable routine. You saw people going about their business, and you too were somebody also going about your business. Things were in motion and the world was as it should be. In your own room with the door shut you had privacy when you wanted it. If you wanted activity or the presence of others, you could go downstairs and find it. When I was no longer connected to a hive of activity as before, I began to feel a vague sense of unease.

Pattie and Jeri-Ann had busy schedules at the tea ceremony school and were never home during the day. Pattie taught English most weeknights and I worked at the restaurant several nights a week. Jeri-Ann was a quiet, considerate roommate. She kept to herself most of the time. Though we three roommates ate dinner together at least once a week, I had barely spoken three sentences to Jeri-Ann.

Pattie and I had chosen to occupy the upstairs bedroom. Jeri-Ann preferred the small room off of the *genkan*. We left the main master bedroom unoccupied.

Jeri-Ann Morasky was ten years older than Pattie and older than the other women in the Murasaki no Kai, the tea ceremony school for foreigners at Honsenke. She was lean and fit, and at home she dressed in jeans and a simple tank top. She had several small tattoos on her upper arms, all flowers, and a few others that she said you would have to know her better to see. Her natural hair color was somewhere between dark brown and auburn and she wore it boyishly short. She didn't speak much, but when she did, what she said was succinct and to the point; sometimes profound and sometimes just spacy and trippy. She looked more like someone you would meet at a bar frequented by motorcycle gangs than someone who was studying Japanese tea ceremony at Urasenke. I couldn't even begin to imagine her in a kimono.

It wasn't until we'd been living together for a few weeks that I got a chance to actually talk to Jeri-Ann. It was just after dinner. Jeri-Ann had just finished making herself a tuna fish sandwich. Pattie was off somewhere teaching English. I had eaten out at my favorite *chu-ka* restaurant, Osho, near Sanjo Keihan where the *gyoza* and *chahan* dinner went for ¥150. Jeri-Ann invited me to join her in a glass of sparkling *nigori* sake that someone had given her as a present.

Jeri-Ann cracked open the bottle and poured some sake into two little rough but attractive handblown Okinawa glass cups. We clinked cups and drank. The sake was nice. Jeri-Ann looked over at me, expecting me to speak first.

"I have to be honest," I said. "You don't look like a person who would be studying tea ceremony."

Jeri-Ann laughed.

"No, I suppose not. When I'm in class I do my best to look the part. I think I can pull it off. You don't think so?"

"Pattie says you do. I guess Pattie would be mad at me for saying that. Out loud to you, I mean."

"Say whatever you want to. I don't mind."

Jeri-Ann poured us both more sake.

"Nice," I said.

"It's from someone at Honsenke. They only get the good stuff. Nothing but the best."

We drank some more.

"Pattie says you're seriously studying Japanese," Jeri-Ann said. "She says you can even read and write."

"True."

"She also says you don't really approve of the study of the tea ceremony."

"True. I don't really get it. Sorry, but I don't."

"Don't apologize. I agree with you. It's complete bullshit. It's nothing but a business. A rather dishonest business, actually. And I should know."

"Does Pattie know that's what you think?"

"Probably not. I can't tell if she buys into the whole thing or if she just prefers not to think about it. You tell me. You know her better than I do."

"I think she thinks she's doing something . . . something spiritual and culturally valuable. Like Zen. I think she feels that if you're going to be in some kind of a business, you should be in one that's . . . noble, in some way."

Jeri-Ann laughed.

"Oh God," she said. "What bullshit. More sake?"

I held out my glass for a refill.

"So . . . if that's what you think, what are you doing spending all your time studying tea ceremony at Honsenke?"

"Has Pattie mentioned to you that I'm Sen Sosuke's mistress?"

"Sen Sosuke? The head of Honsenke? No. You are?"

"Yes. Pattie hasn't said anything about that?"

"No. How, uh . . . how did *that* happen?"

"Long story. You have time to hear it?"

"We still have another half bottle of *sake* left."

"We do. All right then. I'm originally from a little town just south of San Francisco. I married my high school sweetheart just out of college. I worked as a waitress and put him through medical school. When he became a doctor, we bought a big house and I became a bored suburban housewife. I learned to cook fancy meals for my husband who was almost never home to eat them. I took exercise classes to stay in shape for my husband who was too tired to fuck me when he came home from work. One day my husband came home from his hospital and told me he wanted a divorce. He said he'd fallen in love with one of the nurses at the hospital. He said we were very lucky we had no children. He told me to find a lawyer and he moved out."

"Just like that? That's hard."

"Yes, it was actually. Aside from getting married and raising a family, I had never once thought of doing anything else with my life. I didn't take it very well. But I pulled myself together and got over it, as much as you can get over something like that. I think we all need to have our hearts broken at least once. Or at least we should expect to."

"Everyone?"

"Eternal bliss with that special someone is an illusion. I hope you realize that. Anyway, one of my still happily married friends told me she'd heard from her sister about a brand-new airline company that was hiring stewardesses. International travel seemed like a good idea. I'd never even been out of California. I obviously needed a change. Why not try something different?"

"You were still young. The rest of your life ahead of you. Newly single."

"Yes. Yes I was. And my hair was longer. The airline company was called Air America. You know it?"

"No."

"It flew all over Southeast Asia and only Southeast Asia. Bangkok, Kuala Lumpur, Manila, Saigon, Taipei. Places no girl should go through life without visiting. I had no idea that the airline was actually a front for the CIA. The passengers were very interesting. The pilots were a lot of fun. Exotic locales. Good times. Money. It really was the perfect cure for a bad divorce."

"And?"

"And then it all ended. The war in Vietnam began to wind down. The airline's funding vanished. And that was that. I was in Bangkok when I got the news. The company just shut down one day. They gave us all six months salary and a free plane ticket to anywhere in the world on a real airline. I had never been to Japan. I thought, why not? I cut my hair short. I liked living in the present and letting the future worry about itself. I got a job working as a bar hostess in one of the fancy clubs in the Ginza. We foreign girls are very exotic here. I think the short hair makes me seem even more exotic, don't you think?"

"Very exotic."

"One of the other foreign hostesses also worked as a model sometimes. There was a job in Osaka. They needed another girl. I'd never worn a real kimono. I thought it would be fun. Good money. All expenses paid. A ride on the Bullet Train. The modeling turned out to be boring. But Honsenke had some connection with one of the sponsors and Mr. Sen Sosuke himself was there and asked if he could meet me and take me out to dinner. We went to some *kaiseki* place that was more like a private restaurant. We were both in kimono if you can imagine. Really gorgeous kimonos. The private room we had in the restaurant was beautiful. It opened onto its own little garden. I loved it. I never even went back to Tokyo."

"So . . . you don't really speak Japanese, right?"

"Don't be shy. Go ahead and ask."

"So how do you . . . communicate with each other? Does he speak English?"

"About as little as I speak Japanese. Maybe less."

"So how do you . . . ?"

"I know. You would think it would have ended by now. He likes to take me out and show me off. Which is also kind of funny, because in his position he really can't afford to be seen with a *gaijin* mistress. Especially the same *gaijin* mistress over time. So there are only certain private and exclusive places where we can go together. Some of these lovely old traditional restaurants are set up so you can have sex there. Such amazingly refined places that most people will never see. And he likes to buy me presents. You wouldn't believe some of the things he's given me. The kimonos. I have some of them here. Sometime I'll take them out and show you. I'm afraid to show Pattie the tea bowls. I think it might make her angry."

"Because she doesn't approve of the relationship?"

"I think she'd rather pretend not to know. Maybe she really doesn't know."

"So how exactly do you . . . "

"Keep things interesting? I don't mind talking about it. Not at all. You see, the reason he likes to show me off is so that the people that matter to him, that matter to his organization, won't know that he's gay."

"Sen Sosuke is gay?"

"I suppose technically you would have to say bisexual. But really, gay. He's a very charming man with very refined tastes. I like fucking him because he has a very open and curious attitude about it. He's curious about heterosexual sex and some day he knows he's going to have to marry and produce an heir. He wants to seem experienced when the time comes. We have fun. We do it in such wonderful places. And he can't do this with a Japanese mistress because she might discover that he's gay. Or his mother will, if she doesn't already know. His mother is the real power at Honsenke. So-*chan* is more of a figurehead. Sex with him is a lot more fun than sex with my ex-husband ever was."

"So studying the tea ceremony is for you . . . a kind of pretense?"

"Well, yes and no. There is a certain beauty to it. All the rules and everything are ridiculous. And the mystique around it is pure bullshit. It's a lovely way to spend a day. I do like the discipline. The controlled movements. It's kind of like a little floor ballet with hot liquids and sometimes food. And it allows me to stay in Kyoto. I love Kyoto. Don't you?"

"Yes. I do. Very much. But it sounds like you're seeing parts of it that most of us will never see."

"I suppose. But that's part of the beauty of Kyoto. There are lots of places here that most of us will never see. These places have existed in one form or another for centuries. Really Japanese places. It's part of the thrill of living here. As *gaijin* living here some of us see places that most Japanese will never see. It's too bad in a way. We should remember that and treasure the things we get to see and do here. These private restaurants I've been to . . . every single thing in them is perfect. The sounds, the aromas, the textures, the way the food is presented and served. The tastes. The way everyone wordlessly and gracefully clears out and gives you your privacy when they sense the customers want to have sex. Every single thing in the room and everything that happens in the room feels like a scene in an opera. Feels deliciously perfect."

"Like what tea ceremony is supposed to be."

"Well maybe. Maybe tea ceremony is a more austere version of it.

So many rules. I mean, you might just as well have a sake ceremony or an oyster ceremony. Or a sex ceremony. Imagine. These rooms in the private restaurants are so precious. You've just had a wonderful, simple meal where everything was perfect. You've been drinking sake. You've had sex. You stretch out an arm and slide open the *shoji* door. Outside is a perfect little garden with a stone lantern in it. The lantern is lit! A two-hundred-year-old lantern with a candle in it that's lit. And there's a tiny pond with *koi* in it. The night air sweeps in and there's the scent of flowers. The moon is reflected in the pond. Insects are chirping. It's a fleeting moment of pure joy."

"I think you've just summed up all of Japanese poetry."

"Have I? Well that's actually what it's like. See, they've made the poetry real. For anyone wealthy or powerful enough to afford it. If you have the money, they can create a poem for you that you can spend time inhabiting. It's addictive. Sometimes So-*chan* and I make an overnight trip to someplace just to see a certain kind of flower in bloom. Or not even see it, but just smell it out the window of our room."

"You wear your expensive kimonos to these dinners?"

"Oh yes. It's dress-up. That's part of it."

"And what does he wear?"

"Kimono of course. Very stunning. The head of Honsenke is expected to wear kimono in public. If he's feeling more low key and doesn't expect to be seen, he wears one of his tailor-made Italian suits."

"And the mother who runs Honsenke? She doesn't mind him doing this with you?"

"I'm sure she hates my guts. She's good about not showing it when people are around. She may be happy he's learning about sex with someone who won't make any claims on him. I have no doubt she already knows exactly how and when she will get rid of me. As soon as she decides who to marry him to. I spend enough time with him that I see things that I shouldn't. I don't speak Japanese, so I never really know what's going on. But even still I know things about the company's business dealings that I shouldn't."

"Like what?"

"Well, a couple of weeks ago he was on TV protesting a development in the south of Kyoto that's going to destroy some traditional neighborhoods there. He likes to play the champion of Kyoto traditions, but I know that Honsenke is actually one of the silent partners in the same development he went on TV to protest. He was looking at the plans in his chauffeur-driven limousine on the way to one of our restaurants once and he showed me."

"Have you told Pattie?"

"No, and you shouldn't either."

"Isn't it a bad idea for you and I to have secrets from Pattie?"

Jeri-Ann fixed me with an indulgent look.

"Look, I'm now a person who says what she thinks. I wasn't always. But I am now. You seem to be a straightforward person. Someone who appreciates frankness. You wouldn't want me to bullshit you, right?"

"No."

"It's up to you what you tell Pattie. But if you repeat all of our conversations she won't be happy about your talking to me. I like talking to you and I wouldn't want her to object to our being friends. I like Pattie well enough, but I don't agree with most of the things she believes in. Since I like you, I assume your relationship must be mostly sexual. I can respect that."

I laughed. Pattie and I hadn't had sex since we moved into the old Japanese house. There was something about the house that bothered Pattie and had turned her frigid when it came to sex. I wondered if Jeri-Ann knew that.

We finished the bottle of *nigori* sake.

"I'm also studying the *ichigen koto* with a teacher in Tokyo," Jeri-Ann said. Do you know the instrument?"

"Not really. Is it a *koto* with only one string?"

"Yes. A very classical kind of Japanese music. I have to take the *shinkansen* to Tokyo once a week. It's very Zen. I love it. I love the teacher and spending the afternoon with her. She's eighty-five years old. Even with my generous stipend from Urasenke, it's stupidly expensive to go all the way to Tokyo for that. But these days it's what I live for. That and fucking Mr. Sen in beautiful places."

"I see."

"So what about you? What *are* you doing with someone like Pattie? She's certainly very pretty. And smart. But you strike me as a little too laid-back for her, and she strikes me as a little too ambitious for you. It's none of my business, but I think you should find a better girlfriend. Don't look at me like that. I'm not propositioning you. You can relax. I don't mean me. You don't have to answer. Just think about it."

—

THE CONVERSATION WITH JERI-ANN AND her opinion of my relationship with Pattie had surprised me. Though Pattie and I didn't exactly see eye-to-eye on everything, I didn't think our relationship was just about sex. Especially since once we'd moved into the old house we hadn't been having much sex. Pattie was uncomfortable in the large, open tatami room upstairs where we slept. I loved its two walls of windows with its views out onto the sea of gray-tiled roofs and into the back yards of the neighborhood. The view at different times of the day, in different light and in different weather, was endlessly fascinating and quintessentially Kyoto. Pattie said that being in the room made her feel cold and exposed, as if she were on display.

Schools in Japan had a break between end of term in March and the beginning of April. Both my language school and Pattie's Murasaki no Kai were off for a week, and Pattie wanted to travel to the Inland Sea island of Shikoku to visit a famous *washi* paper maker. Her enthusiasm for Japanese traditional crafts was something we shared.

The trip seemed like a great idea to me, especially because it would afford us the chance to stay for at least one night in a traditional Japanese *ryokan*. The average Japanese *ryokan*, even the really good ones, may not have been poetry made real, but they were absolutely perfect for a romantic get-away.

On day one of our spring vacation, Pattie and I got up early and took a train to Kurashiki. We visited the *mingei* museum and looked at Japanese folk pottery, paper, and fabrics. Then we took a train to the port of Okayama and boarded a ferry to Takamatsu. We managed to take in the garden in Takamatsu for which the city is famous, but barely had time to see it before we were kicked out when the garden closed for the day. I'd gone down to the Japan Tourist Bureau at Kyoto Station to make a reservation at a *ryokan*. The woman in the JTB information kiosk convinced me that the inn at Tokushima was a very good deal. We were headed to Kochi in the west central part of the island, so Tokushima would be out of the way. But the JTB lady had said it was definitely worth the detour.

Pattie wasn't happy about the extra train travel. But she changed her mind when she saw the inn. It was by the sea and very beautiful, although we arrived too late to really see it .

The women in kimono who welcomed us to the inn were attentive and full of useful information. We were shown to our room, which was beautiful and large. It had its own *genkan* with slippers for us all laid out. It had its own attractive bathroom with a small wooden tub and a shower. It had two large, picture-postcard-perfect tatami rooms, one with a low table for sitting and one in the back for sleeping. Both rooms had views of ancient pine trees and the sea, or would have in the morning.

One of the kimono women came in with a pot of tea and some cups on a tray and cookies. We sat and sipped the tea and ate the cookies as she explained the routines of the inn.

"Normally our guests relax a bit, stroll around the grounds or down to the beach, and then come back here to relax. Then they change into *yukata*. We have these for you in the sleeping room. Then a visit to our hot springs bath downstairs. While the guests are in the bath, we bring up dinner and arrange it here on the table, and we make up the futon in the sleeping room."

"That sounds perfect," I said.

"Yes, but because it's very late, the baths may be finished already. I have to check."

"Finished?"

"We drain the baths every night and clean them so they will be ready for bathing the next morning."

The woman in kimono went over to a phone in the room that was sitting on a small table in the corner. After a brief conversation, she came back and reported the status of the baths.

"We have three hot springs baths in the inn. One is for men, one is for women, and one is for families and mixed bathing. The men's bath and the women's bath are closed. But the mixed bathing bath is still open. Would you like to go down now and bathe?"

I looked over at Pattie and realized that I had forgotten to translate any of the conversation. I summarized what the woman had said.

"I would love a bath," Pattie said. "But mixed bathing? I don't think so."

I told the kimono lady what Pattie had said.

"Oh, I don't think you should worry about anyone else using the bath tonight," she said. "All of our guests have already bathed. I'm very sure you will be the only ones using the bath. It's normally closed at this hour, so the other guests wouldn't expect it to be open."

I translated for Pattie. She looked skeptical. She looked at the kimono woman who radiated encouragement.

"I could really use a bath," Pattie said.

"Then let's go," I said.

We went into the bedroom and changed into the inn's *yukata*. The soft blue-and-white cotton robes were of very good quality and had the inn's logo artistically inserted into the design. The kimono woman waited for us while we changed, and when we came out she led us downstairs to the baths.

The first door we came to had its oversized *noren* banner folded. A sign under it said "closed." The door next to it had a *noren* that said "man." Also with a "closed" sign under it. The third door had its *noren* down and there was no "closed" sign. The characters on the *noren* said "family bath."

The kimono woman asked if we knew how the Japanese bath worked. We assured her that we did. But, taking no chances, she made sure that we understood about not getting any soap in the bath itself. Once she was sure there would be no unauthorized use of soap, the kimono woman left us to the bath.

"We're not idiots," Pattie said. "Why do they think we wouldn't understand about the bath? You speak Japanese and we've both obviously lived here for a while. We're not tourists."

"Prior experience maybe. Who knows what we unpredictable *gaijin* might get up to if not properly monitored and instructed?"

Along with the *yukata* in the room we had been issued two small white towels. Each towel was about twice the size of a small washcloth. We had brought them with us down to the bath. We had wanted to go into our bags and get toothbrushes, hairbrushes, and combs, but the kimono lady assured us we would find all those things along with soap and shampoo in the bath.

"Are these little towels what we're supposed to use to dry off after the bath?" Pattie asked. "They're so small."

"I'm sure we'll find more towels down in the changing room," I said.

I was right. In the changing room there was a stack of towels. Each one was about half the size of the small towels we had brought with us.

"I guess we're supposed to air dry," Pattie said.

"Yeah," I said. "That is how it's done in the public baths. I thought a fancy *ryokan* might have bigger towels."

We took off our *yukata* and folded them into the baskets we found on shelves in the changing room. Then, naked, we each took one of the little towels from the stack on the way into the bath. Pattie had her towel from the room with her and I told her she was probably supposed to leave it in the changing room to dry off with later. She thanked me for the advice and said she was taking it in with her.

The hot springs bath was a thing of beauty. Its tiled walls had painted scenes of pine trees and waves crashing against cliffs. The bath itself was long and shallow at the front, and belly-button-deep toward the end. Boulders decorated the sides of the bath and a mound of them marked the place where steaming hot water gurgled up from below. The boulders gave the bath a natural, outdoorsy feel. One wall was all glass and probably looked out to an ocean view, but it was too dark outside to see it. Steam rose gently from the bath and imparted a mildly sulfurous aroma to the room.

Pattie went quickly over to one of the showers, turned on the water and started showering. I did the same. We finished soaping up and rinsed off thoroughly. Then we edged ourselves into the steaming bath. The water was hot enough, but not scalding. If the source was actually natural, as the kimono lady had assured us it was, nature had gotten the temperature perfectly right for human bathing.

Pattie made herself comfortable in a corner at the far end of the bath. She folded her arms in front of her and rested her chin on them at edge of the pool and stared out into the darkness through the steamed-up windows. Her smooth white legs drifted to the surface and she kicked them gently to keep them afloat. I sat next to her with my back against the wall of the pool, the water lapping at my chin.

After a while Pattie pushed off from the wall, executed a graceful 180° full-body swivel and ended up in my lap.

"Mm, it's so nice here," Pattie said. "But I wish we'd got here earlier. I bet the view of the sea out those windows is terrific during the day. We should come back in the morning."

"We should, but when we come back we won't be able to enjoy it together. You'll be in the women's bath and I'll be in the men's bath."

Pattie laughed.

"I forgot," she said. "I suppose the little bath in our room won't have a view."

"This is the only view I'm interested in," I said looking at her.

Pattie came off my lap and arranged herself next to me on the floor of the pool. Then she pivoted and pressed herself against me and we kissed. I luxuriated in the feel of the slippery, wet, curves of her body.

As we were kissing and fondling in what we had assumed was our private bath, two ten-year-old Japanese boys, barefoot but with their clothes on, came rushing in. Each boy had a large squirt gun in the shape of a ray gun. They were chasing each other around the bath and trying to squirt each other with the ray guns.

Pattie and I froze where we were. It was a few minutes before the boys noticed that they were not alone. Then they froze in place. Each of their mouths formed a large O. For fifteen or twenty seconds they just stood in shocked silence staring at the alien beings in the bath. Then they ran out of the room.

Pattie and I exhaled, laughed, and then went back to our aquatic foreplay.

It was less than ten minutes before the first of the young fathers decided to come in for a second bath. Altogether, five fathers came in for an additional evening bath.

At first the Japanese men congregated at the opposite end of the bath from where Pattie and I were. Pattie was mortified. She had her little towel from the room with her and she tried, with not a lot of success, to cover herself with it.

One of the men ventured nearer and began to engage *me* in ordinary travel conversation. From where? Staying how long? Leaving when? Planning to see what else? He seemed to be making an effort not to be looking at the naked blond female in the corner, but his eyes wandered after every question.

The other men came over and were also making a pretense of wanting to talk to me, and not just being there to ogle the naked blond *gaijin*. Pattie meanwhile was edging back along the side of the pool toward the exit and desperately trying to cover herself with the tiny towel. I handed her my little washcloth towel to give her a little more cover. She snatched if from me, but it didn't really make a lot of difference.

As the men continued to pretend to engage me in conversation, Pattie made her escape back into the changing room. As she emerged from the pool and rushed toward the exit as quickly she could without slipping on the wet floor and breaking her neck, the men stopped pretending and turned to watch her go. They were treated to a view of her naked backside in full retreat.

I looked at the men standing around me in the bath. They were all in their mid-thirties. In good shape. Not old at all. They were still asking me questions when I turned to join Pattie in the changing room. By now she'd had time to change back into her *yukata*. I ignored the questions. There didn't seem any reason to go along with their pretense.

Back in the room Pattie didn't seem to be angry or upset about the way our bath had been interrupted.

"Tomorrow morning I'm definitely going for a bath," Pattie said. "Their wives should have a chance to see what all the fuss was about."

The meal was brought into our room by a small army of kimono ladies. It contained every single type of seafood native to Tokushima, raw, boiled, broiled, steamed, stuffed, filleted, whole, in the shell, out of the shell, cut into pieces, custardized, puréed, or deep fried. The meal came with a large bottle of beer for each of us and two little beakers of sake. Everything was very, very good, and Pattie and I managed to eat and drink all of it.

The kimono ladies had laid out our sleeping *futon* in the sleeping room while we were in the bath. When we finished eating, we retreated to the bedroom and slid the *fusuma* doors closed behind us. The kimono ladies came back and we could hear them in the next room quietly and discreetly clearing away the things from dinner. Once they were gone, Pattie and I nestled between the crisp cotton sheets of our double *futon* bed and got down to enthusiastic and altogether satisfying *ryokan* sex.

—

THE NEXT DAY AFTER BREAKFAST in one of the inn's common rooms we caught a train to Tsukuda where we would change to a train for Kochi. When we traveled, Pattie spent her time reading books about Zen Buddhism. I spent my time looking out the train window and taking pictures with my beat-up Asahi Pentax SLR, their first model to incorporate a light meter into the camera.

Tsukuda was a transfer stop in the middle of nowhere. We had a forty-five-minute wait there for the train to Kochi. While Pattie read, I wandered to the edge of the platform and watched a group of men working on the side of the tracks about a hundred yards away. One of the men stood up and watched me watching him. Then he began to walk toward me.

The man was in his late fifties or early sixties. He was dressed in a standard-issue Japanese National Railways workman's jumpsuit. When he reached me, he removed his standard-issue JNR safety helmet.

"American?" he asked in an accent that was neither Kansai nor Kanto.

"Yes." I said.

"We don't see many Americans here," the man said. "Not much to see here. Not like in Takamatsu or Tokushima. Where else have you been?"

"We live in Kyoto."

"Studying Japanese?"

"Yes."

"I'm from Hiroshima. Originally. Have you been there?"

"No. This is the furthest west I've been so far."

"You should visit Hiroshima. It was very beautiful once. I was a soldier in the war when they dropped the atomic bomb. I was stationed in Malaysia. When I came back my family and my relatives and everyone I knew were killed by the *genshibaku*. Every place I knew was destroyed. I came here. I wasn't there when the bomb was dropped. I don't qualify as a *hibakusha*. Not officially a victim."

"I'm very sorry to hear it. It must have been a very terrible thing to see."

"Yes, it was. Of course we did very bad things too. The Japanese Army. I was a soldier. I saw the things we did. I don't blame Americans. War is a terrible thing. I just wanted to tell you that. Where are you headed to now? To Kochi?"

"Yes. We're visiting a famous Japanese *washi* paper maker there."

"*Washi*? All the way from Kyoto to visit a Japanese *washi* maker?"

"Yes."

The man put on his bright yellow helmet and extended a hand for me to shake. I shook hands with him. Then he turned and walked away.

"What was that about?" Pattie wanted to know.

"A man from Hiroshima," I said. "He just wanted to let us know he doesn't blame us for the atom bomb."

When Pattie and I reached Kochi and got off the train, people were looking at us like we were visitors from another planet. There were no kiosks with pretty young women in blue uniforms to provide information. When I tried to ask directions, the reaction I got was one of stunned silence. People gathered around to watch us if we stopped to try to talk to someone. Old women cautiously approached Pattie and touched her hair.

At one point, surrounded by a crowd of stunned mutes, an elderly gentleman stepped forward and extracted us from the gawkers.

"They don't see so many foreign peoples here," the man said in English. "They are not used to foreign peoples and don't know the proper way they should behave. Where do you wish to go?"

I took out the slip of paper I had with the name and address of the famous paper maker and showed it to the elderly gentleman.

"Oh," the man said. "This paper is written in the Japanese language. Are you able to read it?"

"Yes," I said. "I can read it, but I don't know where this place is or how to get there."

"Oh!" he said, "then you can speak some Japanese language. My English is very poor. May we speak in Japanese?"

I said OK, and the man told me that the address on the paper was in a remote suburb of the city. He said the only way to get there was by bus, and that busses to that part of town were very infrequent. Then he led us to the place where we could get the bus as I explained to Pattie what the man had said.

At the bus stop the man checked the bus schedule.

"You are very lucky," the man said, "there will be a bus in fifteen minutes. How long are you planning to stay at the address which you have shown me?"

"He's a famous maker of *washi* paper," I said. "We just plan to stay a few hours at most and then come back here to catch a train back to Tokushima."

"I see," the man said. "Then there may be a problem. The last bus of the day leaves from there just over an hour after you arrive. Is the person you mentioned expecting your visit?"

"No," I said. "We were just planning to drop in unannounced."

"I see," the man said. "Perhaps I had better accompany you."

On the bus ride out of Kochi, Pattie and the old gentlemen carried on a very painfully slow conversation in English. Pattie had a great deal of patience for that kind of conversation. I spent the time looking out the window at the scenery. Whatever it was the old gentleman had planned for the day, he had dropped it out of concern that we would not be able to find the famous paper maker, and that we would not be able to find our way back to Kochi.

We got off the bus in a rural area surrounded by dusty farmers' fields. The old gentleman asked for directions and eventually we found the house of the famous paper maker. Everyone who was asked for directions expressed surprise that anyone would be looking for the paper maker's house. By the time we reached the house we were trailing a small gang of children and a few teenaged boys who seemed awed by the personage of a blond American female.

The famous paper maker's wife answered the door and eyed the backpack-toting *gaijin* and the old Japanese gentleman warily. She seemed very surprised that anyone would come all the way to Kochi to visit her husband. Possibly she thought we meant to stay overnight. When she eventually invited us in, the old gentleman said he would be going. I reminded him that it might be a long wait for the next bus, but he said, unconvincingly, that he had someplace to be and that he had better get going. I thanked him for bringing us to the paper maker. We shook hands, and he left.

The paper maker's wife went to get her husband. When the man himself came in, he looked as if he had just been dragged out of bed. His long salt-and-pepper hair was uncombed and he badly needed a shave. When I explained why we had come, the man seemed perplexed that anyone would travel, unannounced, all the way to Kochi to meet him.

The wife came in with tea. We sat on the tatami floor and sipped tea.

Pattie explained how she had heard of the paper maker and why she had wanted to come and see him in person. I translated. The man continued to look perplexed. Pattie asked if he had examples of his paper or things he had made from his paper to show her and which she might buy. I did my best to try and make this sound less abrupt and less commercial.

The man said he didn't have anything. He said that everything he made was shipped to a *mingei* store in Kyoto where it was sold. The wife interrupted to say that she might be able to find a few items. The man said he was just finishing some paper now, and would we like to come down and see how it was made? We said yes.

The paper maker's workshop took up what in most houses would have been the garage. Along one wall were three enormous sinks. Perched on the sinks were large wooden frames. The frames had mesh bottoms for draining water. In the middle of the room was a very long table, on top of which were more of the wooden frames.

The paper maker explained how he hiked in the nearby woodlands and collected certain local plants from which the paper was made. The plant material was then mashed and soaked and mashed and soaked repeatedly until its fibrous material began to decompose. Then it was mixed with a kind of paste, the contents of which were secret. The resulting mash was then poured into a frame and left in the sun to dry. Any color the paper took on was from the plants themselves. No artificial dyes or anything artificial was used in the process.

We saw some of the nearly finished paper drying in the sun. It was a very rough kind of paper, with bits and pieces of the plant matter still visible in the final product. It was not the kind of *washi* that colorful little sewing boxes or things like that could be made from.

When we went back into the house we saw a few of the man's paper products laid out on the tatami floor. There were about a dozen sheets of the paper, a basket made from *washi*, and three little dolls, also made from *washi*.

Pattie asked the wife, "How much?" in Japanese, and the woman winced just perceptibly at the bluntness of the question.

The paper maker said, oh no, since we had traveled all the way from Kyoto, he would make us a present of the items. I asked him to please allow us to pay for them. I said he had been generous with his time and we had been very rude to arrive unannounced.

The wife said she would take ¥2,000 and I quickly handed her the money.

She said she would bring in more tea.

I thanked her and her husband again for their generosity. I apologized and said we were very sorry but that we didn't realize there would be so few busses, and we had to catch the last bus back to Kochi. Everyone stood up. We all bowed. And then Pattie and I left.

The army of children picked us up again on the way to the bus stop and waited with us until the bus came. They watched us get on the bus, and when the bus pulled away they waved to us and ran alongside the bus for a while. Pattie opened the bus window. She leaned out and waved back at them until they were out of sight.

We got back to Kochi and caught a train to Awa-Ikeda, and then one from Awa-Ikeda to Naruto. We were fortunate in the timing and the transfer was smooth and easy. We arrived at Naruto in the early evening and found a cheap business hotel. Then we dumped our bags and went outside to walk around. The bare-bones cheap hotel gave us an even greater appreciation for the *ryokan* at Tokushima.

In the early morning Pattie and I walked to the port and found the ferry to Awaji Shima. I had insisted that we go back by this route. I had always wanted to see the famous Naruto Whirlpool between Shikoku and Awaji Island. It's depicted in some famous Edo-period woodblock prints. Once in Tokyo I had seen a performance of Awaji Island's famous puppet theater, the Awaji Ningyo. Awaji Shima was off the beaten path and inconvenient to public transportation. But we were in the area and I thought we should see the island.

At the ferry terminal I bought two tickets. We then had to wait to see which of the ferry boats would be making the crossing. It seemed to depend on how many passengers there were. Tethered to the dock were a large ferry boat, two medium-sized ferry boats, and a small ferry boat. The large boat had space to take cars on board.

The medium-sized boat had two decks and took passengers only. The small boat was more like a large fishing boat and didn't seem much like a commercial ferry boat at all. When it was time to depart, Pattie and I and ten other people were ushered onto the smallest boat.

There was an inside cabin where the passengers stowed their luggage. One or two of the people elected to make the trip sitting in the cabin. The rest of us arranged ourselves outside on the strip of wooden deck that ran from the middle of the boat to the stern on either side of the boat. The more experienced passengers had already claimed the more comfortable outdoor space at the stern. The boat was steered by a muscular man from a spot on the roof of the cabin toward the rear of the boat. Altogether there were three crewmen on the boat.

It was a lovely gray morning with a good breeze. There had been a very bad storm about a week earlier. Fifteen minutes into our trip we came upon the wreck of an enormous freighter. The ship's bridge and a forest of navigational antennae came into view as we approached the sunken ship. The sight of this gigantic dead ship in the water was truly horrifying. More so because we knew this was something that had happened only a week ago.

The ferry's skipper brought us very close to the wrecked ship. Just beyond it was the whirlpool itself. The whirlpool looked every bit like a comic-book depiction of a whirlpool. It was very large, and it was made up of distinct rings. The outer rings were swirling inward at a leisurely pace. The middle rings were moving faster. The water in the inner rings was moving faster still. And at the very center of the whirlpool the water was roiling and boiling and roaring downward like the inner spout of a tornado.

The ferry veered away from the whirlpool but headed for its outermost ring. When it reached the outer ring, an astonishing thing happened. The ferry boat captain shut off the boat's engines. The passengers all paused mid-conversation and went silent. The quiet was punctuated only by the sounds of a gentle morning sea breeze.

Several gulls wheeling overhead commented dryly from above. The bridge of the wrecked freighter loomed ominously across the vortex. As the boat silently began circling the whirlpool and gaining speed, the sucking, churning sound of sea water racing toward the middle of the whirlpool grew louder. I looked up at the ferryboat captain and saw a very big grin spread across his weathered face.

Pattie's fingers dug into my arm.

"I don't think this is supposed to be happening," she said.

I looked around at the other passengers. All of them were old people and looked like farmers. Pattie and I were the only tourists. Half of the other passengers looked mildly worried and the other half looked mildly amused. No one looked like they thought we were on the doorstep of death. I looked back up at the captain. He was still smiling.

"I think he's doing it on purpose," I said. "He doesn't look worried. None of the other passengers look too worried."

"Asians believe in karma," Pattie said. "They accept their fate. They never look worried."

The boat began to pick up speed and circle around the whirlpool like a child's boat in a bathtub with the drain plug pulled. Bit by bit we were getting closer to the center. The boat continued like this for what seemed like a very long time. I kept checking back on the other passengers and the captain. Some of the other passengers were also checking on the captain. No one spoke. Everyone watched the whirlpool and the bridge of the massive sunken freighter beyond.

Pattie's fingernails dug deeper into my arm.

When we hit the middle rings of the whirlpool the boat really began to pick up speed. That was when the captain turned the engines back on and gave it full throttle. The boat lurched a little and strained against the current at first. But the timing of its thrust had been perfect and the boat rode the current's arching momentum away from the whirlpool and out toward the calmer waters around Awaji Shima.

"That was exciting," I said.

"Admit it. You were just as frightened as I was," Pattie said.

"The captain seemed to know what he was doing. The guy must have done that a thousand times. For all we know, that's what they have to do to get across."

"I doubt that."

"Well, maybe not. Maybe it's an old salt's thing. Or a local traditional thing for boat captains. In Spain they have bullfighting to demonstrate their manliness. Here they have whirlpool baiting. Anyway, we saw the famous whirlpool. It was pretty awesome and I'm glad we did it."

There was almost nothing at the place where the boat docked on Awaji Shima. Besides the ferry terminal there was a large barn-like structure where you could watch performances of the Awaji Ningyo puppet theater, the one thing for which Awaji was famous. It was very much like the more well-known Bunraku puppet theater. Awaji's puppets were larger and the costumes they wore were a little less refined. There were no performances on the day Pattie and I arrived on Awaji Shima.

This was just as well, because we had less than a half hour to catch the next bus to the eastern end of the island where we would get a ferry to Kobe. We spent our time until the bus came, exploring the Awaji Ningyo barn. There was a selection of the theater's puppets on display and an exhibit showing how the puppets were made. There was a souvenir stand that was open. It sold various Awaji Ningyo merchandise and some other local products that Awaji Island claimed to be famous for. Pattie and I bought grape juice and rice balls for the bus trip which would take just under two hours.

When we got back to the ferry and bus terminal I discovered that I'd made a mistake. I had assumed that the only passengers would be the people from the ferry we had arrived on. But other passengers had materialized from somewhere, and not only was the bus already full, but some of the passengers were standing.

"Should we get the next bus?" Pattie said.

"The next bus isn't for another two hours."

"I don't want to wait here for another two hours. Let's get on. Maybe I can use my feminine charm to get us a seat."

"Maybe the bus stops along the way and some people will get off."

We got on the bus. Pattie smiled brightly at the seated passengers. The driver closed the bus door and we were off.

Most of the passengers seemed to be farmers. Some of the younger male passengers were dressed in suits and might have been businessmen or traveling salesmen. No one looked at all sympathetic or even interested in *gaijin*. No one offered Pattie a seat.

After a half hour of standing, Pattie said she was feeling sick. Her face was an unusual shade of green and she did not look well. I made my appeal for a seat for the American woman who was feeling sick. There were no takers. Not only that, but hardly anyone bothered to look away in embarrassment. They just watched us, their faces stone cold.

"I really am sick," Pattie said. "No joke. I think I might pass out. Try again, please."

I made another appeal for the sick American woman. No one offered a seat. And then Pattie collapsed onto the floor of the bus. Some of the people who were standing squeezed further into the back of the bus and made room for her on the floor. The bus driver glanced over his shoulder to see what was happening, hesitated for a moment, but then kept on driving down the narrow highway. The young men in suits who were seated broke off eye contact. Some of the old women clucked and fretted a little. Most of the other passengers just looked on with cold, stony faces.

Pattie made the rest of the trip curled up on the floor of the bus and moaning. I knelt next to her holding her hand. She really was very sick.

"What kind of people are these?" Pattie moaned. "How can they just sit there and not offer to help?"

I made one last appeal, but no one offered a seat. When the bus reached its destination, some of the passengers immediately pushed past us, nearly stomping on Pattie's head in their rush to get off the bus. Other passengers were more considerate, and two of the old ladies even tried to help Pattie up from the floor. But Pattie was too angry to let them and didn't want to be touched. She slapped away their hands. I helped her off the bus. We found a bench and sat.

"I think I just need some air," Pattie said. "Maybe we can walk around a little. I don't think I can face another ferry ride just now."

The ferry terminal for the boat to Kobe was again in the middle of nowhere. It was like a big train station with nothing else around it. The only thing for sale in the terminal's vending machines was beer. It did seem to be true that no one went out of their way to visit Awaji Shima. From what I had been able to see out of the windows of the bus, it was a very flat, uninteresting place given over mostly to farming and fishing.

Pattie soldiered through the short, uneventful ferry ride to Kobe. She cheered up when we found one of the Western-style bakeries Kobe was famous for. We had tea and cake and bought sandwiches for the train ride back to Kyoto. The sandwiches were really delicious.

A NEW GUY WAS ADMITTED to Pattie's meditation group at Daitoku-ji. His name was Ed. When I had asked if I could join the group Pattie had said it was full and that they would not be admitting new members, especially new *gaijin* members.

Ed had graduated Princeton with a degree in physics. After a year of graduate school at Harvard and an MS in rocket science, he transferred into the Harvard Business School. He parlayed his Harvard MBA into a job at McKinsey & Company, the preeminent worldwide management consulting firm. He worked at McKinsey in New York for a year, McKinsey in Tokyo for another year, and then dropped out of the commercial world to move to Kyoto for a life of meditation and spiritual discovery.

Pattie didn't consult with Jeri-Ann, our other roommate, or me, in advance, but rather informed us that Ed would be living with us. Ed had a quiet, Southern charm. He was from Virginia and from old money. Ed and Pattie bonded over their Zen experiences and soon Pattie was spending much more time with Ed than she was with me. I saw her at night in bed and that was about it. Ed had the big bedroom downstairs off the garden that we had left unused.

One day I was meeting Pattie at Sanjo to go out for dinner. We had arranged to meet at five p.m. at the midpoint of the Sanjo Ohashi bridge. It was where couples in Kyoto usually met up.

I arrived at about a quarter to five and stood on the bridge watching the ceaseless flow of the Kamogawa river. Though all of the water in the river flowing past just then was that day's water, the river itself was eternal. That was something written down for posterity by the twelfth-century Japanese poet Kamo no Chomei who lived in a little hut somewhere after being kicked out of a job as an imperial functionary.

The lovely twilight view of the distant Mt. Hiei to the north was possibly not much changed from the days of Kamo no Chomei. Lavender and rose hues flushed appealingly on the undersides of the strips of cloud that wreathed the purple mountain's peak. Stray beams of fading sunlight scattered little sparkles over the Kamogawa's rushing waters. The lights in nearby shops and restaurants were just beginning to come on.

As the sky began to darken, couples met up on the bridge and wandered down to take seats in the shadows on the concrete abutments that lined either side of the river. The seated couples somehow maintained precisely the same distance between themselves and the adjacent couples all the way down the river. The precision and exactness of their spacing seemed both unnatural and a mild rebuke to the river's original wildness.

Then it got really dark and Pattie had still failed to materialize. I had pretty much used up the observations that had kept me amused for more than an hour: observations of the sky, the river, the water in the river, the magnificent white herons that fished on the river and no one seemed to notice, and the evenly spaced couples seated along the river. In those days when your date failed to show up, you had two choices. You could stand there and continue to wait. Or you could leave. I knew I should have chosen the latter. But I chose the former.

In all, I waited on the bridge for about two hours. Then Pattie arrived. She was with a tall, good-looking guy whom I had never seen before. Someone she had just met. Someone who was in Kyoto studying karate and who meditated at Daitoku-ji in a different group in a different sub-temple than the one where she meditated. They had stopped at a nearby bar for a drink. Was she really very late? Sorry. They had simply lost track of the time.

That happened a second time, and then a third, but not with the same guy. About a week after the third time, I was informed by Pattie that she and Ed had decided that it would be best if I moved out and found my own place. There was nothing going on between her and Ed, she said, or for that matter, between her and anyone else. But my unreasonable jealousy was casting a pall of bad vibrations over the whole house, and it would be better for everyone if I moved out. Jeri-Ann spoke up to disagree, but we were outvoted two to two.

And so, Pattie and I were no longer a thing. Like Kamo no Chomei, I was cast out to discover my own Ten Foot Square Hut.

Bamboo and Stone

MY FRIEND PETER FRANKS HAD lived in Kyoto for just over two years. Peter held the most coveted English conversation teaching job in all of western Japan: the Thursday night English-conversation class at the Asahi Chemical Company in Osaka. When Peter was finally making plans to leave Japan and return home to Australia, he passed this teaching job on to me.

The English class at Asahi Chemical was in itself unremarkable. It was a company-sponsored class for employees that lasted two hours. There were twenty-five to thirty indifferent students in the class, both male and female. Though the class was not much fun to teach, it paid extremely well. The real bonus came after the class was over. For some unknown or long-forgotten reason, the job at Asahi Chemical included a private session afterward with the president of a distantly related company, Kansai Paint. This private session was conducted not in a classroom but in a series of small hard-to-find Japanese restaurants and private hostess bars scattered throughout the Dotonbori section of Osaka.

Every Thursday I would take the tram from Hi no Oka to the Sanjo Keihan train station and catch the 4:36 p.m. Special Limited Tokyu Express to Yodoyabashi Station in Osaka. This train had comfortable forward-facing seats and live-feed TV. You didn't even have to pay extra to ride it. The train originated at Sanjo Keihan so I always got a seat.

The train followed a route that made just sitting and looking out the window worthwhile. It emerged from the crowded working-class neighborhoods of southern Kyoto into a narrow strip of lush green rice fields bordered by low mountains draped in a purple haze. Notable Shinto shrines and Buddhist temples could be glimpsed along the way as the train zipped by.

Just before reaching the commercial center of Osaka, the train passed through a tangle of residential suburbs, pulled up alongside Osaka Castle, an iconic remnant of feudal Japan, and then plunged underground for its final stop. For the hour it took to reach Osaka, if simply sitting and studying the scenery weren't enough, you could read a book, or watch a baseball game on the train's TV monitor. The train was fast and comfortable, and it was always on time.

After exiting the underground Yodoyabashi train station I would pause to look at the big city's reflected lights in the murky Yodogawa river. While Kyoto's river, the Kamogawa, was fast-moving, clear, and shallow, Osaka's river was slow, deep, and heavily polluted. The big city's lights looked all the more bright and colorful reflected in the river's oily black waters. Their undulating patterns swirled and shimmered as the river flowed leisurely out toward the sea.

Having meditated on the lights and colors reflected in the river, and how the water in the river on this Thursday was not the water in the river of last Thursday, while the steel and concrete buildings along its banks were probably the same ones of Thursday last, I headed over to the Asahi Chemical Building a few blocks away.

The subject of the class I taught was English conversation. It was an advanced class that had been running for some time. The mostly male engineers were reluctant to speak. English sentences were extracted from them only gradually and painfully. What they had to say when they managed to say it was predictable, dull, and boring. The two hours of class time passed very, very slowly.

The few females in the class were better at talking but they seldom did, allowing the men in the class to have their say before any of them spoke. The women were being careful not to appear smarter or more competent than their male counterparts. The men wore business suits. The women dressed in the kind of blue OL ("Office Lady") uniforms that women working in large Japanese corporations were required to wear. The women in the class were all trained and qualified as engineers, and on paper they held the same jobs as the men. But the women, in addition to the jobs they were trained and hired for, were required to serve tea, clean the common room where the tea was made, and neaten up the men's desks at the close of the workday. They were also paid less than the men for doing the same jobs.

None of this was unusual in a Japanese company. The surprise for me was that everyone was comfortable talking about it as if this was the best possible way to run a company. It wasn't just that this was the way things were done in Japan, and everyone but me was used to it. The people at Asahi Chemical had no problems at all with the way men and women were treated differently.

I was also surprised that you could just ask people what their salaries were and they would tell you. Everyone in the company actually knew what everyone else's salary was, and they were happy to volunteer that information in a public forum. Apparently this was also normal in Japan. Only my curiosity about this seemed to interest the class.

I had expected the women in the class to resent the way they were treated in a Japanese company, though I didn't necessarily expect them to admit it in a class full of their male colleagues. But they seemed genuinely happy with the status quo. So what, I began to wonder, was I missing here? Then I began to wonder, were the women in the company in a stronger position than an inexperienced *gaijin* might be able to understand simply by showing up once a week and talking to them in English?

Perhaps the men in the company were more dependent on the women than they realized. The women in the company helped the men with their work and let the men take credit for it. That kind of invisible support, because it is invisible, could be easily withdrawn.

When you get used to having other people do things for you, even small things like making tea or cleaning, perhaps it gets harder to have to do it for yourself.

I'd learned in class that some of the women in the company sometimes dated the men they worked with, eventually marrying them and then quitting to become full-time homemakers. And the very class that I taught, the company English class, was where some of these romances first blossomed.

As interesting as it was to learn something about the psychology of a Japanese corporate workplace, it didn't prevent me from keeping a close eye on the big clock on the wall in the classroom. When my two hours were up, I heaved an inward sigh of relief, dismissed the class, got in the elevator, and descended the six floors to the lobby of the building. Outside, I spotted the Kansai Paint Company's black Toyota Century town car. The driver stood holding the back door to the car open for me. I got into the car. Mr. Takeishi, the president of the company, was comfortably seated in the back of the car waiting.

Takeishi-san had the relaxed and unhurried air of a man who had nothing but time on his hands and nowhere in particular to go. He never seemed anxious or bothered by anything. Everything about him was slow, measured, and dignified. He seemed to me like a man from another era. A true samurai in spirit, but one from the age when their weapon was the abacus and not the sword.

I got into the car. Takeishi-san and I exchanged greetings in the formal spoken English of the non-recent past. The chauffeur got back into the driver's seat. Takeishi-san told the driver to go, and we were off into the maze of narrow alleys and the sea of bright, multi-hued neon that was Osaka's Dotonbori pleasure district.

"Good evening Mr. Asha. So nice of you to join me this evening. I trust we find you well and in high spirits."

"Yes, excellent, thank you, Mr. Takeishi. And you?"

"Why quite fine indeed and thank you so much for asking. Today I have chosen a very interesting restaurant for our dinner. They prepare the food in a very old-fashioned Osaka style that is not seen much these days. I would like very much for you to experience this with me. I think you will find it a great boon to your study of our Japanese culture and language."

I was not paid to meet Takeishi-san and converse with him in English. It was understood that I would only speak to him in English, and that in return he would educate me in two of the areas he thought important for a culturally sophisticated male person to master: exceptionally good Japanese food and hostess bars. There was also one other thing. He wanted me to learn about and appreciate the music of the great American songwriter Stephen Foster.

"The place I have chosen is rather small. I hope you don't mind."

The restaurants where we ate were always small. They never seated more than a dozen customers, and typically they seated only eight. They were usually in or around the Dotonbori in small, unprepossessing buildings that stood out from their neighbors only by being older and in some cases looking like they might soon be, or had already been, condemned and slated for demolition. Unlike Kyoto, tradition didn't keep sweet old buildings in Osaka from the wrecking ball when the commercial prospects of an area improved.

The Dotonbori was a maze of back alleys and narrow streets where you could find pretty much every kind of entertainment that there was. Traditional Japanese entertainment. Fine dining. Ramen shops or sushi bars that were no more than holes in the wall with two-hour-long lines of people waiting to eat there. Movie theaters, theaters for stage productions, little restaurants, bars by the tens of thousands, bath houses, love hotels, and a lively red-light district. The Yamaguchi-gumi kept its headquarters there, and its *yakuza* made sure everything in the district ran smoothly.

The places Takeishi-san took me to were always the most refined and special. In the best Kansai style, they were the kind of places whose refinement was not apparent from the outside. You didn't realize how fine a thing it was that you had been invited to until you were actually inside. Expensive and exclusive. Not just anyone could walk in off the street. Not just anyone could afford it.

As the car inched through the narrow streets and became mired in its stop-and-go traffic, Takeishi-san lectured me on the different types of traditional Osaka cooking. For the most part, the nuances were lost on me. I grasped the concepts but failed to identify them in practice. My own ability to evaluate the many meals I had with Takeishi-san was limited. I could tell if something was very good, really good, or truly great, but unable to say exactly why. Even if I had ever been able to accumulate enough money to afford these places on my own, I would never have been able to find them again. Or they would have been long gone, their aging chefs retired, or the restaurants morphed into something else.

What I was tasting and seeing with Takeishi-san were in some sense the remnants of an older and possibly vanishing world. In those days, when it came to traditions and the traditional arts, people like Takeishi-san seemed to have given up on the next generation of Japanese. Their hope seemed to be that interest from curious *gaijin* like myself, and the international recognition it could bring, might stir things up and perhaps allow the old traditions to survive and even thrive.

As for Takeishi-san himself, he embodied the traditional Japanese concept of how a man, a samurai perhaps, should behave. Humble, quiet, slow to anger, respectful of authority, reliable, incorruptible, skillful, and strong, but keeping his strength hidden and accepting his fate with dignity, whatever that fate might be. Did I think it odd to be looking for these qualities in visits to restaurants or to hostess bars? Yes. But I was prepared to entertain the concept.

On the very first evening I spent with Takeishi-san, we arrived at a nondescript small wooden building on a quiet back street that was sandwiched between two totally unremarkable concrete structures. One housed a plumbing supplies business. The other one was home to a printing shop. A sign on the wooden building identified it as a restaurant but gave no indication of what kind of restaurant it was. We entered and were deferentially but quietly welcomed by a woman in a kimono. The entire restaurant staff consisted of the chef and his wife, both in their mid- or late sixties.

We were relieved of our jackets by the kimono-clad wife and seated on tiny square wooden stools facing a bar. The bar was made of a single magnificent slab of a pale, well-worn wood and ran the length of the small room. The chef, a small man with a head of snow-white hair, stood behind the bar facing us. Takeishi-san engaged him in a discussion about the meal to come. It was not so much that Takeishi-san was ordering anything. More that he was hearing from the chef what was especially good in season and how it would be prepared. I expected to be asked, as I usually was, if there was anything the *gaijin* wouldn't eat, but I wasn't asked. That small sign of respect had more to do with Takeishi-san than with me.

Although the restaurant had seats for eight, we were so far the only diners. The interior of the restaurant on our side of the counter was adorned only with a simple vase containing a single flower and a *sumie* ink scroll painting of mountains in mist, both in an alcove behind us. The chef's side of the bar was an uncluttered and uncrowded workspace with containers of ingredients, implements, and utensils all set out and ready for use. There was a very worn cutting board on which rested an assortment of Japanese knives in various sizes, mostly the kind used by sushi chefs.

The meal that followed, at a very, very slow pace, was accompanied by clear, cool sake served in profoundly simple earthenware *tokkuri* sake flasks with matching *guinomi* cups. The plates and little dishes for the dipping sauces were all examples of fine Japanese pottery from places like Bizen, Karatsu, and Shigaraki. Each thing came on its own special plate with its own special garnish and followed the general rules for multicourse meals in Japan. Something raw, something broiled, something steamed, something fried, and something simmered in a stew. Each was amazing. The flavors emerged with the first bite, deepened, lingered briefly on the palate, and then faded slowly away. There was conversation between courses, mostly about the seasonal availability of ingredients and regret that the old places, along with the old ways, were beginning to disappear.

Though I had been told, I could not remember the names of the dishes I'd tasted, or the names of the main ingredients that were in them, or their places of origin, or the herbs or spices that had been used to season them. Nor could I ever recall the names of the superb sake we had drunk, not that I would ever have been able to find any of them on my own. Each dish was briefly and intensely wonderful and then gone. My sake cup, apparently made by a famous potter in Bizen, was never empty. Takeishi-san's conversation with the chef continued throughout the meal, punctuated by periods of silence, or of murmured sounds of appreciation. The chef never spoke to his wife but communicated with her in glances or half-formed gestures when something was required. Rice, pickles, and tea came and then the meal was over.

The chef's wife handed Takeishi-san a small slip of paper. He glanced at it, withdrew a small stack of ¥10,000 notes from an envelope inside his jacket, and handed them over to the chef's wife.

There was bowing.

We ambled out to the waiting Toyota Century, satisfied and a little drunk.

Then we were off to visit a hostess bar.

"HAS MR. FRANKS MENTIONED TO you my great interest in your countryman, Stephen Foster? You are of course familiar with Mr. Stephen Foster?"

"Stephen Foster? Yes," I said without conviction.

"Stephen Foster has written several of your country's musical masterpieces. 'Beautiful Dreamer,' 'Camp Town Races,' 'Oh!

Susannah,' 'Swanee River,' and especially 'My Old Kentucky Home.'"

"Stephen Foster. Uh . . . Yes of course."

I did not know that Stephen Foster had written any of those songs. These were songs that my parents, or even my grandparents, would have considered old-fashioned.

"I am especially fond of 'My Old Kentucky Home.' You know," Takeishi-san continued, "I think it is really very much like our own Japanese classic, 'Moonlight on the Old Castle.' Do you know it?"

"'Moonlight on the Old Castle'? No, I don't think I do know it."

"Ah! Well I shall have to sing it for you. You see, it has been my great project to translate both of these songs. I have translated 'My Old Kentucky Home' into Japanese, and I have translated 'Moonlight on the Old Castle' into English. Really I feel they are almost the same song."

We arrived at a narrow concrete building that contained the hostess bar we were about to visit. It was one of an endless sea of similar buildings in a back alley in the Dotonbori. The outside of the building bristled with neon signs. The tenants in these buildings were hostess bars, clubs, karaoke bars, or "snacks." A snack was a kind of private club that was less public and less fancy than a hostess bar.

Lines of blue taxis, black Nissan Presidents, and black Toyota Centuries had already begun to form on the street. The drivers inside the cars read sports newspapers or napped. Casual corporate visitors to the hostess bars began to leave the area by ten or ten-thirty. The more serious visitors remained until after midnight.

There was nothing you could tell from the outside of the buildings about the enterprises they housed. The same building might house the city's cheapest hostess bar and its most expensive one. A bar might be American-cowboy themed. Another in the same building might be a jazz age knock-off. One might have Filipino and Thai hostesses. Another might feature blond hostesses from Sweden. There was no window-shopping. You had to know what you were getting into. And you had to be known.

The woman who had greeted Takeishi-san at the door was about forty years old and very beautiful. She wore an expensive low-cut evening gown and she ushered us into the big living room with elegance, grace, and charm. Takeishi-san called her Mama-san, and she complained that he never came to see her anymore. He said that she was as beautiful as ever and that he would have to do something about visiting more often. She pouted a little and said that he most definitely should. She took Takeishi-san's arm and moved closer to him as they walked. It wasn't until we were about to be seated that Takeishi-san remembered to introduce me.

We sat. The Mama-san already knew that Mr. Takeishi would want champagne to begin with and Chivas Regal after, but what would Mr. Ascher care for? Mr. Ascher had no idea what you drank in a place like this and the first thing that came to mind was Jack Daniels, something he had never even tasted. There were knowing smiles all around. Of course the *gaijin* would want to drink Jack Daniels. That's what a real *gaijin*, an American, *would* drink. It was a surprise to me, but I was pleased that everyone seemed to approve of my choice.

Takeishi-san and I were seated on a large, comfortable sofa. It sat in a room that might have been the living room of a California real estate broker or a retired Florida orthodontist. The sofa was part of a set that included two easy chairs and a handsome low metal and glass coffee table. There were three similar sets of furniture in the room. One set faced a grand piano. The other was situated near a well-stocked private bar. Behind the bar was a bartender in a red uniform jacket with brass buttons. The bartender was tall and good-looking, and his muscular build made the uniform jacket look too small.

There was some conversation with reference to hostesses who had been with the establishment but were no longer there. There was conversation about women who both Takeishi-san and the Mama-san knew who owned other bars. The Mama-san observed that though

Mr. Takeishi was a very hard man to please, she had some new girls whom she was sure he and his American friend would like very much.

Takeishi-san and the Mama-san sat close together at one end of the big sofa while I was seated at the other end with a good deal of space between us. I studied the room. Except for the fact that it had two too many living room sets in it, it probably fit the average Japanese person's concept of every well-off American's living room. The set of sofas and easy chairs nearest the piano was unoccupied. The third set held a trio of Japanese businessmen. They seemed to be very drunk. They were being entertained by three very-good-looking young Japanese women dressed in brightly colored, tight-fitting, low-cut evening dresses. The businessmen appeared to be getting perhaps a little too friendly with their hostesses.

The Mama-san glanced in their direction and looked annoyed. She detached herself from Takeishi-san, made her apologies, bowed, and joined the other group. The muscular barman in the red uniform jacket was edging around the bar and toward the businessmen. When the Mama-san arrived, things settled back down and the barman resumed his position behind the bar. The Mama-san got up and went over to speak to the barman. Then she slipped into a back hallway and disappeared from the room.

A man appeared from the same back hallway and went and sat down at the piano. The Mama-san came back into the room and escorted Takeishi-san and me over to the sofa near the piano. The man leaned over from the piano to show Takeishi-san the music sheets he had with him. Takeishi-san looked them over and nodded his assent. There was a pause. The pianist composed himself at the piano. Then he began to play.

Takeishi-san stood up and began to sing. The tune seemed to be Japanese. The words were hard to understand. I thought it might be the translation of the Japanese folk song "Moonlight on the Old Castle" that Takeishi-san had mentioned. I couldn't tell if he was singing in Japanese or in English. The businessmen in the other part of the room seemed not to notice the singing, though their hostesses quieted down and turned respectfully toward the piano. When I concentrated hard, I could catch some of the lyrics.

On the meadow, hill and stones
Glimmer light of moons.
Ruined the castle carbon door,
Shadow o'er the ruins.

With such sorrow, past delight,
Darkness chills the bones.
Yes we can go not to null
My old Kentucky home.

The song went on for about five or six verses. The other verses might have been in Japanese. The music finished. Takeishi-san thanked the pianist and sat back down on the sofa.

"Don't you agree, Asha-san? If Stephen Foster had been Japanese, this is how he would have sung."

"Yes, perhaps he would have."

The pianist played a medley of Stephen Foster tunes. Takeishi-san listened to them with rapt concentration. As the music continued, the Japanese businessmen began to get rowdy. They began objecting to the music, and the ruckus they were making was interfering with it. I glanced back at the businessmen, and it looked like they were planning an assault on the piano.

The Mama-san looked embarrassed. She gave the piano player a look. He stopped playing, bowed, and left the room. The Mama-san ushered Takeishi-san and me back to our original places on the first sofa. We sat.

In our absence, an array of plates and glasses had materialized on the low table in front of our sofa. There were cubes of processed cheese and little straight-out-of-the-can Vienna sausages on fine china plates. There were small bowls of wasabi-coated peanuts and rice crackers wrapped in seaweed. There were six champagne glasses, a silver pitcher of water, and a matching silver bowl of ice cubes. Next to the table was a bucket of ice on a stand. In it was an opened bottle of Dom Perignon champagne. Next to a trio of glasses was a bottle of Chivas Regal and a bottle of Jack Daniels. I had learned in a college bartending course that the glasses were called Old-Fashioned glasses or rocks glasses.

We were joined by three very beautiful hostesses. Two of them sat on either side of Takeishi-san. One of them sat next to me. We now formed two separate but related groups on the big sofa. It being my first hostess experience, I didn't know how a hostess bar worked. Apparently I was going to be on my own with my hostess. I had no idea what I was supposed to do or how I was supposed to behave.

One of Takeishi-san's hostesses snuggled up close to him and began purring into his ear. The other began fussing with the things on the table. My hostess snuggled up next to me. She was very beautiful and in her late twenties. Her makeup and low-cut, tight-fitting, expensive-looking evening dress may have made her look older and more sophisticated than she really was. I'd never sat so close to such a beautiful woman before. I was definitely underdressed and under-experienced for this.

The Mama-san poured the champagne into the champagne glasses. My hostess and one of Takeishi-san's hostesses helped her distribute them.

A toast was offered to Stephen Foster. We all drank champagne. My glass and Takeishi-san's glass were refilled and the bottle of champagne was finished. The bartender came over to remove the bottle, the champagne glasses, and the bucket of ice and its stand. The Mama-san bowed to us and told us to please relax and enjoy ourselves. Then she went over to join the Japanese businessmen.

The hostess who had been cooing into Takeishi-san's ear leaned forward and began to make him a glass of Chivas on the rocks.

His other hostess began engaging him in conversation. My hostess reached for the bottle of Jack Daniels and one of the Old-Fashioned glasses and looked up at me inquisitively. I didn't know how a person who ordered Jack Daniels was supposed to drink it. In my bartending class we had only covered mixed drinks. I told my hostess "straight" and she gave me a warm smile, as if I'd made the perfect choice. Then she poured the Jack Daniels into the glass.

She had to lean forward to pick up the glass and then hand it to me. This afforded me a generous view down the front of her dress. She held that position longer than was necessary. I tried not to just be staring at the woman's lovely, round, soft-looking pale breasts, out and exposed just to the point where the nipples almost showed. By the time I realized that I was actually meant to look, the view had gone.

I glanced over at Takeishi-san. His cuddling hostess was leaning forward and preparing to offer him his Chivas with a splash of water on the rocks. The point of the low coffee table, it now dawned on me, was that it made it necessary for the hostesses to lean forward every time they had to get something from the table or put something back. Takeishi-san was paying no attention to this smaller, cuter hostess whose bosoms were on display for his benefit and who was feeding him and serving his drinks. His attention was focused on his other hostess. She was doing the talking, and Takeishi-san was paying rapt attention to what she was saying.

I was curious and wanted to join that conversation. But they were sitting too far away, too close together, and my own hostess was between them and me. I was in need of guidance. The assumption seemed to be that since I was male, I would just know. But I didn't. The only thing I did understand was that a classy hostess bar is not a brothel and you had to keep your hands off of the girls. The hostesses can touch you, but you can't touch them.

Nevertheless, when I looked across the room I saw that the Japanese businessmen were pawing their hostesses. I looked at Takeishi-san sitting comfortably on the sofa ignoring his sexy hostess and politely listening to the other attractive but less sexy one.

You find yourself in a living room with a beautiful woman dressed expensively in formal evening wear. She's handed you a real drink and now she's looking at you with a seductive smile on her face. She's close. You've had a few drinks. She might be inviting you to touch her or kiss her but you know you had better not. If this were a date you might be trying to get to know her. To see who she is and if you might have common interests or would maybe like to do things together. But this beautiful woman is being paid to sit with you and entertain you. So shouldn't she be making the first move? But no. She's just looking at you. Your move pal. What would *you* like to do?

What I would like to do, the thing that this lovely woman in an evening gown was doing her best to make me want to do, I couldn't do. Or could I? That, I supposed, was the game.

On the plus side, if all we did was talk, my Japanese could certainly use the practice. Shouldn't I just do whatever Takeishi-san was doing? He was, after all, my mentor. And I was his guest.

I turned and smiled at my hostess. She smiled at me. She handed me my glass of Jack Daniels. She really was beautiful.

"You're not drinking with me?" I asked.

"Would you like me to?" she purred. She had a nice voice.

"Yes," I said.

I expected her to make some excuse and have the bartender bring her some other kind of drink, but she didn't. She leaned over again and poured some Jack Daniels into a rocks glass. The top one-third of her that was mostly naked and on display was truly spectacular. This time I did look. She gave herself the same amount of Jack Daniels that she had poured for me, and she took it neat, the way I had.

We clinked glasses and took sips of our drinks.

Wow. So that was Jack Daniels. I had no idea. Definitely an adult drink. I tried hard not to let my hostess know that it was my first taste of the stuff. She seemed to be savoring hers.

I smiled at the woman and she smiled back at me. She was without a doubt the most beautiful woman I had ever been allowed to sit next to and examine at close range. As the Jack Daniels began to slowly warm my inner self, I began to feel more comfortable just looking at the beautiful creature seated next to me. The lavender-colored gown she wore was made from a richly smooth and silky material. It made her into a very appealing package.

My hostess and I were sitting close together. She moved closer. Her perfume was pleasant and subtle, so probably not cheap. Her hair was worn up, exposing a very lovely long neck. Her skin was pale. It didn't seem to be the kind of skin you found on ordinary women. It radiated a kind of buttery lushness. There was a lot of it to look at. A vast expanse of it. Chest, collar bones, neck, shoulders, and bare-naked arms. A strong chin, full, kissable lips, abbreviated nose, and big, deep, dark eyes.

We sipped our drinks and continued looking at each other.

"So," I said, "How do you like being a bar hostess?"

The woman looked mildly surprised. Also amused at the stupidity of the question.

"I mean," I said undeterred, "I suppose it beats working in an office, especially if you like being out at night. And I guess it probably pays well. You meet interesting people."

I was still getting the mildly amused, partly indulgent smile.

"Or," I continued, "do you also have a day job? Or maybe you just use your free time during the day to do things. You know, like a hobby or something."

My hostess put down her glass and took one of my arms in both her hands. She unbuttoned the cuff of my sleeve and rolled it up just past the elbow. She held onto my arm with one hand and began lightly stroking it with the tips of her fingers. Every few strokes she would turn over her hand so that she teased my arm with her perfectly manicured nails. The nails were painted a shade of lavender that matched her dress.

"*Gaijin* are very hairy," my hostess purred. Her voice was soft and a little husky.

"Even your arms are very hairy. But you have such lovely blond hair on your arms. Very soft. Did you know that Japanese women like this kind of hair?"

"Do they?"

"Yes, I think so. I do, anyway. It's not like the coarse black hair that Japanese men have. But the soft, blond kind like this . . . I like it very much. Very much."

The woman began to sample the skin on my arm with her elegant fingers the way a person might sift fine beach sand through them. She purred softly as she did this. She made the kind of sounds a person makes when enjoying a nice hot bath.

The woman moved in even closer. I could feel the soft curve of her hip and a soft thigh nestled against my leg. Her body was radiating sexual heat. Even through my khaki chinos and her gown material I could feel the lush fineness of her body. There was a soft feminine rustling sound when she moved. I supposed it was whatever she wore underneath the gown rubbing against the gown.

"Do you have this kind of hair all over your body?" my hostess whispered.

"Yes, I think so."

She reached over and unbuttoned one of the middle buttons of my shirt.

"Could I see if you have this hair on your chest?"

I nodded.

Her hand slipped inside my shirt and she began gently stroking my chest, doing to it what she had been doing to my arm.

"Ah," she said with a little smile. "You have it here, too. I like this. And you have a very nice chest. Very firm. Very masculine. Japanese men have such flat chests."

The hostess had her hand inside my shirt. Her eyes were locked on mine. She was smiling.

I wanted to touch her the way she was touching me, but understood that if I did that, the bartender would come over and break my arm.

I removed the hand from my chest and rebuttoned my shirt.

"You don't enjoy being touched like this?" she said.

"I do. Yeah. But maybe we could just talk."

"Ah, you speak Japanese very, very well," she said.

"I speak Japanese well for a *gaijin* you mean? Realistically I put my ability somewhere between third grade and junior high school."

"No," she insisted. "Your Japanese is *very* good."

"I haven't said much. How would you know?"

"We're talking now, aren't we? And you're doing very well."

"Am I?"

"Yes," the hostess purred. "Yes you are."

"Someone I know told me that *gaijin* men speak Japanese like women. Do you think that's true?"

A flash of surprise flickered across the beautiful face. Then the smile came back.

"I think you're very masculine."

"So you don't think I speak Japanese like a woman?"

She considered.

"I think you may know a little about Japanese people. Maybe even a little more than might be good for you."

She backed away a little and reached down for her drink. She sipped it and studied me over the top of her glass. The little smile was still there.

"So," I said, "why don't you tell me a little about you?"

"About me?" she said still smiling. "There's nothing interesting about me. I want to hear more about you. Why you're in Japan. What you're doing here. How you came to learn Japanese."

"We can do that. But I'd rather you tell me something about you."

The hostess held my eyes and the smile still played on her lips. But now it seemed like she might be working to keep it there. The fingers on the hand in her lap were playing distractedly with the material of her dress. She seemed to be recalculating her approach.

As we sat looking at each other, a commotion was developing on the other side of the room. The three middle-aged Japanese businessmen across the room were getting extremely friendly with their three hostesses. They seemed to be very drunk. Two of them sat and cuddled their hostesses, their faces an alarming shade of red. The hostesses were struggling to keep things hands-free.

The third businessman and his hostess in a blue gown were standing. They seemed to have been dancing, but the dancing had turned into wrestling. The businessman was winning. He had one hand thrust inside the top of the hostess's shimmering blue dress and the other hand up the woman's skirt. The gown was a tight fit without anyone's arms inside it, and now both the businessman's hands and arms were trapped there. The man and his hostess were locked together and swaying awkwardly. The businessman was trying to get the hands in further. The hostess was trying to get them out. They teetered, then collapsed onto the sofa, and then rolled onto the floor.

The hostess had been looking to her companions for help. The other two hostesses only seemed amused. They offered no help. The other two businessmen got up and tried to pull their comrade off the hostess. The muscular barman came over, effortlessly brushed the two businessmen aside, reached down and seized the man on the floor by the collar of his shirt and the back of his belt. He lifted the businessman up and shook him free of the hostess. He did this as if the businessman were a weightless sack of feathers. Then he slammed the businessman back down onto the sofa very hard and gave him a look that said try to get up and I will end you. The businessman stayed put.

The hostess in blue stood up, trying to smooth out her gown and restore her dignity. No one helped her. The other hostesses sat on the sofa with their charges laughing and making fun of her. The hostess in blue said something to a hostess in red sitting on the sofa. The hostess in red stood up. They glared at each other. It looked like they might even start to fight, but the muscular bartender was there before it could happen. He put his arms around the hostess in blue and walked her off into the back somewhere. She struggled a little and turned to shout something at the hostess in red before she disappeared. It was the kind of useful Japanese I had always wanted to learn but couldn't find anyone to teach me.

The Mama-san came out looking angry and acutely embarrassed. She went over to speak to one of the businessmen. The man seemed to be apologizing. The bartender returned. The drunken salaryman sat on the sofa in a daze. The other two resumed their drinking and talking with their hostesses as if nothing had happened.

During all this, my hostess had taken one of my hands and tried to keep my attention focused on her. I looked over at Takeishi-san. He seemed not to even have noticed the commotion at all. He was engaged in conversation with one of his hostesses just as before. His outside girl was the younger and the prettier of the two. She snuggled close to Takeishi-san and touched him frequently. When he drank she refilled his glass. When she thought he might want to eat, she handed him something to eat. She seemed to follow the conversation between Takeishi-san and the other hostess and now and then punctuated their conversation with soft, breathy female noises.

Takeishi-san and the other hostess seemed to be having a real and engrossing conversation. He listened intently when she spoke. He responded with feeling. Her eyes danced when he spoke. She made no attempt to flatter him or to touch him. He didn't seem to notice or care how beautiful she was. They were having a serious conversation about something. Possibly about Stephen Foster.

I turned back to my hostess.

"So what *do* you do when you're not doing this?" I asked.

Blank look.

"Day job? Hobbies? Other interests?"

"I'm a student."

"High school?"

"No, obviously. College."

"Where?"

"Osaka Gaidai."

"Studying what?"

"English."

"Sorry, I don't mean this to be rude, but you . . . you look a little old to be a college girl."

The woman in the ball gown smiled sweetly at me.

"I've always looked mature for my age."

"It must be the way you dress. Maybe the makeup and the hair."

She leaned back inviting me to examine her.

"Do you like what you see?"

"Yes. You're very beautiful."

"So you like me then?"

"I like you very much."

"Then come a little closer and try to look like you're having a good time. Mama won't be happy with me if she thinks I don't please you."

"I would like to come a little closer, but I'm afraid to come too close."

My hostess bathed me in a smile and moved closer.

"Come on. I won't bite you. Come closer."

Out of the corner of my eye I saw the Mama-san come out from the back and hand one of the businessmen a little tray with a slip of paper on it. The businessman stood up and had a look at the slip of paper, then did a kind of double-take. His face seemed to go pale and he looked concerned. He backed up a little and then took a fat envelope out of his suit-jacket pocket. Then he removed a pile of ¥10,000 notes from the envelope and placed them on the tray. He bowed to the mama-san, then signaled his two companions. The other two men got up and the Mama-san escorted the three of them to the elevator. The man who had paid seemed to be apologizing to her.

My hostess noticed me watching the exchange.

"They won't be back," she said. "Mama doesn't like men who misbehave."

I moved to put a little distance between me and my hostess.

"I told you I won't bite you," she said and closed the distance between us again.

Then she leaned down to pick up the bottle of Jack Daniels and poured some into my glass and hers. I almost passed out at the sight of so much luscious skin on display. I had stopped pretending not to be looking down her dress as she leaned forward.

She handed me my glass and she picked up hers. We clinked glasses and drank. I might have been getting used to the Jack Daniels.

"You know," I said, "I don't think we were formally introduced. Can I ask your name?"

"It's Sakura."

I couldn't suppress a laugh. Sakura made a show of looking hurt.

"Really? Your name is Sakura?"

"Yes."

I laughed again.

"Really? Sakura? You're saying that's your real name?"

The hostess took a sip of her Jack Daniels and held me with her eyes until I took another sip of mine.

"No, of course Sakura isn't my real name. It's my name when I'm here."

"And what's your name when you're not here?"

"I'm not supposed to tell you that," she said.

She took another sip of Jack Daniels and made a show of looking around to see if anyone was watching us.

"If you come a little closer," she said conspiratorially, "I'll whisper my real name in your ear."

I moved closer to her. Her silken gown rustled as she leaned in toward me. Her beautiful skin seemed to glow. I fully understood the Japanese businessman's impulse to grope his hostess.

"My name is Sachiko," she whispered in a low voice. I could feel her warm breath on my cheek as she said this. The subtle fragrance of her perfume nearly paralyzed me. She held me there for a few moments and then leaned back a little.

"It's a very boring and ordinary name, don't you think?" she whispered.

"No. No, I think it's a very nice name. Kind of old-fashioned."

"Yes. Old-fashioned and plain. An old lady's name."

"Maybe, but it suits you. Uh . . . Not that you're old. It sits well with your . . . youthful beauty. The old-fashioned name, I mean."

"You like to talk, don't you?" Sachiko said. "Wouldn't you like to touch me a little? You can you know?"

"I . . . I, uh . . . I thought that it's not allowed."

"Well of course you can't do anything crude. But we can hold hands. I can sit on your lap. Why don't I sit on your lap. Then if you still want to talk . . . "

"No. Why don't we just stay like this and talk?"

"If I sit on your lap wouldn't that be . . . "

"No. That would probably kill me. Or the bartender would come over and kill me."

Sachiko seemed amused.

"Unless you want to go outside somewhere," I said. "Then we could do whatever we want."

Sachiko sighed.

"You're worried about the bartender? He's very gentle, really. And very understanding."

"Understanding how?"

"He sees how men behave when they drink too much. Maybe you don't know this, but Japanese people are very forgiving when it comes to what people do when they drink too much. In Japan, you can be pardoned for anything you do if you were drunk when you did it."

"Am I drunk enough to be forgiven for whatever I might do?"

"You? No, I don't think so."

"But, if everyone is forgiven for whatever they do when they're drunk, doesn't that make what you do here . . . your work . . . uh . . . dangerous?"

Sachiko picked up her glass and took a sip. She waited for me to pick up mine and drink a little more Jack Daniels. Then she moved even closer to me. Any closer and she would have been sitting on my lap.

"Yes," she said. "I earn my living in a very dangerous profession. Would you like to touch me? You can touch me a little. It's all right. I'll let you know if you break any rules."

"I don't think I should."

"Don't be afraid. I won't hurt you."

"But I am afraid."

Sachiko sighed. She edged back a little. She took another sip of her drink and waited for me to do the same.

"All right then," she said. "We'll talk. What would you like to talk about?"

"You."

"What about me would you like to know?"

"What's your real name?"

"I've already told you. It's Sachiko."

"I doubt that. Where are you from?"

"I'm from a small town near Okayama. Do you know Okayama?"

"It's famous for its *kibidango*."

"*Kibidango*? Yes. Yes, I suppose it is. How do you know about *kibidango*? Do you even know what a *kibidango* is?"

"It's some kind of *okashi*. Some kind of sweet thing. I saw girls selling them in the Okayama train station. They were calling out 'Okayama *meibutsu*! *Kibidango*!' I suppose you grew up eating them for breakfast."

"They weren't popular in the town where I come from."

"Why did you become a bar hostess?"

"I like dressing up like this. I like being with men. And the money is very good."

"But . . . being a bar hostess is kind of . . . "

"Yes . . . ?"

"I don't know if I have the right word. Kind of disreputable. Isn't it? Don't people kind of look down on bar hostesses?"

"I suppose they do. But I like wearing expensive dresses and having expensive things. I like to eat well. For that you need money. Where do you think someone like me would get that kind of money?"

"I don't know, since you won't tell me anything about you."

"There's really nothing interesting about me to tell. I'm just an ordinary Japanese girl."

"I know you're very beautiful. Very poised. You speak well. You graduated from college. Osaka Gaidai. Aren't there many other things you could do? A lot of girls try to marry well for those kinds of things. I'm sure men would be standing in line to marry you."

"So you do find me attractive?"

"Yes, of course."

"Then why don't you show me you do?"

"I show it by being afraid of you."

"Wouldn't you like to kiss me? Just a little?"

"Really? Kissing is allowed here?"

"Don't you want to find out?"

I looked over at Takeishi-san. He was still engaged in deep conversation with one hostess and being stroked and fed by the other one. The Mama-san had gone to the elevator to usher in a new trio of Japanese businessmen. These were older and more distinguished-looking men than the ones they replaced. A quintet of new hostesses came out from the back. None of them were the three that had been there before. Somewhere in the back there must be a whole stable of hostesses. A bullpen of relief hostesses.

I looked at Sachiko who was watching the new group of businessmen settle in. She looked back at me and smiled.

"Do *you* think bar hostesses are disreputable?" she said. "I think that's the word you used."

"I think, like anything else, some are and some are not. You're a college graduate. It's a part-time job. I think, when you've got what you want out of it, you'll move on to something else."

"Why would I do that? Working as a bar hostess is so pleasant. And so easy. Anyone could do it. You sit with people and smile and make conversation. If you like them, you let them touch you a little. You never know who you might meet in a job like this."

"So then, you *like* working as a bar hostess? It's your number-one career choice?"

"I wonder, do people really choose the life they want to live? Do they just say, this is what I want to do and then go and do it? You're born a certain way. You use what you were born with. How I look is what I have to work with. Being a bar hostess is a tough business. Do you have the right clothes? The right hair? The right makeup? Is your style up to date? Do you have enough different dresses to entertain the same clients on different occasions? Are you nice enough to the customers? Do they like you? Is one of the other girls stealing your customers? Can you keep your customers interested enough to keep asking for you?"

"Right, I see."

"No, I don't think you do. You wanted to talk. You wanted to know about me. Go ahead. Ask away. The gentleman over there is paying for you to enjoy yourself. If all you want to do is talk to me, about me, fine."

"Actually, I think the gentleman over there is paying for my education. His idea of enjoyment is something that comes from discipline and learning. The best entertainments are the ones you have to work hard to appreciate."

"Nonsense. If that were true, why is he here? What happens between man and woman is very simple. It doesn't have to be so complicated. Education doesn't help. I can show you if you'll let me."

"No, I don't think you can. We *gaijin* are funny. For some reason we want everything to be real. Not somebody's fantasy. I don't want to be seduced by Sakura or by Sachiko. I want to be seduced by the actual you. Tanaka Kazuko, or whoever you are. If something were to happen between you and me, which it certainly will not, I would want it to be . . . real. Not imaginary. Not paid for. Do you know what I mean?"

Sachiko gave me a look that was wistful and a little sad.

"You should relax and let me show you what I can do. Why don't you? You'd be surprised how good I am."

The new group of Japanese businessmen had requested music. The hostess bar had a good set of speakers somewhere in the back and the sound quality was very good. They were playing the kind of music people dance to at weddings or bar mitzvahs. The Japanese businessmen and their hostesses were now swaying inexpertly to the music in the space in front of the bar.

Sachiko smiled at me. She'd been drinking Jack Daniels with me, and I could see the color in her face through her pale makeup. She brought the face close to mine, and for a moment I thought she was going to kiss me.

"Why don't we get up and dance?" she said. "There's music on."

"I'm not really much of a dancer."

"Oh come on. I told you my name. Dance with me."

"All right. As long as you don't expect me to be able to really dance."

Sachiko stood up and held out a hand for me to join her. I did. The hand she gave me was soft and warm. I was a little unsteady on my feet. She was a little unsteady on her feet. Between us we had drunk more than a third of the bottle of Jack Daniels.

When we reached the dance floor, Sachiko removed herself to arm's length so that I could get a good full-length look at her standing. She was very beautiful in her gown and very much worth looking at. She opened her arms, inviting me to step in and hold her.

I really do not know how to dance. But slow dancing is a kind of ambulatory hugging and can be faked. The bartender lowered the lights. Sachiko and I began to sway together slowly.

At first I tried not to let myself feel Sachiko's body. But once we began to sway together in tight circles that went nowhere, that became impossible. Sachiko pressed herself against me as we swayed gently to the music. She put her cheek to my cheek. I could feel the shape of her breasts against my chest. They rose and fell as she breathed. Her soft, luscious thighs pressed against my thighs. She had a small round belly and curvy hips that made their presence known as she moved. Her naked shoulders and arms felt the way silver or fine crystal sounds when it's pinged.

The music that had been playing finished. Next up was another slow dance. "Can't Take My Eyes Off You" by the Four Seasons. Sachiko kept me with her on the dance floor. We swayed together to the music. I inhaled her fragrance, felt her warm, smooth body move to the music, and relaxed into her.

The room around us began to dissolve as we swayed slowly to the music. My hands roamed the contours of Sachiko's womanly body and caressed them at will. I drew her closer. Sachiko sighed and put her head on my shoulder. We swayed to the music. Frankie Valli sang. Sachiko breathed in and out. Her breasts rose and fell. Her head came up off my shoulder and she looked up at me. Her eyes closed. Her full, moist lips parted slightly and prepared to receive a kiss. I leaned in. My lips sought her lips. I was hers.

And then suddenly, something just went bang. In the space of an instant my hands were empty and Sachiko was gone. Without a word or a glance, Sachiko had slipped my embrace, turned, and hurried straight out of the room. Before I even grasped what had happened, I was dancing with another hostess. A hostess in a pink dress. She was a little shorter and slightly plumper than Sachiko. She wore her strawberry-tinted hair short. She was just as pretty as Sachiko, but perkier and much less sultry. She smiled up at me pleasantly as we danced.

When Frankie Valli stopped singing, the new hostess and I went back and sat down on the sofa where I had been sitting with Sachiko. The hostess in pink filled my glass. Sachiko's glass was gone. I asked the new hostess if she would like some Jack Daniels. She smiled at me and said no. I asked her if she would care for something else. She smiled and glanced over at the bartender. He brought her a glass of a caramel-colored liquid with ice cubes in it. The hostess in pink smiled at me. I smiled at her. She asked me how long I had been in Japan. I told her.

I looked over at Takeishi-san. The hostess who had been cooing into his ear was now gone. The other one was gone too. Two new hostesses had replaced them. The Mama-san also sat on the sofa talking to Takeishi-san. Takeishi-san didn't look at the new hostesses. He looked only at the Mama-san.

The hostess in pink and I sat smiling at each other and drinking our drinks. She asked me if I thought she was pretty and I told her that I thought she was. She told me that I spoke Japanese very well and I thanked her. The hollow back-and-forth went on for a while. Then Takeishi-san and the Mama-san stood up and looked over at me. It was time to go.

I stood up and the hostess in pink stood up. The four of us walked over to the elevator. The Mama-san was telling Takeishi-san that he shouldn't be such a stranger. Her girls missed him and he shouldn't wait so long before coming back. She said he should be sure to bring his foreign friend the next time he came. The elevator arrived and the doors opened. We were about to get in when Sachiko suddenly arrived. She said she wanted to say goodbye to her foreign guest.

There was a moment of confusion. Sachiko took my arm and said we could walk down the six flights of stairs. The Mama-san looked mildly concerned for a moment and then nodded her assent. The hostess in pink bowed to me and melted away.

There was a door next to the elevator. Sachiko opened it and we went into a dingy stairwell.

"I wanted to say goodbye properly before you left," Sachiko said. "I hope you don't mind."

I said I didn't mind.

I wasn't sure what I was supposed to do. Sachiko looked like she wanted to be kissed, so I kissed her. The kiss didn't last very long, but it was a very fine, very warm, very memorable kiss. Then Sachiko and I walked down six flights of stairs holding hands.

Outside, the formal bowing had begun and Takeishi-san was getting ready to get into a taxi. His chauffer was holding the door of the Toyota Century open for me to get in. Sachiko thanked me for visiting her bar and said she hoped I would come and see her again. Then she stepped back onto the sidewalk with the Mama-san. Takeishi-san got into the taxi. I got into the town car. The chauffer got in, put the car in gear and we drove away.

Sitting alone in the back seat of the Toyota Century, being driven back to Kyoto and with Sachiko's kiss still on my lips, I thought about my first hostess bar experience. It occurred to me that I was very fortunate not to have enough money to spend on hostess bars. If there were hostess bars that specialized in providing live renditions of Stephen Foster songs, then the number of different fantasies that these Japanese bars were set up to satisfy must be infinite. If you found the right fantasy, the hostess bar habit would be very hard to shake.

Takeishi-san and I visited many hostess bars in the time that I knew him. But we never once returned to that first bar. And there never was another Sachiko.

Gion: What's Love Got to Do with It?

THREE DAYS A WEEK FROM late morning to early afternoon I taught English conversation to a group of five Japanese women at the Oxford Academy of English in downtown Kyoto near the Kyoto train station. Mrs. Tanaka ran a barber shop with her husband. Mrs. Watanabe's husband was a salaryman in a large manufacturing company. Miss Itoh was unmarried, lived with her parents, and worked for the phone company. Miss Katoh, also unmarried, was first cellist with the Kyoto Municipal Symphony Orchestra. And Mrs. Ogawa's husband ran his family's generations-old kimono business.

At some point, and not due to any guidance from me, conversation in the class had become a sharing of some of the women's most intimate secrets. Mrs. Tanaka, the barber, once had a German lover whom she met in a hotel every few weeks. Miss Katoh, the unmarried cellist, was sleeping with the married guest conductor of her orchestra. Miss Itoh, a telephone operator who worked the night shift, was falling in love with one of her female co-workers and was hoping to make it a sexual relationship. Mrs. Watanabe was planning revenge sex because her husband was sleeping with his company-paid American English teacher. And Mrs. Ogawa had discovered that her husband had a secret lover.

When they weren't sharing their own secrets, the women in the class expressed sympathy for the sad state my life was in at the time. I was getting over the break-up of a relationship. I had lost a girlfriend, a place to live, and most of my money. I was living in a small tatami room behind the classroom in the Oxford Academy where I taught English. I seldom went outside or met up with other people. Miss Itoh had invited me to join her for dinner with her parents near Otsu on Lake Biwa. Miss Katoh had asked me to spend a weekend with her at her parents' home in Himeji. Mrs. Watanabe invited me to visit her at home while her husband was at work. Mrs. Tanaka invited me to join a wife-swapping club. And Mrs. Ogawa bathed me in a warm smile that said she understood and felt my pain.

On one particularly sun-drenched autumn afternoon when the class had finished and the other women had said goodbye, Mrs. Ogawa lingered. Mrs. Ogawa was a refined, elegant, and handsome woman in her early-forties. She was wealthy. Her clothes were expensive. She had taste to go with her money. In the shabby, run-down neighborhood just north of Kyoto Station where the class I taught was held, you would never expect to see someone like Mrs. Ogawa. She had enough money to hire a private tutor to come in and teach her at home. So what was she doing in my class?

After the other women in the class had left and the door to the classroom had been closed, Mrs. Ogawa arranged herself comfortably on the sofa in the classroom and waited for me to come over and sit down. I chose the chair facing her. She patted the spot on the sofa next to her.

"Come over here, Ascher-*sensei*. Come on. Come closer please. I don't want anyone else to hear what I have to say to you."

"The door is closed. No one can hear us."

"Come over here."

I did as requested.

Whatever it was she had to say to me, she wasn't going to waste time trying to say it in English.

"Ascher-*sensei*," she began, "you've told the class that you studied Japanese literature. You said you've read Japanese novels from the Meiji and Taisho periods. You speak Japanese reasonably well. Tell me, what do you know about geisha? Do you know what they actually do?"

"Well, I think I have a general idea. I know they're not prostitutes, if that's what you mean. I know they train in traditional Japanese arts like fan dancing and playing the *shamisen* or the *koto*."

"Have you ever been in a room with a real geisha?"

"Ah. I've heard that takes a lot of money. More money than I'm likely to ever have. I used to work in a *shabu-shabu* restaurant up on Higashiyama. Some geisha were called in to entertain customers once when I was there. I had a chance to talk to one of them when she came into the back of the restaurant to take a break and have a cigarette."

"That wouldn't have been a real Kyoto geisha. A real Kyoto geisha wouldn't entertain at a *shabu-shabu* restaurant. And she certainly wouldn't allow herself to be seen smoking a cigarette."

"She seemed real. It was in the back room. Restaurant employees only."

Mrs. Ogawa regarded me with a look of pity. She had a very lovely face and pity sat well on it.

"Ascher-*sensei*, if you've studied Japanese literature you should know that real geisha have certain standards. Especially Kyoto geisha. They have their reputations and their traditions to uphold. Outside of Gion you can only find them in the official *chaya*, the small private restaurants where geisha are permitted to entertain."

"But I've heard stories about geisha entertaining at weddings. Someone I know has a friend who took a geisha to a *kissaten*."

"Again, not a real Kyoto geisha. Your friend probably lives in Tokyo."

"Yes. He met her at a wedding. They got to talking. He thought he was having an innocent conversation with an attractive woman. He asked her out for coffee and she said yes. He was shocked when he got her bill and realized he had to pay ¥200,000 for an hour of conversation and coffee."

"Believe me Ascher-*sensei*, a Kyoto geisha would never do anything like that. Their ways of attracting and trapping men are far more subtle."

"To be honest, I'm not sure I see the attraction. I mean, they're dressed in elaborate, stiff kimonos. Their hair is made up into big swooping wings held in place with all kinds of dangly ornaments. And their faces are coated in a thick layer of white makeup. It's hard to believe that men find that kind of thing . . . uh . . . sexy. But then again, I guess they must be doing something right to still be in business for over three hundred years."

"That's only your impression as an outsider. Of course there's much more to it than that. The traditional part of it is important. This is Kyoto after all. What you see from the outside and what you see from the inside are very different. And there's also the appeal of the traditional. I thought you would understand that. Didn't you say your American girlfriend is studying Japanese tea ceremony?"

"Ex-girlfriend. Yes."

"There are things in traditional Japanese culture that have been refined over centuries. For some of us, their appeal is still very strong."

"Okay, but why all of a sudden this lecture on Japanese culture and geisha? Are you thinking of becoming one?"

Mrs. Ogawa smiled. She had a very nice smile.

"Do you think I'd make a good one?"

"Well, you have a classically attractive face. I'd have to see you dressed up in the rest of the outfit."

"I'm not planning to become a geisha. I'm going to Gion to visit one. And I want you to come with me."

"Me? You're going to Gion to visit a geisha and you want *me* to come with you?"

"Yes. Wouldn't you like to?"

"Um, yeah . . . a real geisha . . . in Gion. Of course I would. But why? I don't want to seem ungrateful and I've always wanted to see the inside of Gion, but why do you want *me* to go with you? Won't it be expensive? It cost my friend's friend in Tokyo ¥200,000 just to have a cup of coffee with a geisha. And as you said, she wasn't even a Kyoto geisha."

"Don't worry about the money. That's my concern."

"Okay . . . but *why* then? Why would we be doing this?"

"The geisha I am going to take you to meet is not just any geisha. She is my husband's girlfriend."

"Your husband's . . . girlfriend?"

"Yes."

"Your husband has a girlfriend and you know about it?"

"Yes."

"And she's a geisha?"

"Yes."

"And you're okay with this? I mean, you don't mind that your husband has a girlfriend? A girlfriend that's a geisha?"

Mrs. Ogawa looked away for a moment. She rested the heels of her hands in her lap and flexed her long, elegant fingers, spreading them wide and looking down to examine her perfectly trimmed and polished nails. When she looked back up at me her lovely face had hardened.

"Let's just say that I'm trying not to mind."

"I believe you said in class that you and your husband are about the same age. I mean, excuse me but, he's not the kind of older, wealthy Japanese man who might be keeping a geisha as a mistress in a secret apartment or something, right?"

"No, he's not."

"So when you say girlfriend, you don't mean some kind of relationship based on money? You mean . . . a girlfriend. Like the one I've been telling the class about. The one who kicked me out of the house where we used to live together. A girlfriend in the romantic sense. I guess I didn't think a geisha would just be someone's girlfriend. Unless they're planning to go away somewhere and commit *shinju*, lovers' suicide, together. Oh . . . I didn't mean . . . "

"Ascher-*sensei*, this isn't the Edo period. Perhaps you've read too many Japanese novels. No one has done anything like that for three hundred years, if they ever really did. My husband and I love each other. We have a marriage that may be different from other Japanese people's marriages. Perhaps more like European people's marriages. We're not just married to each other and lovers, but we are also best friends and partners in everything."

"I see."

"You probably know how typical Japanese families are. The husband works very late. Lots of entertaining customers. Late nights with colleagues and business associates. Golf on the weekends. The husband is never home. The wife manages the home life. She's the *okusama*, the *kanai*, the one who stays home. But my husband and I aren't like that at all."

"No?"

"No. We do everything together, just like before we were married. We go out to dinner. To concerts and to movies. We play golf and tennis. We have a good sex life. Is sex life what you call it in English? Or is it love life?"

"Either."

"But yes, my husband does stay out late sometimes. He's a successful businessman. It's a part of Japanese business. It can't be helped. Yes, he does go to bars with people from work, and with business clients. And yes, the bars he sometimes goes to are the kind that have bar hostesses. At first he was a little shy about it. He didn't like to tell me about it, but after a while he did. He did, and I said why don't you take me with you to these hostess bars? He laughed and he thought I was just joking, but I kept after him and then he did take me. I went with him."

"To a hostess bar?"

"Yes."

"And, was it . . . uncomfortable?"

"No, not at all. We enjoyed it. It's just talking with those girls, you know. They're very pretty girls, very lively, and very good at entertaining people. We went together and I enjoyed it with him, with my husband."

"I see."

"Men in Japan don't usually do that. Do things with their wives."

"No, I don't think they do take their wives to hostess bars. I've been to a few and I've never seen any wives there."

"No. I suppose they don't. But I think it's important for a good marriage to share in everything as a couple. For it to last. It's important to do things together. So we did. And because of it everything has always been good between us. Everything has been fine until recently. Recently I found out about his geisha. Don't ask how I found out. I just did. So one night I just asked him, why do you need this geisha? Everything has been so perfect between us. Why all of a sudden do you need a geisha for a mistress?"

"And he didn't deny it?"

"My husband laughed and said she wasn't his mistress. He said that no man who wasn't old, rich, and foolish could afford to have a geisha for a mistress. He said he didn't have a mistress and wasn't I getting a little carried away? Yes, he said, he did go to see a geisha from time to time, but only to entertain certain big clients. There was one particular geisha he used for this. He and she had even become friends in a way. She gave him advice on how to entertain certain clients. But she certainly wasn't his mistress. So I said fine, when you go to see her, take me along as well. He laughed again and said that I knew very well he couldn't take *me* along. Not when he was entertaining. And no, he was not prepared to pay what it would cost to be entertained by a geisha when it wasn't for business."

"That's true, right? Japanese customers. Wives not welcome. Very expensive."

"Yes. Since he wouldn't take me, and he wouldn't even tell me her name, I found out on my own who she is. She lives in one of the big geisha houses right in the middle of Gion. And now you and I are going to go and see her."

"But . . . why am I going? Not that I don't want to."

"I can't go there alone. And I certainly don't want anyone else to know about this."

"Are you sure this is a good idea?"

"Yes."

"So, what exactly will we do when we meet this geisha? You're not planning anything violent, are you? I don't know what you've heard about *gaijin*, but we really don't all carry guns."

"We're just going to talk to her. Talk is all we're going to do."

"I see."

"No, I don't think you do see. But you might see if you meet her. So please come with me to meet her in Gion. Just you and me and the geisha."

—

MRS. OGAWA CAME BY TO pick me up for our trip to Gion at eight p.m. after one of my large Tuesday evening classes. She stood in the back for the last five minutes of the class, overdressed and over-lovely for the shabby classroom.

Once the students had left, I slipped into the walled-off section of the big room that was my bedroom and changed into my only set of good clothes. Mrs. Ogawa waited in the classroom for the five minutes it took me to change.

I had one pair of charcoal-gray flannel trousers from Brooks Brothers that my parents had bought me in the vain hope that I would someday wear them to a job interview. I almost never wore them. I kept the pants for special occasions. They were my only pair that weren't jeans. The blue oxford shirt that went with them was also rarely worn. I didn't waste my good clothes for teaching.

"My, don't we look nice this evening?" Mrs. Ogawa said when I came back into the classroom.

Before I could tell her how lovely she looked, Mrs. Ogawa handed me a necktie. It was a very beautiful, very expensive-looking necktie. It seemed to have been worn once or twice but was almost new.

"I brought this along for you. I knew you wouldn't have one. My husband has so many he probably doesn't remember which ones he still has. You can keep it if you like. Shall I tie it for you?"

"You may have to. I'm not sure I still remember how. You look especially beautiful this evening, by the way."

Mrs. Ogawa flushed a little at the compliment. She always looked lovely in class, but now she looked lovely with an added dash of late-night sparkle. She came over with the tie and put it around my neck and tied it for me. I couldn't help being aware of her delicate fingers on my shoulders and chest as she executed a perfect Windsor knot for me.

I knew I was going to feel underdressed next to Mrs. Ogawa. But her shimmering purplish-blue evening dress, her serious dark stockings, and her sleek Italian-made high-heeled shoes put me on a different planet from her altogether. That and the small fortune's worth of pearls and otherwise understated but expensive jewelry she had on. Her hair was worn up, revealing her long white neck, and held in place by a diamond-studded silver clip. I had a hard time seeing myself as her escort. Her husband's necktie didn't change that.

"Are you sure I'll be OK like this?" I said. "You realize you look far too gorgeous to be seen outside of this room with me."

"That's very nice of you to say, but we need to get going. Are those the only shoes you have?"

"Yes."

My worn pair of hiking boots were the only shoes I owned.

"Well, I suppose it doesn't matter. You won't be wearing them once we get inside. Come on, let's go."

We took the elevator downstairs. Inside the confined space of the tiny, slow-moving elevator, I was getting the full benefit of Mrs. Ogawa's womanly allure.

A cab was waiting for us out on the street. It wasn't a regular taxi. It was a large black taxi, the kind you called ahead for and hired for special occasions.

"I had the driver wait," Mrs. Ogawa said. "In this neighborhood it's very hard to find a cab."

"I wouldn't know."

I held the door for Mrs. Ogawa. She slithered into the taxi in her shimmering, body-hugging dress. Then I got in with her. I had always found Mrs. Ogawa attractive. Now, at extreme close range in the back seat of the taxi, her attractiveness was becoming much less theoretical.

"Are you excited?" Mrs. Ogawa asked once the taxi pulled out into the road.

"Uh . . . about going to Gion you mean? Yes. Yes, I am. I mean, you pass by Gion all the time and you don't really give it much thought. It's either a kind of Japanese Disneyland for tourists, or a place where older men pay ridiculous sums of money to sit for a few hours and be seduced by women pretending to be from the sixteenth century."

"So you don't approve?"

"No, I . . . it's not that I don't approve."

"Then what?"

"Not that I have any real experience, but hasn't the whole thing been updated very effectively by the high-end hostess bars here and in Osaka? Much as I love Japanese traditional art and culture, I think paying a lot of money for an hour or two in the company of women with their faces painted white and wearing elaborate, impractical kimonos is crazy. They make wonderful props for taking photos, but other than that, I think if you live here in Kyoto, as a regular person and not a tourist I mean, you assume Gion has nothing to do with you and you just ignore it. From the outside there's nothing to see."

"Well, now you'll have a chance to go inside."

"Yes. It should be great for my study of Meiji and Taisho Japanese novels. It's not very often you get to step back into another era. So I'm excited to be going to Gion and meeting a real geisha. But how are *you* feeling about it? Are you . . . anxious? I mean . . . ”

Mrs. Ogawa didn’t say anything but just kept looking at me. It was dark in the back of the taxi, and I couldn’t clearly see the expression on her face. I thought about the confessions that the women in my afternoon class shared aloud. What they often said was surprising and unexpected. It made me realize that even though I sometimes thought I understood what these women were thinking, it was an illusion. The mysterious and unexpectedly complicated mind of the Japanese female was something you underestimated at your own risk.

“You and I are going to have an adventure,” Mrs. Ogawa finally said. “But I want you to remember one thing. A geisha never does anything except for money or for advantage. Please remember that. Don’t let them fool you and don’t let yourself be seduced by them. Do you understand?”

“Sure. I think so.”

“I doubt it, but please try not to forget.”

The hired car pulled up at the edge of the Gion district. Mrs. Ogawa had the driver go a little farther in from the main street. Gion at night was a big, fat, dark blob of a place with a single main building and a collection of ramshackle wooden buildings attached to it, all of them windowless and none of them lighted. At the corner near Shijo there was a formal public entrance and a large theater where tourists came to see geisha perform and have their pictures taken with them. But that was only a small part of it. Once the evening’s shows had ended and the tourists had gone, the lights went off and Gion melted into the darkness.

I got out of the taxi and waited for Mrs. Ogawa to pay. I extended a hand to help her out of the cab. Her grip was firm and the touch of her hand was smooth. It felt very strange to be dressed in a good shirt and expensive tie and walking down a completely dark, deserted alley alongside an attractive woman dressed for a formal night out.

The sound of her Italian heels clicked brightly on the pavement as we walked.

We arrived at a kind of break in a wall surrounding I wasn't sure what. In the dark we slipped quietly into a gap between two buildings like a pair of cat burglars and then found ourselves in what might have been someone's back yard. At the back of a crumbling wall was a small door. Mrs. Ogawa pushed it open. We had to bend at the waist to get through it. We were now in an unadorned empty courtyard. It might have been a garden once but was now neglected and unused. Three wooden steps led up to another door at the back of a ramshackle building. Mrs. Ogawa opened the door and we entered.

We were now in a fairly wide *genkan*. It seemed to be a back entrance to something. A large man in his mid-fifties wearing a shortish blue *happi* coat was standing next to the door where we had entered, more watching the entrance than guarding it. His *happi* coat bore the logo of a restaurant, possibly the establishment we were now inside of. He was broad-shouldered and stout, like a bouncer at a club, but older. He might have been a retired sumo wrestler. He wore a *hachimaki* wrapped around his forehead that bore the same logo as the *happi* coat. The man nodded briefly to Mrs. Ogawa as we entered, approximating but not exactly executing a formal bow, and then ignored us.

One step up from the *genkan* was a narrow passageway, and along it were sliding *fusuma* doors leading to interior rooms. They were all closed so there was no way to tell what might be inside them. At the head of the *genkan* was a small wooden table. On top of the table was a *bonsai* tree in a ceramic pot. The tree was a *momiji*, a Japanese maple, its leaves a fiery red, perfectly evoking the season. Everything in sight seemed faded and slightly shabby.

Mrs. Ogawa leaned into the passageway from the *genkan* and called out loudly, "*Gomen kudasai!*"

A voice from inside called back, "*Hai! Donata desho ka?*"

There was the sound of small, *tabi*-clad feet shuffling down the hallway, and in a moment a frail woman in her late seventies appeared. She was wearing a very subdued, dark brown kimono and she smiled pleasantly as she welcomed Mrs. Ogawa.

"Ah, Ogawa-*sama*, I'm so very glad you could join us this evening. It's been so long. So good of you to come to see us. I see you have brought a friend with you."

"Yes, and I'm so very sorry to be so much trouble."

"Nonsense, you're no trouble at all," the woman said.

Though she was old, the woman's movements were surprisingly agile. She reached down into the *genkan* to slide open the door to a small wooden chest. She brought out two pairs of ordinary, plain, green vinyl house slippers. She kept up a patter of conversation as she arranged the slippers at the top of the *genkan* for her guests to step into.

Mrs. Ogawa swiveled adroitly, stepping out of her high heels and up into the slippers. Then she turned and bent, very gracefully, to rearrange her shoes in the *genkan* so that they faced outward. My heavy hiking shoes refused to come off and I had to sit on the edge of the *genkan* to get out of them, a major breach of Japanese shoe-removing etiquette. I came heavily up from the *genkan* and was unable to get my feet exactly into the slippers. Then I nearly fell over when trying to bend down and neatly rearrange my own shoes so they faced outward. Mrs. Ogawa had to bend down and do it for me.

"Foreigners have such big feet, don't they?" the old woman said with a sweet, grandmotherly smile.

Mrs. Ogawa straightened up, got me into my slippers, and then managed a smile.

"This is my English teacher," Mrs. Ogawa said. "His name is Ascher. Ascher-*sensei*. Ascher-*sensei*, this is Okiku. Okiku is a retired geisha. She doesn't come out anymore. She only teaches the younger geisha."

"Don't be silly. I don't teach anyone anything," the old woman said. "What would any of these young girls learn from an old woman like me? Or did you forget who you were talking to?"

Okiku turned to me and said, "We older geisha all look the same to these housewives. She probably has me mixed up with someone else."

"Okiku, don't be so modest. You know you have quite a lot to teach to others. You're still one of the most famous geisha in Gion."

Okiku turned to me again, as if confidentially providing me with helpful commentary.

"She's just trying to butter me up by flattering me. What a lot of nonsense. I'm the one who's over seventy, and which of us do you think is more old-fashioned? Is she always like this?"

Okiku turned and started briskly down the passage to the right. "All right, come along you two. We have a very nice table waiting for you."

Mrs. Ogawa and I followed Okiku down one of the narrow hallways. As I passed near the *bonsai* on the table at the head of the *genkan*, I noticed the ceramic vessel that it was planted in. I paused to look at it. It could have used a little cleaning, but it seemed to be a museum-quality Edo-period piece of Kakiemon porcelain. Something even more valuable and costly than the million-yen tea ceremony bowls that my ex-girlfriend sometimes borrowed from her tea ceremony school. And there it was, just sitting in the middle of a drab back hallway.

Further down the hall, one of the doors we passed was open just a crack. I stopped to peek into it. It was a kitchen. Men dressed in white lab coats with white chef's hats were preparing food. One man was gutting a large fish with a stouter version of the kind of knife that sushi chefs use. Another man was grating a wasabi root on a block of wood covered in what looked like real sharkskin. A younger assistant was plucking small flowers from a glass vase and setting them aside to be used for decorating finished plates of food. I was impressed by the way each man gave his full concentration to the task at hand and worked with perfect efficiency and economy of movement. No one in the kitchen was talking, laughing, or chatting.

When I looked back at the hallway I could no longer see or hear the two women I was with. They had turned into one of the narrow corridors ahead and I couldn't tell which one.

I stood where I was for a minute or two. Then I heard Okiku padding back toward me. She still had the benevolent, grandmotherly smile on her face.

"Mr. Smith, lost already? You have those great big mountain hiking shoes. Do you use them for hiking much? I'll bet you get lost in the woods all the time."

"Well, I . . . "

"Oh, you were looking in there, eh? It's a kitchen. You know, where they cut up the food and then try to make it look nice. Which country did you say you were from? England was it? You must have kitchens in England don't you? Of course Japanese kitchens are probably much simpler than kitchens in England. We Japanese eat everything raw you know. Not much actual cooking. That makes everything so very much easier don't you think?"

"Well, it . . . "

"All right, come along. We don't want to keep everyone waiting."

Okiku turned and padded briskly back down the hall. I followed her. The place seemed to be a maze of narrow hallways. After a few more turns, Okiku stopped at a big door. It was an over-large, solid-wood double door, Western style, with a pair if big brass doorknobs. Okiku pulled the door open and we went inside. The room that came into view was astonishing.

The entrance to the room was about a half a story higher than the room itself. The stairway that led down into it was a work of art. It was a flight of seven or eight steps. Each of the steps was made of a single large slab of a handsome hardwood, polished to show off its grain. The whole thing was supported by a hand-forged black iron frame. At the bottom of the steps were pairs of leather slippers to change into. The leather of the slippers was buttery soft and caramel-colored.

The room was a very sleek, modern bar. It was so completely

different from anything I had seen since we entered the building that the effect of seeing it was like being smacked in the face. I had to pause to clear my head.

Everything in the room was fashioned from richly burnished wood or glass or polished metal. The floor of the room was made from square tiles of a very smooth black stone. The lighting was soft and intimate. Certain areas had brighter accents to highlight their features. Certain areas were left in shadow for added privacy or intimacy. It was a small room. A dozen people at most would fill it. But the design of it and the way everything in it was purposefully arranged was startlingly sophisticated.

On one side of the room a floor-to-ceiling wall of glass showcased a small garden, backlit for dramatic effect. Everything in the garden was lush and green. There were hanging plants, climbing plants, potted plants, and a small stand of bamboo. Large, moss-covered boulders were artfully arranged to suggest a mountain stream with a slow-motion waterfall trickling down from somewhere unseen.

Adjacent to the glass wall was a bar made of a polished dark wood. But there were no stools or chairs for people to sit on. A tall, trim, athletic-looking, handsome man in a black silk vest and a black shirt stood behind the bar. Behind him, bottles of liquor were displayed on lighted glass shelves. All the bottles were displayed so that their well-known premium brands could be recognized.

The room was irregularly shaped and there were more than four walls. Inside the room you somehow lost track of the dark walls altogether. They just melted away into the shadows. To the side of the stairway and facing the bar was a kind of sheltered alcove with two tables in it, two steps higher than the floor of the room. The tables had picnic-style benches instead of chairs. The tables and the benches were made of handsome slabs of the same dark wood as the bar. There were thick cotton *zabuton* cushions in traditional blue-and-white patterns on the benches to make sitting there more comfortable.

It was hard to believe that this spectacular modern room was buried in the bowels of a ramshackle jumble of old-fashioned chambers and hallways.

Mrs. Ogawa was already seated at one of the two tables in the raised alcove. Okiku and I joined her. Okiku motioned for me to sit down on the opposite side of the table from Mrs. Ogawa. Seated now, I could see that the design of the room made it seem more spacious than it actually was. Anywhere you sat in it seemed private. Anywhere you looked from where you sat was gorgeous. The objects in the room were few, practical, and very finely made. The room managed to be simultaneously splendid and yet seem understated.

The two women seemed to be less awed by the room than I was.

"What can we get you to drink?" Okiku asked. "Oharu will be down in a minute. She's just saying goodbye to some other guests."

"I think we'll wait for her before we start," Mrs. Ogawa said.

"Oh? All right then, let me have them bring you some tea."

Okiku stood up and shuffled over to the bar. The soft leather slippers she wore over her *tabi* were too big for her. They made her look comical as she made her way over to the bar. She spoke briefly to the barman and then came back to sit at the table. Okiku and Mrs. Ogawa made small talk, mostly about the weather.

The barman brought the things for tea over on a handsome wooden tray. Both women busied themselves setting out the cups on beautifully handcrafted coasters. The coasters were made out of polished tin with the marks of the tools used to form them intentionally left visible. The teapot was made of a dark unglazed clay that showed scorch marks from the kiln. Okiku made a show of pouring the tea, distributing it evenly between three rough and simple teacups that matched the teapot.

I very much disliked Japanese green tea, but even I could tell that the tea in the cups was excellent and very special. It was more refined and had more tea flavor than any tea I had ever tasted. I almost even liked it. A special Japanese sweet came with the tea. It was a tasteless gelatinous blob covered with a powder the consistency and flavor of sawdust. The blob sat in a very lovely, black-glazed ceramic dish. The blob had been cut into nine squares roughly the same size. We each got our own gorgeous little ceramic plate and a very small, hand-hewn bamboo skewer to eat the pieces with.

I was managing to eat my allotted three squares but with difficulty. You needed the tea to get the sawdust-covered blobs down. The tea turned out to taste better when paired with the blobs.

Okiku seemed to enjoy watching me eat and drink.

"So tell me, Mr. Smith," she said, "would you mind if I asked you a question?"

"No," I said.

"Well, I hear that foreign men have very large penises. Is that really true?"

I accidently inhaled some of the sawdust covering my tea sweet which led to a brief coughing fit. Okiku was looking at me benevolently and patiently waiting for her answer. Mrs. Ogawa sighed and peered into her teacup.

"Take your time, Mr. Smith," Okiku said. "Here, have a little tea to clear your throat."

She poured me some more tea.

"Shall I repeat the question?"

I drank some tea and held up a hand.

"No," I said. "Sorry, I think I got the question. Well, I don't think it's my place to speak for the entire non-Japanese male population."

"I see. Your own personal opinion will do. Do *you* yourself have a very large penis?"

"Me? Ah . . . well . . . I . . . "

I was saved from having to answer by the sound of the wooden door opening and the brisk footsteps of a woman descending the stairs.

"Ah," Okiku said. "Here's Oharu now."

OHARU CAME AND SAT ON the bench next to Mrs. Ogawa. Okiku was sitting next to me and across from Mrs. Ogawa. Oharu sat directly across from me. She had slipped quietly onto her place on the bench so casually that you would have thought she had been there all along. It wasn't an entrance so much as a seamless blending in. Oharu had made no attempt to greet anyone or say anything. There were no bows, smiles, apologies for being late, or any formalities at all. I had never seen a Japanese woman behave like this. Ever. Oharu had simply come in, sat down, and tuned into the conversation.

Everything about Oharu seemed quiet and understated. The kimono she wore was a muted shade of dark green. The *obi* was rust-colored. Kimono were not made for sitting on benches or in chairs and it amazed me that a woman could look so comfortable in one while doing what an expensive kimono was not made to do. Oharu wore hers like it was a part of her.

Okiku had given up on getting an answer from me to her question and had launched into her own observations about foreigners in general. She was saying that in most things *gaijin* seemed to prefer size to value. Japanese, she said, were so much better at working with and appreciating the world on a smaller scale. She said that insisting on making everything large and fast dulled the senses and made people truly unable to appreciate the beauty in ordinary, everyday, unadorned things. Then she remembered that I hadn't yet been introduced to Oharu.

"Haru-*chan*, this is Mrs. Ogawa's English teacher, Mr. Smith. He's from England."

"Actually," Mrs. Ogawa corrected, "his name is Ascher. Ascher-*sensei* is an American. Ascher-*sensei* has been studying Japanese literature at a famous American university in New York. He is very interested in traditional Japan."

Oharu simply nodded in my general direction without smiling. The women returned to their conversation about foreigners in general and then again about the weather. Oharu tuned back in to that conversation. I took the opportunity to inspect the woman in the kimono seated directly across the table from me. She gave no sign that she was aware of me looking at her.

If I hadn't been told who Oharu was, I would never have imagined that she might be a geisha. She was an attractive, serious, and thoughtful-looking Japanese woman who seemed comfortable in a kimono. Except for the kimono she might even have been a corporate businesswoman. I had always thought of an expensive kimono, especially a geisha's kimono, as something that was brightly colored and elaborately decorated. Gaudy even. But Oharu's kimono was nothing like that at all.

At first glance the kimono had seemed single-colored and plain. But as I looked more closely I could now see that the fabric was actually finer than anything I'd ever seen before. Besides the richness of its color, there was an unusual suppleness to the fabric itself. While artfully concealing the woman's body inside the kimono, it offered an excellent feel for the shape of her body without seeming to do that. And it seemed to make the garment more comfortable to wear.

I knew from my job at the *shabu-shabu* restaurant where I had worked part-time that all kimono are exactly the same size and that there is an art to wearing a kimono. The way it looks on a particular woman depends on her skill in draping the garment to fit her body. Oharu's kimono fit her in a way that both flattered her figure and made the kimono seem like something any modern woman might naturally wear. The size and stiffness of the wide *obi* that held the kimono in place, and its placement just above Oharu's waist, was exactly perfect for showing off the curve of her hips and a hint of the delicate shape of her breasts.

The kimono's color was not plain at all, but a luscious shade of green that changed in subtle ways depending on how the light struck it. The color of the wide *obi* contrasted appealingly with the color of the kimono and allowed both colors to look their best. The *obi*'s color was a seasonally appropriate subdued autumnal hue, not rust, but perhaps the color of the flesh of a baked sweet potato or a *kabocha* squash. A delicate scattering of a few embroidered *momiji*, Japanese maple leaves in bright reds, oranges, pale greens, and yellows, swirled across the *obi* in an unseen breeze. These added just the right touch of understated decoration to the effect of the whole.

As for the woman in the kimono, at first I wouldn't have said that Oharu was beautiful. You had to really look at her to see it. But once you did look you couldn't miss it. It was a kind of beauty that owed as much to a thoughtful intelligence as it did to an arrangement of fine features. Oharu hadn't smiled or switched on the charm as some beautiful women can do with little effort. She didn't seem to be trying to be beautiful. She seemed more interested in what was going on around her than in herself, though not entirely unaware of her own beauty. She was not haughty or proud. And she was apparently a woman who could ignore the conventions of ordinary Japanese etiquette.

It was hard to say how old Oharu was. She might have been several years younger than Mrs. Ogawa. But the seriousness of her manner made her seem older than she probably was. If Oharu was uncomfortable at being seated at a table with the wife of her lover, she didn't show it. But she didn't seem exactly pleased about it either. She seemed relaxed but somehow also alert.

I was so fascinated by Oharu that I had lost track of where the conversation at the table had gone. It had apparently lost track of me. Names that I didn't know were mentioned. They could have been talking about restaurants, politics, business, or the weather. Okiku was still doing most of the talking while the other two women simply listened, nodding their heads, and occasionally interjecting something or just making the appropriate female noises. I still had no idea what my role in all this was. It seemed I was being allowed to just sit and look. So I got back to my study of Oharu, by far the most fascinating thing in the room.

Oharu wore her hair up, but not formally done up into one of those hairstyles geisha display in public or when they pose for pictures. Her dark, lustrous hair was loosely, almost casually piled on top of her head and held imperfectly in place by a pair of simple amber hair ornaments. The skin of her neck and face was perfectly smooth and very pale. There was no trace of what might be called a healthy outdoor glow. This was an indoor woman.

When loose strands of her hair fell across the side of Oharu's neck or across her cheek, she casually brushed them aside with the tips of her elegant fingers. The arm that emerged from Oharu's kimono sleeve as she did this was firm and shapely, like the arm of an athlete or a dancer. Her hands were the hands of an artist or musician, unencumbered by adornment of any kind. Unlike Mrs. Ogawa, Oharu wore no jewelry and seemed to be wearing no makeup at all.

Oharu was following the conversation at the table, though her eyes betrayed the faintest hint of disinterest. It would have been impossible to even guess what a woman like this might be like or what she might be thinking. There was no hint in her face or in her body language of what she thought of being invited to sit with her lover's wife and the wife's English-conversation teacher. I tried to imagine Oharu dressed in normal clothing and failed. It was impossible to imagine her wearing anything but a kimono.

Only once during the women's conversation did Oharu turn to look at me. She seemed to have noticed and then to be carefully studying my expensive necktie. I supposed that it was probably at odds with the rest of what I was wearing. Too fine and too costly. When there was finally a lull in the conversation, Oharu turned to me.

"So, Ascher-san," Oharu said, "I hope Okiku hasn't been teasing you. Has she asked you about the size of your penis? She thinks foreigners find that sort of question shocking coming from a woman her age."

Oharu had a very appealing voice. It was a voice that spoke the Japanese language with absolute distinctness and clarity. It was somehow lusher and lower in register than a voice you usually heard coming out of a Japanese woman. There was a barely perceptible hint of bourbon and tobacco in Oharu's voice. It was a voice that made you feel that what she said was spontaneous and meant for you alone. Like the voice of a good friend speaking to you flatly, soberly, and truthfully. There was no trace at all of the exaggerated formality or rise in pitch that Japanese women usually employ when speaking to outsiders.

"Ah, yes . . . yes," I said. "As a matter of fact, uh . . . Okiku did ask me. . . . "

"And were you shocked?"

"Uh . . . no, not really. I guess not."

"It's a kind of game Okiku likes to play when she's entertaining. She likes to pretend she's a simple, innocent old woman. Someone's grandmother I suppose. And then she pounces when you least expect it. She's really quite good at it. I think it's a talent that could have served her well in another profession. Running a small bar or *oden* restaurant somewhere in town near the river perhaps. She's actually very sophisticated, though she prefers to hide it."

"Why Haru-*chan*," Okiku protested, "why would you say a thing like that? You know very well I'm just a simple old woman. A very traditional old woman. Of course I am. Don't look at me like that. I've lived here in Kyoto all my life. Right here in Gion. How sophisticated could I possibly be? Perhaps I *am* interested in how big the penis of a foreign man might be. What of it? I certainly don't get to see them any anymore. The very topic makes me feel nostalgic for the old days. And why not? Everyone needs a little hobby to keep them going. A kind of special interest. Penises are my special interest. I don't see anything wrong with it. I'm sure Mr. Smith here doesn't mind. Or Mrs. Ogawa. Am I right Mrs. Ogawa?"

Mrs. Ogawa seemed uncomfortable with the topic. She sat and studied her empty teacup.

"No," Oharu said. "If you didn't think there was anything wrong with it you wouldn't say it. And you know perfectly well that this young man's name isn't Smith. I think Mrs. Ogawa expects something a little more sophisticated from us. She wants her foreign friend's experience of real Kyoto geisha to be something more educational. He's not one of the clueless foreign businessmen you're used to entertaining."

Mrs. Ogawa looked up and seemed to want to protest that I was not her foreign friend but her English teacher. But Okiku spoke before she could say anything.

"Oh dear. Haru-*chan*, you're not in one of your moods are you? Obviously, I'm old and out of touch with the new ways of doing things. But it's very unkind of you to point it out in front of outsiders."

"Now don't pretend I've hurt your feelings. I know you too well for that."

"Ah. Haru-*chan*, I think you know a thing or two about pretending too. It makes me sad to see you unhappy. All the other girls here always seem so happy in their work. They're very proud to be geisha. Not just geisha but Kyoto geisha. But you pretend you're not satisfied with this life. I know you don't want to end up like me, a sad old retired geisha with nothing to show for her years of service here, padding around inside these same old walls forever. Perhaps you've even thought about giving it all up and getting married. Oh my! What a really big mistake that would be! Wouldn't it be a mistake, Mrs. Ogawa? Ask Mrs. Ogawa. I'm sure she'll tell you what a big mistake it would be for you to get married."

Oharu looked impassively back at the older geisha. Her face was completely expressionless but I thought I detected the slightest trace of amusement dancing in the corners her eyes. Mrs. Ogawa looked unhappy but said nothing and absently tightened her grip on her empty teacup.

Oharu nodded just perceptibly to the older woman. Okiku stood up to leave.

"Well, very nice to have met you Mr. Smith. I hope you will come and see us again. Mrs. Ogawa, please give my regards to your charming husband."

Okiku padded over to the bartender and exchanged a few words with him. Then she went over to the staircase, slipped off her soft leather slippers, got back into the green plastic slip-ons, and quietly left the room.

—

ONCE OKIKU LEFT, THE CONVERSATION came to a halt. Oharu seemed to be in no particular hurry to speak. Mrs. Ogawa seemed unsure of what it was she wanted to say. I had no idea why I was there or what my role was supposed to be. There was nothing to do but sit patiently across the table from these two very attractive women and try to enjoy the strange and exotic bar in the middle of Gion that I was sure I would never see again.

Mrs. Ogawa filled our teacups and we sat and sipped tea. Oharu, radiating mystery and youthful old-world elegance, looked relaxed but alert. Mrs. Ogawa, radiating privilege, breeding, and wealth, looked tense and uncomfortable. The silent message Oharu seemed to be sending to Mrs. Ogawa was, "It's your show. If you have something to say, say it because I have better things to do tonight." No one said anything for a while.

Oharu finally broke the silence.

"Do you mind if I smoke?" she said. "We're really not supposed to in front of outsiders, but since we're here just to relax and chat, I hope you don't mind if we're casual with each other."

Without waiting for permission, Oharu drew a silver cigarette case from inside the sleeve of her kimono. She opened it and extracted a long thin cigarette. The brand might have been Virginia Slims.

There was a matchbox in a large ashtray on the table. I reached for it and took out one of the wooden matchsticks. As I lit it, Oharu leaned toward me to accept the light. I was still having a very hard time trying to imagine this woman with her face painted white and wearing an elaborate kimono doing a traditional dance on a stage, or kneeling and playing the *shamisen* or *koto*. But apparently she did all of that.

Oharu inhaled deeply, drawing smoke from the thin cigarette. Then she leaned back a little and released the smoke slowly into the air.

"Mr. Ascher," Oharu said, "I'm afraid we've been neglecting you. I see Okiku has had you served with Japanese tea and old-fashioned Japanese sweets. She's fond of her little jokes. Can I get you something more adult to drink. What would you like? A whiskey? Some beer? A glass of French wine? We have almost anything."

"Thank you," I said. "Anything is fine. I'll have whatever you're having."

Oharu paused to look me over again, her eyes resting on my face, and then again on my borrowed necktie. Then she turned to Mrs. Ogawa.

"You see that, Sumi-*chan*? American men are so much more considerate than Japanese men. Don't you think so? They care about what it is that *we* want."

Mrs. Ogawa seemed unhappy to be addressed by what I assumed was the familiar or diminutive of her first name. She was so surprised that she seemed to have missed the question entirely.

"Let's have champagne then. Would that be all right with you Ascher-*san*?"

"Yes," I said.

"Sumi-*chan*?"

Sumi-*chan* remained unresponsive.

Oharu looked over at the bartender and he came over. She said something to him which I didn't quite catch, and he left.

Oharu smoked her cigarette. Mrs. Ogawa sat looking uneasy. I watched the two women.

The bartender came back with a tray holding three crystal

champagne glasses and a bottle of champagne in an ice bucket. He set down the glasses and went about opening the champagne. The label on the elegant green bottle had a French name on it that was not one of the bigger well-known champagne names, at least not one that I would have recognized. The bartender peeled back the gold foil and popped the cork. Then he quickly poured champagne into each of our glasses. He returned the bottle to its ice bath, turned, and went back to the bar.

Oharu raised her glass and offered a toast.

"Thank you for coming, and welcome," Oharu said.

We all clinked glasses formally and drank. I had limited experience with champagne and wasn't a big fan of it. But this one tasted terrific. I'd sometimes wondered what all the fuss about champagne was and why it was so expensive. This one answered the question.

Mrs. Ogawa finished her glass in a single gulp. I reached for the bottle and refilled her glass for her.

"You see that, Sumi-*chan*? What Japanese man would think to pour a woman's drink when there was another woman nearby? I find that very appealing."

"Yes, I'm sure you do. Personally, I think it's just the way *gaijin* are brought up. They treat women a certain way out of habit and custom. It doesn't mean anything."

A man in a *happi* coat came in with a tray and began setting plates down on the table. There was a selection of soft French cheeses with white or bluish moldy crusts, some whole-grain Swedish crackers for the cheese, a little bowl of grayish-black caviar, things to eat with the caviar, chopped eggs, diced onions and toast triangles, and a large dish of very fresh-looking assorted *sashimi*.

Oharu poured more champagne for me. When Mrs. Ogawa reached for the bottle to pour for Oharu, Oharu waved her off.

"Please," she said. "Let's not stand on ceremony. We're all friends here."

We were each given elegant lacquered chopsticks and individual saucers and plates to eat off of. There was a set of tiny silver implements for the caviar. I picked up one of the plates and examined it.

"Mashiko?" I asked.

"Oh? Are you interested in Japanese pottery, Ascher-*san*?" Oharu asked.

"A little," I said. "I know the ones that are easy to identify. Bizen, Shigaraki, Oribe, and Shino. The large plate holding the *sashimi* . . . could that actually be by Hamada Shoji?"

"Very good. Yes it is."

"And you're using it to display an assortment of raw fish? Isn't that . . . "

"Sacrilege? Is that what you were about to say? I don't think so. It's a plate, and it was made to be used as a plate, wasn't it? Would you rather see it confined to a museum?"

"If it *was* in a museum, I would be able to go and see it anytime for ¥200."

"But here you can see it, touch it, and use it. Isn't that what a thing like this is actually made for? To be handled and used? They're very beautiful, yes, but they're not just pretty baubles to look at. What makes them really special is how well-crafted they are for the purpose for which they were made. Perhaps time has played a little trick on them, making them . . . expensive . . . so that only a very few people can touch them or get to use them. We happen to have some of them here. So wouldn't it be wrong of us not to use them? Our collection of *tokkuri* and *guinomi* is especially nice. If I had known you were interested in Japanese pottery I would have asked for Japanese sake."

"Thanks, but the champagne is fine. It's really good, actually."

"Yes. They tell me it's quite hard to get. That increases the enjoyment of it, don't you think?"

"I suppose I don't have enough experience to really answer that."

"Yes, if you haven't experienced the very best example of a thing, how would you be able to judge what it is that makes that thing special?"

"I think you're making my argument for putting the best things in museums. Otherwise it would be only the very rich who would be able to judge."

"Yes, and perhaps also a fortunate few who are simply lucky. And what would be wrong with that?"

"Well, I . . . "

"Sumi-*chan*, your friend seems to have an appreciation for rare Japanese things. You should have let us know. We could have chosen a more traditional Japanese room to meet in."

Mrs. Ogawa had been busy making a plate of food for me. She looked up at the mention of her name.

"We're here for Ascher-*sensei*'s benefit and for his education," Mrs. Ogawa said. "I don't think it matters which room we happen to be in."

I looked over at Oharu as she stubbed out her cigarette in the large plate she was using as an ashtray.

"Yes, the ashtray is by Kawai Kanjiro," Oharu said. "Did you notice that, Ascher-*san*?"

"I thought it might be, but . . ."

"Quite right. Not originally made to be used as an ashtray. I'm afraid we have no shame here, as you see."

We sipped our champagne and ate.

"I think," Oharu said, "if you're going to really enjoy special things to eat and drink, you should also pay attention to the way they're served and the things that are used to serve them. Why not use the very best things? If you can afford to do it, then you should do it, is what I say. Don't you agree, Sumi-*chan*?"

Oharu looked over at Mrs. Ogawa. Mrs. Ogawa looked unhappy.

Oharu finished the champagne in her glass and I picked up the bottle and poured more for her and for Mrs. Ogawa and for myself.

We lifted our glasses in automatic salute and drank, and turned our attention back to the caviar, cheese, and raw fish.

"So, Ascher-*san*," Oharu said, "has Sumi-*chan* been telling you that she thinks I'm sleeping with her husband?"

Mrs. Ogawa drank down the champagne in her glass. Oharu refilled it for her.

"Please don't be offended, Ascher-*san*," Oharu said. "But I really can't imagine why Sumi-*chan* has brought *you* with her. The last time Sumi-*chan* and I met, I told her that I was not sleeping with her husband, but it seems that she doesn't believe me. Or am I wrong about that Sumi-*chan*?"

Mrs. Ogawa looked more annoyed than angry. She kept her voice even.

"You're so very direct, aren't you, Haru-*chan*? Direct, straightforward, and plain. Isn't that right?"

Oharu didn't say anything. She sipped her champagne and looked at Mrs. Ogawa.

"Does my husband call you by your geisha name, or does he call you by some private name?"

Oharu smiled.

"You know I'm not a bar hostess, though I sometimes wonder if I'd be any good at it. When I became a geisha I took a geisha name and that became my name. It was so long ago I don't think I even remember what my name was before I joined this house."

Mrs. Ogawa looked angry, though she seemed to be trying not to show it. Oharu filled my glass, finally emptying the bottle.

"So tell me, Ascher-*san*. This business of being a geisha. What do you really think of it? The costumes, the dances, the performances. Have you ever seen them?"

"Only in movies."

"So? What's your impression? Is it something you yourself would find entertaining? Don't be afraid to tell me what you really think."

"To be honest, I don't think I would like it."

"You speak Japanese. You live here in Kyoto. You don't appreciate the traditional Japanese arts?"

"Some of the traditional Japanese performing arts I do appreciate. When I first arrived in Japan I saw a performance of Awaji Ningyo. I couldn't understand ninety percent of the words, but the beauty of the movements, the skill of the performers, and the raw emotion of it was amazing. I liked it very much. But I was once taken to see a Noh play. It was an outdoor performance in the countryside in a village pretty far outside Kyoto. Honestly, I found it so boring I wanted to scream. It went on forever. Sitting there on the ground trying to follow it, outdoors in the cold, it was . . . not pleasant. But, when I looked around at the other people in the audience, they seemed transfixed and absorbed by the performance. Everyone but me seemed to be really enjoying it. I think that for me, the kind of dancing and singing that geisha do would be more like the Noh play. Sorry."

"But you've never seen an actual geisha perform. Perhaps I should invite you."

"I don't think seeing *you* perform would improve Ascher-*sensei*'s impression of your art," Mrs. Ogawa said. "He's seeing you perform now. That should satisfy him."

"I'm sorry but I really don't know what you mean."

"Don't you?" Mrs. Ogawa said. "Everything about this place. It's all so calculated. For such a simple woman, you certainly seem to have expensive tastes."

"Simple doesn't mean inexpensive. The French have something called a truffle. It's a kind of mushroom or fungus. Pigs dig them out of the ground in the forest. They're ugly, lumpen little things, but pound for pound they're more expensive than gold or platinum. The taste is so subtle, most people wouldn't even notice it. Like our *matsutake*, but not quite so flavorful or attractive."

"And that's you, is it? Is that what you mean? A subtly flavored mushroom? Difficult to appreciate and expensive?"

"I don't know about subtle. My actual profession involves wearing an elaborate costume and performing. I suppose you've never seen me do the *uchiwa odori* or heard me play the *shamisen*? But you do realize that I do these things? You seem to forget that it's what makes me a geisha."

"If that's all there was to it, you wouldn't need a place like this. You'd have a theater like the Kabuki-za for performances and you could meet your fans and admirers in expensive public restaurants like other performers do. All those little exclusive private restaurants not open to the public. The *chaya*. What's all this mystery and secrecy for? That's the part of it that makes you a Kyoto geisha, isn't it? The places where only the chosen are allowed to go. Men are fooled by it and you take advantage of them."

"You see that Ascher-*san*? There's a certain fantasy attached to our profession. I think people assume that Gion hasn't changed in hundreds of years. How could that possibly be true? Most of the women who lived and worked in this house in the Edo period were sold into it by poor farmers with daughters they couldn't afford to feed. These days being a geisha is a profession of choice. We do this because we choose to do it."

"And if you didn't do the things you claim that you don't do, would there be any demand for performances of the *uchiwa odori* or the *shamisen*?"

"That's very unkind of you. We live in Kyoto where people still value a traditional Japanese life and cherish the traditions and special culture of Japan."

"Traditional Japan? Don't make me laugh. A fake kind of Japan for tourists."

"Really? You do realize that the way your husband earns his living, and for that matter yours, depends on our traditional Japanese way of life."

This seemed to make Mrs. Ogawa angry. She seemed to want to say more, but she hesitated and said nothing.

Oharu turned to look at me.

"You would like to see me perform, wouldn't you Ascher-*san*? It's much more interesting than a Noh play. And it's indoors."

"He already *is* seeing you perform," Mrs. Ogawa said.

Oharu sighed.

"I see. Well, we've finished the food," she said. "Shall we have something else to eat? Something else to drink? Brandy perhaps? Or scotch? Ascher-*san*?"

"Well . . ."

"Something to drink then. What would you like?"

"Jack Daniels if you have it."

"How American of you. Sumi-*chan*?"

Mrs. Ogawa nodded.

Oharu summoned the bartender and ordered Jack Daniels for all three of us. He came back with the bottle and poured each of us some in very expensive-looking crystal glasses. He left us the bottle and went back to the bar.

We sipped at our Tennessee whiskey.

"Don't you think it's amazing what they can do in a small place like this?" Oharu said. "I don't get to eat here very often. I'd forgotten how much I enjoy being in this room."

I had to agree with her, though I felt I might be betraying Mrs. Ogawa if I seemed to be enjoying myself too much. But it had been a long time since I'd eaten or drunk so well. For a while we just sat quietly sipping Jack Daniels and enjoying the room.

Oharu took out another cigarette from the silver case in her sleeve and I lit it for her.

"You know Ascher-*san*," Oharu said, "when Sumi-*chan* and I last met, she was much more talkative. She said we should be friends. Why not? She was a modern woman. We were all modern people. Well, I suppose *I'm* not really, as you see. But why couldn't we all sit down together and be friends? Her husband, Mr. Ogawa, and I are friends. Business friends, actually, in a way. Why shouldn't we all three meet together, she said, and sit and talk and drink and eat together as friends?"

"Because it would be expensive," Mrs. Ogawa said.

"That's very unfair, Sumi-*chan*. There are costs of some kind or other for everything we do in life. I don't have any secret about mine."

"Everything you do has to do with secrets. Without your little secrets there would be nothing to you."

Oharu sighed and finished the Jack Daniels in her glass.

I picked up the bottle and poured some into Oharu's glass.

"You see that, Sumi-*chan*. I say again, what Japanese man would think to pour a woman's drink when there was another woman nearby? I find that very appealing."

"Yes, I'm sure you do. But why do you? Is it because you think you're winning him over with your unconventional charm?"

"Why is everything about winning or losing with you? You see this, Ascher-*san*? Sumi-*chan* spends so much energy worrying about whether she's winning or losing that she's forgotten how to just relax and enjoy herself."

"And that's what you do? Just enjoy yourself?"

"When I can."

"And when exactly is that?"

Oharu closed her eyes and smiled to herself but didn't answer.

"Please note, Ascher-*san*, that she hasn't answered. She hasn't answered because it's something she doesn't want us to see about her. A geisha lives in a glass box, very much like the one we're in now. She has to charge money to be with people because that's how she earns her living. She can't ever be seen to have someone special because that would close off her opportunities. She always has to appear to have no one special in her life because that would eliminate the possibility of a prince coming to her rescue. And he would have to be a prince because a geisha has expensive tastes, as you see. Look around you Ascher-*san*. None of this is designed for simple happiness or simple pleasures. What you see here is very, very expensive. It's her world, and sometimes I even feel sorry for her because she's trapped in it. She has to pretend that she's showing you a part of herself that she doesn't let others see. That she's herself with you, though with others she holds a part of herself back. That's her great art. It's really that simple. It's what men want. The part of her that she holds back from everyone but you."

"That's ridiculous. Really. If all a man wants is the real me, whatever that is, he's more than welcome to it. If that's what he really wants. But I don't think I've ever actually met one who does."

"My husband apparently."

"Your husband is a lovely man and you're very lucky to be married to him. As I keep telling you, your husband and I have a business relationship. I'm sure he would be very happy to explain it to you, if he hasn't already. Are we friends, he and I? Yes. Do we enjoy doing certain things together? We do. But we're not sleeping together."

"Would you actually tell me if you were?"

"I shouldn't have to tell you if I were. That's what I find so strange about this whole thing."

"And these things you do together, you don't mind charging him for your time, even though you are friends. You meet as friends but you still charge for your services. For sharing a bit of yourself and your little vices with others. Does a geisha ever do anything at all that she doesn't charge for?"

"Would it be awful of me to remind you that meeting like this was your idea and not mine? I didn't ask you to come. I honored your request."

"Because my husband is your friend?"

"Yes."

"Your special friend?"

Oharu sighed.

"All right Sumi-*chan*. You know I don't like to admit it, but I'm not so very popular these days, and I don't have anywhere to rush off to. But I think you ought to tell us, Ascher-*san* and myself, what the point of this meeting has been."

"As I told you before, I wanted Ascher-*sensei* to have the

opportunity to see a real Kyoto geisha. And yes, also to remind you that marriage is a thing for only two. Two only."

Now Oharu looked unhappy. And she was beginning to look tired.

"I see. And as I've told you before, Sumiko, your husband and I are really just friends. I don't require him to pay for my time. He insists on doing it. We don't meet at the traditional *chaya* because both of us hate those places. And why is Ascher-*san* really here?"

"Ascher-*sensei* is here for his education. He seems to have a very deep affection for Japan, and I wanted to show him something very special. Very special and uniquely Japanese."

"Oh, I almost forgot that I'm the living embodiment of Japanese culture. I should have chosen a different room and we should have had a proper Japanese meal. I wish you had told me."

"I think Ascher-*sensei* has gotten a much more complete picture as it is."

"I hope so and I'm sorry if you haven't got what you came for. You're mistaken if you expect me to report back to your husband about our little get-together this evening. If nothing else, we Kyoto geisha are very discreet. And now I think our time is about up. But I would like to ask just one little favor before you go. Please leave Ascher-*san* here with me for just a little while longer. You and I have done most of the talking and I've hardly had a chance to get to know him. Leave him with me for a little while. I won't even charge you for the time."

"Certainly not."

"Don't worry, I'll send him home safe and sound and in one piece. Ascher-*san* doesn't mind, do you?"

"I'm sure Ascher-*sensei* appreciates your invitation, but he came with me and he's leaving with me."

There was a pause as both women turned to look at me. If I hesitated it was only because I'd had a lot of champagne and Jack Daniels to drink and things for me were moving more slowly than usual.

"As Ogawa-*san* explained earlier," I said, "I've been brought up in a certain way with certain habits and customs. We *gaijin* think a guy should leave with the lady who brought him. Though I do appreciate your invitation to stay and get to know you better."

"A shame," Oharu said. "It would have been very educational. Shall we call it an evening then? I'll have someone call you a taxi."

Oharu signaled the bartender. We finished our drinks and then we all stood and moved toward the stairs. Oharu led the way up. I found myself shamelessly trying to imagine the body that inhabited her kimono as she made her way up the short flight of stairs.

Oharu stopped at the first turn in the labyrinth of corridors. One of the servers in a *happi* coat was there to meet us.

"I'll say goodbye here," Oharu said. "Kimura will take you the rest of the way to the outer door. Ascher-*san*, you are always welcome to come back and see me."

"I don't think he'll be able to afford it," Mrs. Ogawa said.

Oharu came forward a little to look at me. Her lovely face wore an expression of sadness mixed with curiosity. She really was very beautiful. She leaned in very close to me. For a moment, I thought Oharu was going to kiss me. Instead she whispered into my ear.

"Love and marriage, Ascher-*san*. Where do you think the silly idea that they should go together came from?"

Then she leaned back and said aloud, "Please come back again, Ascher-*san*, if you ever do get rich, and we'll show you exactly what it is that we do here."

"If he ever does, you'll be much too old for him," Mrs. Ogawa said.

"Which is why I prefer to live in the present whenever possible. I wish you both a pleasant rest of the evening. Thank you for coming."

IT WAS VERY COOL AND quiet in the night air outside. There was almost no light at all coming from the sprawling buildings of the Gion quarter.

Out on the street a black bespoke taxi was waiting. Mrs. Ogawa and I got in and she gave the driver the address of my building.

"Why did you bring me with you, really?" I asked once the taxi pulled out into the street.

"I couldn't go alone, obviously. Who else could I get to go with me?"

"But Oharu said you'd been there before. I had the impression you went alone."

Mrs. Ogawa didn't say anything for a while. It was dark in the taxi and I couldn't really see her face.

Then she said, "I suppose I thought if someone else were there it would help me to keep control of myself. I thought if I had a witness with me, someone who saw how I behaved, it would keep me from making a fool of myself in front of that woman. I couldn't bring any of my friends."

"You and I barely know each other. Why would you care what I think? Why would my opinion of you keep you from doing anything?"

"I suppose that's just how I am. I seem to care what anybody thinks of me. Except those geisha. I could care less what women like that think of me."

We rode together in the taxi in silence for a while. We'd had enough to drink that neither of us was completely sober. We were sitting close together in the middle of the back seat of the cab. Probably too close together.

The taxi was approaching my building.

"You do realize," Mrs. Ogawa said, "that nothing would have happened if you had stayed. She didn't really expect you to stay."

"Sure."

"Do you really understand that?"

"It doesn't matter, does it?"

"What did she say to you as we were leaving?"

"That marriage shouldn't be about love."

The taxi pulled up in front of my building. The cab driver was coming around to open the door on my side. I leaned over to thank Mrs. Ogawa for a very interesting and very educational evening. Our eyes met. I wanted to kiss her. I'm sure she would have let me.

I hesitated.

Mrs. Ogawa sat on the edge of the back seat of the cab looking at me.

I thanked Mrs. Ogawa again for taking me to see a geisha and got out of the cab.

She blinked once or twice and then smiled, more to herself than at me. And then she transformed back into the woman who showed up at my late morning to early afternoon English conversation classes every week.

I bowed slightly. She bowed slightly. The taxi door closed.

Then the taxi sped away into the night.

AUTHOR'S NOTE

I'D LIKE TO THANK Sheldon (Don) Ascher for allowing me to use his experiences in Kyoto as the basis for this book. He in turn would like to thank the special women he knew in Kyoto who graciously allowed him into their lives and, to some small extent, to share them.

ALSO BY STEVE ALPERT

Sharing a House with the Never-Ending Man: 15 Years at Studio Ghibli

p-ISBN 978-1-61172-057-0 / e-ISBN 978-1-61172-941-2

Available at booksellers worldwide and online

sbp@stonebridge.com / www.stonebridge.com

CPSIA information can be obtained
at www.ICGtesting.com
Printed in the USA
JSHW020909070622
26779JS00001B/1

9 781611 720747